PROMISE
AT DAWN

PROMISE
AT DAWN

A MEMOIR BY
ROMAIN GARY

"...But I have promises to keep,
And miles to go before I sleep..."
ROBERT FROST

Translated by John Markham Beach

A NEW DIRECTIONS BOOK

Copyright © 1961 by Romain Gary

Manufactured in the United States of America
This translation of *La Promesse de l'Aube* by John Markham Beach was first published by Harper & Brothers in 1961.
First published as New Directions Paperbook 635 in 1987 as part of the *Revived Modern Classics Series*
Published simultaneously in Canada by Penguin Books Canada Limited

Library of Congress Cataloging-in-Publication Data
Gary, Romain.
    Promise at dawn.
    (New Directions paperbook; 635)
    Translation of: La promesse de l'aube.
    Reprint. Originally published: New York: Harper,
1961.
    1. Gary, Romain   Biography.   2. Authors, French—
20th century—Biography.   I. Title.
PQ2613.A58Z47413   1987   843.912 [B] 86-23737
ISBN 0-8112-1016-2 (pbk.)

New Directions Books are published for James Laughlin
by New Directions Publishing Corporation,
80 Eighth Avenue, New York 10011

PROMISE
AT DAWN

CHAPTER *1*

IT IS OVER. THE BEACH AT BIG SUR IS EMPTY and cool and the gentle sand is kind to the fallen. The sea mist blurs all things except memories; between ocean and sky not a mast to be seen; on a rock before me, thousands of birds; on another, a family of seals; the father keeps emerging from the waves with a fish in his mouth, a shiny and devoted parent. Sea gulls land, often so near that I hold my breath and the old longing stirs in me again; in a moment or two, they will settle on my shoulders, in my arms, press their feathers against my neck and against my face, cover me completely. . . . At the age of forty-four, I still catch myself dreaming of some universal and total tenderness. So long have I been lying motionless where I fell that cormorants and pelicans have formed a circle around me, and, just after sunrise, a seal let the surf carry him close to my feet. He stayed there quite a while, raised on his flippers, staring at me, before returning into the sea. I smiled, but he kept staring at me seriously and a little sadly, as though he knew.

The day war was declared my mother drove five hours in a taxi to say good-by and to wish me, in her own words, "A hundred victories in the sky"—I was at that time gunnery instructor at the Air Force Academy in Salon-de-Provence. The taxi was an ancient, flat-nosed Renault, ready to breathe its last. At one time my mother had owned a twenty-five per cent share in the vehicle, but for many years now the taxi had been the exclusive property of her former partner, a chauffeur named Rinaldi. She still considered, however, that she had a moral right to free use of the car, and since Rinaldi was a gentle, timid and impressionable soul, whenever he saw my mother walking toward his taxi with a determined air he usually took refuge in flight—both from her and from his own good nature. Long after the war, dear old Rinaldi—he still runs a taxi in Nice and you can hire him at the corner of the rue de France and the Boulevard Gambetta—told me with grudging admiration how my mother had "requisitioned" him.

"She flung open the door of the cab and, with a commanding sweep of her cane, told me: 'Take me to Salon-de-Provence. I wish to say good-by to my heroic son.' I tried to argue— a ten-hour drive it was, there and back, and I knew that she wasn't going to pay me. She told me I was a bad Frenchman, because there was a war on and I was refusing to do my bit. Then she just climbed into the cab, loaded with all those parcels for you—sausages, ham, pots of jam—and sat there sternly, waiting. I refused to budge, and so we both sat there for I don't know how long. Then she began to cry, looking suddenly like a dumb, hurt and lost animal—you know the way she looked sometimes—and still blubbering something about her 'heroic son.' I held out for a moment; but then, what the hell, I told myself, I was too old for the war, no son of my own, and the whole world had gone crazy anyway, so I might as well do my bit, as she had put it. 'All right,' I told her, adding, just to save face, 'but you'll pay for the gas'—I damn well knew she wouldn't. She always thought she had a claim on the car, just because we had been partners years back. Yes, Monsieur Romain, you can say that you've been loved in your life—there is nothing she wouldn't have done for you. . . ."

I saw her step down from the taxi in front of the canteen, leaning on her cane, a Gauloise in the corner of her mouth, under the interested eyes of the assembled soldiery. It was too late for me to hide; I rose from my table, buckling my belt and smiling bravely, while, with a fine theatrical gesture, she threw her arms wide and stood there, her face radiant, waiting for her little boy to fling himself into her embrace.

I walked over to her slowly, rolling my shoulders, with my cap tilted cockily over one eye and my hands stuffed into the pockets of one of those almost legendary dashing leather jackets, which did so much to recruit young Frenchmen into the Air Force. I was thoroughly embarrassed by this intolerable intrusion of a mother into the virile world in which I enjoyed a hard-won reputation as a tough and even a slightly dangerous, devil-may-care character.

I remained a moment locked in her arms, sweating profusely, and then with all the amused and protective nonchalance of which I was capable I tried to maneuver her discreetly out of sight behind the taxi. But no: she took a step back to gaze at my face and into my eyes with naïve admiration, sniffing noisily, which was always with her a sign of deep satisfaction. Then, in a voice loud enough for all to hear, and with a strong Russian accent, she announced:

"Guynemer! You will be a second Guynemer! Your mother has always been right!"

I could hear the roar of laughter behind my back and for the first time she, too, became aware of the mocking audience. She grabbed her cane and, with a threatening gesture toward the soldiery, she delivered, in an inspired tone, another prophecy:

"You will be a great hero, a general, Gabriele d'Annunzio, Ambassador of France! This rabble doesn't know who you are!"

"The rabble" was enjoying itself thoroughly. As for myself, I don't believe there ever was a son who hated his mother as much as I did at that moment. But when I tried, in a furious whisper, to tell her that she was ruining me in the eyes of our Air Force, and made a renewed effort to push her behind the taxi, her lips began to tremble, a hurt, bewildered look came into her eyes and I heard once more the words that I had heard so often and dreaded so much:

"You are ashamed of your old mother!"

That did it: all the trappings of sham virility, of laboriously assumed toughness collapsed to the ground. I put an arm around her shoulders and held her tight, while my free hand defied the soldiery with that rude but expressive gesture known to all armies of the world, with the difference that in Anglo-Saxon society two fingers are necessary, while one suffices in the Latin world. It is all a matter of sunshine and temperament.

I no longer heard the laughter or saw the mocking faces of my Air Force buddies; we were back once more, the two of us, on our secret and private planet, a wonderland where all the beauty lies, so completely fanciful, and yet so much more real to us than the very earth of Provence on which we stood, a magical world, born out of a mother's murmur into a child's ear, a promise whispered at dawn of future triumphs and greatness, of justice and love. I held her shoulders tightly with my right arm, looking confidently at the sky, so empty and thus so open to my future deeds; I was thinking of the day when I should return to her victorious, having given a meaning to her life of self-denial and sacrifice, in a world I had freed, at last, from the grip of those dark enemies whose names and faces I had come to know so well.

Even now, when the battle is over and all has been said, as I lie where I have fallen, on the shore of Big Sur, in the vast and soothing emptiness on the ocean's edge where only the seals utter their cries and a lone whale passes by with its minuscule and derisory jet of white water like a flea's jump into immensity —even now, I have only to raise my eyes to see the enemy legions leaning over me, eagerly watchful for any sign of submission and defeat.

I was only a child when my mother first told me of their existence; long before Snow White and Puss in Boots, before the Seven Dwarfs and the Wicked Fairy, they crowded into my nursery and have never left my side since; my mother pointed them out to me one by one, whispering their names; I was too young to understand, and yet I knew already that a day would come when for her sake I would challenge and destroy them; I felt scared, and bewildered, and yet determined; with each year that passed I became more aware of their presence around me, and their ugly features became more apparent to me; with each new blow they struck at us I felt growing in me the heart and soul of a rebel; today, when I have lived, I can still see them grinning in the darkening shadows of Big Sur, and the sound of their mocking and triumphant laughter rises above the ocean's roar; their names, once more, come one by one to my lips and my aging eyes challenge them with all the earnestness of a child six years old.

First comes Totoche, the god of Stupidity, with his scarlet monkey's behind, the swollen head of a doctrinaire and a passionate love for abstractions; he has always been the Germans' pet, but today he prospers almost everywhere, always ready to oblige; he is now devoting himself more and more to pure research and technology, and can be seen frequently grinning over the shoulders of our scientists; with each nuclear explosion his grin grows wider and wider and his shadow looms larger over the earth; his favorite trick is to hide his stupidity under the guise of scientific genius, and to enlist support among our great men to ensure our own destruction.

Then there is Merzavka, the god of Absolute Truth and Total Righteousness, the lord of all true believers and bigots; whip in hand, a Cossack's fur cap over one eye, he stands knee-deep in a heap of corpses, the eldest of our lords and masters, since time immemorial the most respected and obeyed; since the dawn of history he has had us killed, tortured and oppressed in the name of Absolute Truth, Religious Truth, Political Truth, Moral Truth; always with a capital "T" raised high above our heads, like a scaffold. One half of the human race obsequiously licks his boots, and this causes him immense amusement, for well he knows that there is no such thing as absolute truth, the oldest trick to goad us into slavery or to drive us at each other's throats; and even as I write these words, I can hear above the barking of the seals and the cries of the cormorants the sound of his triumphant laughter rolling toward me from the other end of the earth, so loud that even my brother the ocean cannot raise his voice above it.

Then there is Filoche, the god of Mediocrity, full of bilious scorn and rabid prejudice, of hatred and petulance, screaming at the top of his voice, "You dirty Jew! You nigger! Jap! Down with the Yanks! Kill the yellow rats! Wipe out capitalists! Imperialists! Communists!"—lover of holy wars, a Great Inquisitor, who is always there to pull the rope at a lynching, to command a firing squad, to keep the jails full; with his mangy coat, his hyena's head and his deadly breath, he is one of the most powerful of the gods and the most eagerly listened to; he is to be found in every political camp, from right to left, lurking behind every cause, behind every ideal, always present, rubbing his hands whenever a dream of human dignity is stamped into the mud.

And Trembloche, the god of Acceptance and Servility, of survival at all costs, shaking with abject fear, covered with goose flesh, running with the hare and hunting with the hounds; a skilled persuader, he knows how to worm his way into a tired heart, and his white reptilian snout always appears before you when it is so easy to give up and to remain alive takes only a little cowardice.

There are other gods, less easy to unmask, shifty and shrouded in mystery; their cohorts are innumerable and innumerable are the traitors amongst us ready to serve them; my mother knew them all; often, when the going was very hard, she would press my cheek against hers and point them out to me one by one; I listened, holding my breath, to the warning murmur and its promise of final victory, and soon those evil giants who bestride the world became for me more real than the most familiar objects in my nursery, and their towering shadows remain looming over me to this very day; I have only to raise my eyes to see the glitter of their armor in the sky, and their lances aimed at me in every beam of light.

We are old enemies now, they and I, and it is of my battle with them that I shall tell here; my mother had been one of their favorite toys; they never left her in peace; from the snows of Russia to the shores of France, with her child in her arms, it was in vain that she tried to escape from them; they followed her everywhere; I grew up longing for the day when I could tear down the veil of darkness and absurdity concealing the true face of the universe and discover at last a smile of kindness and wisdom; I grew up in the certitude that one day I should help my fellow men to wrest the world from our enemies and give back the earth to those who ennoble it with their courage and warm it with their love.

CHAPTER 2

I WAS THIRTEEN YEARS OLD WHEN A CLEAR REV-
elation of my life's purpose dawned on me for the first time.

We were living in Nice then. Each morning we left the house
together and walked, discussing our radiant future, along the
Promenade des Anglais; I was on my way to school, leaving
my mother at the Hotel Negresco, where she rented a showcase, displaying on its shelves a few *articles de luxe* borrowed
from the local shops. On each scarf, belt, clip or sweater sold
she received a commission of ten per cent. She usually charged
more than the agreed price and pocketed the difference. She
sat there all day long, except for a two-hour break at noon
when I came home for lunch, keeping her eyes open for prospective clients and nervously smoking innumerable Gauloises,
since our survival depended entirely upon this humble and
precarious business.

Alone, without husband or lover, without friends, for more
than ten years she had been putting up a brave fight to keep
us going, to pay for bread and butter and rent, school fees,
clothes, shoes and, above all, to achieve that daily miracle, the
beefsteak which she set before me for lunch, with a proud and
happy smile, as though it were the very symbol of her victorious
struggle against adversity. She stood there, her arms crossed,
watching me while I ate, with the contented and dreamy look
of the female suckling her young.

She never touched any of the meat herself, maintaining that

she was on a diet, and that animal fats were forbidden her.

One day, leaving the table, I went into the kitchen for a glass of water.

My mother was seated on a stool, holding the frying pan on her knees. She was carefully sopping up with small chunks of bread the fat in which my steak had been cooked, and then eating the bread with obvious relish. When she saw me, she quickly tried to hide the pan under a napkin, but it was too late: the true reason for her vegetarian diet was now obvious to me.

For a moment I remained motionless, staring at the frying pan, and at the embarrassed smile and guilty look on my mother's face. Then I burst into tears and ran away.

At the far end of the Avenue Shakespeare, where we were then living, there was an almost vertical embankment overlooking the railway line, and it was there that I sought refuge, in the tall weeds under a mimosa tree. The idea of throwing myself under a train and thus escaping my unbearable feeling of shame and helplessness crossed my mind, but almost at once a fierce determination to set the world right started a fire in my blood that burns in me to this day. Pressing my face against the warm earth, with only the weeds for company, I cried; but my friends the tears, which have often been so merciful to me, this time brought no relief. A deep frustration, a strange feeling of manhood drained away, almost of infirmity, took hold of me; as I grew older, this feeling grew with me, until it became a craving, a thirst that neither art nor a woman could quench.

I don't know how my mother found out where I was, but I saw her coming down the slope toward me, her gray hair full of light and of sky. She sat down beside me, holding a lighted cigarette between her lips and the package of Gauloises Bleues in her hand.

"Now," she said. "Now . . . Please don't cry."

"Leave me alone."

"I'm sorry. I hurt you. I won't do it again."

"Leave me alone, I said!"

A train roared past below us. It seemed to me that it was my grief making all that noise.

"You will soon be big enough to take care of me."

I felt a little calmer. We were sitting side by side in the tall grass, looking toward the olive trees on the mountainside across the tracks. The mimosa was in full bloom, the sky was blue, and the sun was doing its best. It occurred to me suddenly that the world was a damn good liar. As far as I can remember, this was my first adult thought.

My mother held out her package of Gauloises. I took one. She had encouraged me to smoke since I was twelve, just as she had encouraged me to wear long trousers, to kiss the hands of ladies, and had watched approvingly when I tried to shave my nonexistent beard: she was in a hurry. Every few days I checked my height with a tape measure; I used also to devour raw carrots by the pound, having heard that they helped one to grow faster.

"Have you done any writing today?"

For the last year I had been "writing," and had already blackened the pages of several exercise books with my poems. I copied them painstakingly in block letters, a humble attempt at creating an illusion of print.

"Yes. I began a new poem this morning. A great metaphysical epic about reincarnation and the migration of souls."

She looked pleased.

"And how are things at school?"

"I got another zero in math."

My mother thought this over for a moment.

"Your teachers don't understand you," she said firmly.

I was inclined to agree. The persistence with which my teachers kept giving me zeros in science subjects seemed to indicate some truly crass ignorance on their part.

"They'll be sorry one day," my mother assured me. "The time will come when your name will be inscribed in letters of gold on the wall of their wretched school. I'll go and tell them so tomorrow."

I shuddered.

"Mother, I forbid you to do anything of the kind!"

"I'll read your latest poems to them. You will be a d'Annunzio, a Victor Hugo, a Nobel Prize winner. They don't know who you are! I'll tell them."

"Mother, you'll only make me look a fool again!"

She wasn't listening. A radiant smile, at once triumphant and naïve, was on her lips, and her eyes had that intense fixity which I knew so well. It was as though, piercing the mists of the future, they had caught a sudden vision of her son, with his old mother on his arm, slowly mounting the steps of the Panthéon in full ceremonial dress, covered with glory, feathers, honors and gold braid.

"The most beautiful women will be dying at your feet!" she proclaimed, shaking a threatening finger at the sky.

The twelve-fifty from Ventimiglia rushed by in a cloud of steam. The passengers standing at the windows must have wondered what it was that the gray-haired woman and the little boy could be watching in the sky with such absolute fascination.

"You must choose a pseudonym," my mother said. "A great French writer who is going to astonish the world can't possibly have a Russian name. If you were a musical genius, it wouldn't matter, in fact it might be a help, but it wouldn't do at all for a giant of French literature."

This time, the "giant of French literature" was in complete agreement. For the last six months I had been spending several hours a day poring over an exercise book, trying out a great variety of noble-sounding pen names, in red ink. That very morning I had settled on Hubert de la Vallée, only to succumb an hour later to the nostalgic charm of Romain de Roncevaux. I could not, I felt, better my first name, Romain: unfortunately there was already a Romain Rolland, and I was not in the least prepared to share my glory with anybody. It was all very difficult. The obvious trouble with pen names, I decided, even with the most inspired and impressive ones, was that they somehow failed to convey truly the full extent of one's literary genius.

I was almost ready to conclude that a pen name was not enough, and that one would still have to write books.

"Of course, if you were a famous violinist, our real name, Kacew, or even better, my stage name, Borisovski, would be excellent," said my mother with a sigh.

This "famous violinist" business had been the cause of one of her greatest disappointments, and I feel guilty about it to this day. Struggling to survive, and seeking some miraculous short cut to the "fame and adulation of the crowd"—she had been an actress once, and the dream of success and applause had always remained with her—she had once nourished the hope that I was going to reveal myself as a child prodigy, a combination of Jascha Heifetz and Yehudi Menuhin. I was barely seven when she presented me with a second-hand violin acquired at a pawnshop in Vilna, the town in eastern Poland in which we found ourselves temporarily stranded on our slow trek west from Russia, and I was solemnly introduced to a tired old gentleman with long hair, an astonishing high and stiff white collar, dressed always in black velvet, whom my mother addressed in a low, respectful voice as "Maestro." Twice a week I plodded through the snow to his house, carrying the violin in a yellow wooden case lined with violet velvet. All I remember today of the "Maestro" is the expression of profound astonishment on his face each time I dutifully applied my bow to the strings; and I can still hear the cry "Ai, ai, ai!" he would utter, covering his ears with both hands, as I was giving my best. He must have been a man who suffered deeply from the lack of universal harmony here below, a lack to which I must have contributed notably during the three weeks that my lessons lasted. One day, no longer able to bear it, he snatched the bow and the violin from my hands, announced that he would speak to my mother and sent me packing. What he told her I shall never know, but my mother spent several days sighing, looking at me tearfully, and pressing me to her bosom in tender forgiveness.

A great dream had left us.

CHAPTER 3

In those days in Vilna my mother survived by making hats to order for a clientele recruited through the mail and through notices posted in shop windows in the better parts of the city: each carefully handwritten notice haughtily informed the prospective customers that "the former head of a famous Paris fashion house, to occupy her leisure time, will agree to make hats to order for a strictly limited and discriminating clientele." She tried to resume this enterprise several years later, shortly after our arrival in Nice in 1928, in a two-room flat we then occupied in the Avenue Shakespeare. It didn't work out, so for a while my mother made lampshades and costumes for the little Provençal dolls then very popular with tourists, administered beauty treatments in the back room of a ladies' hairdresser and then performed the same service for dogs at a kennel in the Avenue de la Victoire. At night, she read palms in restaurants, compensating by her acting abilities and great assurance for her total ignorance of that ancient art. Later came the already-mentioned showcase at the Negresco, the hawking of jewelry from hotel to hotel, the part interest in the taxi and another in a vegetable stall at the Marché de la Buffa. Throughout those years the symbolic beefsteak always appeared punctually before me at noon, and nobody in Nice ever saw me either ill-shod or poorly clothed. There was nothing I could do to help, and my budding virility only deepened my feeling of helplessness and frustration. I felt guilty for having failed her so badly as a child prodigy and I never really forgave myself my lack of musical genius; to this day I cannot hear the names of Menuhin or Heifetz without a pang of remorse. Some thirty years later, when I was French Consul General in Los Angeles, it happened that my official duties called on me to present the Grand Cross of the Legion of Honor to Jascha Heifetz. After pinning the Cross on the chest of the great violinist and reciting the traditional formula: "Monsieur Jascha Heifetz, in the name of the President of the Republic, and by virtue of the powers conferred upon me, I hereby name you Grand Cross of the Legion of Honor," I suddenly heard myself saying, in an only too audible whisper, with my eyes raised to the ceiling: "I can't help it, I just didn't have it in me."

The maestro showed some sign of astonishment: "I beg your pardon, Monsieur le Consul Général?"

I hastily kissed him on both cheeks as tradition required, and thus terminated the ceremony.

I knew that my mother's own artistic ambitions had never been fulfilled and that she was dreaming for me of a career she had never known herself. This longing for something that, for lack of a better definition, I can only call "talent at all costs" led her to dig inside me for some hidden artistic seed, for a nugget of talent, or rather, as she never did things by halves, for a secret bonanza of genius that would lead us both to some supreme triumph, greatness, and material success. Years later, her longing and my own desperate attempts to find in me some trace of a gift, some creative power, gave me the basic theme for my novel *The Talent Scout* and helped me to imagine its central character, José Almayo.

I was determined to do all I could to make her, by proxy, so to speak, through my achievements, a famous and acclaimed artist; it was only a matter of choosing the right field; and, having hesitated for a long time among painting, acting, singing and dancing, after many a heartbreaking failure, we were finally driven to literature, which has always been the last refuge, in this world, for those who do not know where to lay their dreaming heads. The painful word "violin" was never again mentioned between us and soon my mother began to look for some other way to the stars.

Three days a week, carrying my dancing pumps, I obediently followed my mother to the studio of Sacha Jigloff, where, for two solid hours, I conscientiously performed *pas de deux* and *entrechats*, while my mother watched me with a smile of wonder, occasionally exclaiming:

"Nijinsky! Nijinsky! You are going to be a second Nijinsky—I know what I am talking about!"

She kept a hawk's eye on Sacha Jigloff and never left me alone with him, for, as she hinted darkly to me, old Sacha had "a sick mind"—but even so I was utterly surprised and frightened when one day Jigloff tiptoed into the corner where I was taking a shower and tried to bite me—or so I thought in my utter innocence—with the result that I gave vent to a hair-raising howl. I can still see the wretched Jigloff running in circles around the gymnasium pursued by my mother brandishing her cane and uttering the choicest insults from her very rich vocabulary. Thus ended my career as a great ballet dancer. There were other dancing schools in Vilna, but my mother was not taking any more chances. The idea that her son could be lost to the love of women was intolerable to her. I must have been barely eight years old when she began to talk to me about what she called my future "successes," a promise of mysterious and yet interesting delights, of moonlit balconies, of ardent vows at dawn, of sighs and languishing eyes under half-lowered lashes, of hands furtively pressed, of bitter parting tears and of the sweet tears of surrender. There was a slightly guilty smile upon her lips as she thus talked to me, perhaps in spite of herself, looking strangely young, bestowing upon me all the tender tributes which had once been hers by right of beauty: their memory and perhaps a secret and nostalgic regret must have still haunted her. I leaned against her with a nonchalant air, listening to her promise with a far greater attention than she was probably aware of, licking the jam from my slice of bread and butter to keep myself in countenance; I was far too young to understand that she was merely trying to exorcise the loneliness of her own life as a woman, and her own secret longings and memories.

Thus, with the ballet and the violin abandoned by the roadside, and prompted by some instinctive understanding of my mother's dreams, I decided to try my hand at painting. I began to spend long hours brush in hand, and soon found in my schoolboy's water-color box a source of endless wonders. Time flew by unnoticed as I sat in my corner, sucking my tongue, getting slowly drunk on reds and yellows and greens and blues, and experiencing a strange and intoxicating feeling of power—to this day, painting seems to me the only true way of possessing the world.

I was in my tenth year when my drawing master at school spoke to my mother. In his opinion, her son clearly had a talent for painting, and he advised her to take this gift seriously and help it to develop.

The poor man certainly didn't expect the effect his innocent revelation would have upon my mother. I shall never forget the look of terror upon her face when she came into my bedroom, the air of utter discouragement as she sat there facing me with an air of silent supplication. Where painters were concerned, this woman, who never spoke the word "art" in other than a tone of almost religious reverence, was nevertheless hopelessly imbued with the middle-class prejudices of the time; all painters were condemned to poverty, despair, disease and drunkenness. In her mind, painting and ruined lives went hand in hand. Incapable of imagining me moderately gifted, her inflamed imagination rushing at once to extremes, she immediately saw me as a misunderstood genius, drowning my sorrow in alcohol or starved into consumption. What she knew of the tragic careers of Van Gogh and Gauguin—incapable of seeing me in any light but that of a hero, she was now seeing me as an ill-starred one—now put her into a state close to panic and brought tears to her eyes. All this she expressed at last, in a few words that bore the unmistakable mark of a far greater knowledge of the world than I could understand then:

"Maybe you are a genius, and then they will make you pay for it."

From then on, my box of water colors developed a tiresome habit of disappearing, and when, after a threatening scene, I would manage to get it back from her and start painting, she would leave the room, only to come back almost at once, prowling around me like some restless animal, looking at me with such apprehension that one day, sickened by the whole business, I left my paints and brushes alone and never touched them again.

I have never quite forgiven her this, however, and whenever I look at a good painting there is more frustration in me than pleasure, and when I wander into an artist's studio, I shyly pick up the brush and stare at the color-splattered palette with the eyes of a boy eight years old: when I finally turn away, it is almost with the impression of leaving behind an essential part of myself.

Where writing was concerned, however, my mother harbored none of those superstitious fears and prejudices; on the contrary, she gave it her full-hearted approval, regarding literature as if it were some very great lady well received in society, and courted by the very best people.

Goethe, she told me, had been loaded with honors, and died rich, Tolstoy was a count and Victor Hugo President of the Republic—where she got that last idea, I cannot say, but she clung to it tenaciously. Then, just as she was describing literature as blessed with respectability and social recognition, a cloud descended upon her face.

"But there is still the danger of venereal disease," she told me. "You must be very careful. Guy de Maupassant died in madness and Heine was paralyzed."

She sat there under the mimosa tree, over the railway, smoking, and looking worried.

"It starts with a pimple," she warned me.

"I know."

"Then your nose falls off. You must promise to be very careful."

"I will do my best."

My love life at that time had not taken me beyond fascinated peeping under the skirts of Mariette, our daily maid, when she climbed on a stool to wash the walls.

"Perhaps it would be better if we married young—some nice, clean girl," my mother concluded, with an expression of obvious disgust.

We both knew very well that that was not what was expected of me: society women, and only the most beautiful and desirable among them, prima ballerinas, great actresses—Rachel, La Duse and the divine Garbo—to quote only a few chosen at random—nothing else would do. It all seemed very acceptable to me. If only the damn kitchen stool was a little higher, or, even better, if Mariette would understand how important it was for me to start my career at once . . . I was thirteen and a half, and already eager to get on with the job.

And so, with music, dancing and painting out of the way, we resigned ourselves to literature, in spite of the venereal peril, and began to look for a pen name worthy of the masterpieces which the world was to receive from us. I sat day after day in my little room, waiting for inspiration to visit me, trying to invent a pseudonym that would express, in a combination of noble and striking sounds, our dream of artistic achievement, a pen name grand enough to compensate for my own feeling of insecurity and helplessness at the idea of everything my mother expected from me. Now and again, my mother would pop her head discreetly through the door, and lovingly watch her son in the throes of creation. We were both getting terribly impatient to know, at last, under what name we were to become famous, and we were both so far removed from reality, and so deeply immersed in our dream, that the idea that I could have much better employed my time by selling newspapers in the street, running errands, or doing any other kind of work to help my mother make a living never occurred to either of us.

"How is it going?"

I read out aloud to her the immortal words of my inspired labor of the day. I must say that I was never satisfied with my efforts. No name, however noble and resounding, seemed worthy of what I meant to accomplish for her sake:

"Alexandre Natal; Armand de la Torre; Terral; Vasco de la Fernaye . . ."

After each glittering parade of conquering names, we looked at each other, and shook our heads. No, it won't do—it won't do at all. It seemed to us that all the good names had already been taken: "Goethe" had already been grabbed, and so had "Shakespeare" and "Victor Hugo"—and yet that was exactly what I wanted to be for her. As she stood there in the door, listening and smoking nervously, turning over in her mind each new and noble-sounding name I was offering her, there were moments when tears came to my eyes, when I could no longer hear my need to shield and to protect her, and it seemed to me that the world was not large enough to contain all my love.

"What we really need is something like 'Gabriele d'Annunzio,' " my mother said, adding, with a hint of profound admiration and respect: "He made La Duse suffer terribly."

She had always considered it proper that a great artist should make women suffer, and she clearly expected that I would apply myself to that task. She still belonged, and deeply so, to the old-fashioned bourgeois world, where "success with women" ranked with official honors, medals, splendid uniforms, champagne, jewels and ambassadorial receptions as an essential attribute of a man of the world. She was romantic in a way that today can be found only in bad literature, and she tried desperately to make me take my place in a dream of the nineteenth-century Russian girl, in a world of Viennese waltzes and gypsy music, horsemen, camellias, whispers at dawn and tears by candlelight. When she spoke of Vronsky and Anna Karenina, she stroked my hair, looking at me with such a strange mixture of admiration and reproach that there was no mistaking who Vronsky was in her mind. Perhaps deep in the unconscious of this woman who had once been so beautiful, and who had loved deeply a man who had abandoned her, there was a longing for emotional and physical revenge, and so she expected her son to be both triumphant and invulnerable, and to inflict upon others what had been inflicted on her. After an exhausting day, going from door to door, introducing herself to the English tourists in the luxury hotels as an impoverished member of the Russian aristocracy, reduced to selling the "last of my family jewels"—after a day of humiliating and often sterile effort, for she rarely brought off more than one sale a month—she would come into my room, light a cigarette and sit down with a smile, facing the little boy in short pants, who, crushed under the burden of such a love and of his own helplessness and desperate desire to protect her, spent his days in hunting for some name beautiful enough, grand enough, promising and magnificent enough to express all he wanted to give her, a name that would ring loud and clear in his mother's ear, with all the convincing echo of his future victories:

"Roland de Chantecler, Romain de Mysore . . ."

"Perhaps it would be more prudent to choose a less aristocratic name, just in case there is another revolution," said my mother.

None of the pseudonyms I kept inventing ever satisfied her, none of them, she seemed to think, was good enough for me— or was it, perhaps, that she was thus trying to give me confidence in my destiny and the courage to achieve it? She must have been aware how desperate I often felt, how deeply I resented still being only a child who could do nothing for her. For so many penniless years, her life had been a daily battle for survival: I knew this, and yet all I could do to help was to hide my knowledge from her. Each morning, leaning over our balcony, I watched her, as she was setting out for her daily battle down the Avenue Shakespeare, with her cane, her cigarette and her little bag filled with the "family jewels." Often she caught sight of my anxious face, and waved, smiling happily, while both of us wondered whether this time the ring, the watch, the necklace, the gold snuff box, would find a purchaser, so that the rent could be paid, and the debt settled in the grocery shop. And so . . .

"Roland Campéador; Alain Brisar; Hubert de Longpré; Romain Cortès . . ."

But no, I could see from the expression on her face that none of them was good enough, and I was beginning to wonder whether I should ever find a name beautiful and promising enough to fit her dream and everything she wanted for me.

Years later, when for the first time I heard the name of General de Gaulle on the day of his famous call to arms over the London radio, on June 18, 1940, my first reaction was one of anger with myself for not having hit on this magnificent name fifteen years earlier, during my endless search for a good pseudonym. "Charles de Gaulle"—this would certainly have pleased my mother, especially if I had written it with only one "l," like our old Gaul, mother of France. I can only say that life is paved with missed opportunities.

CHAPTER 4

THE MATERNAL LOVE IN WHICH I BASKED SUDdenly presented me with a quite unexpected and extremely gratifying bit of good fortune.

When business was good, that is, when the sale of some of the "family jewels" permitted my mother to look forward to a month of relative material security, her first concern was to pay a visit to a good hairdresser, followed by tea on the terrace of the Hôtel Royal while listening to a gypsy orchestra—she loved gypsy music and songs and, to my embarrassment, she would always pick up some bit of the song with delight but rather too loudly; then, with that optimistic streak in her nature that no hardship or financial disaster could ever dampen, she would hire a daily maid, convinced that our difficulties were over, and that prosperity was there to stay. The only housework that my mother always resented was scrubbing the floors, and for her to have a maid was a supreme luxury and gave her a tremendous feeling of achievement. She had always been extremely status conscious in an old-fashioned, naïve and childish way. Once, during her absence, trying to be helpful, and knowing her distaste for this harmless housework, I armed myself with a floor cloth, a bucket of water and a piece of household soap and proceeded to wash the floor of our little apartment. Unfortunately, my mother returned from her errands earlier than I expected and caught me on all fours, rubbing, scrubbing, polishing and generally doing my best. She looked horror-stricken;

her lips began to tremble and tears came to her eyes as she stared at me with an expression of hurt reproach; I must have spent at least an hour trying to console her, reminding her that we were living in a democratic country where such little household chores were considered quite normal and not in the least degrading.

Mariette, the new maid, was a sturdy young woman with invitingly suggestive thighs, earthy legs, dark, mischievous eyes, and blessed with such a firm, round, lively and truly impressive behind that the haunting vision of that interesting aspect of her personality frequently obscured the face of my math teacher at school. This infinitely absorbing and fascinating vision was actually the sole reason for my wide-eyed and trancelike contemplation of that excellent man's features. My mouth slightly open and my throat dry, my eyes riveted to his face and my cheeks burning, I sat there, unable, needless to say, to pay the slightest attention to what he was saying, and when, turning his back to the class, he would start to write algebra signs on the board, I would make an effort to transfer my hallucinated gaze to the black surface, only to see the object of my dreams take shape there too—ever since then black has always had on me the happiest effect. Whenever the good professor, flattered by my fascinated attention, asked me a question, I rolled my eyes and swallowed hard and stared at Mariette's posterior with an expression of mild surprise, until the irritated voice of Monsieur Valu brought me down to earth.

"It just doesn't make sense," the teacher exclaimed. "You seem to be hanging on my every word and yet you're obviously absorbed in something else!"

This was correct.

With the best of wills it was impossible for me to explain to this excellent man what it was that I saw with such perfection in lieu of his face.

And so Mariette began to play a part in my life which grew larger and more important every day. It got hold of me as soon as I opened my eyes in the morning and would last more or less all day long. As soon as this Mediterranean goddess graced our little apartment with her undulating presence, my heart would jump into my throat and my hair almost stand on end, while I tried to remain motionless on my bed, terribly burdened and awkward. I also often had goose flesh, I shook, and once or twice, when she came too close, I got suddenly covered with hives from head to foot. In spite of this state of semiconsciousness and stupor into which my deity threw me every morning, it slowly dawned on me that Mariette too was observing me with a certain amount of interest. Once or twice she would come very close, put her hands on her hips, stare at me with a dreamy smile, sigh, shake her head, and say with a certain amount of wonder:

"She can never stop talking about you. She just goes on, and on. . . . And all the great things you're going to do and all the beautiful ladies who are going to love you, and this and that. . . . In the end it does something to me. Maybe she thinks I am made of wood, or something."

I felt rather put out. My mother was the last person I wanted to be bothered with just then. Twisted on my bed, doubled in two, knees up, head against the wall, I hardly dared move.

"She speaks of you as if you were a Prince Charming or something. . . . My little Romain here, my little Romain there . . . I know it's only because she's your mother, but in the end, a girl begins to wonder. . . ."

Mariette's voice had a most peculiar effect on me. It was a voice unlike any other I have ever heard. To begin with, it didn't seem to come from her throat at all—though where it did come from I didn't in the least know. And even more strangely, it didn't go where voices are supposed to go. In any case, it certainly didn't go to my ears. It was very odd.

"It gets me, in the end," Mariette concluded. "I begin to wonder what it is that makes you so special. . . ."

She would stare at me for another second, then turn away, and go back to her work. I would lie there on the bed unable to move, reduced from head to foot to the helpless rigidity of a felled tree. Neither of us spoke another word. Now and again Mariette would turn her head in my direction, sigh and go on rubbing the floor: the sight of such an appalling waste was heartbreaking. I desperately wanted to do something about it, but I felt quite literally nailed to the bed. Soon the work would be finished and Mariette would go home. I saw her leave with the feeling that a part of my flesh had left me forever. My life was over. I was a failure. Roland de Chantecler, Artemis Kohinore and Hubert de la Roche Rouge gave up pretending, stuck their fists in their eyes and set up a terrible howling.

But I was soon to learn the famous French saying: a woman's will is God's will. Mariette kept looking at me oddly, her feminine curiosity and, probably, some obscure rivalry or jealousy aroused by my mother's never-ending love song and the highly-colored, romantic and intriguing picture she was constantly conjuring up of the triumphant future awaiting me. And so at last the miracle occurred. I still remember vividly that mischievous face close to mine, the hand gently caressing my cheek, that moment of total deliverance, of strangely satisfying weightlessness, as I was floating somewhere in another and better world and the throaty voice murmuring into my ear:

"You mustn't tell her, Monsieur Romain. It just got me in the end. Course she's your mother, but then the way she speaks about you, as if there had never been anyone like you . . . I just couldn't help it. I just had to find out. Mother or no mother, there will never be another woman to love you the way she does. That's God's honest truth."

It was. But I didn't know it then. It was only after my fortieth winter that I began to understand. It is wrong to have been loved so much so young, so early. At the dawn of life, you thus acquire a bad habit, the worst habit there is: the habit of being loved. You can't get rid of it. You believe that you have it in you, that you have it in you to be loved, that it is your due, that it will always be there around you, that it can always be found again, that the world owes it to you, and you keep looking, thirsting, summoning, until you find yourself on the beach at Big Sur, with only your brother the ocean, and his tortured tumult, with only your brother the ocean able to understand your heart. In your mother's love, life makes you a promise at the dawn of life that it will never keep. You have known something that you will never know again. You will go hungry to the end of your days. Leftovers, cold tidbits, that's what you will find in front of you at each new feast. After that first encounter so early in the dawn, each time a woman takes you in her arms and presses you to her heart and murmurs sweet words into your ear, you will always do your best to forget and to believe, but you will always know better. You will always crawl back to your mother's grave and howl like a lost dog. Never again, never again, never again. Lovely arms embrace your neck, gentle lips whisper sweetly into your ear, and in those eyes you will catch glimpses of beauty now and then, but it's too late, too little, you know where all the beauty lies, and from this first and final knowledge not even the sweetest breast can bribe you away. You have long since found the spring and you have drunk it dry. You will walk through the desert from mirage to mirage, and your thirst will remain such that you will become a drunkard, but each sweet gulp will only rekindle your longing for the one and only source. Wherever you go, you carry within you the poison of comparisons, and you spend your days waiting for something you have already had and will never have again.

I am not saying that mothers should be prevented from loving their young. I am only saying that they should have someone else to love as well. If my mother had had a husband or a lover I would not have spent my days dying of thirst beside so many fountains.

CHAPTER 5

THE MARIETTE EPISODE CAME TO AN END IN AN abrupt and unexpected manner. One morning I sauntered off innocently for school with my satchel under my arm, but soon turned about and ran back home to join my love, who usually made her appearance at the flat at about half past eight. By then my mother was on her way to work, catching, bag in hand, the eight-fifteen bus for Cannes, where she hoped to find buyers for the "family jewels" among the English visitors at the Hôtel Martinez. We had every reason to feel completely safe. But fate, in its usual beastly manner, thought it funny to organize a bus strike that very morning, and so my mother was obliged to turn back. Hardly had she opened the front door when, to her horror, she heard what she thought were cries of pain and, convinced that I was dying on the floor in the throes of acute appendicitis— the threat of a fatal attack of appendicitis was always present in her mind, a humble and prosaic incarnation of Greek tragedy —she rushed to my rescue. I had just come back to my senses, and was submerged in that happy state of beatitude and absence which is one of mankind's greater moments here below. At the age of thirteen and a half I had the feeling that my life had been a complete success, that I had fulfilled my destiny and, from my seat among the gods, I was looking with detachment at my big toe, the only reminder of that lowly earth where common mortals dwelt. It was one of those moments of total serenity which the spiritual part of me, always aspiring to the heights of philosophical detachment, so often compelled me to seek in the days of my meditative youth; one of those moments when all the materialistic and cynical views of life collapse like pathetic fabrications before the sovereign evidence of life's beauty, meaning and wisdom, and when every man experiences the triumphant feeling of an artist of genius who has just entirely expressed himself. In this state of euphoria, I accepted my mother's sudden arrival on the scene as I would have accepted any other manifestation of unleashed elements—that is to say, in a spirit of indulgence. I welcomed her with a mild smile. Mariette's reaction was somewhat different. With a piercing shriek, she jumped out of bed. The ensuing scene did manage, however, to arouse in me some interest, and from my Olympian peak I observed it with a vague curiosity. My mother was still holding her cane in her hand, and, having in a flash grasped the full extent of the disaster, she raised her arm and went into immediate action. The cane descended upon the face of my math teacher with vigor and accuracy. Mariette began to howl and did her best to protect that adorable aspect of her personality. In one instant, the small room filled with a terrifying tumult, above which the old Russian word *kourva* (whore) rose with all the vibrant power of my mother's sense of drama and art of delivery.

She had to the highest degree the sense of invective: in a few well-chosen words her poetic and inspired nature could miraculously create an atmosphere compared to which Gorki's *Lower Depths* would appear ethereal and refined; it took very little for this distinguished-looking white-haired lady, who so deeply impressed by her unmistakably aristocratic poise the purchasers of our "family jewels," to conjure suddenly before the eyes of her flabbergasted audience all the holy Russia of drunken coachmen, swearing moujiks and Volga boatmen; she had been blessed, without any doubt, with a truly impressive talent for holding an audience spellbound, and this stunning and earth-shaking scene, of which I still cannot think without a shudder, seemed to support fully her claim that she had been in her youth a great dramatic artist on the Russian stage.

This last point, however, remains for me to this day rather obscure. True, I had always known that my mother was once a "dramatic artist" and how proud her voice sounded, whenever she uttered those words! I still have a vision of myself, at the age of five or six, sitting beside her in a sleigh, with only the tip of my nose emerging from under the heavy blanket, listening to the melancholy tinkling of the horses' bells as we were driven, through snow-bound wastes, from some freezing factory where my mother had been "giving Chekhov" for an audience of workers, or from some desolate barracks where she had been entertaining the gaping audience of soldiers and sailors of the Revolution with "poetry reading." I can see myself no less clearly sitting on the floor of her dressing room in a Moscow theatre, playing with odds and ends of multicolored stuffs which I was trying to arrange into a harmonious pattern— my earliest attempts at artistic expression. I even remember the name of the play in which she was appearing at that time: *Le Chien du Jardinier*. The mysterious inside world of the theatre is among my earliest childhood memories: the delicious smell of wood and paint, the empty stage where I adventured cautiously in a sham forest, and stopped frozen with fear at the sudden sight of the dark auditorium gaping at me. I can still see the painted faces of the actors, looking strangely yellow, with black and white circles around their eyes, smiling at me; men and women in fantastic clothes and with bright red lips holding me on their knees, while my mother was in front of the footlights. And I remember a Soviet sailor perching me on his shoulders, so that I might see my mother playing the part of Rosa in *The Shipwreck of Hope*, and her stage name written on the door of her dressing room—the first Russian words that I learned to spell out for myself: Nina Borisovskaia. It would seem, therefore, that my mother was not exaggerating when she proudly talked of her "artistic past," and that her position in the small world of the Russian theatre, round about the years

1919-1920, was solidly established. On the other hand, Ivan Mosjoukine, the great movie actor of the silent-picture era, who had known my mother in her earlier days, has always been curiously evasive on the subject of her stage career. Fixing me with his strange pale eyes under the famous Cagliostro brows, he only once referred to the subject in an elusive way, on the terrace of the Grande Bleue, where he often invited me for a cup of coffee when he was making a movie in Nice: "Your mother ought to have studied more, she should have done the conservatoire; unfortunately, circumstances prevented her from developing her talent. Besides, after you were born, young man, nothing and no one else really mattered to her. . . ." And then he would stare at me curiously, with just a cautious trace of irony on his lips. I also knew that my mother was born somewhere in the Russian steppe, at Kursk, to be precise, the daughter of a little Jewish watchmaker, that she had been very beautiful, that she had married very young—at sixteen—and then been divorced, again married and again divorced. And all the rest, all that mattered, were a cheek against mine; a melodious voice whispering into my ear, or speaking to me of a strange faraway land called France, where all the beauty lies, murmuring mysterious tales of wonders awaiting me, singing, laughing—a completely carefree laughter, with that quality of gaiety and happiness that to this day I associate with a woman in love, even though it was only her child's head which she was pressing against her breast—a laughter that I shall hope for, look for, long for till I breathe my last; a whiff of lily-of-the-valley— her favorite perfume, even in old age; a veil of soft dark hair falling over my face—and again, a whisper in my ears, a promise of things to come, of proud victories, of battles won, strange tales of the distant country which I should one day call my own. Dramatic school or no, conservatoire or no she must have been very talented indeed, for her voice has left on me an indelible mark; in evoking France for me, she could summon to her aid all the magic art of eastern storytellers, and a power of conviction from which I have never recovered. To this day there are moments when I find myself *waiting* for France, for that never-never land of which I heard so much, which I have never known and never shall know; for the land of France, which, from my earliest childhood, my mother conjured up for me in her lyrical and inspired descriptions, has become for me a fairy tale, a mythical place, a poetical masterpiece that no fact of life, no contact with reality could ever encompass or reveal. She knew our language remarkably well, though she spoke it with a strong Russian accent, a trace of which, as I am told, I retain in my own voice to this day. How, where, for whom, at what period of her life, she learned to speak French, she never told me. "I have been in Nice and in Paris"—that was all she would ever admit. In her freezing little dressing room at the Moscow theatre, in the flat we shared with three other families of actors, among whom I remember only an old man by the name of Svertchkov—and where a young nursemaid called Aniela looked after me—and later still, in the cattle-and-goods train which took us west—a three-week journey with typhus for company—my mother would kneel beside me, rubbing my numbed fingers, and talk to me about the distant land where my future lay and where all the dreams came true; where all men were free and equal; where artists were received in the best houses; where Victor Hugo had been President of the Republic. The camphor beads which I wore round my neck—a sovereign remedy, my mother was assured, against the typhus-carrying lice—prickled my nose and made me sneeze. I was going to be a great violinist, a great actor, a great poet—the French d'Annunzio, another Nijinsky, Emile Zola; we were kept in quarantine at Lida on the Polish frontier; I was walking with my mother along the railway tracks in the deep snow, firmly grasping in one hand the chamber pot from which, ever since leaving Moscow, I had refused to be parted—I form attachments very easily; they shaved my head; I screamed as they gave me an anti-cholera shot; we were lying on a straw mattress among a hundred other refugees at the Lida railway station; my mother's eyes had a faraway look and there was a smile on her lips as she pressed me against her, whispering in my ear new tales of wonders awaiting me; le Chevalier Bayard; La Dame aux Camélias; shops stuffed with butter and sugar; Napoleon Bonaparte; Sarah Bernhardt; I fought against sleep and forced my eyes wide open, following her faraway look and trying to see what she saw beyond the dirty wall: Maxim's, the Bois de Boulogne, Austerlitz, Wagram; there is a ball at the Opéra . . . until, at last, I fell asleep with my head on her shoulder and my friend the chamber pot clasped in my arms. Later, much later, after fifteen years of daily contact with French realities, at Nice, where we had reached our journey's end, her face now lined, her hair completely white—an old woman now, there was no denying the fact—but having learned nothing, noticed nothing, with the same confidence and the same happy smile, she refused to acknowledge the stark reality, but still kept seeing only the land of marvels which she had brought with her in her wanderer's bundle; as for me, having been brought up in a fairy tale, but not having my mother's extraordinary gift of seeing around her what lived only in her heart, I at first kept looking about me in amazement and rubbing my eyes, and later, when manhood gave me strength and strength gave me courage, I devoted both to the backbreaking task of making a fairy tale come true.

Yes, my mother had talent—and I have never recovered from it.

And yet, the sinister Agroff, a moneylender who dwelt as befits the rat he was in a dark cellar in the Boulevard Gambetta, a flabby, greasy, white-faced individual from the shores of the Black Sea, upon meeting with some difficulties in collecting the ten per cent interest on the loan my mother had contracted in a moment of particularly dire financial stress, told me one day: "Your mother may play the great lady, but when I first knew her, she was singing in third-rate vodka joints and soldiers' dives. That's where she learned the language. I don't feel insulted. A woman like that cannot insult an honest businessman." Being only fourteen at the time, but already feeling able to do at least that much for my mother, I gave the honest businessman a resounding slap on his big snout, the first, as it happened, of many wildly distributed slaps for which I very soon became famous in the neighborhood, thus starting on a long and brilliant career in that field. For from then on, my mother, dazzled by my first noble exploit on her behalf, got into the habit of calling upon my newly-discovered talent whenever she decided, rightly or wrongly, that she had been insulted, invariably concluding her not always very accurate version of what had happened by saying:

"He thinks I have nobody to protect me, that I can be insulted with impunity. Go and show him how wrong he is!"

I always did. I had a horror of such scenes; moreover, I knew that nine times out of ten the insult was imaginary; that my mother was beginning to see insults everywhere, even though she was more often than not the insulting party, sometimes for no reason at all, simply because she was exhausted and her nerves got the best of her. But I played the game—I could do at least that for her. For so many years she had been fighting her own battles in every possible way, and now that she was aging rapidly, and her health was deteriorating, nothing delighted her more than to feel she had a protector by her side, a man to stand up for her. And so good manners be damned and my delicate feelings overboard! As my friend Albert Camus was to say years later in different circumstances: "If I have to choose between my mother and my ideas, I will choose my mother every time." And so, taking my courage in both hands and gulping down my sense of shame, imposing on my childish features the toughest expression I could command, I proceeded forthwith to track down some unfortunate jeweler, butcher, tobacconist or antique dealer. This supposed offender then saw a boy, quivering with suppressed reluctance, enter his shop, plant himself in front of him with clenched fists, and say, in a voice trembling with anger and resentment of the role imposed on him by filial piety: "Monsieur, you have insulted my mother, and I'm going to teach you a lesson!"—this ritual pronouncement instantly followed by a slap in the face, into which I put all my strength, to compensate for my lack of conviction. Thus I soon acquired in the neighborhood of the Boulevard Gambetta and the Marché de la Buffa the reputation of a young hoodlum, and no one suspected how much I loathed these scenes, how deeply they hurt and humiliated me. If some of my victims, or their children, happen to read these pages, I beg their forgiveness, and I wish to assure them that their sense of injury was more than matched by my own; I repeat that I had no choice; my hooliganism was a labor of love; my helplessness can be fully understood only by those who have grown strong through the toil of a sick and aging mother. Once or twice, knowing her complaint to be wholly unjustified, I tried to revolt. Whenever this happened, tears came into her eyes, her mouth sagged, and an expression of such total defeat came over her face that I rose in silence and went off to my dubious battle on her behalf.

I have never been able to endure the sight of a living creature in the grip of what I can only call a lucid incomprehension of its fate. I have never been able to tolerate the sight of helplessness in man or beast, and in her attitudes my mother had a rare gift for assuming what is most heartbreaking in both. And so Agroff had scarcely stopped speaking when the resounding slap hit him on the cheek, followed by another, for symmetry's sake, to which his only reply was a black look, and: "Hooligan! Just what I'd expect from the offspring of an adventuress and a cad." It was in this sudden and unexpected way that the truth about my interesting origins was revealed to me. Not that the news in the least impressed me, since I attached no importance whatsoever to my past or present; all that mattered was that I knew myself destined to reach those dizzy heights so clearly visible to my mother's eyes; nothing on earth could prevent me from reaching them for her sake. I had always known that my mission on earth was one of retribution; that I existed, as it were, only by proxy; that the mysterious force presiding over our destiny had cast me onto the scale so as to balance by the weight of my achievement my mother's life of toil, loneliness and sacrifice. I believed that in life's darkest crannies there lay concealed a secret, smiling, and compassionate logic; that justice always triumphed in the end; I believed deeply in all those clichés that had for centuries assured man's survival on this earth; I could not see a look of total helplessness on my mother's face without feeling surging within me an extraordinary confidence in my destiny. At the darkest moments of the war, in the thick of the battle, I always faced peril with a feeling of invincibility. Nothing could happen to me because I was her happy ending. In that system of weights and measures which men try so desperately to impose upon the universe, I always saw myself as *her* victory.

This conviction did not come to me by chance. It was but a reflection of the faith which my mother had since his earliest childhood placed in her son. I was, I think, eight years old when my mother's grandiose vision of my future led to a scene the horror, comedy, and shame of which will continue to haunt me as long as I live.

CHAPTER 6

WE WERE STRANDED AT THAT TIME IN THE then Polish, formerly Lithuanian, and now Russian town of Vilna, "a temporary halt," as my mother never failed to point out, on our way to France, a country where we were to make our permanent home, which was eagerly awaiting me, and where I was to "grow up, study, and become *somebody*." This last word was always underlined and accompanied by a particularly meaningful stare. With the usual inventiveness and energy she showed whenever our survival was at stake, and without any previous experience in the field, she was busily engaged in designing women's hats in our flat, haughtily publicized through the mail and display cards as the "Grand Salon de Modes de Paris." A clever use of false labels tricked our distinguished clientele into believing that the hats were the work of a then famous Parisian king of fashion, Paul Poiret. My mother went from house to house with her hatboxes, a woman still young, with large green eyes and a face radiant with a mother's indomitable will, entirely beyond the reach of discouragement or doubt. I remained at home with Aniela, who had followed us from Moscow a year earlier. The last of our family jewels—real ones, this time—had been long gone, and the winter was bitterly cold in Vilna, where the snow slowly piled up on the wooden sidewalks against the dirty gray walls. The hats were selling badly. Often, when my mother returned exhausted and frozen from her rounds, the owner of the building would be waiting for her on the stairs and shout at her, threatening to throw us into the street if the rent wasn't paid within twenty-four hours. It was always paid, though how I shall never know. All I can say is that the rent was always paid, the stove lit, tea, bread, butter and eggs were put before me, and my mother would kiss me, her cheeks still icy and smelling of snow, and then look at me, her eyes aglow with that bright flame of pride and triumph which I so well remember. We were then truly at the very bottom—I won't say at the bottom of the "abyss" because I have since learned that the abyss is bottomless and that all records of falling and sinking can be broken there without ever exhausting the possibilities of that interesting institution. Often, when she had come back from her expeditions through the snow-blanketed town, and had stacked her hatboxes in a corner, my mother would sit down, light a cigarette, cross her legs and look at me with a knowing smile.

"What is it, Mother?"

"Nothing. Give me a kiss."

I would kiss her. She held me in her arms, her eyes fixed over my shoulder on some mysterious, bright point in our future, visible only to her in the magical land where all the beauty lies.

"You are going to be a French ambassador," she would say, or rather state, with absolute conviction; I had not the slightest idea what the word meant, but that did not in the least keep me from agreeing with her. I was only eight, but I had already made up my mind: whatever my mother wanted I would accomplish for her—there was absolutely nothing that I would let stand in the way.

"You are going to be a French ambassador."

"Good," I would say with a nonchalant air.

Aniela, sitting close to the stove, gave me a respectful look, while my mother wiped her tears of happiness and hugged me tight.

"You will have a motorcar."

She had been walking the streets all day, with the temperature well below freezing.

"All it will take is a little patience."

The wood was crackling in the porcelain stove. Outside, the snow gave the world a strange denseness, and a dimension of silence which the bell of an occasional sleigh seemed to intensify. Aniela, bent over her work, was sewing another forged PAUL POIRET, MADE IN PARIS label into the last of the day's hats. My mother's face was completely peaceful. All traces of fatigue and anxiety had vanished. Her gaze was still lost in the land of all marvels, and so compelling was her stare, and so convincing her smile, that, in spite of myself, I turned my head in that direction, as I almost always did, trying to catch at least a glimpse of what she was seeing. She spoke to me of France as other mothers speak to their children of Snow White and Puss in Boots. Try as I may, I have never entirely succeeded in ridding myself of that image of France seen as a never-never land of shining heroes and exemplary virtues. I am probably one of the few men alive who have remained completely loyal to a nursery tale.

Unfortunately my mother was not the woman to keep to herself the consoling dream of my future greatness which dwelt within her. Everything with her was instantly proclaimed, spoken aloud, trumpeted abroad, announced to all, projected over the heads of the incredulous populace, more often than not to the accompaniment of lava, stones and thunder.

We had neighbors, and those neighbors did not like my mother. The petite bourgeoisie of Vilna was just as stupid and prejudiced as it is everywhere, and the comings and goings of this foreigner in the black leather coat, with her mysterious boxes, were soon reported to the Polish police, who were then extremely suspicious of Russian refugees. My mother was denounced as a receiver of stolen goods. She had no difficulty in confounding her detractors, but shame, grief, and indignation assumed, as always with her, an explosive and aggressive character. After the police had left she spent some time crying among her hats—women's hats have since remained one of my smaller phobias—then she took me by the hand, and, announcing to Aniela that "they don't know whom they are dealing with, but they'll soon find out," led me out of the flat onto the stairs. What followed was one of the most painful experiences of my life—and I have known quite a few.

She went from door to door, ringing, knocking, and ordering the tenants to "crawl out of their holes." When the first insults had been exchanged—and in the matter of insults my mother always and undeniably had the best of it—she drew me to her side, and, exhibiting me with a noble theatrical gesture to the assembled company, announced with pride and vehemence, in a voice which still resounds with an uncanny clarity in my ears:

"Dirty little bourgeois bedbugs, you don't seem to realize with whom you have the honor of speaking! My son will be an Ambassador of France, a Chevalier of the Legion of Honor, a great dramatic author, a second Ibsen, a new Gabriele d'Annunzio. . . . He . . ."

She was searching her mind for something crashingly final, for a supreme and unanswerable proof of worldly success and supreme achievement: "He will have his suits made in London!"

Even as my hand writes these words I can hear the loud, coarse laughter of the "dirty bourgeois bedbugs."

The blood still rushes to my cheeks, and I can remember every wounding word they spat at us, and I see around me their stupid, mocking faces, so superior, so full of hatred and contempt. I know today that they were just ordinary human faces, full of ordinary hatred and contempt, such as one meets with every day. But I was only a child then—I didn't know, and they appeared horrible to me. And perhaps I shall be allowed to say, for the clarity of this tale, and comical as it may sound, I am today a Consul General of France, an officer of the Legion of Honor, and if I failed to become either an Ibsen or a d'Annunzio, the world knows my name, and if you wish you can laugh at me for saying this—you are welcome to: I am long past any fear of ridicule, and anyway, I am writing this for those who have a heart.

And make no mistake about it: I have my suits made in

London. I have a strong dislike of the English "cut," but I have no choice.

I believe that nothing has played a more important part in my life than the burst of laughter flung in my face on the staircase of an old block of flats at Number 16, Grand Pohulanka in the town of Vilna. To it I owe everything I am today. For better or worse, that laughter has become me.

My mother stood there straight and proud, facing the storm, pressing me against her with both arms, her head held high. She showed no trace of embarrassment or humiliation. She *knew*. My life in the weeks that followed was not very pleasant. Though I was only eight, my sense of ridicule was highly developed— my mother, naturally, had something to do with that. But I have gradually come to terms with it. Slowly but surely I have learned how to lose my pants in public without feeling in the least embarrassed. I have learned that a man is something that cannot be ridiculed.

But during those few terrible minutes on the stairs, under the jibes, the crushing comments and the insults, I felt that my breast had become a cage from which an animal in the grip of pain and panic was desperately trying to escape.

There was, at that time, a woodshed in the courtyard of our block, and my favorite hiding place was at the very heart of the pile of logs. I felt marvelously secure when, after much expert and acrobatic wriggling—the stacks of wood were two floors high—I had succeeded in working my way inside it, protected from the world by walls of damp, sweet-smelling timber. I spent long hours in my secret kingdom, completely happy, out of reach. Parents strictly forbade their children to go near that fragile and menacing structure: one disturbed log, one accidental push, and the whole thing might come crashing down and bury one inside of it. I had acquired a high degree of skill in worming my way along the narrow passage of this universe over which I ruled as lord and master, where a single false move would provoke an avalanche, but where I felt at home. By cunningly shifting the logs I had constructed a whole maze of galleries and secret passages, a system of burrows, a safe and friendly world, so different from the other, into which I slithered like a ferret. I would lie hidden there in spite of the dampness which would gradually soak the bottom of my pants. I knew exactly which logs to move when I wanted to open a passage, and always carefully replaced them behind me so as to increase still more my feeling of inaccessibility.

And so I made straight for my wooden hide-out as soon as I could do so decently—that is, without giving the impression that I was abandoning my mother and leaving her to face the enemy alone. We remained together on the battlefield until the end and were the last to withdraw.

With a few expert movements I worked my way into the maze, replacing each log behind me, soon reaching the very center of the edifice, and there, with fifteen or eighteen feet of protecting carapace around me, I burst into tears. I cried for a long time, and then proceeded to examine the logs, choosing those I would have to shift to bring my wooden fastness crashing down on me and so deliver me from the world forever. I touched them, one by one, with a feeling of gratitude. I can still remember their friendly and reassuring contact, and the sense of peace that came over me at the idea that I was never again to be humiliated and unhappy. All I had to do was to push the logs simultaneously with my feet and back.

I worked myself into the right position.

Then I remembered that I had in my pocket a piece of poppy-seed cake which I had stolen that morning from the back of the pastry shop, while the owner was busy serving customers. I ate the cake. Then I reassumed my position, sighed, and got ready to push.

I was saved by a cat. I suddenly caught sight of its face between two of the logs. For a moment, we stared at each other in astonishment. It was an incredibly skinny, mangy, marmalade-colored tom, with torn ears and that knowing, speculative look which all toms acquire as a result of rich and varied experience.

He studied me attentively and then proceeded to lick my face. I had no illusions about the motive for this sudden display of affection on the part of a stranger: there were still some crumbs of cake stuck to my cheeks and chin. His caresses were strictly self-interested. But I did not let that worry me unduly. The feel of the rough, warm tongue on my face made me smile with delight. I shut my eyes and surrendered to the moment— neither then nor later, in the course of my life, have I ever attempted to find out what, exactly, lay behind the marks of affection lavished upon me. What matters is a friendly muzzle, a warm and diligent tongue which comes and goes over your face with every appearance of friendliness and compassion. That is all I need to feel happy.

By the time the tom had come to the end of his attentions, I felt a great deal better. The world was still full of pleasant possibilities and friendships. My marmalade savior was now rubbing himself against my face and purring loudly. I did my best to imitate him, and we had a whale of a time seeing which of us could purr the louder. I scraped up the last crumbs of cake from my pocket and offered them to him. He showed a marked interest and graciously deigned to lean against my face, with tail held stiff and straight. He nibbled my ear. In short, life was once again worth living. A few minutes later I scrambled out of my wooden shelter and made for the house, my hands in my pockets, whistling a tune, with the cat at my heels.

I have always thought since that it is better to have a few crumbs of cake handy, if one wants to be loved in a truly disinterested manner.

It goes without saying that the words *frantzuski poslannik*— French Ambassador—followed me for months wherever I went, and when the pastry cook, whose name was Michka, finally caught me tiptoeing out of his shop with a splendid piece of poppy-seed cake in my hand, all and sundry were called to witness that diplomatic immunity did not cover a certain well-known part of my person.

CHAPTER 7

Not all the members of the audience found
so screamingly funny the dramatic revelation of my future greatness made by my mother to the tenants of Number 16, Grand
Pohulanka. There was among them a certain Mr. Piekielny—which in
Polish means "infernal." I do not know in what circumstances
the ancestors of this excellent man came by such an unusual
name, and perhaps there were some among them who did something to deserve it. But not so our neighbor. Mr. Piekielny
looked like a melancholy mouse, meticulously clean and with
a gentle, preoccupied air. He was as self-effacing as a man can
be when, by force of nature, he is compelled to rise, if only
so little, above the surface of the earth. He was an impressionable soul, and the complete assurance with which my mother
had launched her prophecy, laying her hand on my head in
the best biblical manner, had a profound and lasting effect upon
him. Whenever he passed me on the stairs, he gave me a serious
and respectful look. Once or twice he ventured to pat my head.
He gave me a dozen lead soldiers and a cardboard Foreign
Legion fort. Then, one day, he took me into his flat, where he
plied me with pastry and Turkish delight. While I stuffed myself to the bursting point—who can say what tomorrow may
bring?—the little fellow sat on the edge of the chair facing me,
stroking his goatee stained yellow with nicotine. He invited me
several times—and then one day came the moving request, the

cry of the heart, the confession of the devouring and proud ambition which this kindly human mouse had been carrying hidden beneath his vest.

"When you become . . ."

He looked away with an embarrassed stare, as though conscious of his naïveté and yet unable to control it:

"When you become . . . everything your mother says . . ."

I studied him with absorbed attention. I had eaten the raisin cake but I had as yet scarcely touched the box of Turkish delight. I guessed instinctively that I had no right to it except by reason of the dazzling future which my mother had predicted for me.

"I'm going to be a French Ambassador," I said with complete self-assurance.

"Have some more Turkish delight," said Mr. Piekielny, pushing the box toward me.

I helped myself. He coughed discreetly.

"Mothers," he remarked, "have a way of feeling these things. Perhaps you will really be someone of true importance. . . . Perhaps you will meet the famous and the great of this world. . . ."

He leaned across and laid his hand on my knee.

"Well then, when you meet them, when you talk to them, promise me one thing. Promise me to tell them . . ."

His voice shook a little and there was a wild, crazy light of hope in the eyes of the mouse: "Tell them there was once a Mr. Piekielny who lived at Number 16, Grand Pohulanka, in Vilna. . . ."

He stared into my eyes with a dumb look of supplication. His hand was still resting on my knee. I ate my Turkish delight, gazing at him for a while without committing myself, and then I nodded briefly.

At the end of the war, in England, where I had gone to continue the struggle after the fall of France, Her Majesty Queen Elizabeth, mother of the present sovereign, came to inspect my squadron at the Hartford Bridge Airfield. When she stopped opposite me and, with the sweet smile which had made her so deservedly popular, asked from what part of France I came, I tactfully answered "from Nice," so as not to complicate matters unnecessarily for Her Gracious Majesty. Then something happened in me. I could almost see the little man jumping up and down, stamping his feet and tearing at his goatee in a desperate attempt to attract my attention and remind me of my promise. I tried to choke back the words, but they rose unbidden to my lips, and, suddenly determined to fulfill the dream of greatness of one little mouse at least, I heard myself announce to the Queen in a loud and perfectly audible voice:

"At Number 16, Grand Pohulanka, in the town of Vilna there lived a certain Mr. Piekielny. . . ."

Her Majesty politely inclined her head and moved on. The officer commanding the "Lorraine" Squadron, my dear friend Henri de Rancourt, shot at me, as he followed her, a venomous look.

But I didn't care: I had at last earned my Turkish delight.

The friendly mouse of Vilna long ago terminated his tiny existence in a Nazi crematorium, along with several million other European Jews.

I, however, continue scrupulously to keep my promise in my various encounters with the great ones of the earth. From the United Nations building in New York to the French Embassy in London, from the Federal Palace in Berne to the Elysée in Paris, from Charles de Gaulle and Vishinsky to ambassadors and high dignitaries everywhere, I have never failed to mention the existence of the little man, and during my years in America I often had the pleasure of telling millions of television viewers that at Number 16, Grand Pohulanka in Vilna, there lived a certain Mr. Piekielny, may God bless his soul.

But what has been done cannot be undone, and the little man's bones, transformed into soap, have long since served to satisfy the German people's famous longing for cleanliness.

I still have a passion for Turkish delight. However, since my mother always saw me as a combination of Lord Byron, Garibaldi, d'Annunzio, d'Artagnan, Robin Hood and Richard the Lion-hearted, I now have to keep a watchful eye upon my waistline. I have not been able to achieve any of the immortal deeds which she expected of me, but at least I have managed not to develop too prominent a paunch. Every day I twist and turn on the floor and twice a week I go for a run—I run, I run, I run—oh, how I run!—but somehow I never manage either to reach, or to leave behind—I don't know which. I also indulge in other attempts at mastery—fencing, archery, target shooting, weight lifting, writing, juggling: it is, I agree, rather foolish, in your forty-fifth year, to believe everything your mother told and foretold you, but I can't help that. I was to be a shining hero, a champion of the world, and what is left of me today still keeps trying, longing, remembering. I have not succeeded in reforming the world, in defeating the gods of stupidity, of prejudice, of hatred, in establishing a reign of dignity and justice among men, but I did win the ping-pong tournament in Nice in 1932, and so I can say that I have truly done my best.

CHAPTER 8

JUST AS WINTER WAS BEGINNING ITS SLOW RE-
treat from the streets of Vilna and the first larks were appearing in the sky, our future suddenly began to look brighter. By
April, the hats "made in Paris" were enjoying a considerable
success, and soon two girls were working busily in Aniela's
room to deal with the increasing demand. My mother no longer
spent her time going from door to door: the "distinguished
clientele" was now flooding to our showroom, and a plate appeared on our door, bearing an inscription in letters of gold:
MAISON NOUVELLE, GRAND SALON DE HAUTE COUTURE DE PARIS. A
new advertisement prominently displayed in the local newspaper
proclaimed that "as the result of a special arrangement with
Monsieur Paul Poiret" and "under the personal supervision of
that great artist," the firm had been granted the exclusive representation not only for hats, but for dresses as well. My mother
never did things by halves. We were now standing on the
threshold of success, but she still felt that we needed something
that would push the door wide open, some masterly stroke of
good fortune, or at least of imagination, that would transform
our modest progress into a final and crushing victory. Sitting on
the little pink sofa in the showroom, her legs crossed, a cigarette
dangling from her lips, with an inspired look in her eyes, she
stared into the distance, and I could tell that a daring plan was
already taking shape in her mind, for her face gradually began
to assume the expression which I was getting to know so well—

a combination of cunning and naïveté—a smile that was both triumphant and a little guilty. I snuggled in an arm chair, a poppy-seed cake in my hand—this time legitimately acquired. Now and again I followed the direction of her gaze, straining my eyes, but could see nothing. The sight of my mother working on her fabulous schemes always plunged me into a state of awed suspense. I forgot my cake and hardly dared to move, watching her open mouthed and brimming over with pride and admiration.

I must say that even in a little town like Vilna, in that distant province neither Lithuanian, Polish nor Russian, where publicity photographs were almost unknown, even there the daring plan devised by my mother might well have ended in disaster, and sent us once more tramping the roads, with our bundles on our backs.

But she had taken the plunge, and soon it was brought to the attention of the "fashionable society of Vilna" that Monsieur Paul Poiret was coming in person from Paris for the official opening of the "Maison Nouvelle, Grand Salon de Haute Couture de Paris," 16 Grand Pohulanka, at four o'clock in the afternoon.

As I have said, once my mother had taken a decision, she followed it through to the very end, and sometimes even a bit further. When the great day came and the flat was crammed to bursting with excited fat ladies, she did not announce that "Monsieur Paul Poiret, owing to unforeseen circumstances, has been prevented from leaving Paris, and begs to be excused." Such trivia were completely foreign to her nature. Determined to do things on a grand scale, at precisely four o'clock my mother opened the doors of her "Salon" and produced Monsieur Poiret in person before the dazzled audience.

In the days of her "theatrical career" in Russia, she had known a small-time actor-singer, one of those pathetic figures without talent or hope, whose life is a perpetually empty theatre on a perpetual tour. His name was Alex—Sacha, to his friends—Gubernatis. He was then leading a nameless existence in Warsaw, where he had set himself up as a theatrical wig maker, having tightened the belt of his ambition by several holes, that is, from a bottle of brandy to a bottle of vodka a day. My mother sent him a railway ticket, and eight days later, under the dazzling chandeliers of "Maison Nouvelle," Alex Gubernatis was assuming the role of that famous master of the Paris fashion world, Paul Poiret, on our brightly polished floor. It must be said in all fairness that he put his best into his performance. Wrapped in an incredible Scottish plaid, wearing the tightest imaginable checkered trousers which, when he bent to kiss a lady's hand, revealed two most remarkable pointed, bony buttocks, a French *lavallière* tie flowing under an enormous Adam's apple, arrogantly spread all over an armchair, with his interminable legs reflected on the shining floor, a glass of sparkling wine in his hand, he spoke in a thin falsetto voice of the intoxicating splendors of Parisian "high life," dropping once glorious names of the Boulevard stage who had not been heard from for twenty years, passing his thin fingers through his wig, like a drunken Paganini without a violin. Unfortunately, toward the end of the afternoon, losing his head completely, basking in admiration and longing for more, he called for silence and proceeded to recite to the assembled company the second act of *L'Aiglon*, after which, his true nature taking over, he started to sing in an unbelievably pederast voice excerpts from his old burlesque repertory, the interesting and somewhat enigmatic refrain of which has stuck in my memory:

> *"Ah! Tu l'as voulu, tu l'as voulu, tu l'as voulu*
> *Tu l'as bien eu, ma Pomponette!"*

this last line punctuated with a kick of his heels on the floor, the snapping of his bony fingers and a particularly roguish wink directed at the wife of the conductor of the Municipal Orchestra. At that point, my mother thought it wiser to take him into Aniela's room, where she left him stretched on the bed, still humming and snapping his fingers, behind double-locked doors. That same evening, he took his Scottish plaid and his bruised and battered artist's soul back to Warsaw, vehemently protesting such ingratitude, such failure to understand and appreciate the gifts which Heaven had lavished upon him.

Dressed in a black velvet suit, I had been allowed to be present throughout the ceremony; my admiring eyes were riveted to the superb Monsieur Gubernatis, and some twenty-five years later I used the poor fellow as unfaithfully as I could as a model for the character of Sacha Darlington in my novel *The Company of Men*.

I do not believe that this minor swindle was inspired merely by motives of publicity. My mother was always waiting for the intrusion of the magical and marvelous into her life, for some *deus ex machina* that would suddenly come to her rescue, confound the doubters and the mockers, take the side of the dreamer and see to it that justice was done. When, in the weeks preceding the opening, she kept pressing me against her with that faraway look, I think I know what her eyes saw. They saw the real Monsieur Paul Poiret appearing before her dazzled customers, lifting his hand for silence and, with a dramatic gesture toward her, delivering for all to hear a eulogy of the taste, the talent and the artistic inspiration of his exclusive representative in Vilna. But that deeply realistic and even astute side of her nature which always kept a strong hand on her imagination nevertheless told her in a prudent whisper that miracles occur but seldom on this earth, and that Heaven had other fish to fry. And so with one of her slightly guilty smiles, torn between her common sense and her longing, she had created her own miracle, and had forced the hand of Fate a little—but let us admit that Fate is a lot guiltier than my mother and more in need of forgiveness.

Anyway, as far as I know, the little *combinazione* was never exposed, and "Maison Nouvelle, Grand Salon de Haute Couture de Paris" was launched like a proud ship upon the high seas of commerce. Within a few months, "the best people"—to use Aniela's expression—were getting their clothes from us. Money poured in from all sides. The flat was redecorated; thick, soft carpets covered the floor; I stuffed myself with Turkish delight and watched the lovely ladies undress in front of me. For reasons of her own, my mother always insisted on my being present as often as possible during the fittings; she was, I have come to think, obeying some unconscious impulse and perhaps some dream of revenge—stories of a lioness teaching her cubs to hunt come to my mind, for there is no question that she was trying to raise me to resemble someone she had loved, to whose hunting instinct she herself had fallen victim. It is not a matter on which I wish to dwell; I shall only say that the sweet and noble memory of her own love made me fail, fortunately, where she wanted me to succeed. Day after day, dressed in silk and velvet, I was exhibited to those of the ladies toward whom my mother felt graciously disposed; I was led to the window, then told to raise my eyes so that their blue could be properly observed and admired. The ladies were politely ecstatic, and those who were astute enough to show more than an ordinary enthusiasm were usually granted a substantial reduction on the price of the latest "Paris model." Having already no other ambition than to please my mother, I dutifully performed my act, raising my eyes to the light even before I was asked to do so, adding with a quickly acquired sense of showmanship a trick or two of my own, like wiggling my ears—a new and exciting art I had just learned from my playmates in the yard. Then, seated in the corner on a Louis XVI chair, I was present at the fitting, observing with growing curiosity all those interesting adornments of female anatomy which were then so strange and new to me.

I can still remember a certain singer from the Vilna opera, whose stage name was Mademoiselle La Rare. I was then a little more than eight years old.

My mother had left the room with the fitter, to put some finishing touches on the "Paris model," and I was left alone with Mademoiselle La Rare, who was in a state of considerable undress. I looked her over inch by inch, dreamily licking my Turkish delight. Something in my expression must have seemed very familiar to the lovely singer, for she suddenly seized her dress from the chair and covered herself with it. Then, since I continued my detailed inspection, she took refuge behind the dressing table. I was furious and, walking around the obstacle, planted myself solidly in front of her, with my legs apart and my stomach pushed forward, and went on licking my Turkish delight. When my mother returned, she found us standing motionless, facing one another in an icy silence.

I remember that, having led me from the showroom, she clasped me in her arms, and looked at me with a smile of extraordinary pride, as though I had at last begun to justify the hopes which she had placed in me.

Unfortunately, from then on the salon became forbidden ground for me. I often tell myself that, with a little more cunning, and with a little less frankness in my stare, I might well have enriched my experience by at least six months.

CHAPTER 9

THE FRUITS OF OUR PROSPERITY WERE SHOWERED upon me. I acquired a French governess and sported elegant velvet suits, silk shirts with broad lace collars, and Pompadour ties. In cold weather I was made to wear a most revolting, to my budding manhood, coat of squirrel fur; their poor little tails shook as I walked, to the great delight of my playmates, who mercilessly pulled them. I was given lessons in deportment, was taught to kiss ladies' hands, to bow before them, when introduced, with a formal plunge of the upper part of the body, at the same time clicking my heels, and the delicate art of choosing and offering flowers to members of the beautiful sex was revealed to me. On these two points, the kissing of ladies' hands and the homage of flowers, my mother was particularly firm.

"Without that," she told me, rather mysteriously, "you will never get anywhere."

Often, before falling asleep, I saw my mother come into my room. She leaned over me with a sad smile and whispered: "Raise your eyes, Roma. . . ."

I sleepily raised my eyes. She remained leaning over me for a long while. Then she would throw herself suddenly forward, put her arms around me, and press me against her bosom, shaking with sobs. I could feel her tears on my face and always ended by crying myself, out of some sort of obscure, heartbroken sympathy. I felt confusedly that there was a mystery behind those tears, that there was something strange in my eyes, and

I began to stare at them in the mirror, wondering what there was in their color or shape that made my mother cry. One day I took the bull by the horns and put the question to Aniela, who with our newly attained and steadily increasing prosperity had been promoted to the rank of "personal assistant," and given a handsome salary. She detested my French governess, whom she accused of keeping me away from her, and did all she could to make life difficult for the "Mamselle," as she called her.

"Aniela, what is there in my eyes that makes my mother cry?"

Aniela showed some signs of embarrassment: she had been with us since my birth and there was very little she didn't know.

"It's their color."

"But why? Is something wrong with my eyes?"

"They make her dream," she said evasively, with a sigh, and turned away.

It took me several years to understand that answer. But a day came when there was nothing more left for me to know. My mother was by that time sixty and I was twenty-four, but she still kept looking into my eyes as if she were leaning over some secret source of memories, and I knew that it was not at me that she was looking and that in her sighs and tears I played no part. She didn't have to ask me any longer: I had become a grown man, there were things she could no longer ask, and so, God forgive me, I often deliberately raised my eyes to the sun and held them thus as long as I could, helping her to remember. I always did everything I could for her.

Nothing was omitted from the education I was receiving, the purpose of which was to make me a thorough man of the world. She herself taught me the polka and the waltz, the only dances she knew, or at least cared to remember.

As soon as the last of the customers had departed, the carpets were rolled back in the brightly lit showroom and the gramophone was placed on the table. My mother settled herself in one of the recently acquired Louis XVI chairs, I bowed, clicked my heels, took her hand and, one-two-three! one-two-three! off we went on the floor under the slightly disapproving eyes of Aniela.

"Keep your back straight! Mark the beat with your right foot! Raise your head, look proudly at your partner with an enchanted air!"

I raised my head proudly, looked at my partner with an enchanted air, and . . . *one*-two-three! *one*-two-three! we hopped along on the polished floor. Then I led her back to her chair, kissed her hand and bowed. She thanked me with a gracious movement of the head and fanned herself. She sighed and sometimes said with admiration while trying to recover her breath: "You will win prizes at the *Concours Hippique!*"

No doubt she saw me in the white uniform of the guards officer, leaping obstacles under the lovelorn eyes of Anna Karenina. There was something astonishingly old-fashioned in the nature of her imagination, a sort of outmoded romanticism. She longed for the world of the Russian novels before 1900, the date at which, for her, all truly great literature had come to a stop. Pushkin and Lermontov were her gods; she saw me as Eugene Onegin, and recited that lovely poem to me so often that, without ever actually learning it, I know to this day a great deal of it by heart.

Three times a week, she took my hand and led me to the riding school–shooting gallery–gymnasium presided over by Lieutenant Sverdlovski, where I was initiated into the arts of riding, fencing and pistol shooting. The lieutenant was a tall, elderly, dried-up man with a bony, martial face and a white mustache à la Lyautey. At the age of eight, I was certainly the youngest of his pupils, and had great difficulty in lifting the enormous pistol which he held out to me. After half an hour with the foils, half an hour with the pistol—a friend of my mother's, who still lives in Nice, claims that the sight of the little boy with the enormous pistol in his hand was one of the most outrageous sights he had ever seen—and half an hour in the saddle, I was given a round of gymnastics and breathing exercises. My mother sat in the corner, her legs crossed, smoking a cigarette, observing my progress with a delighted smile.

Lieutenant Sverdlovski, who spoke in a sepulchral voice and seemed to have no other passion in life than to "score a bull" and "aim at the heart," had an unbounded admiration for my mother. We were always warmly welcomed. I took my place at the barrier in the company of my fellow shots—officers of the reserve, retired generals and elegant young bloods with nothing to do—put one hand on my hip, rested the heavy pistol muzzle over the lieutenant's outstretched arm, held my breath and fired. The target was then presented to my mother for inspection, she looked at the little holes, commented on my progress, and gave a satisfied sniff with a rather menacing air. After a particularly successful session, she put the target in her bag and took it home. It was not difficult to guess the longing in the lonely woman's heart: she must have been hurt badly and often. She frequently asked me: "You'll always defend me, won't you, Romouchka? They'll see. In a few years' time . . ."

This with a wide, vague, sweeping gesture, a truly Russian gesture. As for Lieutenant Sverdlovski, he stroked his long, stiff mustache, kissed my mother's hand, clicked his heels and said: "We'll make a cavalier of him."

He himself gave me fencing lessons, and he took me on long tramps across the country with a military rucksack strapped on my shoulders. At home, I was taught French, Latin and German— English at that time did not exist in those Eastern provinces. A Mademoiselle Gladys gave me fox trot and shimmy lessons, and I was introduced to the tango. On the days when my mother was giving a party, I was frequently wakened from my sleep, dressed, led into the showroom and asked to recite some of La Fontaine's fables. I was obedient, eager to please, completely bewildered, but instantly rewarded whenever I saw on my mother's face a smile of happiness. With such a program, I had no time for school; however, since the local schools taught, quite naturally, not in French but in Polish, as far as we were concerned they might as well not have existed at all. Vilna, in my mother's mind, had never been anything but a temporary stop, a resting place, on our journey to the land where all the beauty lies.

I was taught arithmetic, geography, French history and French literature by a succession of tutors whose names and faces have left no more trace on my memory than the subjects they were trying to teach me.

Sometimes my mother would say: "Tonight we will go to the movies."

Then, when darkness fell, warmly dressed in my squirrel fur coat with its tails or, if the weather happened to be pleasant, wearing a white raincoat and a sailor's cap, I sauntered along the wooden sidewalks of the town with my mother on my arm. She kept a fiercely watchful eye on my manners. I had always to hasten ahead of her to open the door and hold it wide until she had passed through. When one day in Warsaw I politely stood back to let her step from the tram ahead of me, she started a row in the presence of twenty persons queueing at the tram stop, and I was informed that the male escort should always get out first and help the lady down. As for hand kissing, although seven years of soldiering and adventures have, to be quite frank, taken care of most of my good manners, this is one habit I have never managed to get rid of, in spite of all my other successful efforts to adjust. I don't know why this particular mark of courtesy has become so deeply part of my nature, but I can't dispense with it. In the United States, it has been a source of constant misunderstanding. Nine times out of ten when, after a considerable muscular struggle, I succeed in raising the hand of an American lady to my lips, I am either rewarded with a surprised and blushing "Oh! thank you!" or else, taking my courteous mark of attention for a more sinister kind of approach, she hastily snatches her hand away with a quick, worried glance toward her husband. Worst of all, particularly when the lady in question happens to be of a rather ripe age, she gives me such a coquettish smile that I have the most irritating feeling of having just confirmed some of the more trashy and corny aspects of the reputation Frenchmen enjoy abroad.

I do not know whether it was one of the movies we thus saw together, or my mother's behavior after the show, which left me with such a strange and uneasy impression. The famous star, then completely unknown to me, who was playing the lead, wore a black Tcherkesse uniform and fur hat. His pale eyes under the wide brows raised like open wings seemed to keep staring at me from the screen, while the pianist was playing a halting and nostalgic little tune. When the picture was over, and we were walking back hand in hand through the empty streets, I felt my mother's fingers pressing mine so hard that it almost hurt. When I looked at her reproachfully, I saw that she was crying. As soon as we reached home and she had helped me to undress and tucked me into bed, she leaned over me with her handkerchief pressed against her face, and then, of course, came the old request, which I had been hearing for so many years. I did as I was told, rather bored, and stared at the ceiling lamp. For a long time, she remained leaning over me, with a curious smile of triumph, of conquest and possession upon her lips. Then she dried her tears and kissed me good night.

It so happened that some time after this particular visit to the cinema a fancy-dress ball was given for the children of the fashionable society in our town. Naturally, I was invited. My mother reigned supreme over local fashion, and we were then much sought after. No sooner had the invitation arrived than the girls in the workroom devoted themselves excitedly to the job of making my costume.

I hardly need to add that I went to the ball dressed as a Tcherkesse officer, exactly modeled after the uniform worn by the man in the picture, complete with the dagger, dashing fur hat, breast cartridges, silver spurs and all the *tra la la.*

CHAPTER *10*

ONE DAY AN UNEXPECTED PRESENT REACHED ME, apparently out of the blue: a miniature bicycle exactly appropriate to my size. The origin of the mysterious gift was not revealed to me, and all my questions on the subject were left unanswered. Aniela, after staring for a long while at the bicycle, merely said, with a strong note of animosity in her voice: "It comes from very far."

There was a long whispered animated discussion between her and my mother, the purpose of which was to decide if I should be allowed to keep the present or if it should be returned to the sender. I was not allowed to join in this all-important argument. Sweating with apprehension at the thought of the marvelous machine being, perhaps, snatched from me, I did some anxious eavesdropping at the door and caught a few odd words of a mysterious dialogue: "We don't need him any longer."

It was Aniela who was speaking and my mother was crying in the corner. Aniela pressed her point: "It's a bit late in the day, for him, after all these years, to remember our existence."

Then I heard my mother's voice, strangely timid and almost beseeching: "All the same, it's nice of him."

Aniela had the last word: "He might have thought about us sooner."

The only thing that interested me just then was whether I was to be allowed to keep the bicycle. Finally, my mother gave me her permission. It was a habit with her to surround me with a crowd of "professors"—a "professor" of elocution, a "professor" of deportment—there again I did not show much aptitude, and the only thing I remember of all he tried to teach me was that I must not stick out my little finger when holding a cup of tea—"professors" of swimming, of shooting, of fencing, of . . . A father would have done far more for me. And so, having acquired a bicycle, I also acquired a "professor" of cycling and, after a few customary falls and minor disasters, I could soon be seen proudly pedaling my miniature machine over the cobbles of Vilna, in the wake of a tall and melancholy young man who wore a straw hat and who was famous in our neighborhood for his sporting accomplishments. I was strictly forbidden to ride unaccompanied in the streets.

One fine day, on returning from a ride with my "professor," I found a small crowd gathered near the entrance to our block, gaping in admiration at a huge yellow Packard convertible drawn up outside our house. A liveried chauffeur was seated at the wheel. My mouth opened wide, my eyes goggled and I remained as though rooted to the ground before this marvel of all marvels. Motorcars were still a rare sight in the streets of Vilna, and certainly none of them could compare with the prodigious bright yellow creation of human genius which I saw before me. A buddy of mine, the son of the local shoemaker, whispered respectfully in my ear: "They are in your apartment." Dropping my bicycle, I dashed upstairs.

The door was opened by Aniela. Without a word of explanation, she grabbed me by the hand and dragged me into my bedroom. There she subjected me to a tremendous process of cleansing, the like of which I have never known before or since. The workroom girls helped her in her task and they all set upon me like maternal hawks, rubbing, brushing, washing, undressing, dressing, perfuming, combing, pomading and otherwise attending to me with a devotion the memory of which still fills me with nostalgia. Often, I light a cigar, plump myself down in an armchair, and wait for somebody to come and do something about me. But I wait in vain. I try to find consolation in the thought that no throne is safe these days, but the little prince in me still keeps waiting. In the end, I have to take off my shoes and change my clothes without assistance, and even run a bath for myself. I am afraid that I have lost my kingdom for good.

For almost half an hour Aniela, Maria, Stefka and Halinka buzzed busily around me. At last, with my ears bright scarlet from much hair brushing, dressed in blue pants and white shirt, with an immense silk Pompadour tie around my neck and blue ribbons in my shoes, I was shown into the salon.

The visitor was sitting in an armchair with his legs stretched out in front of him. There was something almost animal in the fixity of his pale eyes, staring at me from under sweeping brows like open wings, something slightly disturbing in the hint of an ironic smile on his immobile lips. I had seen it two or three times on the screen, and recognized him at once. He looked me over, coldly and leisurely, with a sort of detached curiosity. My ears were still hot and buzzing from Aniela's attention, the smell of eau de cologne in which I had been drenched made me sneeze, I had a confused feeling that something important was happening, but I was completely at sea about what it could be. I was still in the very early stages of my progress as a man of the world. And so, already stunned by the girls' ferocious attack at me with brush and soap, thrown off by the stranger's fixed stare and enigmatic smile, by the curious silence which had greeted me, as well as by my mother's stricken appearance—I had never seen her so pale and so tense, and her face looked like a mask—in short, utterly confused, I committed a most dreadful *faux pas*. Like a performing dog who goes on automatically doing its tricks, I stepped forward, bowed, clicked my heels, kissed the hand of the lady who accompanied the stranger, and then, losing my head completely, I saluted the gentleman in the same manner, kissing his hand as well.

My blunder had the happiest results. The atmosphere of icy constraint suddenly melted. My mother took me in her arms. The beautiful lady in the apricot-colored dress kissed my cheek, and her companion took me from my mother and perched me on his knee. Only too conscious of the enormity of my slip and of the irreparable damage I had done to my reputation as a man of the world, I burst into tears, and so our visitor suggested a drive in his car, a proposal which made me prick up my ears and forget my tears instantly.

I was destined to see a great deal of Ivan Mosjoukine in the years to come. Our meetings usually took place in Nice, on the terrace of the *Grande Bleue* overlooking the sea, where he would frequently treat me to a coffee. He was a great star of the silent screen. When the "talkies" came, the strong Russian accent of his speech gradually put an end to his career, and he soon hit upon difficult times. He used to get me small jobs as an extra whenever he made a picture in Nice, my last appearance on the screen dating back to 1935 or 1936 in a story in which he played the lead—a gun runner, who meets his end in a cloud of smoke when his ship is gunned and sunk by Harry Baur. The picture was called *Nitchevo,* and I was paid fifty francs a day—a real fortune for me. All I was asked to do was to lean on the ship's rail and look at the sea. I tried to find out from the director what I was supposed to be expressing in that scene but he didn't seem to care. It was the greatest part I was ever called upon to play.

Mosjoukine died shortly after the end of the war, forgotten and impoverished. Up to the very end, the pale, savage and piercing light kept burning in his eyes, and his air of physical dignity, discreet and yet slightly arrogant, ironical and detached, never left him. I liked him.

I often arrange for a showing of his old movies at film societies. He always plays the part of romantic heroes and noble adventurers; he conquers empires single-handed; reigns supreme with sword and pistol; gallops under the eyes of lovely ladies in the white uniform of a guards officer; carries off beautiful captives thrown across the saddle of his horse; endures the most appalling tortures in the service of the Tsar, and always, always, women die of love at his feet. . . . I leave the theatre deeply conscious of all that my mother expected of me, and I dutifully perform my physical exercises every morning to keep myself in shape, just in case.

Our impressive guest left us that evening, though not without making a generous and exciting gesture. For a whole week the canary-colored Packard and the liveried chauffeur were put at our disposal. The weather was lovely and it would have been delightful to leave the town for a drive in the Lithuanian forest.

But my mother was not a woman to lose her head under the intoxicating caress of spring. She knew what was important to her; she also had a taste for revenge and would have gone to any length to confound her enemies. It was for this purpose, and for this purpose alone, that the car was employed. Each morning about eleven o'clock I was made to put on my most eccentric clothes—she herself always dressed with discreet good taste—the chauffeur, cap in hand, held the door open, we stepped in and for the next two hours the open car paraded slowly through the town, taking us to all the favorite haunts of the local "best society," to the Café Rudnicki, to the Botanical Gardens, while my mother nodded with the most condescending smile to all those who had treated her badly, who had been rude to her, or had closed the door in her face, in the days when she went from house to house with her hatboxes.

To children of seven or eight who have reached this point in my story, and who, like myself, may have lived their greatest love too early and never ever recovered from it, I wish to give some practical advice. I am assuming that they all suffer, as I do, from a chronic longing for warmth, and spend long hours in the sun in a vain attempt to recapture something that always eludes them. I agree that a blazing fire is not to be despised, and I suppose that alcohol can be of some assistance, and there is always the solution devised by a little friend of mine, who is now the ambassador of his country somewhere in the world, and who sleeps in electrically heated pajamas under an electric blanket on a mattress that is electrically warmed. It may well be worth trying, but my advice to all the little boys is quite firm: stop trying. There is a lot of sunlight on earth, and many a pair of warm lovely arms, but I tell you, stop trying. You've had it. You've had it—and you'll never have it again.

I feel the moment has also come for me to raise a rather delicate point, and to make a frank confession, at the risk of shocking and disappointing some of my readers, and being perhaps regarded as an unnatural son by the fervent disciples of the great Freud: I have never had incestuous leanings toward my mother.

I fully realize that this naïve refusal to face facts will bring a knowing smile to the lips of the well-informed, and also that no one can vouch for one's unconscious mind. I also hasten to assure them that even a barbarian like myself regards the Oedipus complex with the greatest admiration and respect; I consider that its discovery does high honor to our Western civilization, and should encourage us to go on digging for the benefit of all; with the recent finding of oil in the Sahara it ranks unquestionably among the most fruitful explorations of our underground resources. Nor is that all. Painfully aware of my Asiatic origins, and in order to show myself worthy of the truly civilized and progressive Western community which has so graciously accepted me, I have frequently and determinedly tried to evoke the image of my mother in the proper libidinous light, not only to free myself from my complex, of which I have been so painfully and embarrassingly unaware, but also to show my deep respect for our spiritual values, and to prove that Western civilization, in all its noble and progressive endeavors, could rely on me to the end. But try as I may, I somehow always failed to strike in myself even the most modest spark of libido. And yet, there must have been among my Tartar ancestors many a savage horseman who, if their reputation is at all founded, never hesitated before rape, incest, or any other form of indulgence in our earth-shaking taboos. Here again, without in any way looking for excuses for my total lack of enthusiasm for incest, I think I can present my defense.

Though it is perfectly true that I have never felt any physical desire for my mother, the reason was not so much, I feel, in the blood relationship existing between us, but simply because she was a person advanced in age, and for me, for some reason or other, the sexual act has always been linked with a certain degree of youth and physical freshness. I must even say that my oriental blood has always made me peculiarly sensitive to the tender attractions of youth and I am sorry to add that this tendency has grown stronger in me as I grow older—an almost general rule, I am told, among the satraps of Asia. I feel, therefore, free to say that I have never had for my mother, whom I never knew, or even remembered, as a young woman, any other impulse than those dictated by the most natural and affectionate feelings. I know that this sort of naïve statement will be immediately interpreted according to the rules of the book, that is, upside down, by those wriggling little suckers of the human soul, otherwise called psychoanalysts, presently engaged in bleeding it white at the rate of fifty dollars an hour, who always remind me, except for their size, of sharks feeding on refuse underwater. Some of the most outspoken among them have explained to me with that great subtlety and calm, realistic assurance which, so often, go with arrogant idiocy that if, for example, you are excessively fond of women, it is because you are really a panic-stricken homosexual, who desperately tries to escape from his obsession. If the idea of an accidental physical contact with a male body is repulsive to you—may I be allowed to confess that this is exactly the case with me—it is really because you are just a teeny-weeny little bit queerish and tempted; and, to go to the extreme of this splendid psychoanalytical logic, as I told one of those gentlemen on some television panel, if the contact with a corpse in the morgue revolts you and repels you utterly, the explanation, I suppose, lies in the fact that, in your unconscious, you are a teeny-weeny little bit necrophiliac and deliciously attracted, both as a male and a female, by the sight of all that splendid rigidity.

Psychoanalysis today, like most of our ideas, has assumed a totalitarian form; it irresistibly tends to imprison us in the strait jacket of its own excesses and perversions. It has occupied the ground left vacant by the retreat of superstition; its dialectics, brilliantly and almost artistically developed, assume more and more toward the human soul the approach of Communism toward the individual; the clientele is largely recruited through a subtle, scientific form of intimidation and psychological blackmail, much as Chicago racketeers used to impose their protection. There are some honest and true artists among psychoanalysts, but they know where to stop, what to respect; and they do not view human nature as a sickness in itself. But a great many of the so-called therapists are nothing more than charlatans, operating on Dr. Knock's famous dictum that health is something that bodes no good to those who are temporarily stricken with it.

I therefore leave to the demagogues who hold the upper hand today in so many fields the freedom to see in my love for my mother the sign of some pathological puffiness in my soul. If we consider what liberty, fraternity and so many of the noblest aspirations of mankind have become in their hands, I see no reason why the simplicity of filial love should escape unscathed the distorting process of their twisted minds.

If it pleases them to throw the dark mantle of Oedipus over my shoulders and to shake their heads knowingly at my naïveté, I welcome them. Anyway, I have never regarded incest in that glare of eternal damnation and hair-raising horror which our so-called morality casts on a form of sexual aberration occupying, it seems to me, a rather modest place on the monumental scale of our degradations. All the frenzies of incest strike me as infinitely more acceptable than those of Hiroshima, of Buchenwald, of firing squads, of police torture, of forced-labor camps and starving millions; I see a thousand times less evil in the insanity of incest than in the nuclear pursuits of our inspired scientists, who have taken over from syphilis the task of poisoning the genes of the unborn. No one will ever persuade me that sexual behavior is the ultimate criterion of good and evil. That sinister countenance, the sudden sight of which may well be fatal to pregnant women, of one of the most demoniac fathers of the hydrogen bomb, clamoring in favor of more and better nuclear explosions, is to me infinitely more sickening and odious than the very unpalatable idea of a son having a physical relationship with his mother. Compared with the intellectual, scientific and political aberrations of the present century, all the sexual ones appear to me utterly unimportant, since, after all, they only shake the bed and not the world. The unfortunate prostitute who obliges her customer is, in my eyes, a very innocent soul, a provider of daily bread, when one compares her humble venality with the prostitution of our great scientists, always willing to gratify the appetite of authority and to help in the preparation of genetic poisoning or atomic terror. Compared with the perversion of the mind, spirit, and ideal to which these traitors to our species are lending themselves, all our pathetic sexual frenzies, venal or not, incestuous or not, confer on our three lowly sphincters all the angelic innocence of an infant's smile.

Finally, to complete this vicious circle, let me say again that I am quite aware that this way of minimizing incest may be cleverly interpreted as a defense mechanism of the unconscious, and that all my indignation and reasoning can be easily presented as an attempt to exorcise in myself an obscure feeling of guilt—and having thus made my polite bows to all our fashionable fetishes, and danced dutifully to the tune of that dear old Viennese waltz, I shall now return to my humble and innocent love.

For I scarcely need say that what prompts me to tell my story is the fraternal, universal, and recognizable nature of my love: there was nothing new, nothing different, nothing exceptional in my feelings—I loved my mother no more, no less than you loved yours. The only difference, perhaps, is that my juvenile attempt to accomplish everything she expected from me and to lay the world at her feet was, to a very great extent, impersonal, and prompted by an almost mystical longing to discover some inner, humane and triumphant logic in life. Whatever the nature of the link which bound us so deeply and often so painfully to one another—and each of you will have to decide this for himself—one thing, at least, appears quite clear to me today, as I cast a last look at what has been my life: in my attempt, I was driven far more by a fierce determination to cast a light of dignity and justice over the hidden face of the universe, to tear down its mask of absurdity and chaos, than by the mere wish to see a smile of happiness on my mother's face.

CHAPTER *11*

I WAS ALREADY NEARLY NINE WHEN I WAS sucked down, hook, line and sinker, by a passion so violent and so absorbing that it completely poisoned my existence, and almost cost me my life.

She was eight years old, her name was Valentine and she was lovely. Her hair was dark, her eyes light, her figure was admirable, she was wearing a white dress and she carried a ball in her hand. She appeared before me near the woodshed, where the field nettles began, and I cannot describe the violence of the feelings this sudden vision of beauty stirred in me: all I know is that my knees began to shake, blood rushed to my head, my sight became blurred and I raised, rather obviously, my hand to my heart, in my mother's best romantic manner. Determined to win her then and there forever, so that there would never be room in her life for another man, I immediately threw in my trump card and, leaning negligently against the woodpile, raised my eyes to the light. But Valentine refused to be impressed. There I stood, gazing into the sun until the tears rolled down my cheeks, but the heartless creature went on playing with her ball. My eyes were bulging and almost bursting, the world around me turned to fire and flame, and yet Valentine did not so much as give me a glance. Completely put out by this indifference, so unexpected after everything my mother had told me, I made one more desperate attempt to keep the blue of my eyes exposed to the light; then, having so to speak exhausted all my ammunition, I wiped away my tears, and, in a gesture of unconditional surrender, held out to her the three green apples I had just stolen from the orchard next door. She accepted my surrender as though it were the most ordinary thing in the world, and announced:

"Janek ate his whole stamp collection for me."

Such was the beginning of my long martyrdom. In the course of the next few days I ate for Valentine several handfuls of earthworms, her father's collection of rare butterflies, a mouse, a good many decaying leaves and, as a crowning achievement, I can say that at nine years of age—far more precociously than Casanova—I took my place among the greatest lovers of all time and accomplished a deed of amorous prowess no man, to the best of my knowledge, has ever equaled. I ate for my lady one of my rubber galoshes.

Here I feel compelled to open a parenthesis.

I am well aware that men are rather too apt to boast about their amorous exploits. To hear them, one would believe that their virile accomplishments know no limits, and they are always willing to indulge in statistics, without sparing you a single detail.

I do not, therefore, expect anyone to believe me when I say that, for my well-beloved, after a few pounds of cherries—Valentine was kind enough to lighten my task by eating the flesh and handing me the stones—I also consumed a Japanese fan, ten yards of cotton thread, a complete paperback novel called *Nat Pinkerton* and three goldfish we stole from her music teacher's aquarium.

God knows what women have made me swallow in the course of my life, but I have never known anybody so insatiable. After my experiences with her, there was nothing left for me to learn about love. My education was completed. I knew.

My adorable Messalina with the freckled nose was only eight, but her physical demands went beyond anything I have ever read about. She would run ahead of me in the yard, pointing out some interesting object for me to swallow—sometimes a rotting piece of lace, sometimes a couple of old corks, or just a mere handful of earth, and I eagerly acquitted myself of my man's task—always only too willing to provide satisfaction. Once she started to gather a bouquet of daisies—with apprehension I watched it grow bigger in her hand—but I ate the daisies too, under her very watchful eyes—she knew already that men tend to cheat at games of that sort.

In those days, children were taught nothing about the mysteries of sex, and as I swallowed one thing after another, I was convinced—quite rightly, as a matter of fact—that this was the way people made love.

It was in vain that I looked for the slightest flicker of esteem in her eyes. Scarcely had I finished swallowing the daisies than she casually observed: "Janek ate ten spiders for me, and then stopped only because Mother called us in for tea."

I trembled. No sooner was my back turned than she was being unfaithful to me with my best friend. But I swallowed that too. That was what love was about, after all.

"May I kiss you?"

"Yes. But you mustn't wet my cheek. I don't like it."

I kissed her, doing my best not to wet her cheek. We were kneeling behind the nettles and I kissed her again and again, while she twiddled her hoop around her finger with an indifferent look: the story of my life.

"How many times have you kissed me?"

"Eighty-seven. May I go up to a thousand?"

"How many is a thousand?"

"I don't know. May I kiss you on the shoulder too?"

"Yes."

I kissed her shoulder. But no, that wasn't it. Something was missing. Something essential: but I didn't have the slightest idea what it could possibly be. My heart was beating very hard, and I kissed her nose, her hair, her neck—but no, I was still off the mark, something else was required, something else was expected from me. I kissed her on the ear, and on the neck, but some deep, obscure impulse was pushing me further, much further, I didn't know where and, finally, crazed by love, and at the very peak of my erotic frenzy, I sat down and took off one of my rubber galoshes.

"I'll eat this for you, if you wish me to."

If she wished me to! Ha! Of course, she wished me to. She was a true little woman. As I took out my penknife and cut into the rubber, I thought I at last saw a gleam of admiration in her eyes. I asked for nothing more. She laid her hoop on the ground and watched closely.

"Are you going to eat it raw?"

"Yes."

I gulped down one morsel, then another; under her warm and at last grateful gaze I truly felt that I was becoming a man—a perfectly correct impression, for this was my first taste of things to come. I cut more deeply into the rubber, puffing and blowing a little with each mouthful, and continued with my labor of love even after a cold sweat began to appear on my forehead. My eyes were bulging, I was fighting against a growing nausea, gathering all my virile strength in an effort to give satisfaction, and to remain undefeated on the field, as I've had to do so often since then, with as little luck.

I was very ill. They took me to the hospital. My mother sobbed, Aniela screamed, the workroom girls ran around in panic while I was carried to the ambulance on a stretcher. I was very proud of myself.

Twenty years later this puppy love inspired my first novel, *A European Education*, and also some passages in *The Company of Men*.

For more than twenty years, in the course of my wanderings, I carried among my belongings a child's rubber galosh with four large holes in it. Wherever I went, it was always within easy reach of my hand. I waited and waited. But it never happened again, or perhaps I had given once and for all everything I had in me. In the end, when I was more than forty years old, I left the galosh behind me, somewhere along my way. It's no use pretending; one lives only once.

My affair with Valentine lasted for almost a year. It brought about a complete change in me. It forced me to compete, to engage in pitched battles with my rivals; to assert and prove my virility I had to walk on my hands, steal from shops, smash windows and fight, always fight—defending myself on all fronts. One of my torments was a Polish boy whose name I have forgotten but who courted Valentine by juggling with five apples —and there were times, after hours and hours of desperate attempts at juggling, the apples scattered around me, when I hung my head and felt that life was not worth living. But even today I can still keep three apples in the air at the same time, and often, on my hill at Big Sur, when the challenge of the sea and the sky's immensity sparks in me some last trace of defiance, I grab three apples, raise my head nobly, advance one foot and perform my exploit, just to show that I am still a man to be reckoned with.

In winter we used to dash down the hills on our sleds, and since I could not do this standing up, like that beast Jan, I felt compelled to jump into the snow from a height of fifteen feet while Valentine watched, and I dislocated my shoulder. That awful Jan, how I loathed and how I still loathe him! I never found out exactly what there was between him and Valentine, and even now I prefer not to think about it, but he was almost a year older than I was, and could do everything I could do, only much better. He had the look of a gutter cat, was incredibly agile and could spit five yards, hitting the bull's eye. He had a particularly impressive way of whistling between his teeth, a trick which I have never learned to this day and which I have never known anyone to perform with the same stridency, with two exceptions: my friend, Ambassador Jaime de Castro and Countess Nelly de Vogue. I owe to Valentine my slow realization that my mother's love and the warmth and affection surrounding me at home were not typical of what life and the world had in store for me. Jan, with an uncanny genius for finding the right insult, had nicknamed me "the little blue one." I cannot say why I found it especially offensive, but in order to demonstrate, for all to see, that there was nothing of the tenderfoot in me, I had to multiply the proofs of my toughness and daring, with the result that I very rapidly became the terror of the neighborhood. I can say without boasting that I broke more windows, stole more boxes of dates and Greek *halva*, pulled more doorbells and poured more cold water over the heads of passers-by than any other diplomat in the French Foreign Office. I also learned to risk my life with a facility which stood me in good stead during the war when that sort of thing was so much appreciated.

I remember particularly a certain "death game" which Jan and I played on a fourth-floor window sill. It mattered little to us that Valentine was not there to admire us—we both knew that she was the fair lady for whom this duel was fought. The game was very simple, but I am inclined to think that the famous Russian roulette is safe by comparison. We climbed to the fourth floor of the building, opened the window and sat on the sill with our legs dangling outside. The game consisted in pushing the other fellow in the back, just hard enough to make him slide from the window sill onto the ledge—not more than ten inches wide—without actually plunging into the void.

We played this strangely desperate game an incredible number of times. Whenever a quarrel broke out between us, and sometimes for no apparent reason other than a blind and deep-rooted hostility, we would look at each other defiantly and then proceed without a word to the fourth floor of the building, and "play the game."

The truly desperate, and yet, at the same time, peculiarly loyal character of this duel derived from the fact that you put yourself entirely at the mercy of your greatest enemy; if the force of the push were miscalculated, deliberately or not, the victim would be sent to certain death on the stones below. I still have a very vivid recollection of my legs dangling over emptiness, of the cold metallic sill under my bare thighs and the feel of my rival's hand on my back, ready to push.

Jan is today an important member of the Polish Communist

party. Some ten years ago, I met him in Paris at an official reception at the Polish Embassy. I recognized him at once. He had changed astonishingly little. At thirty-five, he had the same gaunt look, the same thin body, the same feline movements and the same hard, narrow eyes as in the old days. Since we were both attending the reception in an official capacity as representatives of our respective countries, we treated one another with studied courtesy. The name of Valentine was never mentioned. We drank vodka and exchanged toasts. He spoke to me about his fighting days in the Polish Resistance and I told him something of my battles in the Royal Air Force. We treated ourselves to another glass of vodka. Somehow the atmosphere was growing tense and the little freckled nose could almost be seen sniffing the atmosphere voluptuously.

"I was tortured by the Gestapo," Jan said.

"I was wounded three times," I countered.

We glared at each other. Then, without a word, setting down our glasses, we made for the stairs. We climbed to the second floor and Jan opened the window and bowed politely. After all, we were in the Polish Embassy and I was a guest. I already had one leg over the window sill when the Ambassador's wife, a most charming lady, well worthy of her country's finest love poems, emerged from one of the reception rooms. I hastily withdrew my leg and bowed with a pleasant smile. She took us both by the arm and off we went to the buffet.

I must say that I find myself occasionally wondering what the world press would have said if, at the very height of the Cold War, an important Polish Communist or a French diplomat had been found lying on the pavement, thrown from one of the upper windows of the Polish Embassy in Paris.

CHAPTER *12*

THE IMPRESSION LEFT IN MY MIND BY THE
courtyard of Number 16, Grand Pohulanka, is that of an immense arena where I served my apprenticeship for life's future
battles. One entered it from the street through a huge tunnel-
like porte-cochère. In the middle of the yard rose a great pile of
bricks, the last remains of a munitions factory which had been
blown up by the partisans during the patriotic struggles between
the Lithuanian and Polish armies. Beyond was the woodshed,
and a thick field of nettles against which, armed with my wooden
sword, I fought bravely in the name of France, under a "tricolor" flag specially made for me by the girls in the workroom,
with the words *liberté, égalité, fraternité* lovingly embroidered
in letters of gold by my mother herself. At the far end was the
fence of an apple orchard. To the right was a row of old barns;
a fairly easy access into them could be gained from the roofs,
after taking out a few planks. The barns were used by the
tenants as storehouses. They were filled with trunks and boxes
which I inspected thoroughly after forcing the locks. I would
lift the lid of a trunk, and in a pervasive smell of mothballs
there would lie glittering under my eyes a whole mysterious life
of strange objects, a forgotten world of unwanted and discarded
traces of past lives. I spent hours of wonder there, in an atmosphere of shipwrecks, sunken treasures and mysterious messages.
Each old-fashioned hat, each casket of ribbons and medals, each
sharply-pointed tantalizing lady's slipper spoke to me of a re-

mote and bizarre universe, of private worlds once glittering with life and now buried in darkness; and echoes of ghostly laughter, of ghostly joys, sorrows and loves reached me like a light from a long-dead star. A fur scarf; strange costume jewelry; the contents of a theatrical wardrobe; a toreador's headdress, a top hat, a ballerina's *tutu*, yellow and shabby with age; cracked mirrors with drowned, forgotten eyes peering out at me; tail coats, black lace drawers, tattered mantillas, a uniform of one of the Tsar's regiments, with the red, black and white ribbons of decorations, albums of sepia photographs and picture post-cards; dolls, wooden horses—the whole pathetic bric-a-brac which humanity leaves behind on the bank as it flows on, as present becomes past and oblivion, and all that is left on the deserted shore are discarded objects, the battered and humble traces of a thousand vanished encampments. I would sit there, looking at the objects, trying to help them, to bring them back to life by imagining what they meant, to whom they had belonged—ancient atlases, broken watches, black velvet masks, empty perfume bottles, bouquets of artificial violets, gorgeous evening dresses still longing for beautiful shoulders and a lovely neck; gloves with something almost imploring in their outstretched, torn fingers.

One afternoon, having climbed to the roof and removed the planks, I saw, lying among my treasures, beside a tail coat, a fur scarf and a wooden tailor's dummy, an extremely busy couple. I modestly replaced the plank, leaving a crack just wide enough for my eyes to peer through in the interest of science. The man was Michka, the pastry cook, the girl, Antonia, one of the servants who worked in the building. I must say that what I saw intrigued me so much that more than once I nearly fell from the roof in my attempts to make out what, exactly, was happening. Later, when I described to my friends what my eyes had seen, they indignantly accused me of lying, and the kindlier souls among them explained that, since I had been looking from the roof, I must have been seeing everything upside down, which could possibly account for my obviously mistaken conclusions. I, however, had seen what I had seen, and I vigorously stuck to my story. It was finally decided that all of us should take turns acting as watchman on the roof, armed with a Polish flag borrowed from the porter. As soon as the couple showed up, the flag would be waved and the gang would make a beeline for the observation post, so that, by putting our heads together, some sense could be made out of all this.

The first to witness the hair-raising events was little Marek Luka, a lame youngster with corn-colored hair, and he became so completely fascinated by what he saw that he forgot to wave the flag, to the despair of all of us. He confirmed, however, detail by detail, the description I had given of the extraordinary goings-on, and he did it with a mimicry so lively, and with such a zeal to communicate his experience, that he bit his finger quite badly in an excess of realism. We held a long discussion in an attempt to explain the motives of such crazy behavior; finally, it was Marek himself who presented the only plausible explanation:

"Perhaps they don't know how to go about it, and so they keep looking everywhere."

Next day, it was the local pharmacist's son who took his turn on watch. It was three o'clock in the afternoon when we saw the Polish flag triumphantly waving from the roof of the barn. A few seconds later, six or seven boys were making a dash for the rallying point. The plank was carefully drawn aside a little farther, and for more than two hours we were given our first lesson in artistic greatness.

On that day, Michka, the pastry cook, surpassed himself, as though his generous nature had guessed the presence of six angelic faces leaning above his labors.

I have always loved good pastry, but I have never been able, since that memorable day, to look at cakes with quite the same eyes. This particular pastry cook was a great artist. Pons, Rumpelmeyer and the famous Lours of Warsaw should all bow low before him. True enough, at our tender age we lacked the knowledge to indulge in comparisons, but today, having traveled widely, having tasted the *petit fours* at Florian's in Venice, the incomparable strudel and Sacher torte of Vienna and, generally, having visited the best teashops of two continents, I remain convinced that Michka was a very great pastry cook. If, instead of settling in a small, remote town of eastern Europe, he had set up shop in Paris, he would have become rich, famous and decorated. The loveliest ladies of the French capital would have delighted in his cakes. In the field of pastry he had no equal, and it is heartbreaking to think that his talents never found a more extensive market. I do not know whether he is still alive—something tells me that he died young—but I wish to bow my head in reverence to the memory of this great artist, with all the humility of a mere scribe.

So moving was the spectacle and, in some ways, so disturbing that the youngest member of our group, little Kazik, who couldn't have been more than six years old, became frightened and began to cry. We were all shaken, but what we feared above all was to disturb the artist and cut short his inspiration, and so we lost several precious moments covering the innocent's mouth with our hands to silence his howls.

When, at last, Michka's inspiration left him, and all that remained on the ground was a crushed top hat, a twisted fur scarf, and a stunned tailor's dummy, it was a little group of silent and exhausted boys who descended from the roof. A story was going around at the time of a boy named Stas who had lain down between the rails under a passing train, and whose hair, as a result of this experience, had turned white. Since none of us found that our hair had turned white after Michka's tumultuous passage, I regard this story as apocryphal. There was a solemn look on our faces as we huddled together in a strange, respectful silence, as if we had just visited sacred ground. I think we were gripped by an almost mystical feeling of wonder at the revelation of the prodigious and mysterious force men carry within them.

Little Kazek seems to have been particularly impressed. I came upon him next morning behind the woodpile. He had pulled down his pants and was lost in contemplation of his male organ. There was a frown on his forehead and a look of profound meditation on his face as he held the object delicately between his thumb and first finger, with his little finger lifted, precisely as my professor of deportment had forbidden me to do when I held a cup of tea in my hand. He had not seen me coming, and when I shouted "Boo!" in his ear he jumped high into the air, and then took to his heels, holding his pants with both hands, and I can still see him scampering at full speed across the yard like a startled rabbit.

I have never forgotten the sight of that great artist at work. I often think of him. I recently saw a film about Picasso, and as I followed the Spaniard's brush moving quickly across the canvas, the image of the pastry cook of Vilna came irresistibly to my mind. It is difficult to be an artist, to keep one's inspiration intact, to believe in the masterpiece, to possess the world over and over again—the dream of perfection, of total fulfillment, of permanent and completely satisfying mastery. I watched the painter's brush in its frenzied pursuit of the absolute, and a great sadness came upon me at the sight of this bare-chested gladiator whom no new triumph could save from being defeated in the end.

But it is still more difficult to become resigned. How many times, since I first raised my eyes toward those dizzy heights, have I found myself clinging to the flying trapeze, launched across a yawning void, trying to grasp, to attain, to give, to get there, my heart ready to burst, my teeth clenched and every fiber of my body at the breaking point; and while you thus hang on by the skin of your teeth, trying to postpone the inevitable fall, you still have to bother about style, give an impression of ease and grace; and when you are back on earth, empty of strength but secure, so you think, in the certainty of your fine performance, the trapeze is lowered toward you once more, the page is blank once more, and you throw yourself forward again, seeking new heights and trying to reach something that is there only to elude you.

The artist's compulsion, the obsessive pursuit of the master-piece, in spite of all the beauty I have seen, in spite of all the greatness I have witnessed, and in spite of all my own efforts on the flying trapeze, has remained for me unto this day no less of a mystery than it was thirty-five years ago, when I leaned from a roof over the inspired labors of the greatest pastry cook in the world.

CHAPTER *13*

WHILE I WAS THUS OPENING MY EYES FOR THE
first time on the mysterious world of art, my mother was devoting herself to the task of discovering in me the nugget of some
hidden talent. The violin and the ballet set aside once and for
all, and painting rejected as the cause of many a damned and
unhappy life, I was next introduced to singing. The great masters
of the local opera were invited to interest themselves in my
vocal cords and discover, if they could, the seed of a new
Chaliapin, destined to the applause of multitudes against a
background of dazzling lights, of purple and gold. Much to
my regret, after more than thirty years of hesitation and stubborn hope, I have to admit that the most malicious misunderstanding has crept in between me and my vocal cords. I have
no ear and no voice. I don't know how it happened but I have
to face the fact: I am not the great *basso profundo* I have always dreamed of being. For some reason that escapes me, it was
Chaliapin yesterday and Boris Christoff today who have been
given *my* voice. This has not been by any means the only misunderstanding in my life, but it still hurts deeply. I cannot tell
at what precise moment, as a result of what sinister machina-
tion, the substitution took place, but those who wish to hear
my true voice are invited to buy one of Chaliapin's records.
They should, for instance, listen to Moussorgsky's "The Flea":
they will hear me at my best. They have only to imagine me
standing on the stage, one hand proudly posed on my chest, and

thundering: "Ha! ha! ha! *blokha!*" [1] in my magnificent bass, to see how good I am. Unfortunately, what emerges from my throat when, one foot forward and my head held high, I give free rein to my vocal powers is to me a constant source of surprise and melancholy. There is not the slightest doubt about it: I have been robbed. It wouldn't have mattered at all if I didn't have it in me. But I do. I have never admitted this to anyone, not even to my mother, but what point is there in still concealing the fact? I am the true Chaliapin, even if everything was taken away from me and given to someone else. I am a great and noble *basso profundo* who has been tragically misunderstood, and I shall remain so until the end of my days.

Some years ago, during a performance of *Faust* at the Metropolitan in New York, I sat next to Rudolf Bing in his box. I sat there silently, my arms folded on my chest, my eyebrows twisted into a Mephistophelian knot, an enigmatic smile on my lips while, on the stage, an understudy was doing what he could with *my* part. I found something piquant in the thought that I was sitting next to one of the greatest operatic experts in the world and that he *did not know*. If, on that occasion, Mr. Bing felt some surprise at my diabolical and mysterious facial expression, here is the explanation, and I beg him to forgive me for not revealing my true identity to him.

My mother adored opera, she had for Chaliapin an almost religious awe and admiration, and I have, therefore, no excuse. Often, when I was eight or nine, catching one of those tender and yet, it seemed to me, reproachful expressions on her face, I ran to my treasure island in the barn, and there, drawing a deep breath and assuming the proper heroic pose, my mouth twisted into a diabolical snarl, I burst forth with a magnificent "Ha! ha! ha! *blokha!*" destined to shake the world. But alas! My voice had gone to live with another.

If only once, just once, it had been granted me to appear before my mother in her royal box at the Paris Opéra, or even, more modestly, at La Scala of Milan, while a dazzled audience

[1] "The Flea."

applauded me in my triumphant performance of Boris Godunov, I know that her artistic longings would at last have been fulfilled. But it was not to be. The only moment of triumph I had managed to give her was in 1932, when I won the ping-pong. championship of Nice, in my eighteenth year. I won it once, but I have always been beaten since.

The singing lessons were discreetly abandoned. I heard one of my coaches refer to me as "the child prodigy": he claimed that he had never in his life seen a youngster so completely devoid of ear, voice or talent.

Even now I often put on my record player the record of Chaliapin singing my part in "The Flea" and listen somberly to my real voice that had left me for another man. And yet I was prepared to give it everything I had in me, and I think we could have been very happy together.

Forced to admit at last that I possessed no special gift or hidden talent whatsoever, my mother decided, as so many parents have done before, that there was only one solution left open to us: diplomacy. Once this idea had taken root in her mind her spirits rose considerably, and since it appeared to her only natural that I should have the best the world had to offer, the least I could do was to become Ambassador of France— she would never have settled for less.

The love, or rather the adoration, which my mother had for France has always been a source of considerable astonishment to me. I hope that I am not being misunderstood: I myself have always been a great Francophile. But it was not my fault: I was brought up in such a way that I had no choice. Try to listen, as a child, to the legends of France told you in the depths of the Lithuanian forest; look at the beauty of that mythical country reflected in your mother's eyes; identify it once and for all with her smile of happiness and with her loving whisper, while she holds you in her arms; listen, sitting by a crackling fire, while the snow, outside, silences the world as if to help you hear better, listen, in that deep silence, to France being told you as if it were "Puss in Boots" or "Red Riding Hood";

listen to Jeanne d'Arc, and then open your eyes in wonder and hear voices every time you meet a shepherdess; gather your army of lead soldiers on the nursery floor and tell them that "from the top of these pyramids forty centuries are watching you"; take the Bastille at the head of your troops, and give the world liberty by attacking the nettles and the thistles with a wooden sword; learn to read by reading the fables of La Fontaine, and come to feel that French is your mother tongue —and then try to forget, try to see with your own eyes, try to get rid of the fairy tale. Even a prolonged residence in France won't help you to achieve this.

It goes without saying that the day came when that highly imaginary and theoretical vision of France as seen from the depth of a Lithuanian forest collided violently with the tumultuous and contradictory reality of my country. But it was already too late, much too late: I was stuck with the fairy tale.

In the whole course of my life, I have heard only two people speak of France in the same tone: my mother and General de Gaulle. Both physically and otherwise they were as unlike as it is possible to be. But when, after the fall of France, I heard De Gaulle's call to arms on the 18th of June, 1940, it was the voice of the old lady who sold hats at Number 16, Grand Pohulanka, as much as the General's immortal words, to which I rallied without hesitation.

From the age of eight, whenever we hit on difficult times— and we seldom hit on anything else—my mother would come and sit opposite me, her face weary and a haunted expression in her eyes. She would smoke a cigarette, look at me for a long time with a knowing and satisfied eye, and state with calm assurance: "You are going to be an Ambassador of France; your mother knows what she is saying."

All the same, one thing puzzles me. Why didn't she ever make me President of the Republic while she was at it? Perhaps there was more reserve, more caution in her than I gave her credit for. More likely, in that romantic world of Anna Karenina and aristocratic officers in which she secretly lived, a President of the Republic did not truly belong to the "best people," and an Ambassador in his dress uniform cut a more distinguished figure in her eyes.

More and more often I sought refuge in my secret hide-out among the sweet-smelling logs, and, after pondering for a while all the fabulous things that my mother expected from me, I would cry bitterly, silently; I just didn't know how to go about it.

Then I would climb out, with a heavy heart, trot back home and learn yet another of La Fontaine's fables: it was all I could do for her for the time being.

I am unable to tell exactly what sort of idea my mother had of the diplomatic career and diplomats generally, but one day she came into my bedroom with a preoccupied look. She sat down, waited a moment silently, and then embarked on a long discourse, the gist of which, for want of a better title, I can only call "the art of giving presents to ladies."

"Remember that it is far more effective to call in person with a small bouquet than to send a larger one by messenger. Never trust women that have several fur coats—they always expect another—have nothing to do with them, unless it is absolutely necessary. Always choose your gifts thoughtfully: if the woman is not very cultured, if she has no literary leanings, give her a good book. On the contrary, if she is intelligent, modest and truly interested in culture, give her some item of luxury, a bottle of scent or a beautiful shawl. Be careful, when you give her something to wear, to remember the color of her eyes and hair. With small objects—clips, rings, earrings—see that they go well with her eyes. If it is a dress, or a coat, choose it to go with the color of her hair. Women whose eyes and hair are the same color are easy to dress and will cost you less. Above all . . ."

She looked at me with a deeply worried expression: "Above all, you must never accept money from a woman. Never. I would rather die than learn that you had. Swear that you will never accept money from a woman; swear it on your mother's head."

I raised my hand and swore solemnly. It was a point to which she constantly returned and always with that worried and uneasy air.

"You may accept presents as long as they are objects, a fountain pen, for instance, a wallet, even a Rolls-Royce if she insists, or a house, but money—never!"

Nothing was ever neglected in my training as a man of the world. She read aloud to me *La dame aux camélias,* and when tears came into her eyes, and her voice broke so that she had to pause in her reading, I knew whom she saw as Armand, in her mind. Among other pieces of edifying literature which she read aloud to me, with her strong Russian accent, I remember particularly the works of MM. Déroulède, Béranger and Victor Hugo. She was not content merely to *read* poetry, but faithful to her past as a "dramatic artist" she declaimed, standing in the salon under the glittering chandeliers, with gusto, gesture and feeling. I remember a certain rendering of Victor Hugo's tragic evocation of Napoleon's defeat, with its sinister line: *"Waterloo, Waterloo, Waterloo, field of gloom . . ."* which gave me goose flesh: perched nervously on the edge of my chair, I watched and listened as she stood there, the book in one hand, the other raised in a most impressive manner toward the ceiling; her power of evocation sent cold shivers down my spine; my eyes wide, my knees pressed closely together, I stared at the "field of gloom" and I am sure that Napoleon himself, had he been present, would have been most impressed.

Another important item in my French education was, naturally, the "Marseillaise." We sang it together, my mother seated at the piano, and I standing beside her with one hand pressed to my heart, the other outstretched and pointing to the barricade, gazing defiantly into one another's eyes; when we came to *"Aux armes, citoyens!"* she brought both hands crashing down on the keyboard, while I raised a clenched fist with a somber and threatening expression on my face; having reached *"Qu'un sang impur abreuve nos sillons,"* she gave the keyboard a last punishing blow and sat with her two hands suspended in the air, while I, stamping my foot and assuming an implacable and determined look, imitated her gesture, fists clenched and head thrown back, and thus we remained for a moment, staring at each other, until the last chord had ceased to vibrate between the four walls of the salon.

CHAPTER 14

MY FATHER HAD LEFT US ALMOST IMMEDIATELY after I was born; whenever I mentioned his name, which was seldom, my mother and Aniela exchanged a quick glance and hurriedly changed the subject. I soon came to the conclusion that there was something embarrassing and even painful about the whole business, and learned to avoid it altogether.

I knew that the man who had given me his name had a wife and children, that he traveled a great deal and had gone to America. I met him several times. He was rather stout, had beautifully kept hands and kind eyes. With me he was always slightly uneasy and a little sad, though very nice, and when he looked at me with his gentle and, it seemed to me, reproachful eyes, I would lower my own guiltily—he always gave me the impression that I had done him a bad turn.

He really entered my life only after his death, and in a way that I shall never forget. I knew that he had died during the war in a German gas chamber, disposed of as a Jew, together with his wife and two children aged, I believe, fifteen and sixteen. It was only in 1958, however, that I learned of a particularly revolting detail connected with his tragic end.

I had come from Bolivia, where I was in charge of the French Embassy, to Paris, where I was to receive the Prix Goncourt for my novel *The Roots of Heaven*. Among the many letters which I received on that occasion was one that gave me certain details about the death of the man I had known so slightly.

He did not die in the gas chamber, as I had been told. He died of fright, on his way to execution, a few yards from the entrance. My correspondent had seen it all with his own eyes: he had been acting as doorman or as receptionist—I don't know what to call him, what the official title was that went with this sort of job.

The man wrote me, thinking, no doubt, that it would please me to know that my father had escaped the gas chamber, that he had fallen stone dead of a heart attack before he could enter it.

I sat for a long time with the letter in my hand. I didn't feel anything and my head was completely empty. I put the letter in my pocket, walked out to the staircase of the N.R.F. publishing house, where I had come to collect my mail, and I leaned against the banister for I don't know how long, in the clothes which had been made in London, with my title of Chargé d'Affaires of France, my Cross of the Liberation, my rosette of the Legion of Honor, and my Prix Goncourt.

Albert Camus happened to pass by, and seeing that I was unwell took me into his office.

The man who died of fear on his way to the gas chamber was little more to me than a total stranger, but on that day he truly became my father, and I want him to be known as such.

I continued to recite the fables of La Fontaine, the poems of Déroulède and Béranger, and to read a book entitled *Edifying Scenes of Great Men's Lives,* a fat volume in a pale blue binding with an engraving in gold representing the shipwreck of Paul and Virginie. My mother adored the story, which she considered to have a particularly inspiring moral tone. She often read aloud to me the noble passage in which Virginie, on the deck of the sinking ship, prefers to drown rather than take off her clothes in front of Paul. My mother never failed to sniff with satisfaction each time she read it to me. I listened politely, but already felt very skeptical. I was of the opinion that Paul didn't know how to go about it, and that was all there was to it.

So that I might learn how to maintain with dignity the important position awaiting me, I was made to study another fat volume, entitled *Lives of Illustrious Frenchmen*. This masterpiece too was read aloud to me, and my mother, having conjured up some admirable deed of Pasteur, Joan of Arc or Roland de Roncevaux, would lay the book down on her lap and give me a long look of admiration and love. The only occasion on which I saw her show any sign of rebellion was when she came upon certain unexpected corrections made by the authors in their treatment of history. They described the battle of Borodino as a French victory. My mother brooded for a moment about this paragraph and then, her Russian soul taking for once the lead over her love for France, she shut the book and, in a shocked voice, stated firmly:

"That is not true. Borodino was a great Russian victory. They seem to be overdoing it here."

There was nothing, on the other hand, to prevent me from admiring Joan of Arc and Pasteur, Victor Hugo and St. Louis, the Roi Soleil and the French Revolution—here I must say that in that wholly laudable universe which France was in my mother's eyes, she viewed everything with the same approval, and, calmly putting in the same basket the heads of Marie Antoinette, Robespierre, Charlotte Corday and Marat, Napoleon and the Duc d'Enghien, she served it all up to me with an admiring smile.

It took me a long time to free myself from the influence of those penny plain and tuppenny colored pictures, and to choose from the hundred faces of France the one which seemed to me most deserving of my love. For a long time, the most typically un-French part of me was precisely this refusal or inability to discriminate among them, this total approval given to the most contradictory and conflicting aspects of "my country, right or wrong," this absence of hatred for my countrymen, of indignation at some aspects of our history, and my complete failure to harbor grudges and resent old scores. I had to wait until I was a grown man to get rid of my Francophilia and thus become truly French; it was only around 1935, and most especially about the time of Munich, that I finally began to share my countrymen's dislike for one another, and their faith, cynicism, love, exasperation, rage. The longing to knock some of them on the head, and kick them on the shins, together with a certain nostalgia for the guillotine, at last allowed me to turn my back once and for all on the old nursery tale and to come to grips with the fraternal, difficult, contradictory and exhilarating reality of my country.

Apart from this highly patriotic education I received, from the results of which I found it so difficult to free myself, nothing was omitted or neglected which could extend the range of my experience as a man of the world.

When a theatrical touring company visited our town, an open carriage was ordered and my mother, looking very gay and beautiful under an enormous hat, wearing a lovely dress specially made for the occasion, pearls glittering in her ears and around her neck, took me to see *The Merry Widow* or *The Girl from Maxim's* or some other *Cancan of Paris*. Dressed, as usual, in velvet and silk, a pair of opera glasses pressed to my eyes, I gazed critically at the scenes of my future life, when the time would come for me at last to drink champagne from the shoes of lovely women in the private rooms of garden restaurants on the banks of the Danube, and to be sent by my government to seduce the wife of some Balkan prince, and thus put a spoke in the wheel of a military alliance which was being prepared against us.

My mother frequently made the rounds of the junk shops and returned home with a selection of old picture postcards showing me what she called "the best places" of the world, which were awaiting my appearance.

I soon became familiar with the interior of Maxim's and it was agreed that I should take my mother there at the first opportunity. She looked forward to it with obvious delight. She had dined there once—it was all most respectable, she insisted— in the course of a trip to Paris which she had made before the 1914-18 war.

But her favorite postcards were those, in color, showing military parades, with handsome officers, their swords drawn, following their kings; or great ambassadors in full ceremonial dress riding in open carriages to present their credentials at court; or admirable ladies of the time—Cléo de Mérode, Sarah Bernhardt and Yvette Guilbert. I remember her showing me some violet-robed bishop with his mitre on his head, and saying with approval, "Those people know how to dress." Naturally, she always brought home all the postcards of "illustrious Frenchmen" on which she could lay hands—excluded, however, were those who, though granted posthumous glory, had been something of a failure during their lives. Thus a postcard representing the unfortunate son of Napoleon, l'Aiglon, which had somehow found its way into our album, was promptly removed with this simple comment: "He was consumptive"; whether the reason for this banishment was fear of contagion, or whether she regarded the career of the poor Roi de Rome as an example not to be followed, I cannot say. The painters of genius who had during their lifetime met with nothing but poverty and lack of recognition and the *poètes maudits*—Verlaine, Rimbaud and Baudelaire—especially Baudelaire—great composers who had died mad or had otherwise met with a tragic fate, were refused admission because, to use a well-known English expression, my mother *would stand no nonsense;* she regarded success and fame as something that should be given you in your lifetime, preferably while your mother is still alive. The postcard she most frequently brought home was of Victor Hugo. She was willing to admit that Pushkin, whom she adored, was a greater poet, but he had been killed in a duel when he was only thirty-six, whereas Victor Hugo had lived to a very advanced age and had died in a splendid blaze of glory, with all of France in mourning. She approved of him immensely, and wherever I went in the flat there was always the noble face of Victor Hugo looking at me, and when I say everywhere, I mean it literally. From our domestic Panthéon of yellowing cards she had categorically rejected Mozart—"he died young"; Baudelaire—"you'll understand why later"; Berlioz, Bizet, Chopin—"they were unlucky"; but, strangely enough, and in spite of her horror of illness, and especially of tuberculosis and syphilis, Guy de Maupassant had found sufficient favor in her eyes to gain admission—after a slight show of embarrassment, I must say, and after a brief hesitation. My mother had a marked weakness for him, and the only books I ever saw her buy for herself were a complete collection of his works. I always felt a little uneasy at the idea that Guy de Maupassant might have met her in the days before I was born— I sometimes feel I had a narrow escape.

And so it was that the postcard exhibiting the handsome Guy in a white shirt, with his strong neck and virile mustache, was admitted into my collection, and occupied a place of honor between the young Bonaparte and Madame Récamier. Sometimes, when I turned the pages, my mother would look over my shoulder, and stop my hand just as it was going to turn the page with Maupassant on it. She would stare at him broodingly, and with a guilty and yet almost frivolous smile. Then she would shake her head and sigh.

"Women adored him," she would say, and then add, with seeming irrelevance and a hint of regret: "Oh well, perhaps it would be better for us to marry a nice, clean girl from a good family."

No doubt as a result of gazing too often at the picture of poor Guy, my mother decided that the time had come to issue a solemn warning against the treacherous snares that all too frequently lie in wait for every man of the world. One afternoon, she put me in a cab and dragged me to a most loathsome place called Panopticum, a sort of museum of medical horrors where abominable wax models served the purpose of putting schoolboys on their guard against the consequences of certain forbidden games. I must confess that I was duly impressed. All those collapsed and dissolving noses, slowly vanishing under the merciless attacks of syphilis and leaving nothing but a hole in the face, presented by the authorities for our inspection in a subterranean half-light, made me sick with fear.

For it was always the nose which, for some mysterious and to me incomprehensible reason, was required to pay the price of those fatal pleasures.

The severe warning thus addressed to me in that sinister place had a most salutary effect upon my impressionable nature: all my life I have paid the greatest attention to my nose. I gathered that boxing was a sport which the ecclesiastical hierarchy of Vilna emphatically advised against, and so the ring is one of the few spots into which I have never ventured in my career as a champion of the world. I have always done my best, also, to avoid brawls and fist fights, and can honestly say that, as far as my nose is concerned, the religious authorities have every reason to be pleased with me.

My nose is no longer what it used to be. It had to be entirely reconstructed in an R.A.F. hospital during the war after a nasty flying accident, but it is still there all the same; it stood by me firmly, and helped me to go on breathing through several French Republics. Even now, as I lie in the afternoon mist between heaven and earth, when my old craving for friendship and companionship once more takes hold of me, and I think of all those who have showed me so much devotion and love—my cat Mortimer, buried in a Chelsea garden; my cats Nicholas, Humphrey, Gaucho; and Gaston, my mongrel dog, all of whom left me long ago—I have only to raise my hand and touch the tip of my nose to feel that I am not entirely alone and that I still have company.

CHAPTER *15*

IN ADDITION TO THE EDIFYING READING RECOM-
mended by my mother, I devoured all the books which came
into my hands or, more accurately, on which I managed to lay
my hands in the local bookseller's shop. I carried my booty to
my secret treasure island in the barn, and there I would plunge
into the fabulous worlds of Walter Scott, Karl May, Mayne Reid
and Arsène Lupin. I found the admirable Lupin especially en-
chanting and did my best to impart to my features the caustic,
menacing and superior look with which the artist had endowed
the face of the hero on the book's cover. With that natural
gift children have for mimicry, I succeeded only too well, and
even today I often recognize in my features a vague resemblance to the cheap drawing which a third-rate illustrator had
supplied for the cover of a pulp publication. Walter Scott also
gave me great pleasure and I still occasionally fling myself on
my bed and set off in imaginary pursuit of some noble ideal,
defending poor widows and saving little orphans—the widows
are always remarkably beautiful and inclined to show their
tender gratitude, after first shutting away the little orphans in
the next room.

Another of my favorite books was Robert Louis Stevenson's
Treasure Island. I have never tired of reading it, and the thought
of that wooden chest filled with doubloons, rubies, emeralds and
turquoises—for some reason or other, diamonds have never
tempted me—still haunts my dreams. I remain convinced that

it truly exists somewhere and that I can find it, if only I try hard enough. I still hope, still wait, I am tortured by the feeling that it is there, and that I need only to break the code to be able to understand the great answer that has been there since the beginning of time but that no human mind or heart has ever been able to decipher. How much disappointment and sadness this tantalizing illusion can encompass only the very old star eaters will fully understand. I have never ceased to believe that a marvelous secret lies in wait somewhere around me and I have always walked this earth with the feeling that I am passing close to a buried treasure. When I wander on the San Francisco heights, Nob Hill, Russian Hill, Telegraph Hill, few persons could suspect that the graying gentleman is seeking a hidden sign, an open sesame, that his ironic smile conceals a craving for the master word, that he believes in some fabulous mystery behind the blankness, in a loving smile behind the veil of chaos, in the existence of an answer, a magical formula, a key. My eyes are continually searching heaven and earth; I never stop asking my silent question; I plead, I appeal, I wait. Naturally, I have acquired considerable skill at concealing all this under a courteous and somewhat distant exterior: I have become prudent, I play the grownup, but all the time I am still secretly looking for the golden scarab with a message under his wing, I am waiting for a mysterious beckoning, for a bird to perch upon my shoulder, and, speaking to me in a human voice, to reveal at last the meaning of all this, the why, the how and the what-for.

And yet I cannot pretend that my first contact with magic was very encouraging. I received my initiation behind the woodshed, from the hands of one of the younger boys, nicknamed "Melon" because of the habit he had of observing the world from above a slice of watermelon, so that only his wise and knowing eyes remained visible. His parents kept a fruit and vegetable shop in the building and he almost never emerged from the basement he lived in without a sizable slice of his favorite fruit. He had a way of plunging head first into the succulent flesh which made our mouths water, while his dreamy eyes stared at us above the object of our desires. Melons were common indeed in our part of the world, but every summer there were always a few cases of cholera and typhoid for which they were blamed, and we were strictly forbidden to touch them.

Melon must have been at least two years my junior but I have always been very much influenced by those who are younger than I. Mature men and their advice are entirely wasted upon me. Words of wisdom drop from their lips like dead leaves from a tree, majestic enough perhaps, but from them the sap has vanished. Truth dies young. What old age has "learned" is actually what it has forgotten. The ironic serenity of those who claim to have passed the time of illusions and avoided the pitfalls open to the inexperienced heart always reminds me of the smile of the Cheshire Cat, who has vanished, tail, heart and the rest, and now that ignoble middle age begins to weigh on me and whisper in my ear its tune of wisdom and detachment, I can see the ropes clearly and do not fall for the trick: I know that, in all that truly matters, I have been and shall never be again.

It was little Melon who initiated me into the secrets of magic. I remember my delighted astonishment when he told me that all my wishes would be granted if I knew how to go about it. All I had to do was get hold of a bottle, urinate into it and then fill it, in the following order, with a cat's whiskers, some rats' tails, a considerable number of live ants and flies, the ears of a bat and twenty other ingredients all most difficult to come by in commerce, and all of which I have completely forgotten, so that I begin to wonder if I shall ever have my wishes granted. I started an enthusiastic search for the indispensable magic elements. Flies were everywhere and, in our yard, there was never a lack of dead rats and cats. Bats could be found, and urinating into the talisman offered no insurmountable difficulty. But just try and get living ants into a bottle! You can neither catch them nor keep them; they escape as soon as you grab them; when you lift your finger to push one in, two others rush out, and by the time you have persuaded a fourth to enter, all the others are gone, and the whole business has to begin over and over again. A real task for Don Juan in Hell.

A moment came, however, when Melon, sickened by my frantic efforts, and impatient to get his teeth into the cake I was to give him in exchange for his magic formula, finally declared that the talisman was complete and ready to function. The only thing left for me to do was to make a wish. I began to think.

Seated on the ground with the bottle between my legs, I covered my mother with jewels, presented her with yellow Packards driven by liveried chauffeurs; I built her a palace of marble where all the good society of Vilna was summoned to appear on their knees. But something always was lacking. Between these poor crumbs of reality and the extraordinary need which had suddenly come to life in me there was no common measure. Confused and yet piercing, tyrannical and yet impossible to formulate, completely vague and yet totally commanding, a strange craving stirred in me, a longing for something that had no face, no content or shape, no answer. It was the first bite into my soul of that unlimited thirst for total possession and fulfillment which has nurtured mankind's worst crimes as well as its greatest museums, its most beautiful poetry and its most cruel empires—a longing whose source perhaps lies within our genes like some memory, some microcosmic biological yearning of the ephemeral for the eternal, for that unending immortal flow of time and life from which we become detached when we are born.

It was thus that I made acquaintance with the absolute, and I shall carry its bite within my soul till the end, and shall be haunted by its source as by some infinite and summoning absence.

I was only nine and could scarcely have been expected to guess that I had just felt for the first time the merciless pull upon my heart, soul and mind of what I was to call thirty years later "the roots of heaven" in the novel which bears that title. The absolute had suddenly revealed to me its almost physically felt absence, and already I did not know at which spring to quench my thirst. It was on that day, I think, that I was born as an artist. By that supreme and glorious failure which art is forever condemned to be, man, the eternal self-deceiver, tries to pass off as a satisfactory answer something that has never and can never be more than a tragically and vainly beseeching question.

It seems to me that I am still sitting there in my short pants among the nettles with a magic bottle in my hands. I made the most desperate efforts of imagination, for already, like all artists, I had the feeling that the time at my disposal was strictly limited. But I could find nothing satisfying enough to answer my mysterious, confused and already tyrannical longing, nothing that was worthy of my mother, of my love, of all those masterpieces of accomplishment that I wished to give her. The craving for perfection had just visited me, never again to leave. Gradually, my lips began to tremble, my face assumed an expression of vexation and anger, and I started to howl in fear, astonishment and rage.

Since then, I have grown used to the idea and, instead of howling, I write books.

I buried my talisman deep in the woodshed. I prudently put the top hat on the spot, so as to be able to find it again, but somehow a sort of disenchantment had taken hold on me and I never looked for it again.

CHAPTER *16*

Yᴇᴛ ᴄɪʀᴄᴜᴍꜱᴛᴀɴᴄᴇꜱ ꜱᴀᴡ ᴛᴏ ɪᴛ ᴛʜᴀᴛ, ᴠᴇʀʏ soon, my mother and I found ourselves in need of all the magic we could find.

I fell very ill. Hardly had scarlet fever left me when an acute inflammation of the kidneys set in and the distinguished doctors who had hastened to my bedside pronounced me lost. I have been pronounced lost several times in my life; on one such interesting occasion, extreme unction had been administered to me, and an R.A.F. guard of honor, complete with white gloves and dirks, was mounted around my body, while the Senegalese soldiers were busy with the coffin in the corridor.

During my rare moments of consciousness, I felt very preoccupied. I had an acute sense of my responsibilities, and the idea of leaving my mother in the world with no one to support her was intolerable to me. I was also painfully aware of everything she expected of me, and as I lay there, vomiting black blood, the idea of letting her down caused me more torment than my infected kidneys. I had been a failure. I had become neither Jascha Heifetz nor a French Ambassador, I had neither ear nor voice and, to make matters worse, I was now destined to die like a fool without having had so much as one single success with women and without even becoming a Frenchman! I still shudder at the idea that I might have died then, without having won the ping-pong championship of Nice in 1932.

I imagine that my refusal to evade my responsibilities toward my mother played a major part in my struggle to remain alive. Each time I saw her grief-stricken face leaning over me, I tried to smile and to utter a few coherent words, just to show that I was putting up a good fight, as she had always thought I would, and that things were not as bad as all that.

I did my best. I summoned to my aid d'Artagnan and Arsène Lupin; I spoke French to the doctor and muttered aloud fables of La Fontaine; with an imaginary sword in my hand, I performed prodigies of cut and thrust, flying after the enemy, just as Lieutenant Sverdlovski had taught me. The lieutenant came in person to see me and stayed for a long time by my side, holding my hand in his great paw and violently agitating his mustache; and I felt mightily encouraged by this martial presence. I tried to raise my arm and to score a bull's eye with my pistol; I hummed the "Marseillaise" and gave accurately the birth date of the Roi Soleil; I was winning prizes at the horse show and even had the effrontery to imagine myself standing on the stage, in my black velvet suit, playing the violin before an entranced audience while my mother, in her box, received tributes of flowers. With a monocle in my eye and a top hat on my head—helped, I must admit, by Rouletabille *—I was saving France from the diabolical schemes of the Kaiser, then rushing to London to recover the Queen's diamonds,** and returning just in time to sing *Boris Godunov* at the Vilna Opera.

Everybody knows the story of the willing chameleon. He was put upon a green cloth and obligingly turned green; he was put upon a red cloth and obligingly turned red. Upon a white cloth he turned white, and on a yellow one, yellow. But when they put him upon a Scottish plaid, the little fellow burst.

I did not burst, but I was very ill indeed. However, I put up a good fight, as befits a Frenchman, and I won the battle.

All of us can win many battles in our lives but it takes a lot of courage to get used to the idea that we may be constantly winning battles without ever winning the war. The war goes on

* The hero of sensational novels by Gaston Leroux.
** D'Artagnan's famous exploit in Dumas's *Trois Mousquetaires*.

and on and we die with our hands full of victories. But I believe, and shall always believe, that one day mankind will win the great war it has been waging since the beginning of time, and that one day human hands will succeed where I have failed and tear down the mask of darkness and chaos and absurdity, and look at the face of truth radiant with meaning, justice and love.

As far as my personal battle was concerned, I can only say that I fought in accordance with the best traditions of my country, with the sole purpose of saving the widow and the orphan. I very nearly died all the same, leaving to others the task of representing France abroad.

At one moment, under the eyes and on the advice of three doctors, I was wrapped in a sheet full of ice, a treatment to which I was to be subjected once again in Damascus, in 1941, after a particularly virulent attack of typhoid with intestinal hemorrhages, when the doctors decided they might just as well give me one more delightful experience.

After that, it was unanimously agreed to "decapsulate" my right kidney—whatever that may mean. But at that point my mother reacted in a grand manner worthy of her. She forbade the operation. She forbade it flatly and almost furiously, in spite of the insistence of the great German kidney specialist who had been summoned at enormous expense from Berlin.

I learned in later years that there existed in her mind a very close link between a man's kidneys and his sexual capacities. In vain did the doctors explain to her that the patient might undergo this operation and still have a normal sex life—I am convinced that the word "normal" only confirmed her in her furious opposition: a merely normal sex life was not at all what she envisaged for me. Poor Mother. I have the feeling that I have not been a good son.

But I kept my kidney, and the German specialist took a train for home after declaring that my demise was only a matter of days. But I survived—in spite of all the German specialists with whom I have had to deal since.

As soon as the fever left me, I was put on a stretcher and transported, in a special compartment, to Bordighera, on the Italian Riviera. It was thought that the Mediterranean sun would considerably speed up my recovery.

My first contact with the sea was unforgettable. I had never met anything or anybody, except my mother, who had a more profound effect on me. I am unable to think of the sea as a mere "it"—for me she is the most living, animated, expressive, meaningful, living thing under the sun. I know that she carries the answer to all our questions, if only we could break her coded message, understand what she tries persistently to tell us. Nothing can really happen to me as long as I can let myself fall on some ocean shore. Its salt is like a taste of eternity to my lips, I love it deeply and completely, and it is the only love which gives me peace. Perhaps it reminds me of my mother, and if all the Freudian theories about the return to the womb are even vaguely correct, the seashore is certainly as close as I can get to her now.

I was sleeping peacefully in my compartment when I felt upon my face something like a friendly hand. I woke up and found that it was only a breath of cool and scented air. The train had just stopped at Alassio, and my mother had lowered the window. I propped myself up on my elbows and my mother smiled as she followed the direction of my eyes. I took one glance at the world outside and suddenly, with absolute and final certitude, I knew that I *had arrived.* I saw a blue sea, a beach of pebbles and fishing boats drawn up on their sides. A few palms. Something peculiar—I am unable to tell what it was —happened to me at that moment, in a flash; all I know is that it was a flash of happiness. I had a feeling of infinite peace— I had come back home, at last.

Ever since then, the sea has been for me perhaps a humble but a completely satisfying answer. I do not know how to speak of her. All I can say is that the sea frees me from all my burdens; whenever I come back to her, it is as though no one had ever died.

While I was recovering my strength under the lemon trees and mimosas of Bordighera, my mother made a brief visit to Nice. Her idea was to sell her Vilna establishment and open a fashion house in Nice. Something must have told her that I stood very little chance of becoming a French ambassador if I went on living in a small border town of eastern Poland. But when, six weeks later, we found ourselves back in Vilna, it became only too obvious that her Maison Nouvelle, Grand Salon de Haute Couture de Paris, was no longer something that could be sold, or kept going. My illness had ruined us. During the two or three months it lasted, my mother had neglected her business completely, and to pay the greatest kidney specialists of Europe, whom she had summoned one after another to my bedside, she had become deeply bogged down in debt. Even before I had caused her so much trouble, and although our salon was considered the leading fashion house in town, our prestige had been far ahead of our balance sheet, and our standard of living too high for our means. We lived in the vicious circle of drafts settled by new drafts. The Russian word *wechsel*, draft, sounded constantly in my ears. Aside from my mother's boundless extravagance where I was concerned, and the astonishing stud of "professors" who surrounded me, she had had to keep up, at no matter what cost, a façade of prosperity. In the capricious snobbery which brings customers to a fashion house, the reputation of success and prosperity plays an essential part. At the least hint of financial difficulties, the ladies who formed our clientele would have pursed their lips, made a face and either taken their custom elsewhere or, more likely, grabbed us by the throat, compelling us to reduce our prices more and more, thus accelerating the process of decline beyond the point of recovery. My mother knew this and fought hard to the end in an effort to preserve appearances. She was a past master in the art of giving our patrons the impression that they were chosen by her, accepted and tolerated, that we did not really need them, that, in taking their orders, we were conferring a favor. They battled among themselves for my mother's personal attention, never argued over money, trembling at the idea that a new dress might not be ready for a ball, a first night, a gala performance. Little they knew that during all that time my mother felt at her throat the knife of the moneylenders, for she had been driven to sign more and more promissory notes in order to pay the interest on the money already borrowed. And in the midst of her distress, she had to keep up with the latest fashion, invent new and imaginative designs, put up with interminable fittings without ever letting the customers see how entirely we were at their mercy, and endure with an amused smile the suspense of their "to buy or not to buy," never letting them guess that the issue of their hesitation waltz was, for us, a matter of life and death.

I often saw her come out for a breath of fresh air from a particularly bothersome fitting, sit down in my room, and silently look at me with a smile, as though seeking to recover her strength at the very source of her courage and her life. She remained so without a word, smoking a cigarette, before getting to her feet again with a deep sigh and returning to the field of battle.

Thus it was not at all surprising that my illness and our two months' absence, during which Aniela had been left in charge of the firm, should have dealt the final blow to Maison Nouvelle. A few weeks after our return, in spite of her desperate efforts to refloat the sinking ship, it became only too plain that all was lost. Much to the delight of our competitors, we were declared bankrupt.

Our furniture was seized, and I have a vivid recollection of a bald, fat Pole with a black waxed mustache nosing like a cockroach from room to room, accompanied by two acolytes who might have stepped straight from the pages of Gogol, fingering the dresses in the wardrobes, the armchairs, the sewing machines, touching pensively the breasts of the dressmakers' dummies, and generally sticking his red, large nose everywhere. I do hope that life showed itself unclement to him.

My mother had taken the precaution of concealing from creditors and bailiffs her one precious treasure, a complete collection of old imperial silverware which she had brought with her from Russia, rare collectors' pieces, the value of which, according to her, was considerable. She had always refused to touch this hoard. It was valuable enough to assure our future for some years to come, after we had settled in France; its sale would then make it possible for me to "grow up, complete my studies and become truly *somebody*"—the last word always pronounced in a slightly mysterious, meaningful tone of voice.

Now, for the first time, my mother openly showed her distress, and she turned to me for help and protection with a sort of defeated and disarming femininity. I was already nearly ten, and I did my best. I realized that my first duty was to appear imperturbable, manly and detached, steady as a rock. The moment had come for me to reveal myself at last in that role of cavalier for which Lieutenant Sverdlovski had been so diligently training me.

The bailiff's men had laid their hands on my jodhpurs and my riding crop. I was reduced to facing the world in short pants and with empty hands. I decided that it was all a matter of style.

I moved through our quickly emptying flat under the very noses of the robbers, with an arrogant air, getting in their way, stepping on their feet, planting myself in front of them with my hands in my pockets and my stomach stuck out, whistling a tune to show my unconcern, spitting on the carpet which they were carrying away, giving the piano a push at the right moment that sent it thundering down the stairs, with considerable damage to itself and to the wall, staring the rascals out of countenance, a real man, in short, a cavalier, offering his protection, fully capable of looking after his mother and after himself and ready to get tough at the slightest provocation.

Needless to say, this display was not intended for the bailiff's men, but for my mother. She must be made to see that I was there, by her side, that it was only a matter of time before I would give her back a thousand times all she was losing—the carpets, the Louis XVI chairs, the console, the splendid chandelier and all the mirrors on the wall in their golden frames. She seemed pleased and comforted as she sat in the last remaining armchair, crying only a very little and following me with a loving look.

When the last carpet was taken away, I began to whistle a tango and on the bare floor executed with an imaginary partner some of the most intricate dance steps which Mademoiselle Gladys had taught me. I glided over the floor, closely clasping the waist of my invisible partner, holding high her invisible hand, whistling the tune "Tango Milonga, tango *mych marzen i snow*," * while my mother, a cigarette between her fingers, beat time with her feet.

When at last she had to get up from the armchair and abandon it to the rabble, she did so almost gaily and without taking her eyes off me, joining me in my game of defiance while I continued my skillful movements on the dusty floor, just to show her how tough and unconcerned I was, and to remind her that her most valuable possession had not been taken from her.

A little later we held a long conference to decide what to do next, where to turn. We spoke French so that the Polish rabble couldn't understand what we were saying. The rooms were empty now, and the chandelier, the very symbol of our past splendor, was being lowered from the ceiling.

There was no question of our staying on in Vilna, where my mother's best customers, those who had cajoled and courted her once, now turned up their noses and looked away when they passed us in the street, a behavior that was due not so much to snobbery as to the simple fact that many of them still owed us money: they were thus able to kill two birds with one stone.

I no longer, unfortunately, remember the names of these noble and human creatures, but I sincerely hope that they are still alive, that they have not had time to take their fat behinds out of Lithuania, and that the Communist regime has taught

* Tango Milonga—tango of fancies and dreams.

them a lesson or two. I am not vindictive by nature, and I will say no more.

I sometimes visit the premises of the great Paris couturiers and sit in a corner watching the show. Almost all my friends imagine that I haunt these places to indulge in my favorite pastime, which is looking at pretty girls. They are wrong. I go there to think of the directrice of Maison Nouvelle.

There was not enough money left to enable us to settle in Nice, and my mother refused to sell her precious silver, on which my whole future depended.

With a few hundred *zlotys*, which we had managed to save from the shipwreck, we decided to go first to Warsaw—it was, after all, a step west, that is, in the right direction. My mother had friends and relatives there, and besides, there was one decisive argument in favor of this plan: "There is a French lycée in Warsaw," she announced, with a sniff of satisfaction.

There was no more to be said. We had only to pack our bags—*à façon de parler,* since our luggage had gone the way of everything else. The silver being secretly stored in a secure hiding place, we gathered the rest of our belongings into a bundle, in the best tradition of all fairy tales.

Aniela did not go with us. She was to join her fiancé, who worked for the railroad and who lived in a discarded railroad car with the wheels taken off. It was there that we parted from her, after a heart-rending scene, in which we all sobbed desperately, flinging ourselves into one another's arms, tearing ourselves away, only to return for yet another embrace. I have never howled so much since.

I tried more than once to get news of Aniela, but a discarded railway carriage, even without wheels, is not a very pleasant address, particularly when the whole world is being turned upside down. I should have dearly liked to reassure her, to tell her that I have never as yet fallen victim to tuberculosis, which is what she always feared most for me. She was a handsome young woman, with a well-filled figure, large brown eyes and long black hair but, of course, it was all more than thirty years ago.

We left Vilna without regret. I took with me, in our bundle, the fables of La Fontaine, a volume of Arsène Lupin and my *Lives of Illustrious Frenchmen*. Aniela had managed to save from our disaster the Tcherkesse uniform which I had once worn at the fancy-dress ball, and that, too, we took in our bundle. It was already too small for me and I have never since had occasion to wear a Tcherkesse uniform and probably never will.

CHAPTER *17*

IN WARSAW WE LIVED IN A SUCCESSION OF FUR-
nished rooms. Someone from abroad came to my mother's rescue,
sending her sums of money at irregular intervals which just enabled us to keep alive. I went to school, where every morning,
at the ten o'clock recess, my mother arrived with chocolate in
a Thermos flask and slices of bread and butter. She turned her
hand to a hundred and one things in order to keep us afloat.
She acted as a go-between in the precious-stones market, bought
and sold furs and antiques, and was, I believe, the first person
to think up a new kind of business which turned out to be
modestly lucrative. Through advertisements in the press she informed the public that she was prepared to buy teeth—for lack
of a better term, I can only call them second-hand teeth—containing some proportion of gold or some proportion of platinum,
which she then sold at a good profit. She examined the teeth
under a magnifying glass, after first soaking them in a special
acid to make sure that the filling or the crown was truly of
precious metal. She also acted as scout for a real-estate firm,
sold advertising space and took on several other jobs the precise nature of which I no longer remember. What I do remember is that every morning, at ten, she turned up punctually with
her Thermos flask of hot chocolate, and her bread and butter.
    Nevertheless, there again we suffered a bitter disappointment.
I was unable to enter the French *lycée*. The fees were high—far

and away beyond our means. So, for two years, I had to make do with the Polish school, and I can still speak and write Polish fluently. It is a beautiful language, Mickiewicz has remained one of my favorite poets, and, like all true Frenchmen, I have a tender spot in my heart for Poland.

Five days a week I took a tram to the house of an excellent man, Monsieur Lucien Dieuleveut-Caulec, who taught me my maternal tongue.

Here, I think, I should make a confession. I do not often indulge in lying, because, for me, a lie has a sickly flavor of impotence: it leaves me too far away from the mark. But when I am asked where I pursued my studies in Warsaw, I always answer, at the French *lycée*. It is a question of principle. My mother had done her best, and I don't see why I should deprive her of the fruit of her labors.

I should not like anybody to think that I watched her struggles without trying to help. After having failed in so many fields, I was beginning to feel that I had at last found a hidden bonanza of talent in myself. I had begun juggling in the old Valentine days, in the hope of finding favor in her eyes, and now I was once more devoting myself to that noble art, with a new fire, with my mother in mind.

I juggled with five, six oranges, burning with a mad ambition of eventually achieving seven, and perhaps even eight, or even nine, like the great Rastelli, and so going on to become the greatest juggler of all time, a true champion of the world. My mother deserved that, it would mean the end of all her financial worries, and I spent all my time practicing, practicing.

I juggled with oranges, with plates, with bottles, with brooms, with anything, in fact, that came my way. My passion for art, for perfection, my confused longing for some staggering and unique exploit that would raise us above our vulnerability and perhaps even above mortality itself found suddenly in juggling a naïve but genuine expression, and I flung myself into it heart and soul. Assailed on all sides by poverty, insecurity and fear, I was dreaming of some supreme prowess, a dazzling display of mastery that would astonish the world. I juggled in school, in the streets, I climbed our stairs and entered our room still juggling. I was juggling in my dreams, and whenever I caught sight of a look of deep worry on my mother's exhausted face, I would grab my oranges, or balls, and throw them in the air and stand before her, juggling as gracefully as I could, a silent proclamation of mastery, a promise of even greater deeds to come.

But there again, in spite of all my efforts, in spite of my devouring craving for mastery, the masterpiece always eluded me: I could never get beyond the fifth ball. God knows I tried hard: at times I juggled for seven or eight hours a day. But no matter what I did, the sixth and last ball remained beyond my reach. The masterpiece kept eluding me. I have spent a lifetime trying. It was only when I was approaching my fortieth year that gradually the awful truth dawned on me, and I realized that the last ball did not exist.

It is a sad truth, and it should not be told to children; that is why this book must not be allowed to fall into their hands.

When I see Malraux, the greatest of us all, juggling as few men have ever juggled before him, my heart bleeds at the tragedy whose traces are so clearly visible on his face. In the midst of his most brilliant performances, the last ball remains beyond his reach, and all his work bears the mark of that agonizing certitude.

I also feel it is time that the truth about Faust be made known. Everyone has lied before, Goethe worse than anyone; he has lied with genius. I know that I should not say what I am going to say, for if there is one thing I hate doing, it is depriving men of their hope. But there it is: the tragedy of Faust is not at all that he sold his soul to the devil. The real tragedy is that there is no devil to buy your soul. There is no "taker." No one will help you to catch the last ball, no matter what price you are willing to pay. There is, of course, a gang of smart phonies, who give themselves airs and claim they are prepared to make a deal, and I don't say that one cannot come to terms with them with a certain amount of profit. One can.

They offer success, money, the applause of the mob. But if you have had the misfortune to be born a genius, if you are Michelangelo, Goya, Mozart, Tolstoy, Dostoievsky or Malraux, you are destined to die with the feeling that all you have ever done was sell peanuts.

Having got that off my chest, let me say that I still go on practicing.

Every morning, I step out of my house on the hill above San Francisco and there, in the bright sunlight, into the face of the sky, I juggle defiantly and masterfully with three oranges, which is now as far as I can go.

It is no arrogance on my part, but a simple affirmation of human dignity. I shall never stop trying.

I should not like anyone to conclude from a certain tone of sadness that might occasionally creep into my voice that I have been an unhappy man. That would be a most regrettable error.

I have known in my life, and still know, great moments of happiness. Ever since childhood, for instance, I have always loved pickled cucumbers, either the Russian, the Polish or the Jewish kosher type, which we call in France cucumbers *à la russe*. I often buy a pound at a time, then settle down somewhere in the sun, preferably on the ocean shore, or on the pavement, no matter where, and munch my cucumbers. Those are my only moments of bliss and I truly feel that the great Persian poet Chaim Zyskind did not lie, and that man is indeed the champion of the world, and that everything on this earth belongs to him. If the landscape is beautiful, so much the better: while I look at it, eating my pickled cucumber, I feel that I am eating it too. It is a good way of taking possession of the world. Artistically speaking, I have never been able to possess anything to my heart's content or even truly to bite into it— no mortal has achieved this, not even the greatest poets or painters—and in that desperate hunger for the absolute and for some total fulfillment which the sight of beauty stirs in me, I am somehow reduced to the humble expedient of eating or making love. Give me a pound of kosher cucumbers, called *malosolny* in Russian, and I know that life *is* worth living, that happiness *is* attainable: it is a matter of loving something worth while with all your heart and giving oneself to it completely, without reserve.

My mother watched my efforts to help with gratitude. When she came home dragging some faded old carpet under her arm, or a secondhand lamp, which she proposed to resell, and found me juggling in my room, she well knew that this was a labor of love. She would sit down, watch me, and then say with a smile: "I don't think you will have very much practical sense. But you are going to be a great artist. Your mother is always right."

Her prediction very nearly came true. My class at school had got up a play and, after the elimination of other possible male leads, the principal role in Mickiewicz's dramatic poem *Konrad Wallenrod* was entrusted to me despite the strong Russian accent with which I spoke Polish. It was not by chance that I came through the preliminary heats with flying colors and was given the part.

Every evening, when she had finished her rounds and got our supper ready, my mother spent an hour or two rehearsing with me. She had learned every word of the text and started the proceedings by giving me her own interpretation; then I was told to go through the text again, closely copying her gestures, her poses and her intonations. It was a very dramatic part, and at about eleven o'clock our exhausted neighbors could stand no more and clamored for silence. But my mother was infuriated by such lack of respect for art, and there were many memorable scenes in the corridors during which, her heart still throbbing with the inspiration of truly great poetry, she surpassed herself in invective, defiance and flaming tirades. We did not have long to wait before we were asked to do our declaiming somewhere else, and went to live with one of my mother's relatives in a flat occupied by a lawyer and his sister, who was a dentist. At first, we slept in the waiting room, but later moved to the lawyer's office. Every morning we had to clear up before the arrival of clients and patients.

At long last, the performance took place and, on that evening, I enjoyed my first success upon the boards. When all was over, my mother, still dazed from the applause and with tears of joy still running down her cheeks, took me to eat cakes at Lardelli's, the most chic confectioner in town. She had never got over the habit of holding my hand when we were walking in the street and I, being by then eleven and a half, felt most embarrassed. I always tried, on some plausible pretext, politely to disengage my hand and then conveniently forget to give it back to her, but my mother never failed to grasp it once more firmly in her own.

The streets in the vicinity of the Poznanska were, from afternoon on, much patronized by prostitutes. There were, quite literally, swarms of them in the rue Chmielna, and my mother and I very soon became a familiar sight to these kind young women. When we walked past them, hand in hand, they always respectfully made way for us and complimented my mother on my good looks. When I was alone, they frequently stopped me to question me about my mother, asking why she had never remarried, giving me sweets, and one of them, a thin little redhead with bandy legs, always kissed me on the cheek, after which she would ask me for my handkerchief and carefully rub the place where her lips had touched my skin. I do not know how the news that I was to play an important part in the school production of *Konrad Wallenrod* had spread to the street but, on our way to the confectioner's, the girls surrounded us and anxiously inquired what sort of reception I had had. My mother informed them of my triumph without any foolish modesty and, throughout the ensuing days, presents were rained upon me whenever I walked down the rue Chmielna—little crosses, sacred medals, rosaries, pen knives, slabs of chocolate and statuettes of the Virgin. I was more than once taken by the girls into a small delicatessen nearby, and there, under their admiring glances, I stuffed myself with dill pickles and *halva*.

At Lardelli's, after my fifth cake, as I began to relax, my mother briefly described her plans for the future. At last we had solid ground under our feet. There was no doubt about my talent, the road was marked out and we had only to stride ahead. I would become a great actor, I would make many lovely women unhappy, I would have an immense open yellow car, I would have a contract with the UFA. . . . This time, it was all within our reach: we had made it. Another cake for me, another glass of tea for her. She must have drunk between fifteen and twenty glasses of tea a day. I listened—how shall I put it?—I listened prudently. I can say without boasting that I had not lost my head. I was only eleven and a half, but I had already made up my mind to be the calm, the restraining, the logical French influence in the family. For the moment, the only concrete fact which I saw in all this was the plateful of cakes, of which I left not one. That was wise of me because my great stage and screen career never materialized. It certainly was not for want of trying. For several months, my mother never stopped sending my photo to every theatrical management in Warsaw as well as Berlin, and to the UFA, with a long description of the terrific success I had had in the principal part of *Konrad Wallenrod*. She even got the director of the Polski Theatre to give me an audition. He was a distinguished and cultured gentleman who listened attentively while, one foot forward and one arm raised in the attitude of Rouget de Lisle singing the "Marseillaise," I fervently declaimed on his office floor, with a strong Russian accent, the immortal verses of the Polish bard. I had terrible stage fright, which I tried to conceal by shouting more and more loudly. There were several people in the office who stared hard at me and seemed greatly struck, but I cannot have been at my best in this far from encouraging atmosphere, since the fabulous contract was never offered to me. All the same, the manager heard me through to the end and when, having swallowed poison as the text demanded, I collapsed on the floor, twisting in appalling convulsions while my mother looked with an air of triumph at the audience, he helped me to my feet and, after making sure that I had not hurt myself, vanished so quickly that I still wonder how he did it and through what door he fled.

I never appeared upon the boards again until sixteen years later before a very different public, of which General de Gaulle was the most interesting member. It happened in the heart of Equatorial Africa, at Bangui in the Oubangui-Chari in 1941. I had been there for some while in charge of the three Blenheims of my squadron when we were told that General de Gaulle was coming to inspect us. We decided to honor the leader of Free France with a theatrical performance and at once set to work. An extremely witty revue—according to its authors—was put together on the spot. The text was very light, very gay and sparkling with humor, for those were the days of the great military disasters of 1941, and we were determined to show our leader an unshakable morale and a tremendous optimism.

We gave a tryout performance before the General's arrival, so as to get everything running smoothly, and our success on that occasion was encouraging. The audience applauded loudly, and though an occasional mango dropped from a tree onto the head of one or another of the spectators, the whole thing went off very well. The General turned up next morning and, that same evening, was present at the show with the military Governor and several high political personalities of his entourage: it was a disaster. I swore to myself that never, no matter what dramatic hours my country might be passing through, never again would I act, dance and sing before General de Gaulle. France may ask anything of me, but not that.

Admittedly, the idea of performing a naughty little revue before the man who stood alone in the storm of History, facing at the same time a ruthless enemy and scheming Allies, was not the best invention that could have sprouted in our youthful brains. But I never would have thought that one single man could have such a magical effect upon an audience.

General de Gaulle, in white tropical uniform, sat in the front row, very stiff, his arms crossed and his *képi* on his knees. He did not budge, twitch or show the slightest reaction of any kind from start to finish of our performance. I do seem to remember, however, one fleeting moment when I was doing a lot of high kicking, dancing the can-can, while a fellow actor screamed, as the part demanded, *"Je suis cocu!"*—I do seem to remember that I just caught, out of the corner of my eye, a very slight quiver of the mustache on the face of the leader of Free France. But perhaps I only imagined it. There he sat, very erect, with his arms crossed, and looked at us with a sort of merciless concentration.

The eye was in the audience and it looked on Cain.*

But the most astonishing thing of all was the behavior of the two hundred other spectators. Whereas on the previous evening the whole house had roared with laughter, applauded loudly and showed that they were thoroughly enjoying the fun, we did not, on this occasion, get so much as a smile. And yet the General was sitting in the front row and it was almost impossible for the rest of the audience to see his face. Let those who maintain that General de Gaulle is incapable of making contact with crowds or of communicating his feelings think this over.

Some time after the end of the war, Louis Jouvet staged a production of *Don Juan*. I was present at rehearsal. In the scene in which the statue of the Commander arrives punctually at the rendezvous and carries the libertine off to hell, I suddenly felt that I had seen it all before, somewhere, and, in a flash, recalled Bangui in 1941 and General de Gaulle looking me straight in the eyes. I hope he has forgiven me.

* Reference to Hugo's verse: "The eye was in the tomb and it looked on Cain."

CHAPTER *18*

AND SO, MY STAGE TRIUMPH IN KONRAD
Wallenrod turned out to be merely ephemeral and failed, to
our great surprise, to solve any of the material problems we
were facing. Our last penny was gone. My mother spent every
day walking the streets in search of business, and came home
late, looking exhausted and scared. But I was never cold or
hungry, and she always kept assuring me that a terrific, lucrative deal was just around the corner—there was absolutely nothing to worry about.

I did all I could to help her. I literally surpassed myself in
my efforts to fly to her rescue. I wrote poems which I recited to
her—they were to bring us fame, fortune and the adulation of
applauding crowds. I worked for five or six hours a day polishing my verses and filled many exercise books with stanzas,
alexandrines and sonnets. I even embarked upon a tragedy in
five acts, a prologue and an epilogue, entitled *Alcymène*. Each
time my mother came back empty-handed from one of her expeditions, and sank down on a chair—the first marks of age
were beginning to show in her face—I read aloud the immortal
lines which were to bring the world to her feet. She always
listened with the greatest attention. Little by little, her face
grew brighter, the traces of fatigue vanished and she exclaimed
with absolute conviction: "Lord Byron! Victor Hugo! Pushkin!"

I also went in for greco-roman wrestling in the firm hope of one day becoming a champion of the world, and soon was known at school as "Gentleman Jim." I was far from being stronger than anybody else, but I excelled in striking noble and elegant poses, which gave the impression of quiet power and dignity. I had style. I was almost always floored.

M. Dieuleveut-Caulec gave his kind encouragement to my poetic creations. For it goes without saying that I composed neither in Russian nor in Polish. French was my language. Warsaw was no more than a temporary camping ground on the journey to my true country, and there could be no question of my shirking my duty. I had the greatest admiration for Pushkin, who wrote in Russian, and for Mickiewicz, who wrote in Polish, but I could never really understand why they had not used French in the creation of their masterpieces: it seemed to me rather unpatriotic of them.

I made no attempt to conceal from my young Polish friends the fact that I was one of them only temporarily, that we were planning to "go home" at the first opportunity. Such artless pigheadedness on my part did not make life at school any easier for me. During the breaks, when I wandered about the corridors with a self-important air, a little group of older boys would sometimes gather around me. They looked at me with solemn eyes. Then, one of them would step forward and, addressing me in the third person, as is customary in Poland, would ask me in a tone of deep respect: "Am I right in thinking that *Kolega* * has put off his journey to France?"

I invariably played into his hands. "Yes. It is not worth while arriving in the middle of the school year," I would explain. "One must be there at the beginning."

My baiter would nod agreement, then add: "I trust he has warned them of his intention: otherwise they might be worried."

They nudged one another and I knew that they were making fun of me. But I was far beyond the reach of their insults. My dream was more important to me than my wounded pride and, somehow, their baiting helped to strengthen my belief and my

* Our comrade.

illusions. I stood up to them and very calmly answered their questions. Did I think that the school curriculum in France was more difficult than in Poland? Yes, much more difficult. Sport, too, played a great part in it and I intended to specialize in fencing and greco-roman wrestling. Was uniform obligatory in French schools? Yes. What was it like? It was blue with gilt buttons and a sky-blue *képi*. On Sundays, one wore red trousers and a white plume in the *képi*. Did one wear a sword? Only on Sundays and on the last day of the year. Did one sing the "Marseillaise" before the day's work started? Yes, naturally, one sang the "Marseillaise" every morning. Would I mind singing the "Marseillaise" for them? God forgive me, but there and then I advanced one foot, put one hand on my heart, raised high a clenched fist and gave a rendering of my national anthem in tones of burning enthusiasm. Yes, I played into their hands but I wasn't taken in. I could see their grinning faces and the way they turned aside to give vent to their guffaws. But oddly enough, I didn't care. There I stood in the middle of a group of *banderilleros*, feeling completely indifferent. Conscious that I had a great country behind me, I was impervious to their sarcasm and their gibes. This game might have gone on indefinitely had not my tormentors suddenly touched me on the raw. The routine had begun in its usual way when five or six of the older boys pressed around me, with a thoughtful look on their faces: "So, our friend is still with us? We thought that he had left for France, where he is so eagerly awaited."

I was about to embark upon my usual explanations when the eldest of the group broke in upon me: "They are not very keen about admitting *ex-cocottes*, I suppose."

I no longer remember who the boy was and I certainly do not know where he had picked up this curious piece of information. Need I say that nothing in my mother's past justified such a slanderous statement? She may not, perhaps, have been the "great dramatic artist" of her imagination but, still, she had played in very good Moscow theatres, and those who knew her at that time always described her to me as a proud woman whose exceptional beauty had never turned her head nor led her astray.

But so great was my surprise on this occasion that it took the appearance of cowardice. My heart suddenly sank into a hole, my eyes filled with tears and, for the first and last time in my life, I turned my back on my enemies.

I have never, since then, turned my back on anything or anybody, but on that black day I did, and there is no use denying it. For a moment I was put out of countenance.

When my mother came home, I ran to her and blurted out the whole story. I expected her to fling her arms wide and console me as she knew so well how to do. But what actually happened was staggering. All of a sudden, every vestige of love and tenderness left her face. She did not, as I had been anticipating, let a flood of compassion and affection flow over me. She said nothing and looked at me for a long time, almost coldly. Then she moved away from me, took a cigarette from the table and lit it. She went into the kitchen, which we shared with the owner of the flat, and busied herself about my supper. Her face looked as though it were made of wood, utterly indifferent, and from time to time she turned on me a pair of eyes that were almost hostile. I could not understand what had happened and was filled with a great surge of self-pity. I felt indignant, betrayed, abandoned. She made my bed, still without uttering a word. She did not so much as lie down all that night, and when I woke in the morning, she was still sitting in the same old armchair of pale-green leather, facing the window with a cigarette between her fingers. The floor was covered with stubs—she never cared where she dropped them. Her face was quite expressionless, and she turned her eyes away from me to the window. I believe, today, that I know what she was thinking—at least I imagine that I do. She must have been wondering whether I was worth bothering about, whether there was any meaning in her sacrifices, her efforts and her hopes, whether I was not going to turn out like men all the world over, whether I would not end by treating her as another man had once treated her.

She boiled my three eggs as usual and made my cup of chocolate. She watched me eat. At last a faint hint of tenderness showed in her eyes. She must have been reflecting that, after all, I was only twelve. When I got my books together, ready to start off for school, the same hard expression as before came back into her face.

"You'll never go back there again."

"But . . ."

"You will continue your education in France. Only . . . sit down."

I sat down.

"Listen to me, Romain."

I stared at her in amazement. I was no longer Romantchik-Romouchka. This was the first time she had ever not used the diminutive. This new departure made me feel extremely ill at ease.

"Listen to me carefully. The next time a thing like that happens, the next time your mother is insulted to your face, I'll expect to see you brought home on a stretcher. Do you understand?"

I sat there with my mouth open. Her face was very hard. Almost hostile. There was no trace of pity in her eyes. I could not believe it was my mother who was speaking. How could she say things like that? Was I not her Romouchka, her little prince, her precious treasure?

"I shall expect to see you brought back with blood on your face, do you understand?"

Her voice rose. She leaned toward me. She was almost shouting.

"Unless you realize that, it's not worth our going to France. . . . Not worth going anywhere."

A profound feeling of injustice gripped me. My lips began to tremble, tears came into my eyes, my mouth opened still further. I had no time to do more. I felt a stinging slap on my cheek, then another and another. So great was my stupefaction that the tears vanished as though by enchantment. It was the first time my mother had ever raised her hand against me and, like everything she did, it wasn't done by halves. I sat motionless and petrified under her rain of blows. I didn't even cry out.

"Remember what I've said to you. From now on, you have to defend me. I don't care what they do to you with their fists, that's not what hurts most. If necessary, you'll let yourself be killed."

I again pretended not to understand, to be only twelve, to hide myself. But I understood all right. My cheeks were smarting, I was still seeing stars, but I understood and she saw that I did. It seemed to have a calming effect on her. She breathed noisily—always a sign with her of satisfaction—and poured herself out a cup of tea. She drank it always with a lump of sugar in her mouth, the way Russian peasants do. She was staring into the distance, busily seeking, scheming, calculating. Then she spat what remained of the sugar into the saucer, took her handbag and went out. She went straight to the French Consulate and energetically set about making arrangements to have us admitted as residents in a country where, as she wrote on the application which she got M. Dieuleveut-Caulec to draw up, "it is my son's intention to settle, to study and to grow into a man"—but there, I am sure, the phrase outdistanced her thoughts and she did not fully realize what it was that she was thus demanding of me.

CHAPTER 19

WHAT I CHIEFLY REMEMBER OF MY FIRST CON-
tact with France is the porter at the Nice station, with his long
blue smock, his peaked cap, his leather straps and a hale and
hearty complexion which was the combined product of sun, sea
air and good wine.

The uniform of French porters is much the same today, and
each time I return to the South I am sure of finding that friend
of my childhood. To him we entrusted the box containing all
our future, that is to say the famous set of old Russian silver,
the sale of which was to ensure our prosperity during the years
to come.

We settled into a *pension de famille* in the rue de la Buffa
and my mother gave herself barely time enough to smoke her
first French cigarette—a Gauloise Bleue—before opening the box
in question, taking out a few particularly choice pieces, putting
them into a small suitcase and, with a confident air, setting off
to hunt through Nice for a purchaser. I, meanwhile, burning
with impatience, hurried down to the beach to renew my old
acquaintance with the sea. It recognized me at once and crept
up to lick my toes.

When I got back to the house, I found my mother waiting
for me. She was sitting on the bed, smoking nervously. The expression on her face was one of complete incomprehension, a
sort of prodigious astonishment. She gave me a questioning
look, as though expecting me to supply her with the key to a

riddle. In each shop she had entered with her samples of our treasure, she had met with the coldest of cold receptions. The prices she had been offered were utterly ridiculous. Naturally she had told the various dealers what she thought of them. The jewelers were nothing but professional thieves who had tried to rob her; besides, not one of them was truly French. They were, all of them, Armenians, Russians, perhaps even Germans. To-morrow she would visit *French* shops, kept by real *Frenchmen* and not by dubious refugees from eastern Europe whom France should never have allowed to settle on her territory in the first place. There was nothing for me to worry about: the Imperial silver was worth a fortune and, in any case, we had enough money to see us through several weeks. Meanwhile we were sure of finding a purchaser and then our future would be assured for a number of years. I said nothing, but the distress, the incomprehension which I could clearly read in her staring and somewhat enlarged eyes immediately communicated itself to my bowels, thus renewing the strongest bond between us. I knew already that the silver would not be bought by anyone and that, in a fortnight's time, we should find ourselves penniless in a foreign land. It was the first time that I had thought of France as a foreign land, which only goes to show that we were truly *at home.*

In the course of that fortnight my mother engaged in, and lost, an epic struggle in defense of the good name of old Russian silver. She had set herself the task of educating the jewelers and silversmiths of Nice. I watched her putting on a wonderful act of artistic ecstasy before a decent Armenian in the Avenue de la Victoire—who was later to become our friend—extolling the beauty, the rarity and the perfection of the sugar bowl in her hand, only breaking off for a moment to give vent to a dithyrambic chant in honor of the samovar, the soup tureen and the mustard pot. The Armenian, with eyebrows raised to a great height on the limitless expanse of his scalp, which was barren of all hairy obstacles and creased with a thousand wrinkles of astonishment, followed with a sort of petrified gaze the movements of the ladle and the saltcellar in the air, and assured my mother that he had the highest esteem for the articles in question but was slightly surprised by the price she was asking for them, which seemed to him to be ten or twelve times in excess of the current market value. Confronted by such ignorance, my mother returned her property to the suitcase and left the shop without a word of farewell. She was scarcely more successful in the next shop, kept, this time, by two well-born Frenchmen. She displayed before the eyes of the elder the admirably proportioned samovar and, with truly Virgilian eloquence, conjured up the picture of a flourishing French family gathered about it in an atmosphere of domestic coziness. To this, the charming M. Sérusier—who later was often to employ my mother and to supply her with objects for sale on commission—shook his head and, holding to his eyes a pair of beribboned pince-nez which he never put fairly and squarely on his nose, delivered himself as follows:

"Madame, the samovar has never become a native of these latitudes."

This he said with so heartbroken an air of regret that I could almost see the last herd of samovars expiring in the depths of some Gallic forest.

When received so courteously, my mother gave signs of being abashed—good manners and sweetness always disarmed her— said no more, gave up any attempt at argument and, lowering her eyes, set about silently wrapping each object in paper before putting it back in the suitcase, each object, that is, except the samovar, which was so cumbersome that I had to carry it in my two hands with the greatest care and walk behind her under the wondering eyes of the passers-by.

We had very little money left and the thought of what would happen to us when it should be exhausted made me sick with anxiety. At night, we both pretended to sleep but for a long time I saw the glowing point of her cigarette moving in the darkness. I watched her with a terrible feeling of despair, as powerless as a beetle which has been turned over on its back.

Even today, I cannot see silver, no matter how beautiful, without wanting to vomit.

It was M. Sérusier who came to our rescue, on the very next morning. Being a shrewd man of business, he had at once realized my mother's great talents when it came to singing the praises of her fine and rare "family pieces" to possible buyers, and it occurred to him that he might do worse than make use of her gifts to our mutual advantage. I have an idea, too, that this experienced collector had been much struck by the presence in his shop, among so many other curious objects, of two living specimens of considerable rarity. Adding thus to his natural kindliness the excuse of commercial astuteness, he there and then decided to give us a helping hand. He advanced us a sum of money and, very soon, my mother was making the rounds of all the luxury hotels along the Riviera, offering to the clientele of the Winter Palace, the Hermitage and the Negresco, the "family treasures" which she had managed to take with her when she had fled the Revolution, or which had been entrusted to her by an old friend, a Russian grand duke who, "as the result of circumstances beyond his control" had found himself obliged to dispose of his possessions in as unostentatious a manner as possible.

We were saved, and saved by a Frenchman—which was the more encouraging since, as France had forty million inhabitants, our future looked bright indeed.

Other shopkeepers followed suit, with the result that my mother, tirelessly combing the town for purchasers, was enabled, little by little, to provide for our needs.

As to the famous silver, disgusted by the ridiculous prices she was offered, my mother packed it away in a box, pointing out that this service of twenty-four pieces, all engraved with the Imperial eagle, would be very useful to me in the course of my diplomatic career when I would have to do a lot of "entertaining"—this last word being uttered with a solemn air of mystery.

She gradually extended the field of her activities. She had

showcases for the display of luxury articles in the hotels, acted as intermediary in the selling of apartments and building sites, acquired an interest in a taxi, and a twenty-five per cent share in a lorry which delivered grain to the local poultry farmers, took a larger flat, two rooms of which she sublet, and gave a considerable part of her time to a knitting concern. In the midst of all this, she still found time to surround me with every attention. Her plans for my future had long been made: first, the *lycée*, then naturalization, a degree in law, military service— needless to say, as a cavalry officer—the School of Political Science and, finally, entry into the Diplomatic Service. When she spoke those two words, she lowered her voice respectfully and a shy look of wonderment showed in her face. To reach that ultimate goal—I was in the third form at school—would mean, according to our constantly repeated calculation, a mere nothing of eight or nine years, and she felt quite capable of carrying on till then. She sniffed with satisfaction and looked at me with anticipatory admiration. "Secretary of Embassy," she repeated out loud, the better to absorb those wonderful words. It needed only a little patience. I was already fourteen—almost there! She put on her gray cloak, took her suitcase, and I followed her with my eyes as she strode forward energetically toward that brilliant future, cane in hand. She now had to walk with a cane.

I, however, took a more realistic view. I had no intention of marking time for nine years—anything might happen. I wanted to accomplish something formidable for her at once, without waiting. I decided to win the championship in the junior swimming competition, a five-mile crossing of the Baie des Anges, and I trained every day at the Grande Bleue, but I succeeded only in almost drowning during the race. As a result, I was driven back to literature, like so many other failures. Notebooks piled up on my table filled with more and more eloquent, more and more grandiose, more and more desperate pen names. In my desire to score a bull's-eye with my very first shot, to steal the sacred fire without further waiting, I read the names, new to me, on the covers of the books in the shops: Antoine de Saint-

Exupéry, André Malraux, Paul Valéry, Mallarmé, Montherlant, Apollinaire, and, since they seemed to glow with all the brilliance on which I had set my heart, I felt cheated, and kicked myself for not having been the first to think of using one of them for my own adornment.

I still continued with my efforts to triumph on sea, on land and in the air and to become the champion of the world at something or other. I often had the feeling that I would die of smallness, helplessness and love. I went on with my swimming, running and high-jumping, but it was only at ping-pong that I could really give everything I had in me and return home crowned with laurel. It was the only victory I could offer my mother, and the silver medal, engraved with my name and housed in a violet velvet case, stood on her bedside table until the day of her death.

I also tried my hand at tennis, having been given a racquet by the parents of one of my friends, but to become a member of the Club du Parc Impérial meant paying, and the membership fee was far beyond our means. Seeing that lack of money made it impossible for me to enter the Parc Impérial, my mother became righteously indignant. The matter, she announced, would not rest at that. She stubbed out her cigarette in a saucer, grabbed her cloak and her cane, and ordered me to fetch my racquet and to follow her that very instant to the Club du Parc Impérial. There, the club secretary was summoned, and, since my mother had a very carrying voice, he lost no time in obeying, followed by the club president, who rejoiced in the admirable name of Garibaldi and who also answered the call at full speed. My mother, standing in the middle of the room, with her hat slightly askew, and brandishing her cane, let them know exactly what she thought of them. What! With a little practice I might become a champion of France and defend my country's flag against foreigners, but no, because of some trivial and vulgar matter of money, I was forbidden to go onto the courts! All she was prepared to say to these gentlemen at this time was that they had not the interests of their country at heart, and this she would proclaim at the top of her voice, as the mother of a Frenchman—I was not yet naturalized but that, obviously, was a minor matter—and she insisted on my being admitted to the Club courts, there and then. I had not held a tennis racquet in my hand more than three or four times in my life, and the thought that these gentlemen might suddenly ask me to go onto the court and show what I could do made me tremble. But the two distinguished officials were far too overcome with astonishment to give a thought to my possible talents as a tennis player. It was, I think, M. Garibaldi, who, in the hope of calming my mother, hit on the fatal idea which led to a scene the memory of which fills me with confusion even to this day.

"Madame," he said, "I must ask you to moderate your voice. His Majesty King Gustav of Sweden is sitting only a few steps from here, and I beg you not to make a scandal."

His words had on my mother an almost magical effect. A smile, at once naïve and radiant with wonder, which I knew only too well, showed on her face and she rushed forward.

An old gentleman was taking tea on the lawn under a white parasol. He was wearing white flannel trousers, a blue and black blazer and a straw "boater" slightly tilted over one ear. King Gustav V was a frequent visitor to the Riviera and its tennis courts. His celebrated straw hat appeared regularly on the front page of the local papers.

My mother did not hesitate for a moment. She made a deep curtsy and then, pointing her stick at the president and secretary of the club, exclaimed: "I crave justice of Your Majesty! My young son, who will soon be fourteen, has a quite extraordinary gift for lawn tennis and these bad Frenchmen are making it impossible for him to practice here. The whole of our fortune has been seized by the Bolsheviks and we are unable to pay the subscription. I come to Your Majesty for help and protection."

This performance was conducted according to the best tradition of popular Russian legends in the time of Ivan the Terrible or Peter the Great. At its conclusion, my mother turned triumphant eyes upon the numerous and interested audience. Could I have melted into thin air or dissolved into the earth, my last conscious moment would have been one of tremendous relief. But I was not to be allowed to get off so lightly. I had to stand there under the amused gaze of beautiful women and handsome men and win the only world championship that seemed always to be open to me, that of shame and ridicule. But even there my true laurels were yet to come—I had merely qualified for the finals.

His Majesty Gustav V was, at that time, already a very old man and this, combined no doubt with Swedish phlegm, accounted for the fact that he seemed not in the least surprised. He took the cigar from his lips, gave my mother a solemn look and me a casual glance and, turning to his coach: "Hit a few up with him," he said, "and let's see how he does."

My mother's face brightened. The fact that I was completely inexperienced as a tennis player didn't worry her in the least. She had confidence in me. She knew who I was. She knew that I had it in me. The trivial day-to-day details of life, the little practical considerations didn't count for her. For a second I hesitated, then, at sight of that expression of utter confidence and love, I swallowed my shame and my fear, sighed deeply, lowered my head and went forth to my execution.

It was a quick business, but it sometimes seems to me that I am still on that court. Needless to say, I did my best. I jumped, dived, bounced, pirouetted, ran, fell, bounced up again, flew through the air, clanging and spinning like a disjointed marionette, but the most I can say is that I did, just once, touch the ball, and then only on the wood of my racquet—and all this under the imperturbable gaze of the King of Sweden, who watched me coldly from under his famous straw hat. Some will no doubt ask why I let myself be led to the slaughter, why I ever ventured onto the court at all. The truth of the matter is that I had not forgotten the lesson I had learned in Warsaw, the slap on the face I had received, nor the voice of my mother saying: "Next time I expect to see you brought back home on a stretcher, you understand?" There could be no question of my turning back. For her sake I was prepared to play the clown as well as the hero.

I must also confess that, in spite of my fourteen years, I still believed, just a little bit, in fairy tales. I believed in the magic wand and, when I risked myself on the court, I was not absolutely sure that some just and indulgent Power might not intervene in my favor, that some almighty and mysterious hand might not guide my racquet—and it was just possible that the balls themselves would suddenly come to my rescue. But it was not to be: the miracle was probably busy elsewhere. I am bound to admit that this failure of the wonderful to materialize has left so deep a mark on me that I sometimes wonder whether the story of Puss in Boots is not, perhaps, just an invention, and whether the mice really came in the night and sewed buttons on the coat of the Tailor of Gloucester. In short, at forty-four, I am beginning to ask myself certain questions. But my life as a champion of the world has taken a lot out of me, and too much attention should not be paid to my occasional and passing doubts.

When the coach at last took pity on me, and I went back to the lawn, my mother welcomed me as though I had not disgraced myself. She helped me on with my pullover, she wiped my face and neck with her handkerchief. Then she turned to the audience. How can I describe the silence, the very attentive and reflective manner in which she stared at them with just a trace of an almost inviting smile on her tightly pressed lips? The mockers seemed to be just a shade put out of countenance, and the beautiful ladies, picking up their straws, lowered their eyelashes and gave all their attention to their lemonade. Some vague, humble cliché about the female defending her young may have occurred to them. My mother, however, had no need to go into action. The King of Sweden saved us and the guests from a scene that would be too awful even to try to imagine. The old gentleman touched his straw hat and with infinite courtesy and kindliness—though it used to be reported that he was not an easy man to get on with—said: "I think that these gentlemen will agree with me: we have just witnessed something quite admirable. . . . Monsieur Garibaldi"—and I remember that the word "Monsieur" had a more than usually sepulchral sound on his lips—"I will pay this young man's subscription: he has shown both courage and determination."

Ever since then I have loved Sweden. But I never again set foot in the Parc Impérial.

CHAPTER 20

ALL THESE MISADVENTURES HAD THE EFFECT of making me seek the privacy of my room more and more and devote myself fully to writing. Attacked by reality on every front, forced back on every side and constantly coming up against my own limitations, I developed the habit of seeking refuge in an imaginary world where, by proxy, through the medium of invented characters, I could find a life in which there were meaning, justice and compassion. Instinctively and, so far as I know, unprompted by any literary influence, I discovered in myself a sense of humor, that extraordinary and blessed weapon which makes it possible to take the sting out of reality just when it is preparing to strike. All along my road, humor offered me a constant protection; behind its armor, I felt invincible and secure; it has been a heartening companion, a source of strength, helping me to endure and to prevail, until it has become a living presence, almost a deity, a miracle that has never failed to work. To humor I owe my only genuine triumphs over adversity. No one has ever succeeded in wrenching that weapon from me, and I am the more willing to turn it against myself since, behind the disguise of the "I" and the "me" at which I thus strike out, it is really with the very essence of our human condition that I am at odds. Humor is an affirmation of dignity, a declaration of man's superiority to all that befalls him. Some of my "friends" who are entirely devoid of it say behind my back how grieved they are to see me, in my writing and in my life, always turning its red iron against myself. They speak, the poor darlings, who are so up to date on every piece of Freudian schmaltz, of masochism, of self-hatred and even, when I involve my nearest and my dearest in such liberating and triumphant exercises, of exhibitionism and caddishness. I pity them. The truth of the matter is that the "I" does not exist, and if "me" seems the target, it is against the human situation as a whole, underlying all its ephemeral incarnations of "I" or "me," that I thrust that favorite weapon of mine; it is with our fraternal predicament that my laughter and derision try to come to grips, probing for something much deeper and more significant than myself; it is against the biological, moral, spiritual and metaphysical servitude that has been imposed on us from outside, dictated to us like some ugly Nuremberg law, and not only against my own shortcomings that I raise my mocking voice. In human relationships, this misunderstanding has been for me a constant source of solitude, since nothing isolates one more than to stretch out the brotherly hand of humor to those who sit in blind and pompous self-esteem behind the thick walls of their pathetic little Kingdom of "I."

About that same time, too, I at last began to take an interest in social problems and to wish and write for a world in which women would not be condemned to carry their children on their backs. But I knew already that social justice would never mean to me more than a first step and that I was really demanding of my fellow men that they should become full masters of their fate. I came to think of Man as a revolutionary attempt, as an uprising against the basic facts of his own biological limitations. Whenever I noticed new marks of age and fatigue on my mother's face, I boiled with an almost unbearable sense of injustice, and my determination to reform the world and make of it an honorable place grew with each beating of my heart. I wrote far into the night.

Our financial position was once again deteriorating. The

shock waves of the economic crisis of 1929 had at last reached the Riviera and we were passing through difficult times.

My mother turned one of the rooms of our flat into a kennel where people could board their dogs, cats and birds; she read hands in restaurants and night clubs, took in lodgers, assumed the management of a commercial building and acted as agent in one or two property deals. I helped her as best I could, in her financial struggles, by trying to write an immortal masterpiece. Occasionally I read aloud to her some of the passages of which I was especially proud, and she never failed to give me all the warm admiration I expected of her. I remember, however, that, on one occasion, when she had been listening to one of my poems, she repeated once more with a sort of shyness: "I have the feeling that you'll never have much practical sense in your life, though why that should be I don't know."

It is true that, at school, my marks in the exact sciences remained deplorable up till the time of my graduation. At my oral examination in chemistry, M. Passac, the examiner, asked me to tell him what I knew about plaster and all I could find to say was: "Plaster is used in making walls."

He waited patiently. Then, since it appeared that I had nothing more to say, he remarked: "Is that all?" I gave him a haughty look and, turning to the audience of parents and fellow students, I exclaimed dramatically: "Is that all, indeed! Do away with walls, sir, and ninety-nine per cent of our civilization would collapse!" My mother, who sat in the gallery, applauded loudly and I was saved from failing at my examination only by the exceptionally good marks I had gotten in literature.

Business was going from bad to worse and, one evening, after my mother had spent some time in tears, she sat down at the table and wrote a long letter to somebody. Next morning I was told to go to a photographer, and there a picture was taken of me in a blue blazer with my eyes raised to the light. The photo was enclosed in the letter and, after hesitating for several days and keeping the envelope locked in a drawer, my mother finally put it in the mail.

She spent that evening bent over her strongbox, rereading a packet of letters tied with blue ribbon.

She must at that time have been fifty-two. The letters were old and crumpled. I found them in 1947 hidden away in the cellar. I have read and reread them several times.

A week later, a money order for five hundred francs arrived, from Paris. It had the most extraordinary effect upon my mother. *She looked at me with gratitude.* It was suddenly as though I had done her some tremendous service. She came close to me, took my face between her hands and studied my every feature with astonishing intensity. There were tears in her eyes and a curious feeling of embarrassment came over me. All of a sudden I had the feeling that I was someone else.

For the next eighteen months the money orders continued to reach us, though somewhat irregularly. We entered on a glorious period of peace and prosperity. I was allowed to have a racing bicycle, painted bright orange. I was given two francs a day pocket money and, on my way home from school, I sometimes stopped in the flower market where, for fifty centimes, I bought a sweet-smelling bouquet, which I gave to my mother. In the evenings I took her to hear the gypsy orchestra at the Royal. We stood on the pavement instead of going onto the terrace, where drinks were compulsory. My mother adored gypsy orchestras: together with guards officers, Pushkin's death in a duel, and champagne drunk from women's slippers, they symbolized for her all that was most romantically depraved in the world. She always warned me against gypsy girls, who, according to her, were one of the greatest dangers threatening my future, for they would ruin me physically, morally and financially, and lead me straight to tuberculosis. I was pleasantly titillated by this prospect, which, I am sorry to report, never materialized. The only gypsy girl in whom I ever took an interest as a young man—and then only because of the tempting descriptions which my mother had lavished on me some years earlier—did no more than steal my wallet, my silk scarf and my wrist watch before I even had time to turn round, let alone to catch tuberculosis.

I have always dreamed of being ruined, physically, morally and financially, by a woman: it must be marvelous thus to make something of one's life. I may, even now, get tuberculosis but, at my age, I doubt whether it will be in just that way. Nature has its limits. Besides, something tells me that neither guards officers nor gypsy girls are quite what they used to be.

After the concert, I would give my mother my arm and we would sit on the Promenade des Anglais. The chair there had to be paid for, too, but that was a luxury we could afford.

By carefully choosing one's chair, one could so arrange matters as to be within hearing distance of two orchestras—one at the Lido, the other at the Casino—and so get a double dose of music free. As a rule, my mother took with her, discreetly concealed at the bottom of her elegant bag, some black bread and a few dill pickles wrapped in a newspaper. It was therefore possible at that time, for anyone watching the crowd of idlers on the Promenade des Anglais, to see a distinguished white-haired lady and a youth in a blue blazer, seated unostentatiously with their backs to the railing, listening to music and busily munching dill pickles *à la russe* with black bread, on a sheet of newspaper spread over their knees. It was delicious. But it was not enough. Something even more delicious was missing. Mariette had awakened a hunger in me which no pickle in the world, not even the dilliest, could now appease. It was already two years since she had left our employment, and yet the memory of her was still in my blood. It kept me awake at night. I wish to express here my profound gratitude to that good French woman, who opened for me the door to a better world. Thirty years have passed but I can still say, perhaps more truthfully than the Bourbons, that I have learned nothing since and forgotten nothing. May her old age be happy and tranquil and her conscience at peace in the knowledge that she has done her best with what the good God gave her. . . . I feel that I may start to cry if I go on any longer in this vein, so I had better stop.

Unfortunately, Mariette was no longer there to give me a helping hand. My blood was in such a state of ferment and was pounding with such violence, such insistence, against the door, that the three kilometers which I swam early each morning were powerless to cool it. Seated with my mother on the Promenade des Anglais, I looked at all the enticing young givers of good French bread who passed before my eyes. I drew deep breaths, bowed my head and remained there, utterly dejected, with my pickle in my hand.

But the oldest civilization in the world, with its smiling understanding of human nature and its frailties and failings, with its sense of compromise and arrangements, came to my rescue. The Mediterranean has lived too long with the sun to treat it as an enemy, and leaned above me with its face of a thousand absolutions.

The Nice *lycée,* which was situated between the Place Masséna and the Esplanade du Paillon, was not the only educational establishment that the town could boast. My young friends and I found, in the rue Saint-Michel, a simple and a friendly welcome, at least when the American squadron was not anchored in Villefranche harbor, days of ill omen when the place was out of bounds for us and when dismay reigned in the classrooms, and the blackboard loomed over our heads like the symbol and flag of our melancholy.

All the same, when one had no more than two or three francs in one's pocket, it was difficult to "visit," as they say in the South.

Consequently, strange things began to happen in the house. First one rug, then another, disappeared, and one day on returning from the Casino, where they were giving *Madame Butterfly,* my mother was astounded to find that the little dressing table which she had bought the day before, intending to sell it at a profit, had literally vanished into thin air, though all the doors and windows were tight shut. Boundless astonishment showed on her face. She made a detailed examination of the flat to see whether anything else was missing. Most certainly there was. My tennis racquet, my camera, my watch, my winter overcoat, my collection of postage stamps and the set of Balzac which I had just received as a prize in school had all traveled the same route. I had even succeeded, if not in selling, at least in pawning the famous samovar with an antique dealer in the Old Town. What I got for it had at least served to save me momentarily from solitary embarrassment. My mother stood for a while wrapped in thought and then sat down and looked at me. She studied me for a long time with concentrated attention and then, much to my surprise, instead of the dramatic scene which I had been expecting, an almost solemn look of pride and triumph spread over her face. She sniffed noisily, with immense satisfaction, then looked at me again with gratitude, admiration and devotion. At last I had grown into a man. Her struggles had not been in vain.

That evening she wrote a long letter, in her large, nervous script, still with that look of triumph and satisfaction in her eyes, as though she were in a hurry to announce to someone the fact that I had been a good son. A money order for fifty francs, addressed to me personally, arrived shortly afterward and was followed by many others in the course of a year. For the time being, I was saved. Nevertheless, I was sent to see an old doctor in the rue de France, who, after a good deal of beating about the bush, explained to me that the life of a young man was beset by snares, that the human male was extremely vulnerable, that poisoned arrows were constantly whizzing past his ears, and that even our daring ancestors, the Gauls, never went into battle without their shields—after which, he gave me a small package. I listened politely, as one should to a venerable elder. But the visit I had paid to the Panopticum in Vilna had enlightened me once and for all and I had long ago determined to preserve my nose intact. I might also have told him that he seriously underestimated the respectability and the scrupulousness of the young women whom we "visited." Most of them were devoted mothers, and never, never, would they have allowed us to risk ourselves in the wake of all the navies in the world without first being initiated into those rules of prudence which every navigator with a proper respect for the elements should observe.

Dear Mediterranean! How tolerant and gentle is your Latin wisdom, how sweet and helpful is your knowledge of man, and how indulgently your look of age-old amusement rested on my tormented brow! I come back always to your beaches when the fishing boats return with the setting sun caught in their nets. I have been happy on those pebbles.

CHAPTER *21*

Our life was entering upon a new phase.
I even remember a certain August when my mother went off
into the mountains—her first holiday in years—for three days'
rest. I took her to the bus, holding a bunch of violets in my
hand. Our parting was heartbreaking. It was the first time we
had ever been separated, and my mother cried, thinking, no
doubt, of the many separations that lay ahead. The driver,
having watched this dramatic farewell for a long time, finally
asked with his strong *niçois* accent, so well suited to emotional
outbursts:

"It's for a long while that you two are tearing yourselves
away from each other?"

"For three days," I replied.

He appeared to be much impressed. He looked at us both
with marked respect. Then he said:

"*Eh bien,* you sure have it in you."

My mother returned from her holiday bubbling over with
projects and energy. Business in Nice was beginning to look up
again, and now it was in the company of a genuine Russian
Grand Duke that she made the round of hotels with her "family
jewels." He was new to the job and very embarrassed by the part
he had to play, and she wasted a good deal of time in lecturing
him severely on his lack of moral courage. There were, at that
time, something like ten thousand Russian families living in
Nice, a noble assortment of generals, Cossacks, Ukrainian *ata-*

mans, colonels of the Imperial Guard, princes, Baltic barons and has-beens of every sort and description, who succeeded in creating on the shores of the Mediterranean a dark Dostoievskian atmosphere, minus the genius. During the war they split into two camps, one of which worked for the Germans and supplied a number of recruits to the Gestapo, while the other played an active part in the Resistance. The former were liquidated at the Liberation, the others became wholly assimilated and vanished forever into the fraternal melting pot of Renaults and Citroëns, of holidays with pay, *café-crème* with *croissants*, of disgruntlement and abstention at election time, so that their children do not even speak Russian today, which I find sad.

My mother treated the Grand Duke and his little white goatee with ironic condescension. All the same, she was secretly flattered by the association, and never failed to address him, in Russian, as "Your Serene Highness" even when she made him carry the bag. The Serene Highness, in the presence of possible purchasers, became so terribly embarrassed, so unhappy, and maintained so guilty a silence while my mother was describing the precise degree of his relationship with the late Tsar, the exact number of palaces which he had owned in Russia and the close ties he had with the English Royal Family that the tourists all felt that they were "in on a good thing," that they were exploiting a poor defenseless creature, and so almost invariably clinched the deal. From my mother's point of view he was a valuable asset, and each day, before they set out on their rounds, she gave him twenty drops of his medicine in a glass of water, for he suffered from heart trouble. The two of them could often be seen together on the terrace of the Café de la Buffa, busy making plans for the future, my mother confiding to him her plans to make me a French Ambassador, His Serene Highness describing the kind of life he hoped to lead after the collapse of the Communist regime and the return of the Romanoffs to the throne of Holy Russia.

"I mean to live quietly on my estates, far from the court and public life," announced the Grand Duke.

"My son," said my mother, sipping her tea, "is destined for diplomacy."

This realistic pair could talk thus endlessly, as long as the tea lasted.

I do not know what became of His Serene Highness. There is a Russian Grand Duke buried in the cemetery of Roquebrune village, not far from my own property, but whether it is the same one I do not know. Anyway, without his white goatee I doubt if I would recognize him.

It was just about then that my mother brought off her most successful deal, the sale of a seven-story building on what used to be the Boulevard Carlonne and is now the Boulevard Grosso. She had been hard at work for several months, running through the city like a busy ant, trying to find a buyer; she knew that if the sale materialized it would ensure my first year at the University of Aix-en-Provence. It was quite by accident that the eventual buyer turned up. One day, a Rolls-Royce stopped before our house. A chauffeur opened the door and out stepped a short, roly-poly gentleman, followed by a young woman, twice his height and half his age. She was a former patroness of my mother's fashion house in Vilna, and among the kindlier souls of that foul lot, and the plump little gentleman was her recently acquired husband, who was a "millionaire," the first I had ever met of that fabulous race. It immediately became apparent to us that they had dropped straight from Heaven. Not only did little M. Jedwabnikas buy the building, but, struck like so many others before him by my mother's energy and spirit of enterprise, he decided on the spot to turn it into a hotel and restaurant, of which my mother should be manageress. And so it was that the Hôtel-Pension Mermonts—"Mer" as in *mer* (sea) and "monts" as in *montagnes*—with a freshly painted façade and under "a new management," opened its doors to "the international elite, in an atmosphere of tranquillity, comfort and good taste." I quote the first prospectus word for word, for I was its author. My mother knew nothing of the very special art of *hôtellerie*, but she immediately rose to the occasion and became a true professional in a matter of weeks. I have, since those days, spent a great part of my life in hotels the world over, and, in the light of the experience I have gained, I can say that with very limited material resources she achieved a miracle. Thirty-six bedrooms, two floors of "suites" and a restaurant, run with the help of only two housemaids, one waiter, a chef and a dishwasher—it was quite a task for a beginner. The enterprise got off to a flying start. My own contribution consisted in acting as receptionist, guide on conducted tours, *maître d'hôtel,* and generally making a good impression on the clientele. I was by that time sixteen, but never before had I been exposed to human contacts in quite such massive doses. Our "public" came from every country under the sun, with the English predominating. As a rule they arrived in parties, sent by the travel agencies, and thus diluted by the democracy of numbers they showed a humble gratitude for the least mark of personal attention. Those were the early days of mass tourism, which became the rule shortly before the war, and has greatly developed since, and with few exceptions our "guests" were gentle, submissive, unsure of themselves and easily satisfied. Most of them were women.

My mother got up at six every morning, smoked three or four cigarettes, drank a cup of tea, took her cane and went to the Buffa Market, of which she was the undisputed queen. This market, which was very much smaller than that of the Old Town, where the big hotels got their provisions, mainly served the pensions in the neighborhood of the Boulevard Gambetta. It was and still is today a place of varied accents, smells and colors, where superb curses rose into the air above the quarters of veal, the cutlets, the hams, where truly Latin, dramatic gestures flashed under the eyes of dead fish, where, by some benign Mediterranean miracle, the sweet fragrance of mimosa managed always to rise triumphantly over a thousand far less appealing smells. My mother would handle a slice of veal, ponder over the heart of a melon, reject with scorn a piece of beef—the flabby sound of which, when it was dropped on the marble slab,

seemed to express shame and humility at being thus rejected
—point her stick accusingly at some rusty leaf in a stall of
salads, which its proprietor at once covered with his body, as
if they were his insulted children, at the same time shouting
in despair "don't you go pawing the stuff, now!," sniff at a piece
of Brie, stick her nose into a Camembert—she had, when apply-
ing her nose to a cheese, a filet or a fish, a way of looking doubtful which made the faces of the stall holders turn white with
exasperation—and, having at last rejected once and for all the
wretched merchandise, she would turn away with her head held
high, while a medley of challenging cries, insults, invective and
indignant abuse sounded in our ears the oldest choir of the
Mediterranean. One felt transported in a flash to some Eastern
court of law, where my mother, all of a sudden, pardoned salads,
joints and peas their doubtful quality and exorbitant price, thus
promoting them in a flash from the rank of shoddy merchandise
to that of *"cuisine française de premier ordre,"* in the words of
the above-mentioned prospectus. For several months she would
stop in front of M. Renucci's stall, spend a long time handling
his display of hams without ever buying any of them, in a spirit
of deliberate provocation, inspired by some obscure quarrel,
some personal account to be settled with him, all for the sole
purpose of reminding him how important a customer he had
lost. When the butcher caught sight of my mother sailing in-
exorably, cane in hand, toward his stand, his voice rose like the
warning note of a siren, and he would rush forward, lean his
fat belly on the counter, wave his fist and assume the appearance of a man about to fight to the death in defense of his
merchandise, screaming at his daily tormentor to go away. Then,
while my mother brought her nose close to a piece of ham, with
a grimace, first of incredulity, then of horror, and made it clear
in expressive mimicry that an abominable stench had insulted
her organ of smell, Renucci, with upcast eyes and hands clasped
in prayer, would implore the Madonna to restrain him from
committing murder, while my mother, pushing away the ham
with a scornful and triumphant smile, would sail away to con-

tinue her reign elsewhere, in some kingdom of cheese or fruit, pursued by a storm of laughter, shaking fists, cries of "Santa Madonna!" and tragic oaths.

Whenever I go back to Nice, I pay a visit to the Buffa Market, and I spend long hours among the leeks, the asparagus, the melons, the cuts of beef, the fruit, the flowers and the fish. The noises, the voices, the gestures, the smells and scents have not changed. It needs only very little, almost nothing, for the illusion to be complete, and this I achieve by closing my eyes. Then I wander through the market for hours on end, and the carrots, the chicory and the endives do what they can for me.

My mother always returned home with a load of fruit and flowers. She had a profound belief in the beneficial effect of fruit upon the human organism, and saw to it that I consumed at least a kilo a day; ever since then I have suffered from chronic colitis. Then, she would go down to the kitchens, draw up the menu, see the tradespeople, supervise the *petit déjeuner*, which was always served in the bedrooms, listen to anything the visitors might have to say, see to the packing of picnic baskets for those who were going on excursions, inspect the cellar, do her accounts and attend to every detail of the business.

One day, after going up and down the accursed stairs which led from the restaurant to the kitchens, which she climbed at least twenty times a day, she suddenly collapsed into a chair. Her face and lips were gray; she leaned her head a little to one side and pressed her hand to her breast. Then she began to tremble all over. We were lucky enough to get a doctor quickly, and his diagnosis was rapid and sure. She had given herself too strong an injection of insulin, and was suffering an attack of hypoglycemia.

It was thus that I learned what she had been concealing from me for years: she was a diabetic and each morning gave herself an injection of insulin before starting on the day's work.

I was in a state of abject terror. The memory of her gray face, of her head leaning slightly sideways, of her hand clutching painfully at her breast, never again left me. The idea that she might die before I had done all that she expected of me, that she might leave this world without ever having known *justice*, that projection in the heavens of a human system of weights and measures, seemed to me to be a denial of the most elementary common sense, of good manners and law, and to show a sort of gangsterlike attitude on the part of fate that justified one in calling the police, invoking the moral code and the intervention of some supreme legal authority.

I felt that I must hurry, that I had to write at top speed an immortal masterpiece which, by making me the youngest Tolstoy of all time, would enable me to lay at my mother's feet my laurels as a champion of the world, the reward for all her pains and labors, and thus give meaning not only to her life of love and sacrifice, but to life generally, showing some hidden logic and cleanliness in it.

With her full approval, I ceased going to the *lycée* for a while, and once again, shut in my bedroom, I rushed to her aid. I piled in front of me three thousand sheets of white paper—which, according to my calculations, was the equivalent of *War and Peace*. My mother gave me a dressing gown of ample proportions, modeled on the one which had already made a great literary reputation for Balzac. Five times a day she opened the door, set a plate of food on the table and tiptoed out again. I was, just then, using François Mermonts as a pen name. Since, however, my works were regularly returned to me by the publishers, we decided that it was a bad choice, and substituted for it, on my next effort, that of Lucien Brulard. But this seemed to give the publishers no more satisfaction than its predecessor. I remember how, a little later, when I was busy starving in Paris, one of the godlike beings who, at that time, was wielding a more than usually cutting whip in the editorial offices of the *Nouvelle Revue Française,* told me, handing back a manuscript which I had submitted: "Take a mistress, and come back in ten years. . . ." When I did go back, ten years later, in 1945, he was unfortunately no longer there; he had been shot already, as a collaborationist.

The world had contracted to the size of the sheet of paper against which I flung myself with all the exacerbated lyricism of adolescence. And, in spite of the artlessness of those romantic outpourings, it was then that I realized the importance of the stakes for which I was playing and literary creation became for me a matter of survival, a necessity like air and bread, the only escape from the helplessness and infirmity of being human, a manner of yielding up the soul so as to remain alive.

For the first time, when I saw that gray face, those closed eyes, that leaning head, that groping hand, I began to wonder if life was an honorable endeavor or if one perhaps ought to reject it as a matter of dignity. My answer was immediate, probably dictated to me by my instinct for self-preservation, and I wrote, at feverish speed, a story entitled "The Truth about the Prometheus Affair," which remains for me to this day the truth about the Prometheus affair.

For, no doubt about it, we have been cheated. The real adventure of Prometheus, or rather, the end of it, has been kept from us. It is perfectly true that, because he stole fire from the gods, Prometheus was chained to a rock and that a vulture began to devour his liver. But what we were never told is that when the gods, some time later, took a look at the earth to see what was going on there, they saw, not only that Prometheus had freed himself from his chains, but that he had seized the vulture and was devouring its liver so as to recover his strength and try to grab the sacred fire again. He was an artist.

All the same, I still suffer from my liver. You will, I think, admit that there is good reason for that. I am at my ten thousandth vulture and my digestion is not what it used to be.

But I am doing my best. And when a final stab of the beak chases me from my rock, I will be grateful if the astrologers watch for the appearance of a new sign in the Zodiac—the sign of a human cur clinging with all its teeth to the liver of some celestial vulture.

The Avenue Dante, which led straight from the Hôtel-Pension Mermonts to the Buffa Market, had its starting point directly under my window. From my work table I could see my mother on her way back to the hotel when she was still quite far off. One morning, an irresistible longing came over me to talk about these matters with her and to hear what she thought. She had come into my room for no particular reason, as she often did, for the sole purpose apparently of smoking a cigarette in silence, with me for company. I was in the process of studying, with my graduation in view, some bit of flimsy nonsense about the structure of the universe.

"Mother," I said, "listen to me."

She listened.

"It will be three years before I get my degree, then there will be two years of military service. . . ."

"You will be an officer," she broke in immediately.

"But, for Christmas' sake! that's not the point. . . . I'm afraid of not getting there . . . in time."

This gave her something to think about. Then, with a loud sniff, and with both hands on her knees, she said: "There is such a thing as justice."

And off she went to see that everything was all right in the restaurant.

My mother believed in a more logical, sovereign and coherent structure of the universe than anything my physics book could teach me.

She was wearing a gray dress that day, with a violet tucker, a string of pearls and a gray coat thrown over her shoulders. She had put on a little weight. The doctor had told me there was no reason why she should not live for years. I hid my face in my hands.

If only she could see me in the uniform of a French officer— even if I never became an ambassador and never got the Nobel Prize for literature—one of her fondest dreams would be realized. I was to begin reading law next autumn at the University of Aix-en-Province, and with any luck . . . In three years I might make a triumphal entry into the Hôtel-Pension Mermonts, in the uniform of a second lieutenant in the Air Force. We had long ago, my mother and I, chosen the Air Force. Lindbergh's Atlantic flight had deeply impressed her, and once again I kicked myself for not having thought of it first. I would go with her to the Buffa Market, dressed in blue and gold with wings stuck all over me and be exhibited to the admiring gaze of the carrots and leeks, of Pantaleoni, Renucci, Buppi, Cesari and Fassoli, with my mother on my arm, under a triumphal arch of sausages and onions.

My mother's simple adoration of France still continued to astonish me. When some exasperated tradesman called her a "dirty foreigner" she would smile, wave her stick as though to call the whole Buffa Market to witness, and declare: "My son is an officer of the French Air Force and he tells you *merde!*"

She drew no distinction between "is" and "will be." The gold stripe of a second lieutenant suddenly assumed enormous importance in my eyes, and all my dreams of laurels became temporarily reduced to a most humble one, that of strolling round the Buffa Market with my mother on my arm in the uniform of a second lieutenant. It was not really asking too much.

CHAPTER 22

Mr. Zaremba was a man in his early fifties: a tall, gaunt, gentle and somewhat withdrawn man. He appeared one day on the doorstep of the Hôtel-Pension Mermonts in white tropical clothes, with a panama hat and several expensive-looking suitcases covered with labels bearing the exotic names of faraway places; he asked for a room for a few days and stayed a year.

Nothing in his distinguished appearance, in his detached and beautiful manners, revealed that the elegant, much-traveled man of the world was really a little-boy-lost whom the passing years had buried deeper and deeper in their sands; and even later, when my knowing and cynical eye—I was almost eighteen and, naturally enough, considered myself in the full throes of maturity—began to notice certain interesting and promising signs in our guest's behavior, I was still far from suspecting that men can become old and die or reach high positions while never outgrowing the child within them who sits in the dark in his short pants, longing for attention. With a little less juvenile perspicacity and cynicism, and a little more true understanding, Mr. Zaremba would perhaps have served me as a premonition of things to come: good manners excepted, there is a strong likeness between what he was then and what I am today.

Our new guest didn't look like an artist at all, and when he wrote down his profession in the hotel form, my mother took one look at the word *artiste-peintre* and instantly and very rudely asked for one week's money in advance. He had a long, distinguished face, with sad eyes and a very fine, silky, blond-gray mustache, and his whole personality, his beautiful manners and almost ghostlike discretion struck me as being very much at odds with my mother's oft-voiced opinion that all painters were condemned to drunkenness, poverty, disease and despair. There could be but one explanation for Mr. Zaremba's gentlemanly appearance, and she expressed it quite firmly, long before she even bothered to look at his paintings: the man had no talent whatsoever. This statement of fact was soon confirmed in her eyes when it appeared that Mr. Zaremba was internationally known and successful enough to keep a house in Florida and travel extensively, and so my mother began to treat him with slightly ironic pity. I suspect that she feared he might have a bad influence on me: the sight of a prosperous painter could, God forbid, drive me to take up painting myself once again. I still felt a confused longing for vast canvases, brushes and tubes of paint; but if I showed myself well disposed toward Mr. Zaremba and took to visiting the studio he had rented in the neighborhood, this had nothing to do with my interest in art. The Pole had aroused in me certain hopes, for it soon became clear that this rather romantic and sad-faced figure, who, with his drooping mustache, reminded me of Doré's drawing of Don Quixote, was seeking my mother's company and attention with a discreet and yet unmistakable persistence, and I felt more and more convinced that this delicate situation, if properly handled, could mean a most welcome change in our life.

Mr. Zaremba was a lonely man and, from some casual re-mark, I got the impression that his childhood had been even more lonely than his middle age. His parents had died young, of a rather romantically shared tuberculosis, and were buried in the Russian cemetery at Menton, which he visited from time to time; he had been raised by a bachelor uncle on a rich estate in eastern Poland. We often took to discussing Mr. Zaremba's per-sonal problems with great frankness.

"You are a very young man, Romain," the painter would say

with a sigh, "and your whole life is still ahead of you. Mine is almost over. It would be very nice if I could meet someone who would care for me a little. I say, a little: I am not an exigent man. I would be quite content to take second place in a woman's affections."

"I think you can still be a very happy man," I answered prudently—only a fool would rush in on such delicate ground. "Of course, it would mean a certain amount of responsibility for you—financially, for instance. I don't know if a painter can afford to support a family."

"I am really quite well off," Mr. Zaremba would say, rather sadly. "I even welcome the idea of sharing my material success with someone. It's rather disgusting to spend everything on oneself."

My heart began to beat quite fast. A mad, quite improbable idea of a car—a small car, with me at the wheel—suddenly crossed my mind. A Citroën two-seater convertible it would be. I was not prepared to settle for anything less—and perhaps a trip around the world. I also had noticed that the painter owned a superb, richly embroidered Damascus dressing gown.

But there was more to it: something very much like a chance of escape. There were moments when my mother's overwhelming love crushed me, moments when it was more than I could bear. I needed a little help. It was not that I dreamed of evading the responsibilities that her devotion and self-sacrifice imposed on me: I was still determined to fulfill all her dreams. But I longed for a moment of respite. For someone who could take over, or at least share, while I went out to fight and conquer and came back home to lay the world at her feet.

I soon noticed that my mother was becoming aware that something was afoot, for she began to treat poor Mr. Zaremba with a considerable amount of suspicion and even of hostility, in a certain very feminine and not entirely unprovocative way. And then I became aware of something else. She was in her fifty-third year and, although despite her white hair her features still held traces of earlier beauty, I knew that my shy and distinguished friend had not fallen in love with her simply as a man loves a woman. There was in this sophisticated aristocrat a child who had never received enough affection and who was now aroused to an almost frantic hope by the maternal love that shone so splendidly and uninhibitedly before his eyes. He had obviously decided that there was room for two in it, and so languidly and yet desperately longed to be admitted. It often seemed to me that there was a trace of exasperation, a hurt and even a slightly indignant look on Mr. Zaremba's face whenever my mother, in her moments of what I used to call "expressionism," threw her arms around me in an overflow of emotion, or when she appeared before me in the little garden in front of the hotel with an offering of fruit, cakes or tea and a smile of happiness. He would stand there, watching the scene sadly and a little reproachfully, leaning on his elegant walking stick, with its ivory and silver head, pathetic, lonely and somehow irrevocably an outsider, a man locked out who was quietly and yet stubbornly, even desperately, trying to get in. I must confess that I was young enough and ignorant enough of what awaited me at the other end of the line to enjoy the situation, and was not above throwing in his direction a slightly superior and even ironic look. He had in me a solid ally, but if I ever was to make good in diplomacy this was the moment to show it. He never interfered during my mother's display of love, he never allowed himself to make some pointed remark like "You are spoiling him." He just stood there in his white silk suit, looking hurt. I knew that my mother, although she never mentioned it, was quite aware of the situation, and I think she enjoyed it in a way, for it created a new complicity between us and made us both even more conscious of our bond. And then, one day, after my mother had triumphantly deposited her offering of fruit before me on the garden table, Mr. Zaremba did allow himself something that, coming from him, amounted almost to an open manifestation, a silent and yet vehement proclamation of his feelings. He suddenly sat down at my table, without being invited, and extending a shaking hand, he took one of my apples from the tray and began to eat it, staring defiantly into my mother's eyes. I sat there completely stunned, gaping. Then my mother and I exchanged an indignant glance and she looked at poor Mr. Zaremba with such an expression of coldness and scorn, standing there, her head high, a statue of indignant rejection, that the painter, after one or two more desperate attempts at chewing the apple, put it back on the plate, got up and walked away, his shoulders hunched and his head low.

Soon afterward—in fact, if I remember correctly, exactly three days later—Mr. Zaremba made a more direct attempt at finding in his middle age something he had so clearly missed in his childhood. I was sitting in my room on the ground floor in front of the open window, writing the last chapter of the great novel I was working on at the time. It was a great last chapter. I regret to this day that I somehow never got around to writing the preceding chapters. I have always had a certain tendency to do last things first, a feeling of urgency, an eagerness for achievement that always made me very impatient with mere beginnings. There is something pedestrian and even mediocre about beginnings. In those days I had written at least twenty last chapters, but I somehow could never bother to begin the books that went with them.

My mother was sitting in the garden, drinking tea, and the painter was standing next to her, one hand on an empty chair, waiting for the invitation to sit down and join her that was never forthcoming. There was always one subject of conversation that was sure to find my mother accessible and so it was easy for Mr. Zaremba to find an opening.

"There is something I feel it my duty, as an aging man of experience, to tell you," he said. "It concerns Romain."

My mother had the strange habit of drinking her tea much too hot and then, after burning her lips, she would blow into the tea in an attempt to cool it.

"I'm listening," she said.

"Believe me, Nina," the painter said, "it is very dangerous for a boy to grow up as an only son, to be the only loved one."

"I do not plan to adopt another child," my mother stated abruptly, and it seemed to me sardonically.

I could see the painter full face. I have never met a man more removed from childhood in his physical appearance and giving a greater appearance of mature nobility and poise. And yet he was but a little boy knocking with both fists at a closed door.

"I didn't imply anything of the sort," Mr. Zaremba said, looking at the chair once more.

"Sit down," my mother said.

The painter sat down.

"I was merely implying that it is important at his age to feel that he is not the only man in his mother's life. To learn to share, to give generously to . . . others some of the beauty and warmth he has been given so early in life."

My mother pushed her cup of tea away and took a Gauloise. The painter instantly produced a match and lit it.

"What is it exactly that you are trying to say?" she asked. "You Poles have a way of going around in circles that has made your nation the dizziest and the most mixed up in the world."

"I am merely trying to say that it would be excellent for Romain if he shared the treasures of your love with someone else."

My mother was watching him very carefully with an expression that I can only describe as one of benign hostility.

"Please understand that I am not speaking in any way against a mother's love; on the contrary," Mr. Zaremba said quickly. "I have never known it myself and I realize exactly what I have missed—what I am missing. It is as necessary in making a man as yeast is in making bread. I am an orphan myself. . . ."

"You are certainly the oldest orphan I have ever met," my mother said.

"Age has nothing to do with it," Mr. Zaremba exclaimed almost emphatically. "The heart knows no such thing. I am not talking of any youthful folly, of passion that in the end can only destroy the beauty of a true relationship between a man and a woman. But believe me, if you could bestow some of the affection, the love, the attention on someone else besides your son, Romain would become a much stronger, much more self-reliant young man."

My mother inhaled deeply and noisily through her nose, sat a moment with both her hands on her thighs, then got up. She waited a moment, looking at the pale, imploring face of my friend, and then she said something that even I, at first, failed to understand.

"Cuckoo," she said.

"I beg your pardon?" the poor gentleman murmured.

"Cuckoo in the nest," my mother said, then she smiled scornfully and walked away.

The painter's eyes suddenly met mine. I don't think he had been aware of my discreet presence, and for some reason or other it shook him visibly. With his drooping, graying blond mustache, he looked suddenly as if I had caught him stealing my marbles. I, on the other hand, was a firm believer in letting bygones be bygones. I merely leaned out of the window and smiled pleasantly.

"I wonder if I could borrow fifty francs?" I asked.

The painter's hand instantly went for his pocketbook. He was a nice, kind and obliging man. I liked him.

After this little show of strength, my friend quite wisely decided that the best way to court my mother was to court me. I received a splendid wallet in crocodile skin, with fifteen American dollars in it, then a camera, then a wrist watch, all of which I accepted graciously, not in any mercenary spirit but out of the tactical consideration that it was important to get Mr. Zaremba in the proper mood and to make sure of the true quality of his nature. Thus I soon acquired a Waterman fountain pen and my little library began to prosper as never before. Cinema tickets were always available and I soon caught myself talking to my little friends on the beach about our family's new house in Florida, and then one day I even brought up with Mr. Zaremba the possibility of acquiring a sailboat for our mutual benefit and entertainment. For those readers who tend to judge my behavior severely and term it cynical, I would remind them once more that I was then not yet eighteen years old, that I never had a father and, if Mr. Zaremba was perhaps seeing himself as a son, I was beginning to see him as a father, and was pushing him with both hands into the role.

I succeeded rather well and finally the long-awaited day came when Mr. Zaremba proposed to me. I was lying in bed, with a slight cold, and the painter had come into my room, carrying a tray with some fruit, tea and honey, and my favorite biscuits, Les Petits Beurres Lulu, which still exist to this day, I am happy to say, and which I heartily recommend. I was wearing the painter's pajamas and his dressing gown; his Turkish slippers stood by my bed; it had long been agreed between us that we ought to share everything—no doubt, he had considered this a clever maneuver, thinking of my mother's heart, but practically it had resulted in the free access I had to everything in his room —and I was particularly well disposed toward him. He had chosen his moment well. He put the tray on the bed and sat on a chair, a tall, distinguished figure in gray tweeds, with good, brown earnest eyes. It was obvious that he felt embarrassed. He was swallowing hard and was pressing a handkerchief nervously in his hand.

"My dear Romain," he began in a voice which shook a little. "You know, of course, how I feel about you."

I had a grape. I looked at him kindly, encouragingly; I had the feeling that at last we were getting somewhere—in fact, that I had him exactly where I wanted.

"Of course," Mr. Zaremba said, "you are still a very young man. Perhaps it is difficult for you to understand my feelings."

I looked at him earnestly.

"Listen, Josef . . . may I call you Josef?"

Up to now I had always called him "Pan," that is "Mr." Josef and he called me "Pan" Romain.

"Please do," he said quickly.

"All I can say, Josef, is that I like you very much. You are a great artist and a wonderful person."

I could almost see the faces of my little friends on the Grande Bleue Beach when I suddenly appeared before them in my new sailboat, with beautiful blue sails—I was determined to have blue sails. I was then particularly interested in a little Peruvian girl and my rival was no less a person than Rex Ingram, the famous American movie director. The Peruvian girl was fourteen years old, Rex Ingram was then in his fifties, I was eighteen and so the sails had to be blue. I didn't quite know why.

I could also see myself very well in Florida, a big white mansion, emerald sea, immaculate beaches—that was the life. We would obviously go there for our honeymoon.

Mr. Zaremba took his handkerchief and wiped his perspiring brow. He was a good-looking man, with a typically Polish noble face, an eagle's nose and firm, clean-cut proud features.

"I am no longer a young man," he said. "It is perhaps better to admit that I am asking more than I can offer. Art is a refuge, at best. You are an artist yourself, Romain. But I promise that I will take care of you as well as I can and facilitate your artistic beginnings in life to the best of my ability."

I nodded in silent and grateful acknowledgment. "I feel quite sure that we could be very happy together, Josef."

I was getting a little impatient. I just wanted him to ask his question, without beating around the bush.

"So?" I shot at him bluntly.

"Do you think your mother will marry me?" he asked.

It was a strange moment. I had been angling for this very thing for many months, and now that the man was asking me for my mother's hand I felt a little lost and completely unprepared. Besides, there was no point in making him feel that the goose was already cooked. If I was ever to enter the Diplomatic Service I might as well begin to prepare myself for it at once.

"I don't know," I said gravely. "We have already had several offers."

I felt immediately that these last words were perhaps off key but Mr. Zaremba was obviously shaken.

"Who?" he asked feebly.

"I don't think it's proper for me to mention any names."

Tact, I knew, was an essential quality in a diplomat.

"Excuse me," the painter said. "I didn't mean to be indiscreet. But I would like to know how you feel about it."

I looked at him kindly.

"I like you," I told him. "I like you very much, Josef. But you must understand, of course, that this is an important decision. You mustn't rush me."

"Will you talk to her?"

"At the right moment, yes. But give me time to think it over. Marriage is a serious matter. How old are you exactly?"

The painter sighed. "Fifty-five."

"I'm only eighteen," I told him. "I just can't throw my life in one direction suddenly, without knowing exactly where I am going."

"I am aware of that," Mr. Zaremba said. "I am not a man to shirk my family responsibilities. I am also quite well off. I don't think you would regret your choice."

"I'll think it over," I repeated, rather sternly.

Mr. Zaremba rose from his chair with obvious relief.

"Your mother is an exceptional woman," he said. "I do hope you will find the proper words on my behalf. I'll await your answer most anxiously."

He left the room and it was suddenly as if he had left me all his anxiety and doubts. This was perhaps her last chance—our last chance. But I knew already that it wasn't going to be easy to convince her.

I decided to approach my mother on the subject after her return from the market—she was then usually in her best mood, as if this daily visit to her kingdom helped her to face the rest of the world with tolerance and indulgence. I put my finest clothes on, had a haircut, borrowed one of the painter's ties, a splendid silk affair in blue, embroidered with silver horsemen, bought an enormous bouquet of red roses of the most expensive kind—"Velvet Dawn," they were called—and about 10:30 A.M. found myself pacing the lobby, my heart beating with a nervousness that only Mr. Zaremba, who was cringing in his room, could understand. This was an important moment in my life and I was fully aware of it. It was not that I was anxious to shrug off some measure of the heavy burden of responsibility toward my mother, although I admit that this played a certain part in my wishful thinking. I also fully realized by now that the strange man of the world with the drooping mustache was looking for a mother rather than a wife, but he was a gentleman and I longed to see my mother holding the arm of someone who had better manners, less cruelty or indifference than life itself. Truly, the fact that his paintings sold so well threw a shadow of doubt over his artistic capacities—but, after all, one great artist in the family was quite enough, and this part I, quite naturally, saw falling to myself. Also I had read enough of the history of painting to know that one couldn't be both a great artist and a gentleman, and it was a gentleman that we were acquiring and not his art.

My mother found me in the lounge with my bouquet of flowers, which I presented silently to her, feeling a strange obstacle in my throat. She buried her face in the flowers with delight and then looked at me with apprehension, for they were quite obviously beyond my means.

I gestured to her to sit down and she settled in a chair with the bouquet on her knees, silent and suspicious, and quite obviously prepared for the worst.

"What's happened?" she said.

"Listen," I said.

She listened. But it wasn't easy to find the words.

"He is a gentleman," I began bluntly.

That was quite enough. She knew instantly what it was all about. She took the bouquet of flowers and threw it across the room with a violent, large and final gesture. The bouquet hit a vase and the vase smashed on the floor. Lina, the Italian maid, rushed in, took one look at my mother's face and rushed out.

"He has a house in Florida," I said desperately.

"You want to get rid of me," my mother said.

She began to cry. I didn't know what to say. Or rather, I knew only too well what I wanted to say, but those were desperate words and I could not bring myself to utter them. I wanted to tell her that this was her last chance, that there would never be another man, that she needed company, that I couldn't be with her forever, that sooner or later I would go my own way and she would be alone, that there was nothing that my love couldn't accomplish for her except that one thing, except renouncing my own life. And as those thoughts were filling my mind and while I was fighting away the words that were ready to express them, it appeared to me that, in a way, I *was* trying to get rid of her, after all, of her overpowering love, of her overwhelming emotional pressure on me.

"It's just that I don't want you to work so hard," I said rather lamely. "I can't help you, yet. He can."

"I am not going to adopt a middle-aged son with graying mustaches," my mother said. "There's something very wrong with him. His paintings sell; it's unnatural. I don't think we can trust him."

"He's a very distinguished man," I pleaded. "He has beautiful manners. He dresses well. He . . ."

And it was then that I made the final and fatal mistake. I underestimated my mother's youth of heart and her womanhood.

"He respects you, and he will always treat you like a gentleman," I said.

My mother's eyes filled with tears. She rose from her chair. "Thank you," she said. "I know that I am old. I know that there are things in my life that are gone forever; but I loved a man once, very much. It was a very long time ago—and I still love him. He didn't respect me and he wasn't a gentleman. But he was a man. And I am a woman—an old woman, but I have memories. I have one son and that's enough for me—I won't adopt another."

We stared silently at each other for one long, heartbreaking moment. She knew exactly what was going on in my mind: she knew that I was dreaming of escape. But there was no escape—only loneliness. Her loneliness—and mine today.

It only remained for me now to break the news to my poor friend. It wasn't an easy task and I liked him enough, and loved my mother enough, to feel sad for him, for her and for myself. I just didn't know how to convey this message of rejection without hurting him deeply, for if it is difficult to tell a man that a woman doesn't want him for a husband, it is even more difficult to tell a little boy that he has once more lost a mother. I went to my room and sat gloomily on my bed, staring at the floor and smoking a cigarette. I always had a strong reluctance to hurt people, which is always the best way of hurting oneself. Finally, I hit upon an idea that seemed to be both tactful and eloquent enough. I opened my cupboard. I took the blue silk tie with the silver horses on it, the camera, the silk shirts, the pajamas, the fountain pen and all the other precious things that I had shared with my friend for so long. I took off the watch from my wrist. Then I marched upstairs and knocked on his door. There was a faint, rather shaky "Come in"; and I went in. Mr. Zaremba was sitting in a chair, a very pale, immobile and, it seemed to me suddenly, very old man. He didn't ask any questions. He just looked on silently, with his hurt eyes, as I put all my treasures gently on his bed. Then we remained silent for a moment, avoiding each other's eyes, for there was nothing more to say.

He took the train the next morning, very early, without saying good-by. He left behind the blue tie with the silver horses, carefully wrapped in white paper, and the maid gave it to me when I returned from school. I still have it somewhere, but I seldom wear it: I feel that it makes me look older than my age. I am still quite a few years younger than he was then, twenty-eight years ago.

CHAPTER *23*

Toward the end of that year, I enrolled
in the law school of the University of Aix-en-Provence, and left
Nice in October, 1933. My mother and I were not to see each
other again till Christmas and our farewells were heart-rending. Under the eyes of my fellow passengers I tried hard to
assume a manly and faintly ironic expression, while my mother,
transformed suddenly into a bent old woman, and looking half
her normal size, stood staring at me, with her mouth hanging
open in agonized incomprehension. When the bus started, she
took a few steps along the pavement, then stopped and began
to cry. I can still see in her hand the little bunch of violets
which I had given her. I turned myself into a statue, helped in
my efforts, I must confess, by the presence of a pretty girl who
had her eyes upon me. In order to give my best, I have always
felt the need of an audience. I struck up an acquaintance with
the girl in question, in the course of the journey. She ran a
delicatessen shop in Aix, she told me, and went on to say that
she had only with difficulty refrained from crying during that
good-by scene, and I heard again those words which I was beginning to know so well: "Anyone can see that your mother
adores you"—spoken with a sigh, a dreamy look and a flicker of
curiosity.

My room in the rue Roux-Alphéran at Aix cost sixty francs
a month. My mother, at that time, was making five hundred.
Of this a hundred went for insulin and doctors' fees, another
hundred for cigarettes and sundry expenses. The rest was for

me. In addition there were what my mother called "the little extras." Almost every day the Nice bus brought me some provisions abstracted from the storeroom of the Hôtel-Pension Mermonts and, gradually, the sloping roof round my attic window began to resemble a stand in the Buffa Market. The wind set the strings of onions shaking; the eggs lay in a row in the gutter, much to the astonishment of the pigeons; the cheese swelled under the rain; the hams, the legs of mutton and the joints looked like a still life against the background of tiles. Nothing was ever forgotten, neither the dill pickles, nor the mustard made with tarragon vinegar, the Greek *halva,* nor the dates, figs, oranges and nuts, and to all these good things our friends of the Buffa Market added their own particular specialties: M. Pantaleoni's pizza made with cheese and anchovies; M. Peppi's "garlic pasties," a wonderful invention of his own which looked like perfectly ordinary pie crust, but melted in your mouth to an accompaniment of a succession of unexpected flavors—cheese, anchovies, mushrooms, ending suddenly in an apotheosis of garlic such as I have never since met with; to say nothing of whole quarters of beef, sent by M. Jean in person— the only authentic *boeuf sur le toit,* if I may say so, with apologies to the famous Paris night club of that name. The reputation of my larder spread rapidly in the Cours Mirabeau, and, as a result of it, I made a great many friends—a poet-guitarist called Sainthomme; a young German student and writer whose ambition it was to fecundate the North by the South, or vice versa, I forget which; two students who were attending the philosophy lectures of Professor Segond; and, of course, my delicatessen girl, whom I met again in 1952, by which time she was the mother of nine children—a proof that Providence had kept a careful eye on me, since she never caused me a moment's anxiety. I spent my free time at the Café des Deux Garçons, where I wrote a novel under the plane trees of the Cours Mirabeau. My mother sent me frequent letters, couched in lapidary terms, exhorting me to show courage and tenacity. They resembled the proclamations issued by generals to their troops on the eve of defeat, pulsating with promises of victory and honor, so much so, indeed, that when, in 1940, I read upon the walls that unforgettable "We shall conquer because we are the stronger," issued by the Reynaud Government, I thought of my own especial commander in chief with tender irony. I often thought of her getting up at six o'clock in the morning, lighting her first cigarette, boiling the water for her injection, sticking the needle of the syringe with its load of insulin into her thigh, then snatching up a pencil and scribbling her order of the day, slipping out to post it before going to the market: "Courage, my son; you will return home crowned with laurels. . . ." Yes, it was as simple as that, and she never hesitated before the oldest and most naïve clichés of the human race. I think that she wrote those letters more to convince herself than me, and to bolster up her own courage. She also begged me not to fight any duels, for she had always been haunted by the deaths of Pushkin and Lermontov. Since my literary genius was, in her eyes, the equal of theirs, she was afraid that I might be the third, if I may so express it. I was not neglecting my literary labors, far from it. A new novel was soon finished and sent .off on the round of publishers. For the first time, one of them, Robert Denoël, took the trouble to answer me personally. Apparently, having glanced through a few pages of the manuscript, he had shown it to a well-known psychoanalyst—the Princesse Marie Bonaparte, as it turned out—and now enclosed the conclusions she had come to about the author of *Vin des Morts*. Her report ran to twenty pages. It was perfectly clear, she said, that I was suffering from a castration complex, a fecal complex, that I had necrophilic tendencies and I don't know how many other interesting and exciting aberrations. The only thing missing from the list was the Oedipus complex, and I felt a little annoyed to see that even there the championship eluded me. Anyway, for the first time I had the feeling that I was becoming "somebody," that at last I was beginning to fulfill the hopes my mother had so confidently placed in me.

Though my book was turned down, I felt much flattered by

the psychoanalytic document of which I was the object; I showed it to my friends and they were duly impressed, especially by my fecal complex, which they took to be proof positive of a truly somber and tormented soul. At the Café des Deux Garçons I was undeniably making a mark, and I can say that, for the first time, the light of success touched my brow. Only the delicatessen girl reacted, after reading the document, in the most unexpected way. The demoniac and superhuman side of my nature, the existence of which she had not, thus far, suspected, had the effect of suddenly making her reveal an exigence the satisfaction of which exceeded my powers, demoniac or not. She bitterly reproached me with cruelty when, being endowed, as I was, with a somewhat simple temperament in these matters, I expressed amazement at certain of her whispered suggestions. In short, I fear that I fell far short of my newly acquired reputation. I set myself, however, to cultivate the air of an *"homme fatal,"* such as I imagined would suit someone afflicted with necrophilic tendencies and a castration complex. I never appeared in public without a pair of small scissors, which I opened and shut in a suggestive manner. When anyone asked me why I carried them about with me, I would say: "I don't know. I can't help myself," at which my friends exchanged meaningful glances. At the Cours Mirabeau, where I went about with a sort of fixed grin, and in law school I soon became known as a disciple of Freud, of whom I never spoke though I always carried one of his books about with me. I typed out twenty copies of the report, which I distributed generously among the young women of the university. I sent two of them to my mother. Her reaction was the same as mine: at last I had become famous and judged worthy of a twenty-page document—and written by a princess too. She insisted on reading it to the patrons of the Hôtel-Pension Mermonts, and, when I returned to Nice at the end of my first year as a law student, I was received with a great show of interest and spent my holidays most agreeably. The only thing that worried my mother a little was the castration complex: she feared I might hurt myself.

The Hôtel-Pension Mermonts was thriving. My mother was now making seven hundred francs a month, and it was decided that I should finish my studies in Paris, where I would make a lot of useful contacts. My mother already knew a half-pay Colonel, a former colonial administrator now on the retired list, and a French Vice-Consul in China who had become an opium addict and had come to Nice to undergo a cure. They both showed themselves well disposed toward me, and my mother felt with their backing we had at last a solid base from which to launch into life, and that my future was assured. On the other hand, her diabetes was getting worse, and the increasingly powerful doses of insulin which she was giving herself were producing more and frequent attacks of hypoglycemia. On several occasions, on her way home from the market, she had fallen down in the street in a coma.

She had, however, discovered a very simple way of averting this threat, since a swoon of that kind, unless immediately diagnosed and treated, was generally fatal. She therefore took the precaution of never leaving the house without pinning a little notice on her cloak: "I am a diabetic: if I become unconscious, please see that I swallow the packet of sugar which is in my bag. Thank you." This was an excellent idea. It spared us a great deal of anxiety, and enabled my mother to go out each morning, stick in hand, with a renewed confidence. Sometimes, when I saw her walking down the street, a feeling of terrible anguish laid hold on me, a sense of powerlessness and shame, a panic so horrible that a cold sweat broke out on my forehead. Once I timidly suggested that it might be better if I discontinued my studies and found some work to do which would bring in money. She said nothing, looked at me reproachfully, and began to cry. I never again returned to the subject.

Not once did I hear her complain except about the spiral staircase which led from the restaurant to the kitchens, and which she had to climb twenty times a day. She told me, however, that the doctor had said her heart was sound, and so there was nothing for me to worry about. I was nineteen. I did not have the mentality of a ponce. I suffered cruelly, and became obsessed with the idea that I was a weakling. Against this I struggled as had other men before me who wanted re-assurance of their virility. But that wasn't enough. I was living on her work and on her health. Two years, at least, lay between me and the moment when I could return home with the stripe of a second lieutenant on my sleeve: the first real triumph of her life. I had no right to refuse her help. My self-respect, my virility, my dignity were irrelevant—they couldn't matter less, in fact. The legend of my future was what was keeping her alive. For me there could be no question of noble indignation, of high moral attitudes, of posturings and grimacing, of personal pride: those luxurious goodies would have to wait. "I" didn't matter. I also knew that the cruel lesson I had learned in my flesh and blood since childhood meant that I was condemned to fight for a world where no woman, Chinese, Jewish, Indian or whatever, would have to carry her child uphill on her back: for a world where no one would be left alone. But this disinterested form of self-indulgence would also have to wait. I had to swallow my shame and continue with my race against time in an attempt to keep my promise, to give to an absurd, fond dream at least some small core of reality.

Two more years of law school still lay ahead, then two years more of military service. . . . I spent up to eleven hours a day in writing.

One morning, M. Pantaleoni and M. Bucci brought her back from the market in a taxi. Her face was still gray, her hair in disorder, but already she had a cigarette between her lips and a reassuring smile ready for me.

I do not feel guilty, I am not ashamed of myself. But if my books are filled with so many invocations to dignity and justice, if I make such a to-do about the honor of being a man, that, perhaps, is because I lived until the age of twenty-two on the sweat and toil of a sick and exhausted old woman and I still feel mad at her sometimes.

CHAPTER 24

THE SUMMER WAS ENLIVENED BY A QUITE UN-
expected bolt of lightning. One fine morning a taxi drew up
outside the Hôtel-Pension Mermonts, and out stepped my delicatessen girl. She made straight for my mother, and staged a
tremendous scene—floods of tears, sobs, threats of cut wrists and
of swallowed poison. My mother was tremendously flattered.
This was everything she had expected of me. At last I had become a man of the world. Not a moment was lost; that same
day every stall holder in the Buffa Market was *au courant* and
I was greeted everywhere with respectful glances. The point of
view of my "victim" was simplicity itself: it was now my duty
to marry her. This she supported with the strangest argument
that can ever have been advanced: "He made me read all of
Proust, Tolstoy and Dostoievsky," declared the unfortunate
young woman with an expression on her face which would have
melted the hardest heart. "What is going to happen to me now?
Who will want to marry me?"

I must say that my mother was deeply struck by this flagrant
proof of my intentions. She looked at me reproachfully. I had
obviously gone too far. I myself felt not a little embarrassed,
for it was true that I had made Adèle swallow all of Proust,
volume by volume, in rapid succession, and that, in her eyes,
was as good as telling her that she could go ahead with the
wedding dress. God forgive me!—I had even made her learn by
heart passages from *Thus Spake Zarathustra*. I didn't put her

in a family way, but there was no denying the fact—I may as well come clean with it—that I made her read Flaubert, Gobineau, and—of all people—Lautréamont, and obviously could no longer contemplate slipping away on tiptoe.

I could see that my mother was weakening, and I began to feel really scared. Her attitude toward Adèle had suddenly become all sweetness and kindness, and a sort of female solidarity developed between the two women. They looked at me searchingly and censoriously. They mingled their sighs and whispered to each other. My mother offered Adèle a cup of tea and—supreme mark of good will—made her sample some strawberry jam of her own making, and the delicatessen girl was clever enough to hit on just the right note of praise. I felt that my ship was sinking rapidly. When tea was over, my mother took me into the office.

"Are you really and truly in love with her?"

"No. I love her with all my heart, but not really and truly."

"Then why have you made her promises?"

"I haven't made her any promises."

"How many volumes of Proust are there?"

"Listen, Mother . . ."

She shook her head. "You have not behaved at all well."

All of a sudden her voice broke, and I saw to my amazement that she was crying. She touched my cheek with her fingers and stared at me, her eyes going searchingly and lovingly over every feature of my face, and I knew that she was remembering, that she was trying to find a resemblance. . . . I was almost afraid that she would tell me to go to the window and raise my eyes.

All the same, she did not insist on my marrying the girl, thus sparing the latter a cruel destiny, and when, twenty years later, in Aix-en-Province, Adèle introduced her nine children to me, I felt no surprise at the warm gratitude shown me by the whole family. They owed it all to me. Her husband fully realized this, and wrung my hand effusively. I looked at the nine angelic faces, I felt around me the tranquil prosperity of a happy home, I glanced discreetly at the bookshelf, which contained only *Les aventures des Pieds Nickelés,* and the feeling came to me that I had, once at least, made a success of something in my life, and shown myself to be a good father, by abstention.

Autumn was approaching, and my departure for Paris. A week before I embarked for Babylon my mother had a religious crisis. Until that moment I had never heard her speak of God except in a way that showed a certain bourgeois respect for somebody who had "made good." She had always shown a high degree of consideration for the Creator, but with that purely verbal and impersonal deference which she kept for persons who occupied high positions. So I was rather surprised when, putting on her cloak and taking her stick, she asked me to go with her to the Greek Orthodox Church at the Parc Impérial.

"But I thought we were more or less Jewish."

"That has nothing to do with it: I know the priest."

That seemed to me to be a good enough explanation. My mother believed in the importance of good personal contacts, even in her dealings with the Almighty. As for myself, I had, more than once, in the days of my adolescence, turned to God, and had even gone so far as to be converted for good, though only temporarily, when my mother had had her first diabetic crisis and I had stood by helplessly watching her in a coma. The sight of her ashen face, of her drooping head, of her hand pressed to her breast, of that complete collapse of all her powers of resistance, at a time, too, when there was such a load of responsibility on her shoulders, had been enough to send me, there and then, into the first church my eyes saw, which happened to be that of Notre Dame. I kept it a secret from her, fearing that she would see in this appeal to outside help a sign that I had lost my confidence and faith in her, and also an indication of the gravity of her condition. I thought she might suddenly imagine that I had felt I could no longer rely on her and I was looking for support elsewhere, that, in turning to another, I was abandoning her. But very soon the idea I formed of divine providence seemed to me incompatible with what I saw happening on earth, and it was, after all, *on earth* that I wanted to see a happy smile upon my mother's face. Nevertheless, I find the word "atheist" intolerable. It seems to me stupid and mean, it smells of the bad dust of centuries, it is old-fashioned and narrow-minded in a certain bourgeois and reactionary way which I cannot define though it outrages me, as does everything that smacks of self-satisfaction, and claims, conceitedly, to be emancipated and "knowing."

"We will go to the Russian Church at the Parc Impérial."

I gave her my arm. She still walked fast, with the determined air of those who have a goal in life. She had taken to wearing spectacles, horn-rimmed ones, which accented the beauty of her green eyes. She had very beautiful eyes. Her face was lined and worn and she no longer held herself as upright as she once had. She leaned more and more heavily on her stick, though she was only fifty-four. She suffered too from chronic eczema on her wrists. No one has the right to treat human beings like that. I was beginning to have strange dreams: I dreamed that I had been changed into a tree with a very tough bark or into an elephant whose hide was a hundred times thicker than mine. I had also developed the habit—I have it still—of taking my foil, stepping out into the open, garden, beach or hill, and, without even indulging in the customary salute, crossing swords with every ray of light which struck at me from the sky. I take up my stance, stretching my legs till I almost split in two, I leap, I lunge, I try to hit, I shout: "And here!" and "Take that!" I dash forward, I look for my enemy, I feint, I bounce, in fact I behave much as I once did on the tennis court of the Parc Impérial, when I danced my desperate dance in pursuit of balls I never succeeded in touching.

Among other swashbuckling swordsmen, Malraux has always been the one I most admire. Of all our fighters, he is the one I prefer. Especially in his poem on art Malraux seemed to me to be an author-actor playing his own tragedy: or rather, a mime, a universal mime. When, alone upon my hilltop, with nothing but the sky around me, I juggle with my three balls, just to show what I can do, I think of him. Together with the

Chaplin of the old days, he is, without a doubt, the most moving mime of the human condition this country has known. That lightning flash of thought, condemned to reduce itself to art, that hand outstretched to the eternal, yet finding only another human hand to grasp, that marvelous intelligence compelled to stay contented with itself, that shattering aspiration to pierce, to grasp, to surmount, to transcend, which can never in the end reach beyond beauty, have long been for me, in the field, like the shoulder of a brother-fighter by my side.

We walked along the Boulevard Carlonne toward the Boulevard du Tsarevitch. The church was empty and my mother seemed pleased to have, so to speak, exclusive use of it.

"There is nobody else here," she said. "We shan't have to wait."

She spoke as though God were a doctor who would receive us at once. She crossed herself and I followed suit. She knelt down in front of the altar and I knelt beside her. There were tears upon her cheeks and her lips mumbled old Russian prayers in which the words *Yessouss Christoss* recurred incessantly. I stayed beside her with my eyes cast down. She beat her breast and once, without turning to me, murmured: "Swear to me that you will never take money from women."

"I swear."

The idea that she was herself a woman never seemed to enter her mind.

"O Lord! Help him to stand upright, help him to stand straight, guard him from sickness."

Then, this time turning to me: "Swear to be careful! Promise me not to catch anything!"

"I promise."

For some while longer my mother stayed there, not praying but only crying. Then I helped her to her feet and there we were, back in the street. She wiped her eyes and suddenly appeared to be satisfied. There was even a look of almost childish cunning on her face when she turned toward the church for the last time.

"One never knows," she said.

Next morning I took the bus to Paris. Before starting, I had to sit down and remain seated for a moment so as to keep bad luck away, according to an old Russian superstition. She had given me five hundred francs, which she made me carry in a leather pouch under my shirt, no doubt as a precaution in case the bus should be held up by brigands. I swore to myself that this would be the last sum I accepted from her and, though I have not altogether kept my word, I felt much relieved at the time.

In Paris, I shut myself away in a minuscule hotel room and, wholly neglecting the law school, settled down with determination to my writing. At noon, I walked to the rue Mouffetard, where I bought bread, cheese and, of course, dill pickles. I never managed to get back to my room with the pickles intact but ate them, there and then, in the street. That, for some weeks, was the only satisfaction I had. Not, however, that temptations were lacking. As I stood with my back against a wall, restoring my strength, my eyes were attracted by a young girl of quite incredible beauty. She had black eyes and brown hair of a silkiness without precedent in the history of human hair. She did her shopping at the same time as I did mine and I got into the habit of watching for her to come down the street. I expected absolutely nothing of her—I could not afford even to take her to a cinema. All I wanted was to eat my pickle while feasting my eyes on her. I have always had a tendency to get ravenously hungry when looking at beauty—whether landscapes, colors or women. I am a born consumer. Finally, the girl noticed the odd way in which I stared at her while devouring dill pickles. She must have been struck by my immoderate craving for those estimable vegetables, and by the rapidity with which I swallowed them, and though she never gave me a look, she did smile faintly when she passed me. One fine day when I was surpassing all my former efforts with a truly enormous pickle she could control herself no longer and said, with a note of sincere concern in her voice: "One of these days you'll burst."

We struck up an acquaintanceship. It was a stroke of luck for me that the first girl with whom I fell in love in Paris was totally disinterested. She was a student and, with the single exception of her sister, was quite the prettiest girl in the whole of the Quartier Latin at that time. Young men in cars paid assiduous court to her, and even today, twenty years later, whenever I happen to catch sight of her in Paris, my heart beats faster, my mouth waters and I dash into the first delicatessen shop on my way and buy a pound of pickles.

One morning, when I had no more than fifty francs left and a fresh application to my mother was becoming imperative, I found, on opening the weekly *Gringoire,* one whole page devoted to a short story of mine called "l'Orage," and my name in fat letters in all the appropriate places.

I slowly folded the weekly and went home. I did not feel in the least little bit excited but, on the contrary, sad and tired. I already knew the difference between the ocean and a drop of water and it only made me once more aware of the impossible task ahead.

But no words of mine will serve to describe the sensation which the publication of my story produced in the Buffa Market. An *apéritif* in honor of my mother was given by the traders, toasts and long speeches were read with the most glorious *niçois* accent and in an atmosphere thick with garlic breath. My mother put the copy of *Gringoire* in her bag and never went anywhere without it. At the slightest provocation, she took it out, opened it, stuck the page adorned with my name under the nose of her adversary and said: "I think you forget to whom you have the honor of speaking!"

After which, with her head held high, she stalked victoriously from the field of battle, followed by a host of astonished eyes.

I got a thousand francs for that story and, as a consequence, completely lost my head. I had never before seen such a sum and, going at once to extremes, like someone else of my acquaintance, felt secure from want for the rest of my days. The first thing I did was to go to the Brasserie Balzar, where I stowed two helpings of *choucroute* and a large plateful of *pot-au-feu*. I have always been a big eater. I took a room on the fifth floor of the hotel with a window looking onto the street and wrote a very calm and collected letter to my mother, explaining that I had a regular contract with *Gringoire,* as well as with several other publications, and from now on, if ever she was in want of money, she had only to let me know. I dispatched an enormous bottle of perfume and arranged by telegram for a bouquet to be delivered to her. I bought myself a box of cigars and a sport coat. The cigars made me feel sick but I was determined to live in the grand manner and smoked the lot. Thereupon, seizing my fountain pen, I wrote three stories in rapid succession, all of which were returned to me, not only by *Gringoire* but by every other Paris weekly. For six months not one of my works saw the light of day. They were considered "too literary." At the time I did not understand what was happening to me, but now I do. Encouraged by my first success, I let myself be carried away by my devouring need to catch the last ball no matter what the cost, to go to the bottom of the problem at a single stroke of the pen; and, since the problem had no bottom or, if it had, my arm was not long enough to reach it, I found myself once more reduced to playing the part of the clown dancing on the tennis court at the Parc Impérial. Such an exhibition, tragic and burlesque though it might be, could only dismay the public through my sheer inability to control what I could not even grasp, instead of reassuring them, as do true professionals, by the ease and expertness with which they keep well within their capacities. It took me a long time to admit that the reader was entitled to a certain amount of consideration and that it was necessary to explain to him, as to every newcomer at the Hôtel-Pension Mermonts, the number of his room, the way the switches worked, to give him his key and indicate where he would find all the necessities.

It was not long before my situation became, from the material point of view, well-nigh desperate. Not only had my money melted away with incredible rapidity but I kept on getting letters from my mother overflowing with pride and gratitude, together with a request to let her know, well in advance, the publication dates of my future masterpieces so that she might be in a position to trumpet them all over the *quartier*.

I had not the heart to tell her of my failures. I therefore had recourse to a clever piece of subterfuge of which I feel very proud to this day. I wrote to my mother explaining that the newspaper and magazine editors were demanding stories of so commercial a nature that I was refusing to compromise my literary reputation by signing them with my name and was, so I told her, making use of a variety of pen names for these inferior products unworthy of my pen. I begged her not to breathe a word of this to anyone, since I did not wish to hurt my friends, my masters at the Nice *lycée*, in short, those who believed in my genius and integrity.

Thereafter, each week I coolly cut out the work of other writers appearing in the pages of the Paris weeklies and sent them to my mother with a clear conscience and a feeling that I had done my duty.

This solution disposed of the moral problem, but left the material problem untouched. I no longer had enough money to pay my rent and spent whole days without eating. I would rather have died of starvation than destroy my mother's glorious illusions by asking her for money.

One particularly gloomy evening comes to my mind. I had eaten nothing since the previous day. At that time I was in the habit of going frequently to see one of my friends who lived with his parents not very far from the Lecourbe Métro station and had noticed that, if I calculated the time of my arrival properly, they always asked me to stay to dinner.

My stomach was empty and I thought it might be a good idea to pay a polite call on them. I even took one of my manuscripts to read aloud, for I felt very kindly disposed toward Monsieur and Madame Bondy. I was almost mad with hunger and also with that feeling of indignation, resentment and mean rage which an empty stomach always stirs up in me. I planned to be passing by sheer coincidence—just when the soup would appear upon the table. When I reached the Place de la Contrescarpe, I could already smell in my imagination the delicious brew of potatoes and leeks, though I was still forty-five minutes' walk from the rue Lecourbe—I hadn't enough money to pay for a Métro ticket. My mouth was watering and there must have been a gleam of crazy concupiscence in my eyes, judging from the way such unaccompanied women as I passed gave me a wide berth and increased their pace. I was also pretty certain there would be Hungarian salami too—there always had been, on previous occasions. I don't think I ever went to a lover's tryst with so delicious a sense of anticipation.

When I finally arrived at my destination, overflowing with friendliness, there was no answer to the bell. My friends were out. I sat down on the stairs and waited for an hour, for two hours. But toward eleven o'clock, an elementary concern for my dignity—it always hangs about somewhere—kept me from staying there till midnight for the sole purpose of begging for something to eat.

So I walked all the way back down the infernal rue de Vaugirard, the longest street in Paris, with a sense of frustration that made me feel like murdering the President of the Republic or killing myself. It was then that I reached another peak in my career as a champion of the world.

Having reached the Luxembourg, I had to walk past the Brasserie Médicis. As ill luck would have it I saw, even at that late hour, through the white net curtain, a natty bourgeois in the process of dealing with a porterhouse steak and steamed potatoes. I stopped, took one look at the steak, and fainted dead away. My hunger had nothing to do with it. True, I hadn't eaten for twenty-four hours, but at that period of my life I had a vitality which could stand up to anything and I often went without eating for thirty-six hours without shirking my obligations, of no matter what nature. No: what had made me faint was sheer humiliation, indignation and rage. No human being, I thought, should be placed in such a position, and I still adhere to that belief. I judge political regimes in terms of the amount of nourishment they can guarantee every individual, and when there are any political strings attached to the daily bread, when men can eat only by accepting or submitting, I vomit them. A man should have the right to eat without any conditions.

I was choking with rage. I clenched my fists, everything went dark and I fell full length on the pavement. I must have lain there for quite a while because when I regained my senses I found a crowd around me. I was well dressed, I was even wearing gloves and, fortunately, it never occurred to anyone to guess the reason for my fainting fit. An ambulance had already been sent for and I was much tempted to let myself be driven away: I was sure that I could find some means of filling my stomach at the hospital. But I refused to take that easy way out. With a few muttered words of apology, I extricated myself from the crowd and walked home. The double shock of humiliation and fainting had relegated the demands of my stomach to the background. I lit my lamp, took out my fountain pen and, there and then, started on a story which appeared in *Gringoire* a few weeks later under the title of "Une petite femme."

I also did some soul-searching and decided that I was taking myself too seriously and was lacking both in humility and a sense of humor. I had shown a defeatist attitude toward my fellow men, a lack of confidence in them, and had not even tried to explore the possibilities of human nature, which, after all, could not be entirely devoid of generosity. Next morning I embarked on an experiment, as a result of which my optimistic views turned out to be entirely justified. I began by borrowing a hundred sous from the floor waiter, then went to the Capoulade Café, where, standing at the counter, I ordered a cup of coffee and plunged my hand resolutely into a basket of *croissants*. I ate seven of them with gusto and then called for more coffee; after which I looked the waiter solemnly in the eyes— the poor devil had no idea that, in his person, the whole human race was being put to the test—and asked: "How much do I owe you?"

"How many *croissants?*"

"One."

He glanced at the basket, which was almost empty. Then he glanced at me. Then he glanced again at the basket. Then he shook his head. *"Merde,"* he said. "You lay it on too thick, buddy."

"Maybe two," I said.

"All right, all right, forget it," he said. "I'm not completely dumb. Two coffees and a *croissant*—seventy-five centimes, all told."

I left the place transfigured. Something was singing in my heart—probably the *croissants.* From that day on I became the Capoulade's best customer. Occasionally, the unfortunate Jules —that was the name of this great Frenchman—ventured a timid protest, though without much conviction.

"Couldn't you go stuff yourself someplace else? You're going to get me into trouble with the boss."

"I can't," said I. "You are my father and my mother."

Sometimes he indulged in vague calculations to which I listened with only half an ear.

"Two *croissants?* You can look me in the face and say that? Three minutes ago there were nine in the basket."

I took that remark very coldly. "There are thieves everywhere," I observed.

"Eh bien, merde!" said Jules admiringly. "Some cheek you've got, friend. What are you studying for, if I may ask?"

"Law. I am working for a law degree."

"Some joke," said Jules somberly.

We became friends. When my second story appeared in *Gringoire,* I gave him a signed copy.

I reckon that between 1936 and 1937 I must have got through something like one thousand or one thousand five hundred *croissants* at the Capoulade, without paying. I regarded it as a sort of scholarship awarded me by the establishment.

I have, ever since then, had a particular fondness for *croissants*. I find something sympathetic in their shape, their crispness and their friendly warmth. I don't digest them quite so easily now as I used to and our relationship has become more or less platonic. But I like to think of them lying there in their basket on the counter. They have done more for students than the Third Republic. As General de Gaulle would say, they are good Frenchmen.

CHAPTER 25

THE PUBLICATION OF MY SECOND STORY IN
Gringoire came just in time. The day before, my mother had
written me an indignant letter in which she announced her
intention of unmasking, stick in hand, a lady who had turned
up at the hotel and claimed to be the author of a story which
I had published under the pen name of André Corthis. I was
terrified. André Corthis really did exist, and had, indeed, written the story in question. It was becoming a matter of some
urgency to provide my mother with something to go on. "Une
petite femme" was like an answer to prayer, and, once again, the
trumpets of fame reverberated through the Buffa Market. But
by now I had come to realize that there could be no question
of my living by my pen alone, and I set about looking for
"work," a word which sounded to me mysterious and a little
desperate and which I pronounced with an air of grim resolution.

I was, in succession, a waiter in a Montparnasse restaurant,
a tricyclist deliveryman for a caterer's firm, "Lunch-Diner-Repas
Fins," receptionist at a luxury hotel near the Etoile, a washer-up
at Larue and at the Ritz, a desk clerk at the Hotel Lapérouse;
I worked at the Cirque d'Hiver and at the Mimi Pinson dance
hall, sold advertising space in *Le Temps* to the tourist agencies,
and undertook, for a reporter on the staff of the weekly paper
Voilà, a detailed inquiry into the settings, personnel and atmosphere of more than a hundred Paris brothels. *Voilà* never
published my findings, and I later learned, much to my indig-

nation, for I would have demanded a far larger fee, that I had been working, without knowing it, for an under-the-counter guidebook for the use of visitors to Gay Paree. Of all my jobs, that of receptionist in the hotel near the Etoile was by far the most disagreeable. I was constantly being snubbed by the chief clerk, who had a profound contempt for "intellectuals"—it was a matter of common knowledge that I was a student and an aspiring writer—and all the bellboys were pederasts. The sight of those kids of fourteen offering their services in no uncertain terms made me feel physically sick. By comparison, my round of the brothels for *Voilà* seemed like a breath of fresh air.

I should not like anybody to think that I am making a deliberate attack on homosexuals. I have nothing against them— but I have nothing for them, either. Some of the most eminent pederasts among my friends have discreetly suggested that I ought to have myself psychoanalyzed to see if I could be cured of my weakness, since my fatal preference for women must be the result of some infantile trauma which might be overcome with a little patience and understanding. I am, by nature, prone to meditation and sadness, and I fully realize that in these days, after all that has happened to man in the way of concentration camps, slavery in its various forms and the hydrogen bomb, there is really no reason why he should not accept being ——* as well. We have acquiesced in so many varieties of servitude, humiliation, horror and bestiality that it is difficult to see why we should suddenly become difficult and choosy. However, there is always the future to be considered, and, for that reason, it seems to me a good thing that men in our time keep at least one small part of their persons intact, and in reserve, so that they will still have something left to surrender and to prostitute in times to come.

The job I most enjoyed was that of delivering food on a tricycle. The spectacle of food has always been a pleasure for me, and I found it by no means unpleasant to ride about Paris

* Unprintable.

with a cargo of well-cooked dishes. Wherever I went I could be sure of a warm welcome. On one occasion I had to deliver a delicious little supper—caviar, champagne, foie gras, etc.—at a fifth-floor bachelor flat in the Place des Ternes. I was received by a distinguished-looking gentleman with graying hair, who must have been a few years older than I am today. He was wearing what was then known as an "at home." The table was laid for two. I recognized him as a fashionable writer of the period. He looked dejectedly at what I had brought, and seemed to be extremely downcast.

"Always remember, my lad," he said, "that all women are bitches. I should know. I've written several novels on the subject."

He looked with disgust at the caviar, the champagne and the chicken in aspic. Then he heaved a deep sigh.

"You have a mistress?"

"No," I replied, "I'm broke."

He appeared to be favorably impressed.

"Young though you are," he said, "you seem to know women."

"I have known one or two," I answered modestly.

"Bitches?" he inquired hopefully.

I took a squint at the caviar. The chicken in aspic didn't look too bad either.

"*Oh là là!*" I said, with a deep, heartbroken sigh.

He nodded with satisfaction: "They were mean to you?"

"Mean?" I repeated, with a tragic grin. "The word isn't strong enough!"

"And yet you are young, and by no means bad looking."

"*Maître,*" I said, taking my eyes with difficulty from the chicken: "*Maître,* I have been *cocu,* abominably *cocu.* The only two women I really loved betrayed me with men of fifty—fifty, did I say? Why, one of them was well over sixty."

"Really?" He had cheered up considerably. "Tell me all about it. Sit down. We might as well take advantage of this wretched meal. The sooner it disappears, the better."

I pounced on the caviar. I made but one bite of the foie gras and the chicken in aspic. When I eat, I eat: I don't beat around the bush. I mean business and put all I have into each mouthful. As a rule I don't much care for chicken, which I always find a bit tame, except when it's served with a fine mushroom garnish, or when it's drenched in tarragon sauce. Still, it is edible. I told him how two lovely young creatures, with the most delicately jointed limbs and unforgettable eyes, had left me for two elderly men with gray hair, one of whom was a well-known author.

"It is true that women prefer experienced men," said my host. "There is something reassuring for them in the company of a man who knows life and its ways, and has outlived a certain form of . . . hm!—youthful impetuosity."

I hastily agreed. There were three desserts, and I was getting along splendidly. My host poured me some more champagne.

"You must have a little patience, young man," he said benevolently. "One day you too will be fifty, and then you will, at last, have something to offer women, something they value above all else—authority, wisdom, a calm and assured touch—in other words, maturity. When that day comes, you will know how to love them, and you will be loved by them."

I grabbed the bottle and poured myself some more champagne. There was no point in keeping the gloves on: there was not a crumb of chocolate cake left. I got up. He took one of his own books from the shelves, and inscribed it for me. He laid his hand on my shoulder.

"No need to despair, young man," he said. "Twenty is a difficult age. But it doesn't last—just a painful moment to be lived through. When one of your young women leaves you for an older man, take it for what it is, a promise for the future. One day you too will be a mature man."

"*Merde,*" I thought, uneasily.

My reaction is just the same today, when it has caught up with me all right.

The master went with me to the door. We shook hands, we looked one another straight in the eyes. A fine subject for the

Prix de Rome: Wisdom and Experience Offering a Helping Hand to Youth and Its Illusions.

I carried the book away under my arm. I had no need to read it: I knew what it would be about. I wanted to laugh, to whistle and to talk to the passers-by. The champagne and my twenty years gave wings to my tricycle. The world was my oyster. I pedaled through the Paris of bright lights and shining stars. I broke into song, taking my hands from the handlebar, beating time with my arms and blowing kisses to unaccompanied ladies in cars. I crashed a red light. A cop stopped me with an indignant blast on his whistle.

"What the hell?" he shouted.

"Nothing," I said with a wink. "Life is beautiful, *la vie est belle!*"

"Off you go," he said, grinning, opening up instantly to that password, like a true Frenchman.

CHAPTER 26

I WAS IN MY THIRD YEAR AT LAW SCHOOL WHEN I met an adorable Swedish girl, the type of girl every man in every country has dreamed about since the world first gave the blessed gift of Sweden to mankind. She was gay, pretty, intelligent, and, above all, she had a charming voice, and I have always been sensitive to voices. I have no ear, and between music and me there is a sad, resigned misunderstanding. But to women's voices I am strangely sensitive. Why, I do not know. Perhaps there is something peculiar in the formation of my ears, a nerve, for instance, that somehow got where it shouldn't be at all. I have even gone so far as to have my Eustachian tubes examined by a specialist, but he found nothing wrong. In short, Brigitte had the voice, I had the ear, and we were made to understand one another. As things turned out, we did—admirably. I listened to her, making her speak as much as I could, and I was happy. Rather simple-mindedly, in spite of the world-weary airs I affected, I believed that nothing could threaten such a harmonic and harmonious relationship. We were so happy together that other lodgers in the hotel, students of every color and from every latitude, smiled when they passed us on the stairs each morning. Then I began to notice that Brigitte was becoming pensive. She often went to see an old Swedish lady who lived at the Hôtel des Grands Hommes in the Place du Panthéon. She stayed there until late, sometimes until one or two in the morning.

When she got back, she was always very tired and sad, and stroked my cheek with a melancholy and pitying kindness.

A secret doubt wormed its way into my mind. I began to suspect that something was being hidden from me. My precocious perspicacity was such that it did not take much to arouse my doubts: could it be, I wondered, that the old Swedish lady had fallen ill, in a foreign land, so far away from her dear ones? And what if she was Brigitte's own mother, who had come to Paris to consult one of the great French doctors? Brigitte had such a sweet nature, she adored me with such self-abnegation that she was perfectly capable of concealing her anxiety from me, if only to protect my peace of mind, so important in literary creation—I was busily writing a new novel. One night, about 1 A.M., obsessed by the idea of my poor Brigitte crying her eyes out at the bedside of a dying woman, I could stand the mystery no longer and went to the Hôtel des Grands Hommes. It was raining. The door of the hotel was locked. I took shelter under the portico of the law school, and kept my eyes glued to the façade of the hotel. Suddenly, a light went on in a fourth-floor window, and Brigitte came out onto the balcony. Her hair was undone. She was wearing a man's dressing gown, and stood for a while motionless, with the rain beating down upon her face. I must admit that I was not a little astonished. What was she doing there in a man's dressing gown, and with her hair all loose? Perhaps she had been caught in the storm and the doctor attending the Swedish lady had lent her his dressing gown, while her own clothes were drying? A young man in pajamas appeared on the balcony, and leaned on the rail at Brigitte's side. This time I was positively amazed: I didn't know that the Swedish lady had a son. It was then that the ground opened under my feet, that the portico of the law school collapsed on my head, and hell and damnation took hold upon my heart. The young man put his arm around Brigitte's waist, and my last hope—that perhaps she had merely gone into a neighbor's room to fill her fountain pen—vanished in a flash. The scoundrel clasped Brigitte to him, kissed her on the lips, and led her back into the room. The light was discreetly dimmed but not extinguished: the murderer wanted to see what he was doing. I uttered a horrified yell and rushed across to the hotel entrance, intent on preventing the hideous crime that was about to be committed. There were four flights to climb, but I thought I could arrive in time, provided that the man was not a complete brute and had a modicum of good manners. Unfortunately, the door was shut fast, and I had to bang, ring, holler and dance about like a cat on hot bricks, thus wasting a lot of time, which drove me almost insane with rage and frustration, since my rival up above was almost certainly not having similar difficulties. To make matters worse, I had failed, in my panic, to mark down the exact window, so that when the porter did finally let me in, and I flew like an eagle from floor to floor, I did not know which door was the right one, and when the one I chose opened to my knock, I leaped at the throat of a sweet little thing whom I so terrified that he very nearly fainted in my arms. I had only to take one look at him to realize that he was not at all the type to entertain women in his bedroom—quite the contrary. He gave me a reproachful and entreating look but I was in far too great a hurry to do anything for him. So, back I was on the unlit stairs, wasting still more precious time trying to find the automatic light switch, and hollering all the time at the top of my voice. I was pretty certain now that I would be too late. The murderer had not four flights to climb, no door to break open, his work was all laid out for him, and he was probably gleefully rubbing his hands now. Suddenly, all my strength drained from me. I was a prey to complete despair. I sat down on a stair and wiped the sweat and the rain from my forehead. I heard a timid flop-flop and the willowy youth sat down beside me and took my hand. I lacked the strength even to withdraw it. He set about consoling me, and, so far as I remember, offered me his friendship. He caressed my hand and said that a man like myself should have no difficulty in finding a brotherly soul worthy of him. I looked at him with a vague sort of interest. But, no, there was nothing doing for me in that direction.

193

Women might be abominable sluts, but there was no one else to turn to. They had the monopoly. An immense wave of self-pity broke over me. Not only had I just suffered the most hideous indignity, but there was no one in the whole world but a wretched pansy to console me and hold my hand. I gave him a nasty look, and, turning my back on the Hôtel des Grands Hommes, made my way home. I collapsed on my bed with my mind firmly made up to enlist in the Foreign Legion the very next day.

Brigitte returned round about two in the morning, just as I was beginning to get seriously worried about her: perhaps something had happened to her? She scratched timidly at the door, and I told her, loud and clear, in one word, what I thought of her. For half an hour she tried to soothe my feelings through the door. Then there was a long silence. In my terror lest she might, perhaps, go back to the Hôtel des Grands Hommes, I jumped out of bed and let her in. I slapped her once or twice, halfheartedly, but the blows hurt me more than they hurt her. I have always had the greatest difficulty in raising my hand against a woman: I think I must be lacking in virility. Then I asked her a question which I still consider, looking back on it in the light of twenty-five years' experience, the most idiotic question I have ever asked anyone in my whole career as a champion of the world:

"Why did you do it?"

Brigitte's answer was really superb, I would even say moving. It was a tremendous tribute to the strength of my personality. The blue eyes she turned on me were brimming with tears. Shaking her blond curls, and with a sincere and pathetic effort to explain everything, she said:

"He was so like you!"

I have never recovered from it even now. We were living together, she had me within easy reach, but that wasn't enough for her. Oh no! She had to go out in the rain and walk the best part of a mile to find somebody else, for no better reason than that he reminded her of me. If that's not proof of my magnetism, then I don't know what is! I had to make an effort not to show some conceit: say what you like, I obviously made a great impression on women!

Since then, I have given a great deal of thought to Brigitte's answer, and the conclusions I have reached, though strictly nonexistent, have, all the same, done much to help me in my relationship with women—and with men who are like me. I have never again been deceived by a woman—that is, I have never, since then, waited in the rain.

CHAPTER 27

I WAS NOW IN MY LAST YEAR AT LAW SCHOOL and, of far more importance to us, was about to complete my preparatory military training, which would open to me the doors of the Air Force Academy. The sessions took place twice weekly in a place known as La Vache Noire at Montrouge.

One of my stories was translated and published in America. The fabulous sum of a hundred and fifty dollars which I was paid for it enabled me to make a brief journey to Sweden in pursuit of Brigitte, whom I found married. I tried to come to an arrangement with her husband, but the fellow had no heart and insisted on keeping Brigitte exclusively to himself. Finally, since I was getting slightly out of hand, she exiled me to her aunt's summer house on a small island of the Stockholm archipelago, in a landscape of Swedish legends, and there I wandered gloomily among the pine trees, while the faithless one and her husband indulged in their guilty loves. Brigitte's aunt, in order to calm my nerves, insisted on my bathing every day for a whole hour in the icy waters of the Baltic and sat implacable on the shore, watch in hand, while all my organs shrank, my body gradually withdrew from me and I soaked, frozen, vertical, morose and unhappy. Once, as I lay stretched on a rock, waiting for the sun to thaw the blood in my veins, I saw an airplane with swastika markings cross the sky. That was my first encounter with the enemy.

I had paid but little attention to what was going on in Europe.

Perhaps because I had been brought up by a woman and surrounded with a woman's love, I was incapable of hating anyone for long, and so was lacking in the essential quality which would have made it possible for me to understand Hitler and the Nazis. The silence of France under the impact of his hysterical threats, far from making me uneasy, seemed to me to be a sign of calm strength and self-reliance. I believed in the French Army and in its revered leaders. My mother had built around me, long before the General Staff had constructed it upon our frontiers, a Maginot Line of unshakable certainties and patriotic pictures which no anxieties nor doubts could shake. To give an example, it was only at the Nice *lycéc* that I learned for the first time of our defeat by the Germans in 1870: my mother had forgotten to mention it. I should add that, although I have my good moments, I have always found it difficult to make that prodigious effort of sheer stupidity which one must achieve in order to take war seriously as a solution. I can be stupid enough when I decide to do my best, but I have never managed to reach those glorious asinine heights from which one can gaze on the prospect of slaughter and find it acceptable. I have always considered death to be a regrettable phenomenon, and the idea of inflicting it on anyone is wholly contrary to my nature. True, I have killed men in my time, sometimes with my own hands, in obedience to the unanimous and sacred conventions of the moment, but always without enthusiasm, without anything in the least resembling genuine inspiration. No cause seems to me important enough to warrant such a thing, and my heart is not in it. When it comes to killing my fellow men, I am not enough of a poet. I cannot give myself to it with the necessary zest; I cannot raise my voice in a sacred hymn of hate, and I kill without any satisfaction, stupidly, because I have to.

The fault also lies, I am inclined to think, in my egocentricity. So egocentric am I, indeed, that I see myself in all suffering humanity, and the wounds of others make me bleed. That feeling is not limited to humans but extends to animals and even to plants. An incredible number of people can happily watch a bullfight, unmoved by the sight of the bull's agony. Not I. I *am* the bull. I am always a bit queasy when people cut down trees or hunt the moose, the rabbit or the elephant. On the other hand, the thought of chickens being killed does not much worry me. I cannot see myself in a chicken.

It was on the eve of Munich. There was a great deal of talk about war, and my mother in her letters which reached me in my sentimental exile at Björkö was already sounding a clarion call. One of those noble outpourings, dashed off in an energetic hand and large-sized characters leaning well forward as though already charging the enemy, declared quite firmly that "France will conquer because she is France." Looking back, it seems to me that no one could have predicted more convincingly our defeat of '40, nor better expressed our lack of preparation.

I have often scratched my head, trying to understand the why and the how of an old Russian woman's passionate love for my country, but have never succeeded in finding a really satisfactory answer. No doubt my mother was deeply imbued with the ideas, the scale of values and the opinions current in bourgeois society around about 1900 when France was generally regarded as the pinnacle of creation. Perhaps, too, the origin of her attachment may be found in some secret memory she had kept of her two visits to Paris in her youth, and I, who have retained all my life such a warm place in my heart for Sweden, should be the last person to feel surprised. I have always had a tendency to look, behind the grandiose and noble causes, for some small and intimate impulse, to watch, at the heart of tumultuous symphonies, for the tiny sound of a tender flute suddenly to show the tip of an ear. But the simplest and most probable explanation is that my mother loved France for no specific reason, as is always the case when one truly loves. Be that as it may, it is easy to imagine the part played in the psychological universe in which she lived by the golden stripe soon to adorn my sleeve, as a second lieutenant in the French Air Force. I was actively employed in acquiring it. I had, with great difficulty, achieved my degree in law, but it was in the top listing that I had been accepted into the Air Force Academy.

My mother's patriotism, worked up to fever pitch by the anticipation of my military greatness, now took an unexpected turn.

It was indeed just about this time that my unsuccessful attempt on Hitler's life took place. No mention of it has ever appeared in the press. I did not save France and the world, thus missing an opportunity which, in all probability, will never present itself again.

It happened in 1938 after my return from Sweden. Having abandoned all hope of recovering my beloved and sickened by the behavior of Brigitte's husband, who had no *savoir-vivre*, stunned by the discovery that someone else should have been preferred to me, after all that my mother had promised, I went back to Nice to lick my wounds and spend at home my last weeks before entering the Academy.

I took a taxi from the railway station and, as the cab turned the corner of the Boulevard Gambetta and the rue Dante, I could see the little garden in front of the hotel. It no longer exists, although the Hôtel-Pension Mermonts still stands today, and every time I go back to Nice I look at its entrance and stand there, waiting for the impossible, longing for a miracle.

My mother welcomed me very strangely. I had been expecting tears and embraces, sniffs of emotion and satisfaction, but not these sobs, these despairing looks which are associated more with partings than with homecomings. Weeping, she flung herself into my arms, now and again stepping back to get a clearer view of my face, then clasping me again in a fresh transport of feeling. I began to be uneasy, to wonder about the state of her health. Yet apparently her diabetes was kept in check, the business was flourishing, all was well—but even while she was telling me all this, there was a fresh outburst of tears and stifled sobs. At last, she managed to calm down and, assuming a mysterious air, took my hand and let me into the empty restaurant. We sat down at our usual table in the corner and there, without further delay, she told me of her plan. It was all very simple. I was to go to Berlin and assassinate Hitler, thus saving France and civilization and truly becoming the champion of the world. She had foreseen every eventuality, including my ultimate safety. Supposing I were caught—though she knew me well enough to feel certain that I was perfectly capable of killing Hitler without letting myself be caught—still, just supposing I were caught, it was crystal clear that the Great Powers, France, England and America, would demand my liberation under threat of war, and Germany would be in such a state of confusion and despondency that the result was a foregone conclusion and I would enter Paris on a white horse through the Arch of Triumph, greeted as a national hero by the populace.

I confess that I had a moment's hesitation. I had just done ten different and frequently unpleasant jobs, and had given, both on paper and in the flesh, the best of myself. The idea of starting straight away for Berlin, traveling third class, of course, and assassinating Hitler at the hottest time of the summer, with all that that implied of nervous exhaustion, physical fatigue and preparation, did not appeal to me. I wanted to stay for a while on the shores of the Mediterranean—I have never been able to stay away from it for long without fretting. I would far rather have disposed of the Führer in October, the beginning of the academic year. I contemplated without enthusiasm the prospect of a sleepless night on the hard bench of a third-class carriage in an overcrowded train, to say nothing of the hours I would have to yawn away in the streets of Berlin, waiting for Hitler to put in an appearance. In fact, I showed a lamentable lack of eagerness. But there was no question for me of disappointing her. I was to be a shining hero, the savior of the world, the champion of a just and noble cause, and that was all there was to it.

I made my plans. I was a very good pistol shot and, though I was a bit out of practice, the training I had received in Lieutenant Sverdlovski's gymnasium still enabled me to impress my friends on fairgrounds. I went down to the cellar, took my revolver from the famous family box and went to see about my ticket. I felt slightly better on learning from the papers that Hitler was at Berchtesgaden, since it would be pleasanter to breathe the forest air of the Bavarian Alps than that of a city in mid-July. I also put my manuscripts in order, for I was not at all sure, in spite of my mother's optimism, that I should come out of the business alive. I wrote several farewell letters to the women in my life whom I loved with a unique and undying love, oiled my pistol and borrowed a jacket from a friend who was a good deal fatter than I, so as to be able to conceal my weapon more comfortably. I was irritable and in a bad temper, the more so since the weather was exceptionally hot; the Mediterranean, after our months of separation, seemed more desirable than ever and the Grande Bleue Beach had more intelligent and cultivated Swedish girls on its pebbles than ever before. During all this time my mother never moved from my side. Her look of pride and admiration followed me wherever I went. I got my train ticket and was somewhat flabbergasted to find that the German railways were giving me a thirty per cent reduction—a special arrangement for holiday travelers. Throughout the last forty-eight hours before the time of my departure, I was careful to limit my consumption of dill pickles in order to guard against any intestinal troubles, which might have been interpreted as unheroic by my mother.

On the eve of the Great Day, I had my last swim at the Grande Bleue and looked with emotion at the last smiles of Sweden. It was on my return from the beach that I found my great dramatic artist crumpled up in an armchair. No sooner did she see me than her eyes widened, she joined her hands as though in prayer and, before I had time to make a move, was on her knees with the tears running down her cheeks:

"I beg, I implore you not to do it! Renounce this heroic project of yours! For the sake of your poor old mother, don't, don't! They have no right to ask this of an only son! I have fought so hard to bring you up, to make a man of you, and now . . . O dear God! . . ."

Fear had enlarged her eyes, her face wore a ravaged look, her hands were still clasped. I was not at all astonished. I had been "conditioned" for so long! I knew her so well and I understood her so completely! I took her hand.

"But I've paid for my ticket," I said.

An expression of fierce resolution swept her face clear of terror and despair. "They'll have to refund the money," she announced, grasping her stick. I had no doubt about that.

Thus it is that I didn't kill Hitler. But it was a pretty close thing all the same.

CHAPTER 28

ONLY A FEW MONTHS NOW STOOD BETWEEN MY mother and my second lieutenant's stripe, and the reader can well imagine the impatience with which we both waited for the great moment. Time was running short. Her diabetes was getting worse, and, in spite of the different varieties of diet with which the doctors were experimenting, the sugar content of her blood was increasing dangerously. She had another attack of hypoglycemic coma at the market, where she was laid out on the counter of M. Pantaleoni's vegetable stall, and recovered consciousness only because of the speed with which they poured sugared water down her throat. . . . My race against time was assuming a desperate character, and it showed in my writing. In my determination to write a fabulous masterpiece which should leave the world open-mouthed with admiration, I forced my voice beyond its range, so that it became strident and unpleasant. Aiming at greatness, I achieved only pretentiousness; standing on tiptoe in an attempt to reveal my stature for all to see, I succeeded only in uncovering my lack of it; determined to be a genius, I merely made more clearly visible the limits of my talent. But when one feels the knife at one's throat, it is difficult to sing in tune. Roger Martin du Gard, when asked by some friends to report on one of my manuscripts, during the war, when I was thought to be dead, spoke of me, very rightly, as a *"mouton enrage"*—an enraged lamb. My mother doubtless guessed the agonizing nature of the struggle I was waging, and did everything she could to help me. While I was busy polishing my sentences and seeking the right word to express my noble sentiments, she bore the full brunt of battling with the staff, the agencies, the guides, and dealing with the whims and fancies of a capricious clientele. While I was waiting for inspiration to visit me and the light of genius to touch my brow, while I was seeking some staggering subject of tremendous originality and profundity, worthy of my pen, she ran to the market, fought with our Russian *chef de cuisine* to keep him from drinking, installed a bar in the hall and a café on the roof, checked the accounts, while all the time making it her business to see that nothing should be allowed to disturb my moments of creation. I write these lines without guilt or remorse, still less self-denigration. I was striving to realize her dream, to achieve what, for her, was the sole meaning of her life and of her struggles. . . . She longed to be a great artist, and I was doing my best. In my haste to show her that I was not letting her down, to keep her informed of my strides forward, but, above all, perhaps to reassure myself, to break free from the panic which had hold of me, I would often grab a page or two of my manuscript and go down to the kitchen, where I would turn up just in time to interrupt a violent quarrel with the chef, and read her a passage still hot from the anvil, which seemed to me to be particularly worthy of praise. On such occasions her anger immediately quieted. With a sovereign gesture, she silenced the chef, and listened to me with intense satisfaction.

Her thighs were a mass of punctures. Twice a day she retired to a corner, sat down with her legs crossed and a cigarette between her lips, heated the water in a special boiler, took up her syringe with its load of insulin, and jabbed the needle into her flesh, all the while continuing to issue orders to the staff. With her habitual energy, she watched over the smooth running of the hotel, countenanced no falling-off in the high standards she had set from the start and even tried, without much success, to learn a few words of English so as to be able to follow better the wishes, the phobias and the little fads and fancies of our visitors from across the Channel. The efforts she made to be always amiable, smiling and conciliatory with tourists went dead against the grain of her naturally frank and impulsive nature and aggravated still more her nervous condition. She was going through three packets of Gauloises a day, though it is true that she never smoked a cigarette to the end but stubbed it out almost as soon as she had started on it, instantly lighting another. She had cut out of an illustrated magazine a picture of some military parade and showed it to the guests, particularly to the young women among them, pointing out the handsome Air Force uniform which would be mine in a few short months. I had the greatest difficulty in getting her to allow me to help in the restaurant, to serve at table and to take the breakfast trays up to the bedrooms, as I always had done in the past: she now found such odd jobs incompatible with my imminent status as an officer. She herself would often carry a new arrival's suitcase and try to push me away when I wanted to take it from her. It was obvious, however, from a certain air of gaiety about her, from the triumphant and grateful smile which sometimes lit her face when she looked at me, that she felt herself within sight of victory and that she could imagine no day more wonderful than the day when I would return to the Hôtel-Pension Mermonts wearing my glorious Air Force insignia and my officer's uniform.

I was inducted at Salon-de-Provence on November 4, 1938, and took my place in the special train by which the conscripts were to travel. A crowd of friends and relatives had accompanied the young men to the station, but only my mother had furnished herself with a tricolor flag, which she never ceased waving, at the same time shouting *"Vive la France!"*—a display that caused many hostile or mocking glances and caustic remarks. The class which was being called up was remarkable for its lack of enthusiasm and for a profound conviction—which the events of '40 were to justify to the full—that they were being compelled to take part in a *jeu de con*—"mug's game" would be the closest translation, I suppose. I remember one reluctant young recruit, enraged by my mother's patriotic and jingoistic carryings-on, so contrary to the sound antimilitarist traditions of the times, muttering:

"You can see that she's not French!"

Since I, myself, was infuriated and driven nearly frantic by the uncontrolled exuberance of the old lady with the tricolor flag, I was only too glad of the excuse to give vent to my feelings and plunged head forward, aiming at my neighbor's nose. The brawl at once became general. Cries of "Fascist," "traitor" and "down with the Army" broke out all over the train just as it was jerking into motion, while the tricolor flag still desperately fluttered on the platform. I had just time to fight my way to the window and wave my hand in farewell before plunging back into the providential free-for-all, which enabled me to escape from the emotional upset of the parting.

With my certificate of *Préparation militaire supérieure* and my law degree, the door of the officers' flying school was open to me and I should at once have received my marching orders to Avord. Instead I was kept for very nearly six weeks at Salon-de-Provence. In reply to all my inquiries, the officers and noncoms merely shrugged. They had received no instructions about me. I made representation after representation through the proper official channels, to no avail. At long last, a particularly decent officer, a certain Lieutenant Barbier, took an interest in my case and backed my protests. I was told to report at Avord, where I turned up one full month late, having missed almost a third of the whole course of studies. I did not allow myself to be discouraged. I was there at last; and that was all that mattered. I set to work with a determination of which I did not know myself capable, and, in spite of certain difficulties with the theory of the compass, managed to make up for lost time. My marks were average, except in flying and infantry leadership, in which I suddenly found that I had all my mother's authority of word and gesture. I was happy. I loved the airplanes of that long-vanished day, with their open cockpits, their primitive instruments, which left such a margin to individual flair and initiative, and the devil-may-care attitude of the pilots who flew them in a sky still free from regulations, channels of approach and radio guidance. I enjoyed the long hours which we spent on the airfield in our heavy one-piece leather suits—and a hellish business it was to get into them—floundering in the mud, encased in leather, helmeted, gloved and with goggles on our noses, climbing into the cockpit of the good old Potez-25, which ambled along at about the speed of a draft horse, in a glorious reek of oil, of which my nostrils still retain a nostalgic memory. Imagine the cadet officer hanging half out of the open cockpit of a bomber flying at about 70 m.p.h., or standing upright in the nose, giving hand signals to the pilot of a Leo-20 biplane with its long black, waving wings only a year before the Messerschmitt-110 and eighteen months before the Battle of Britain, and it is easy to see that we were being actively trained, like the French Army, for the war of 1914, with the disastrous consequences now known to all of us.

Time passed quickly, and the day of the graduation parade was drawing near, when we were to be told our graduating rank, and allowed to choose the units to which we were to be posted.

The military tailor had already made the round of the barrack rooms, and our uniforms were ready. My mother had sent me, to pay for my outfit, the sum of five hundred francs, which she had borrowed from M. Pantalconi, our old friend of the Buffa Market. My great problem was the cap. Caps could be ordered with two varieties of visor—short or long. I couldn't make up my mind. The long visor gave me a more rakish look, which was much to be desired, but the short one suited me better. I managed, after a thousand fruitless attempts, to produce a small mustache of the kind then considered very smart by fliers. With a pair of gold wings on my chest, I won't go so far as to say that I cut a stunning figure; still, I looked pretty tough, and thus hidden, the little boy could hope to pass unnoticed.

The graduation parade took place in an atmosphere of happy anticipation. The names of the available stations were written on a blackboard—Paris, Marrakech, Meknès, Maison-Blanche, Biskra. . . . Each cadet could make his choice according to his marks. Those with the highest traditionally settled for Morocco. I earnestly hoped to get a posting in the south of France, so as to be able to visit Nice frequently, and show myself, with my mother on my arm, at the Buffa Market or on the Promenade des Anglais. The Faïence airfield seemed best suited for this purpose, and, as my fellow trainees stood up and declared their preferences, I kept an anxious eye on the blackboard.

I had a good chance of getting a respectable rank, and listened with confidence while the captain read out the names.

Ten names, fifty names, seventy-five names . . . it certainly looked as though Faïence was going to slip through my fingers.

There were two hundred and ninety of us, all told.

Faïence was snapped up by No. 80. I waited. A hundred and twenty names, a hundred and fifty, two hundred . . . Still nothing. The gloomy, muddy airfields of the north were approaching with frightening speed. It wasn't brilliant, to be sure; still, I did not have to tell my mother what my graduation rank had been.

Two hundred and fifty, two hundred and sixty . . .

An appalling hunch suddenly turned my heart to ice. I can still feel the cold sweat breaking out on my forehead. . . . No, it's not a memory: I have just wiped it away with my hand, although more than twenty years have passed since. Pavlov reflex, I suppose. I cannot think, even today, of that abominable moment without feeling that drop of sweat on my forehead.

Out of close on three hundred trainees, I was the only one not to receive commissioned rank.

I was not even made a sergeant, not even a corporal. Contrary to all established custom, and to regulations, I just managed to scrape through as a lance corporal!

For the next few hours I struggled in a sort of nightmare, a hideous fog. I kept a stiff upper lip on parade, surrounded by my silent and appalled companions. All my available strength went into keeping up appearances, trying to look unconcerned, detached, a man who could take it on the chin, trying not to cry, not to break down in sobs. I believe I even smiled.

Generally such a rap over the knuckles was given only for disciplinary reasons. Two pilot trainees had been held back on that account. But it didn't apply in my case. I had never had so much as a reprimand. True, I had missed the opening stages of my training, but from no fault of my own; besides, my *chef de brigade*, Lieutenant Jacquard, a professional soldier from Saint-Cyr Academy, a man with a chilly manner, but as honest and straight as they make them, had told me, and later confirmed his opinion in writing, that my marks would have fully justified a commission. What had happened? Why had I been kept swinging my heels for six weeks at Salon-de-Provence, in defiance of all rules?

My comrades, silent or indignant, crowded around to shake my hand. I smiled: I remained true to the character I had chosen to play, and I kept the little boy well in hand, preventing him from screaming. But I thought I was going to die. And all the time I could see my mother's face, as she stood on the platform at Nice waving her tricolor flag.

At three o'clock that afternoon, while I was lying on my cot, staring at the ceiling, a Corporal Piaille—Piaye?—Paille?—came to look for me. He was not one of the flying personnel, but a pen pusher in the station headquarters. He came to a halt in front of my cot, with his hands in his pockets. He was wearing a leather jacket. He's no right to that, I thought: only flying personnel are entitled to wear leather jackets.

"Do you want to know why they flunked you?"

I looked at him.

"Because you are not French-born. You are Russian-born and your naturalization is too recent. Three years, they feel, is not enough to make a fine Frenchman. There is even a rule that you can't be a flying officer in the Air Force unless your parents were French, or you yourself have been naturalized for more than ten years. But the rule is never applied. There was a row in Parliament about it; they called it undemocratic, discriminating, racist. But they're back at it again."

I don't remember what I said to him. I think it was—"I am French," or something like that, because he suddenly said in a pitying sort of way: "You're just a stupid ass, that's what you are."

But he didn't go away. He seemed to be all worked up and resentful. Perhaps he was one of my sort—wouldn't stand for injustice of any kind.

"Thanks all the same," I said.

"They've been making inquiries about you; that's why they kept you hanging about at Salon for six weeks. There was a lot of argument about whether they'd let you into the Air Force, or turn you into a foot slogger. The Air Ministry said, yes, they'd take you, but this lot here, they said no, in their own dirty way, that is, by flunking you. They just gave you a lousy good-looks mark; that did it!"

The "good-looks," as we called it, or "general aptitude mark," the official name for it, was given to you by your instructors, a sort of all-round comment on your personality and your fitness to become an officer. You could be the number-one cadet at the Air Force Academy, as far as your studies were concerned, and still fail, if the good-looks mark went against you. In the hands of reactionary and politically minded officers, it served to eliminate Jews, left-wingers and various other *métèques*—the closest translation would be "naturalized trash." It was an unfailing weapon, later brought to perfection by the Vichy régime.

"You can't even holler: everything has been played according to the rules. That's what the rules are for."

I just lay on my back. He stayed looking at me for a moment or two. He was the sort of chap who couldn't put his sympathy into words.

"Don't let it get you down," he said. Then he added: *"On les aura!* (We'll get 'em!) "

It was the first time I had ever heard that expression used by a French soldier about the French Army. I had always thought it was reserved strictly for the Germans. I felt neither hate nor resentment, only an overpowering desire to vomit. I tried to think of the Mediterranean and its pretty girls; I shut my eyes and took refuge in their arms, where nothing could touch me, where nothing would be refused. The barrack room was deserted, but I had company. The monkey gods of my childhood, from whom my mother had fought all her life to rescue me, whom she was so sure we had left forever behind us in Poland and Russia, had suddenly raised their ugly heads in this land of France, which I had always thought was forbidden ground to them, and it was their stupid laughter I was hearing now in the homeland of reason. In the dirty trick which had been played on me I had no difficulty in seeing the hand of Totoche, the god of Stupidity, who was very soon going to make Hitler the master of Europe and open the gates of France to German armor, after having first convinced the French General Staff that the theories of a certain Colonel de Gaulle were just a lot of moonshine. But it was Filoche, the petit-bourgeois monkey god of Mediocrity, of rabid scorn and prejudice, whose ugly head I recognized above all, and what broke my heart was that he had put on for this occasion the uniform and braided cap of our Air Force. For, as always, I couldn't bring myself to see enemies in my fellow men. In a vague and inexplicable sort of way, I felt myself the ally and defender even of those who had just stabbed me in the back. I understood well the social, political and historical conditions which lay at the root of my humiliation but, determined though I was to fight against all those poisons, it was to a nobler victory that I kept my eyes turned. Whether there lurks deep down in me some primitive and pagan element I do not know, but at the slightest provocation, I clench my fists and face outward; I do all I can honorably to keep my place in the ranks of our age-old rebellion; I see History as a relay race in which each one of us, before dropping in his tracks, must carry one stage further the challenge of being a man; I refuse to find anything final in our biological, intellectual or physical limitations; my hope knows no frontiers; so confident am I of the outcome of the struggle that the blood of our species sometimes begins to sing in me, and the rumble of my brother the ocean seems then to come from my veins and I experience a gaiety, an intoxication of hope, a certainty of victory so intense that, on our age-old battlefield covered with rusty shields and broken swords, I still feel as if I were standing on the eve of our first fight. That comes, no doubt, from a sort of madness, of simple-mindedness, elementary, primitive but irresistible, which I must have inherited from my mother. I am fully aware of its absurdity, my confidence drives me frantic, but there is nothing I can do about it and it makes my task very difficult, when all it would take is to know how to despair. A spark of confidence, of atavistic gaiety, keeps glowing in me and it only needs a darkening of the shadows around me to blow it into a triumphant flame. Human stupidity may make the angels weep, the uniform of a French officer may serve as a nesting place for mediocrity and rabid prejudice, men's hands—whether French, German, Russian or American—may suddenly show their incredible dirt—it always seems to me that injustice comes from elsewhere and that men are never more clearly its victims than when they are its instruments. At the toughest moment of a fight, whether political or military, I find myself dreaming of some way in which the two sides can come together and join ranks. My egocentrism makes me peculiarly unsuited to fratricidal wars and I cannot see how anything, torn from the hands of those who share my essential destiny, can be called a victory. Nor can I become an entirely political animal, for I always keep recognizing myself in my enemies. It is a real infirmity.

I lay there on my back, tense and eager and smiling in my youthfulness, and I remember that my body was suddenly lifted by an impetuous and imperious physical craving, and that for more than an hour I battled against the savage and primitive call of my blood.

As to the fine captains and their stab in the back, I saw them five years later when they were still captains but certainly less fine. Not the tiniest scrap of ribbon bloomed upon their breasts and it was with a very curious expression on their faces that they looked at that other captain who received them in his office. By that time I was a Companion of the Liberation, Chevalier of the Legion of Honor, Croix de Guerre. I made no attempt to conceal my medals and I am willing to confess that, whenever blood rushes to my face, it is more from anger than from modesty. I chatted with them for a few minutes about our shared memories of Avord—memories that were wholly inoffensive. I felt no animosity toward them. They had long been dead and buried.

Another and somewhat unexpected consequence of the blow I received was that, from then on, I felt myself to be truly a Frenchman. It was as though, by this painful bang on the head of the magic wand, I had become truly assimilated.

It had dawned on me, at last, that the French were not a race apart, that they were not superior beings, that they too could be stupid, ridiculous and as unjust as anyone else—in short, that we were all brothers. I realized that France was compounded of a thousand different faces, beautiful and ugly, noble and hideous, inspiring and repulsive, and that it was for me to choose from among them the one which seemed most to resemble what my mother had told me. I forced myself, without quite succeeding, to become a political animal. I took sides, chose my allegiances, my loyalties, refused to let myself be blinded by a flag, but looked carefully at the faces of those who held it.

There remained my mother. I couldn't make up my mind to tell her the truth. It was all very well my arguing to myself that she was used to being kicked in the teeth: the fact remained that I had to find some way of softening the blow. We were granted a week's leave before reporting to our respective units and I climbed into the train still undecided. On arriving at Marseilles, I felt tempted to jump onto the platform, to desert, to work my passage on a cargo boat, to enlist in the Foreign Legion and so disappear forever. The thought of that worn and wrinkled face lifted to mine, of the look of consternation, of animal incomprehension in those great eyes, was more than I could bear. A sudden spasm of nausea overcame me and I got to the lavatory only just in time. All the way from Marseilles to Cannes I was as sick as a dog. But ten minutes before drawing into Nice, I was suddenly visited by a noble inspiration. The only thing that really mattered was to save the picture of France as the land where all the beauty lies and where justice dwells, which my mother had all her life carried in her head. This I was determined to do. France must be kept out of this—she could not have borne so terrible a disappointment. Knowing her as I did, I thought up a very simple, a very elegant and plausible lie, worthy of a true man of the world, which would not only console her but confirm the high idea she had of me.

As I entered the rue Dante, I saw a tricolor flag floating over the freshly painted façade of the Hôtel-Pension Mermonts. Yet this was no national holiday. One glance at the unadorned windows of the neighboring houses assured me of that. Then, suddenly, I realized the full meaning of the flag. My mother had raised the tricolor in honor of the homecoming of her son, recently promoted to the rank of second lieutenant in the French Air Force. I stopped the taxi. I had just time to pay the driver before being sick again. I finished the journey on foot. My legs felt weak and I was breathing deeply.

My mother was waiting for me in the hotel lobby behind the little reception desk at the far end. She gave one glance at my private's uniform with the red lance corporal's stripe on the sleeve. Her mouth fell open and into her eyes there came that dumb look of incomprehension which I have never been able to endure in men, animals or children. . . . I had pushed my cap over one eye and assumed the hard, cynical expression of a true adventurer. I smiled mysteriously, and after the briefest of kisses, said to her: "Come in here. Something funny has happened. But you must promise me to be very discreet about it. The honor of a woman is at stake."

I led her to our usual corner of the restaurant. "I've not been made an officer, as you can see. I was the only one out of three hundred who didn't get a commission. A little matter of discipline, and only temporary . . ."

Her poor face was all expectation and confidence. She was ready to believe and approve anything I chose to tell her.

"I may have to wait six months or so. You see . . ." I gave a hurried look around me to make sure that nobody was within earshot. ". . . I seduced the wife of my commanding officer. Couldn't resist. The orderly gave us away. The husband decided to make me pay for it. . . ."

My mother's face showed a moment's hesitation. Then the old romantic instinct of Anna Karenina carried the day. Her lips broke into a smile and a look of profound curiosity came into her eyes. "Was she very beautiful?"

"You have no idea," I told her, shaking my head with a sigh. "A fabulous creature! I knew the risk I was taking but didn't hesitate an instant. It was worth it!"

"Have you a photo of her?"

No, I didn't have a photo. "She's going to send me one when things quiet down."

My mother looked at me with extraordinary pride. "Don Juan!" she exclaimed. "Casanova! I always said so!"

I smiled modestly.

"Her husband might have killed you!"

I shrugged.

"Does she love you really and truly?"

"Really and truly."

"And you?"

"Oh well, you know how it is with me," I said with my toughest air.

"You mustn't be like that," said my mother, though without much conviction. "Promise me you'll write to her."

"Oh, I'll write to her all right!"

My mother remained deep in thought for a few moments. Then a new idea came to her: "The only one out of three hundred not to be made a second lieutenant!" she said in a tone of unstinted pride and admiration.

She hurried away to get tea, jam, sandwiches, cakes and fruit. Then she sat down, put both hands on her thighs, and breathed noisily with intense satisfaction.

"Now tell me all about it," she ordered.

My mother loved beautiful stories. I had told her a great many.

CHAPTER 29

HAVING THUS ADROITLY WARDED OFF THE MORE immediate danger, in other words, having saved France from an appalling collapse in my mother's eyes and heart, and explained to her the reason for my setback with the delicacy of a true man of the world, I now had to face a second test which found me much better prepared.

Four months earlier, when I was called to the colors, I enjoyed at Salon-de-Provence the privileged standing which befits a future officer. The noncoms had no authority over me and the privates regarded me with a certain amount of awe. I was now coming back to them as a simple lance corporal.

One can well imagine what sort of life was mine, what I had to put up with, in the way of insults, fatigue, practical jokes, jeers and subtle irony. This was the period when the Army was slowly decomposing among the comforts and delights of that rottenness which finally worked its way into the very souls of some of the defeatists, collaborationists and traitors of 1940. My duties over the weeks that followed my return to Salon-de-Provence took the form of permanent latrine inspection, but I must confess that the sight of latrines was a pleasant change after the faces of certain sergeant majors and sergeants about the camp. Compared with what I had felt when I went back to my mother without her golden officer's stripe, the vexations to which I was exposed were minor troubles and, on the whole, took my mind off my defeat rather than reminding me of it. And I had only to leave the camp to find myself in the Provençal countryside, with its strangely funereal beauty, where the stones scattered among the cypresses suggested some mysterious ruin of the sky.

I was not unhappy. I made a number of friends among the civilian population. I went to Les Baux, where, from the top of the gigantic cliff, troubadours sang in medieval times and the courts of love were held, and I spent hours looking at the stretching sea of olive trees at my feet.

I practiced pistol shooting and put in some fifty hours' clandestine flying time as a pilot, thanks to the complicity of two of my friends, Sergeant Christ and Sergeant Blaise. Finally, somebody, somewhere, awoke to the fact that I held a navigator's diploma, with the result that I was appointed air gunnery instructor. The war caught me thus occupied, with my machine guns pointed at the sky.

The idea that France might lose the war had never occurred to me. My mother's life could not conceivably end on a note of defeat. This extremely logical line of argument inspired me with more confidence in the victory of French arms than all the Maginot Lines and all the clarion calls of our beloved leaders. My own beloved leader could not possibly lose the war, and I felt sure that destiny was keeping in reserve as a reward for her that final victory which, after so long a struggle, so many sacrifices and so much heroism on her part, was her due.

The day war was declared, my mother came to Salon-de-Provence to say good-by to me, in the old Renault taxi already mentioned. She arrived laden with food—hams, tins of jam and preserved fruit, cigarettes—everything, in fact, of which a heroic soldier may dream in the hour of his greatest need.

It transpired, however, that these parcels were not meant for me. There was a cunning look in my mother's face when she held them out, saying: "For your officers."

I was left speechless. I could see the expression on the faces of Captain Longevialle, Captain Moulignat and Captain Turben when a lance corporal entered headquarters and presented them, in his mother's name, with a tribute of sausages, hams, cognac and cakes designed to influence them in his favor. I do not know whether she thought that this type of Oriental *baksheesh* was traditional in the French Army, as it may have been in Russian provincial garrisons in Gogol's time, a hundred years ago, but I took great care to keep my thoughts on the matter to myself. She was perfectly capable of taking these "gifts" in person to my superiors, accompanying their presentation with one of those patriotic tirades of hers which would have brought a blush to the cheeks of Déroulède * himself.

I managed, with considerable difficulty, to shepherd my mother, her effusiveness and her parcels out of range of the curious eyes of the grinning soldiery lounging in front of the canteen, and to lead her to the runway, among the grounded aircraft. She walked across the grass, leaning on her stick and solemnly inspecting our aviation strength. Three years later, it was my good fortune to be present when another great lady reviewed our air crews and their machines on a flying ground in Kent. She was Queen Elizabeth of England and I must say that there was less of a proprietary air about Her Majesty than there was about my mother when she walked past our squadrons on the airfield at Salon.

Having thus taken stock of our military might, my mother felt rather tired and sat down on the grass at the airfield's edge. She lit a cigarette and her face assumed a brooding look. She was frowning and obviously preoccupied. I waited. Without any beating around the bush, she said straight out what she was thinking: "We must attack at once," she declared.

I must have shown some surprise, for she proceeded to make her words more explicit. "We must march straight on Berlin." She said it in Russian: *Nada iti na Bierlinn,* in a tone of profound conviction and absolute certainty.

I have always since regretted that, failing General de Gaulle, the command of the French armies in 1939 was not entrusted to my mother. I feel pretty sure that our great General Staff, which allowed the breakthrough of German armor at Sedan,

* A jingoistic minor French poet of the nineteenth century.

would have found its master in her. She had, to a very high degree, the sense of the offensive and the very rare gift of imparting her energy and initiative even to those who most obviously lacked it. I hope I shall be believed when I say that she was not the woman to remain inactive behind the Maginot Line with her left flank completely uncovered.

I promised her to do my best. This seemed to satisfy her, and she returned to her brooding. "All these machines have open cockpits," she remarked. "Remember that you've always had a delicate throat."

I could not resist pointing out that if all the Luftwaffe was going to give me was a sore throat, I would consider myself very lucky. She smiled and gave me a superior, almost ironical look. "Nothing is going to happen to you," she told me, with perfect tranquillity.

Her face expressed complete confidence. It was as though she *knew,* as though she had made a pact with Fate, as though in exchange for her own botched life she had been given certain guarantees, received certain promises. I myself shared her confidence, but this secret knowledge of hers, by removing all risk, removed also for me all possibility of heroic posturing in the midst of perils and thus suppressed not only the danger but, in a sense, my courage as well, making me feel a little hurt.

"Not one pilot in ten will see the end of the war," I told her proudly. For a moment, a look of blank incomprehension came into her face, a frightened look. Her lips trembled and she began to cry. I took her hand—a thing I very rarely did with her: I could do it only with women.

"Nothing is going to happen to you," she said again, but this time her voice sounded almost imploring.

"No, nothing will happen to me, Mother, I promise you that."

She hesitated. Some struggle was going on inside her and it was reflected in her face. Then she made a little concession. "You may, perhaps, be wounded in the leg," she said.

She was trying to make a deal with Fate. And yet, under that sky of cypresses and white stones, it was difficult not to feel the presence of the oldest of man's destinies, the one that takes no interest and plays no part in his fate. Still, as I measured the anxiety in her eyes, as I listened to that poor woman trying so hard to make a bargain with the gods, I found it more than ever difficult to believe that they were less accessible to pity than Rinaldi, the taxi driver, less understanding than the traders in garlic and pizzas in the Buffa Market, that they could have lived so long with the Mediterranean without learning something from it. Somewhere, above our heads, an honest hand must be holding the scales, and the gods must not be allowed to play with loaded dice against a mother's heart. The whole land of Provence began to sing in my ears with its cicada voice, and it was without so much as a hint of doubt that I said: "Don't worry, Mother, of course nothing is going to happen to me."

As bad luck would have it, on our way back to the taxi, one of my commanding officers, Captain Moulignat, passed us. I saluted smartly and explained to my mother who he was. Fool that I was! In a flash, my mother had opened the door of the cab, fished out a ham, a bottle and two salami sausages and, before I could do anything to stop her, was already bowing before the captain and offering her presents, with a few appropriate words. I thought I would die of shame—as one can see, I still harbored a number of illusions, for, if it were possible to die of shame, the whole human race would long ago have vanished from the face of the earth. The captain glanced at me with astonishment and I looked back at him with such mute eloquence that, like a true gentleman, he hesitated not a moment, grabbed the sausages, the ham and the bottle, thanked my mother politely and, as she turned to the taxi, after withering me with a triumphant glance, he helped her in and saluted. Gravely, and with a royal inclination of the head, she settled herself in the back seat. I was quite certain that she was sniffing with satisfaction, having given one more proof of her tact and *savoir-vivre*, which I, her son, had sometimes had the effrontery to doubt. The taxi started and her expression changed suddenly: it was as though her face had suffered shipwreck; pressed to the window, it gazed at me with intense anxiety; she tried to say something to me through the glass but I could not catch her words and, at last, unable to make me understand what it was she wanted to say, she fixed me with her pathetic eyes and made the sign of the cross.

I must here mention an episode which I have deliberately omitted until now, thus trying to hide from it. Some months before the outbreak of the war, I had fallen in love with a young Hungarian girl who was staying in the Hôtel-Pension Mermonts. We planned to get married. Ilona had black hair and large gray eyes, just to say something about her. She went back to Budapest to see her family, the war separated us and I never saw her again; it was another defeat for me and that is all there is to it. I know that I have broken all the rules by skipping such an episode in an autobiography, but it is still too recent, only twenty years have passed, and to write even these few lines I have had to take advantage of an inflammation of the ear which has confined me to bed in a Mexican hotel: this acute but purely physical pain has acted, in a way, as an anesthetic, and made it possible for me to touch a much more painful wound.

CHAPTER *30*

THE TRAINING SQUADRON TO WHICH I WAS AT-
tached was transferred to Bordeaux-Mérignac and there I spent
five or six hours in the air every day as a bombing and navigation instructor on board a Potez-540. I was soon promoted to
sergeant. The pay wasn't too bad, France stood unshaken, glar-
ing at the enemy, and I shared the view of most of my companions that we had better enjoy life and have a good time since
the war would not go on forever. I had a room in town and
three pairs of silk pajamas, of which I was very proud. In my
eyes, they were the very symbol of luxury living and gave me the
feeling that my career as a man of the world was progressing
favorably. A girl friend of mine in law school days had stolen
them for me when a shop in which her fiancé worked had been
burnt to the ground. Since my relations with Marguerite were
strictly platonic, I felt that the moral code had been scrupulously
observed and I accepted the pajamas gratefully. They had been
slightly scorched and never entirely lost the smell of smoked
fish: but one can't have everything. I was also able, from time
to time, to treat myself to a box of cigars, which I now had
learned to smoke without feeling sick—in short, I was well on
my way to becoming a hardened warrior. At about this time,
however, I had a tiresome flying accident which very nearly cost
me my nose, a loss for which I would never have consoled myself.
I need scarcely say that it was all the fault of the Poles.

The members of the Polish forces were not, just then, very

popular with the French. We rather despised them for having lost the war. They had let themselves be soundly thrashed by the Germans in a matter of weeks and we made no bones about putting into words what we thought of them. In addition to this, the spy mania was at its peak, as is always the case when a social organism is sick and on the very verge of collapse. Every time a Polish soldier lit a cigarette he was immediately accused of communicating with the enemy. Since I spoke Polish fluently, I was employed as an interpreter on training flights, the object of which was to familiarize the Poles with our equipment. Standing between the French and Polish pilots, I translated the comments and orders of the French instructor. It was not long before this original version of combined operations bore fruit. Just as we were coming in to land, making the final approach, the French instructor decided that the Polish pilot was coming in too fast, and too long, and he shouted at me, with a hint of anxiety in his voice:

"Tell the bloody fool to throttle full or he'll have us all in the ditch!"

I at once translated the message. Yes, I can truthfully say, with a completely clear conscience, that I didn't lose a minute in saying: *"Prosze dodac gazu, bo za shwile zawalimy sie w drzewa na koncu lotniska!"*

. . . When I came to, the blood was pouring down my face, the ambulance men were bending over me, and the Pole, who was in pretty sorry shape, though not forgetful of his good manners, was trying to prop himself on one elbow in an attempt to apologize to the French pilot: *"Za pozno mi pan przytlumaczyl . . ."* "He says . . ." I began gallantly.

The French pilot was not much better off, and had only just time to utter one word before he lost consciousness: *"Merde!"*

I gave a faithful translation, after which, my duty done, I passed out. My nose was a nasty mess, but I was told there were no serious internal injuries. They were wrong, and during the next four years my nose gave me a lot of trouble. I was scarcely ever free of appalling headaches, but had to conceal my condition so as not to have my flying career prematurely ended. It was not until 1944 that my nose was completely reconstructed in an R.A.F. hospital. It is no longer the incomparable masterpiece it once was, but it serves its purpose and I have every reason to think that it will keep me company till I breathe my last.

Apart from the time I spent in the air as navigation, gunnery and bombing instructor, my friends often let me take over the controls and I put in, on an average, an hour a day piloting the aircraft. Unfortunately those precious hours had no official existence and could not be entered in my flying log. I therefore kept a second, secret record, each page of which I scrupulously authenticated with the flying-control stamp, thanks to the decency of the clerk in charge. I was convinced that, after the first war losses, the regulations would be relaxed, and that my unofficial hours, already amounting to a good four hundred, would make it possible for me to become a combat pilot.

On April 4, only a few weeks before the German offensive, while I was peacefully smoking a cigar on the airfield, an orderly brought me a telegram: *Mother seriously ill, come at once.*

I stood there in my leather flying jacket, with that ridiculous cigar in my mouth, my cap pulled down jauntily over one eye, my hands in my pockets, and the familiar tough look on my face, while the whole world around me became a strange, foreign place empty of all life. That is what I chiefly remember of that moment today: a feeling of utter strangeness, as though the most familiar things, the houses, the trees, the birds, and the very ground under my feet, all that I had come to regard as certainties, had suddenly become part of an unknown planet which I had never visited before. My whole system of weights and measures, my faith in a secret and hidden logic of life were giving way to nothingness, to a meaningless chaos, to a grinning, grimacing absurdity. I had always known that my love story was bound to end badly because of the difference in age between my mother and myself, and that she would have to be the first to leave. I still could not imagine that the end would come before justice was done. That my mother should die before I had time to fling my weight onto one tray of the scales, to re-establish the balance and demonstrate clearly, irrefutably, the fundamental decency of the world, prove that, deep at the heart of mystery, under the veil of absurdity, was hidden an honorable design, and that a smile of mercy and a light of reason shone at the very essence of things, like some first, sacred, and as yet undiscovered molecule of all matter, seemed to me the negation of the most elementary logic, of all art, of all science, of all possibility of talent or genius, of simple common sense, of the humblest two and two makes four, a final triumph of the monkey gods, reducing life to a pornography, an obscenity that would make not Christ but Hitler the symbol of this world. I do not have to point out to my readers what naïve and juvenile illusions such an attitude implied. Today I am a mature man of much experience. I have lived. I need not say more.

The special train reserved for soldiers on leave took forty-eight hours to get me to Nice. The morale of that wretched train was at its lowest ebb. It was England who had got us into this business; we were going to get it in the arse; Hitler wasn't such a bad chap, after all, we just didn't get him right; we ought to have talked things over with him, instead of listening to the Jews. But there was at least one bright spot in the sky: a new drug had been found which could cure gonorrhea in a matter of days.

Still, there was no real despair in me: I have never been gifted in that direction. The greatest effort of my life has always been the effort to give up, to attain despair and so know peace, at last. But it's no good. There is always something in me which keeps smiling.

I arrived at Nice very early in the morning, and went at once to the Mermonts. I climbed the stairs to the seventh floor, and knocked at the door. My mother occupied the smallest room in the hotel: she had the interests of the proprietor at heart. There was no answer and I walked in. The minute triangular room had a neat and empty look which terrified me. I rushed downstairs again, woke up the concierge and learned that my mother had been taken to the Saint-Antoine clinic. I jumped into a taxi.

The nurses told me later that when they saw me come in they thought at first that it was a holdup. My mother's head was deeply sunk in the pillow. Her cheeks were hollow; her face bore a troubled, worried air. I kissed her and sat down on the bed. I was wearing my leather carapace and my cap was tilted cockily over one eye: I kept my leather carapace. I kept the butt end of a cigar gripped between my teeth for hours on end: I had to have something to cling to. On the bedside table, well in evidence in its violet case, was the silver medal which I had won at the ping-pong championship of Nice in 1932. I sat there; we looked at each other; neither of us said a word. Then she asked me to draw the curtains. I drew the curtains, hesitated for a split second, and then raised my eyes to the light: she didn't have to ask; I spared her that. I remained for quite a while with my eyes raised. That was about all I could do for her. We remained completely silent, all three of us, *all three of us*. I knew that she could see him clearly, that he was present, and that she was still in love with him. I didn't have to turn my head to know that she was crying. I also knew that I had nothing to do with her tears. Then I sat down in the armchair beside the bed, and stayed in that chair for forty-eight hours. All of that time I kept my leather jacket on my back, my cap on my head, a dead cigar stub between my teeth: I needed friendship. Once she asked me whether I had any news of Ilona, my Hungarian. I told her I had not.

"You need a woman by your side," she told me.

I said something like: "All men do."

"Yes," she said. "But it'll be more difficult for you than for others. It's my fault."

We played cards. She was smoking as much as ever. The doctors, she told me, no longer forbade it. There was obviously no point any longer in worrying about her smoking. So she smoked her Gauloises, looking at me from time to time with a concentrated attention, a cunning and calculating air, and I knew that she was scheming once more, that she was cooking up something. But I was very far from suspecting what she had in mind.

I am convinced that it was then that her little scheme first entered her head. I caught a few sly, guilty looks in her eyes and knew perfectly well that she was cooking up something, but it never occurred to me, even knowing her as I did, that she would go to such extremes, that she would play such a dirty, loving trick on me. I have never really forgiven her. I had a few words with the doctor. He was reassuring. She might keep going for several years. "Diabetes, you know . . ." he said with a shrug.

On the evening of the third day, I went to dine at the Masséna, where I made the acquaintance of a Dutch *Mynheer* who was about to fly to South Africa so as to get clear away "before the German invasion starts." Without the slightest provocation on my part, and no doubt pinning his faith to my airman's uniform, he asked me whether I could find him a woman. Come to think of it, the number of men who have made that request to me in my life is pretty shattering: I had always thought that there was something rather distinguished about my appearance, but obviously there ain't. I told him that I was not in very good form that evening and that, anyway, I was on leave. He confided to me that all his money was already safely tucked away in South Africa and we went off to celebrate the good news at the Chat Noir. The *Mynheer* proved himself worthy, as far as hard spirits were concerned; personally, I hate drinking, which always, somehow, sobers me up and makes me see life and the world in their true light; but I know how to master some of my weaknesses, at least, and so we emptied a bottle of whisky between us and then switched to cognac. Very soon the word went round the cabaret that I was the first French "ace" of the war, with many victories to my credit, and two or three veterans of the 1914 war asked to be allowed to shake my hand. Much flattered at being recognized, I distributed autographs, did a good deal of handshaking and accepted round after round of drinks. The *Mynheer* introduced me to the love of his life whom he had just picked up. I had then another opportunity of judging the prestige which the Air Force uniform enjoyed among the hard-working civilian population. The sweet babe offered to make a living for me as long as the war lasted and, if need be, to follow me from one garrison to another. She assured me that she could take on up to twenty men a day. Her talk depressed me because I felt with some sadness that she was offering to do this not really for me personally, but for our heroic Air Force generally. I told her that she was making too much of her patriotism and that I wanted to be loved for myself and not for my uniform. The *Mynheer* ordered champagne and offered to bless our union by laying, so to speak, the first stone. The manager brought me the menu to sign and I was just about to oblige when I noticed a mocking eye fixed on me. The owner of the eye was not wearing a dashing leather jacket and there were no golden wings on his chest, but he could boast a Croix de Guerre with star, which was pretty good for a foot slogger in those early days of the war. I calmed down a bit. The *Mynheer* went upstairs with my patriotic babe, who made me swear to wait for her next day at the Cintra. An Air Force cap over one eye, a pair of gold wings on your chest, a leather jacket on your back, a tough look on your mug—and your financial future is assured. I had a devastating headache and my nose weighed a ton. I left the Chat Noir and plunged into the sweet fragrance of the flower market outside and then home.

I learned later that the girl with the heart of gold waited for several days from 6 P.M. till 2 A.M. at the bar of the Cintra for her sergeant.

I sometimes wonder whether I didn't pass by without knowing the greatest love of my life.

A few days later, I saw the name of my *Mynheer* on the list of victims of an air crash somewhere near Johannesburg, which only goes to show that there is no such thing as complete security for capital today.

My leave came to an end. I spent one more night in the armchair at the clinic and next morning, as soon as the curtains had been drawn, I leaned over the bed to kiss her good-by.

I don't know how to describe that parting. There are no

words. But I put on a good face. I didn't cry or anything—I remembered what she had told me, all her advice about how to behave with women. For twenty-six years, my mother had been living without a man and now, when we were parting, perhaps forever, I was a great deal more anxious to leave with her the image of a man than that of a son.

"Well, so long." I kissed her on the cheek with a smile. What that smile cost me only she could know, because she, too, smiled.

"You must get married when she comes back," she said. "That's exactly the kind of girl you need. She is very lovely."

She must have been wondering what would become of me without a woman at my side. She was right: I have never got used to that.

"Have you a picture of her?"

"Yes."

"Do you think her family has any money?"

"I've no idea."

"When she went to Bruno Walter's concert at Cannes, she didn't take the bus, she went in a taxi. So they must be rich."

"I don't care whether they are or not, Mother."

"When you're in the Diplomatic Service, you will have to do a lot of entertaining. You will have to have servants and your wife must be well dressed. Her parents should realize that."

I took her hand. "Mother," I said. "Mother."

"I'll tell them one or two things, tactfully, of course."

"Really, Mother . . ."

"And don't worry about me. I'm an old warhorse. I've kept going till now and I can carry on for a bit longer. Take off your cap."

I took it off. She made the sign of the cross on my forehead with her finger. *"Blagoslavliayou tiebia*—I give you my blessing."

My mother was a Jewess. But that didn't matter. She had to express herself somehow. In what language was of no importance to her.

I went to the door. We looked at each other once more; we

were both smiling. I felt quite calm. Something of her courage had passed into me and it has remained with me ever since. Her courage and her will continue to burn in me even now and make life very difficult, when it would be so easy to give up, to give in. She has condemned me to gaiety, and to hope.

CHAPTER *31*

I NEVER IMAGINED THAT FRANCE COULD LOSE the war. I knew, of course, that she had already lost one in 1870, but at that time I was not yet born nor, for that matter, was my mother. It was all very different.

On June 13, 1940, when the front was crumbling everywhere, I was returning to base from a bombing mission in a Bloch-210 and landed at Tours to refuel. The Heinkels and Junkers chose that moment to bomb the airfield and I was most ingloriously wounded in the leg. The wound was not serious and I left the splinter in my thigh. I could imagine the pride with which my mother would feel it when I next went on leave.

The lightning successes of the German offensive failed to impress me. We had seen the same sort of thing in the '14-'18 war. We French had a knack for restoring the situation at the very last moment: everyone knew that. The thought of Guderian's tanks plunging ahead through the Sedan gap made me laugh and I pictured our General Staff rubbing its hands as it watched its master plan unfolding stage by stage and those fat-headed Germans once again falling into a well-prepared trap. An invincible belief in the destiny of my fatherland ran in my blood, no doubt bequeathed to me by my Jewish and Tartar ancestors. My commanding officers at Bordeaux-Mérignac must have guessed in me those atavistic qualities of loyalty to our traditions and blind faith, for I was detailed together with two other crews to carry out patriotic air patrols over the working-class districts of Bordeaux. The purpose of these patrols, we were told, was to protect Marshal Pétain, who was determined to continue the struggle against the Germans, and against a Communist fifth column which was preparing to seize power and come to terms with Hitler. Yes: such was the explanation given us during the briefing, and I am happy to say that I am not the only witness, as I was not the only dupe, of this piece of abominable cunning. Brigades of cadets, among them Christian Fouchet, our present ambassador to Denmark, had been told the same fairy tale and stood guard in the streets with their machine guns ready to fire, their hearts overflowing with love and gratitude for the old Marshal who refused to listen to defeatists and was determined to fight to the end. I am still convinced, however, that this adroit piece of trickery had been initiated without orders from the top, by some well-meaning colonels at Mérignac, in the heady political atmosphere of the moment. Completely unaware of this indignity, unable to see Pétain otherwise than as the embodiment of every military virtue, I carried out my low-altitude patrols over Bordeaux, with my machine guns loaded, ready to drop my bombs and to open fire on any suspect mob at the first wireless signal from base. I would have done so without the slightest hesitation, and it never entered my mind that the real fifth column had already won the day and that it was not made up of those who march openly in the streets with flags flying, but was something that worms its way insidiously into the soul, paralyzing the will and corrupting the mind. I was temperamentally incapable of imagining that a legendary leader, who had reached the topmost rank of the oldest and most glorious army in the world and whose name my mother mentioned in a hushed tone of almost religious reverence, could suddenly reveal himself as a defeatist, a man with a deep secret flaw in his make-up, a schemer who could put his personal hatreds, grudges and political passions above the good name of his country. The Dreyfus affair had taught me nothing. In the first place, Esterhazy was not a true Frenchman, having become a French citizen only by naturalization and, anyway, the whole business had been designed to bring dishonor on a Jew, and we all know that, with such a purpose at heart, everything is permissible; our beloved military leaders, at the time of the Dreyfus affair, were simply doing their best. In short, I had kept my faith intact to the bitter end, and to this day I doubt that I have much changed in that respect: disastrous idiocy such as underlies our defeat at Dien Bien Phu, or certain dirty and bloody hands acting behind the scenes in the Algerian struggle, still leave me bewildered and unbelieving.

And so, each time the enemy advanced, each time the front rumbled a bit more, I smiled with a knowing air and waited for that lightning counterstroke of our beloved leaders which was going to come as such a complete surprise to the enemy, for that ironic, dazzling, masterful *"Touché!"* of our military geniuses who had the Germans exactly where they wanted them. My atavistic inaptitude for despair, a flaw in my genes about which I can do nothing, was now taking the form of some happy, congenital idiocy. As the shadows darkened, all I saw in them was a greater opportunity for a dazzling light. As defeat followed defeat, I waited unperturbed for the moment when the genius of France should suddenly become incarnate in a Man of Destiny, in accordance with the best traditions of our history. Yes, I was a fool, and a fool I shall always be, when it is a matter of believing, of fighting, of carrying on, of smiling in the face of nothingness. There is no despair in me and my idiocy is of the kind that death itself cannot defeat. I have always had a tendency to take literally the fine stories which humanity loves to tell about itself in its noble moments of inspiration, and such inspired narrative talent has never been lacking in us French. My mother's dazzling genius, where fairy tales were concerned, suddenly revealed itself in me and soared to unexpected heights. I believed in all our beloved leaders and in each I recognized the Man of Destiny, and as soon as one of them crumbled and vanished from the stage, I was already on to the next. Thus I believed successively in General Gamelin, in General Georges, in General Weygand—I remember with what throbs of emotion I read in the press the description of his rawhide boots and his leather breeches when, as the latest Man of Destiny, he ran jauntily down the steps of his headquarters at the age of seventy-three; I believed in General Huntziger, in General Blanchard, in General Mittelhauser, in Admiral Darlan—and thus arrived at General de Gaulle, always standing to attention and saluting smartly. One can well imagine my relief when my stubborn belief in our final victory and my congenital inability to despair suddenly lit on the right person, and from the very pit of disaster there emerged, exactly as I anticipated, the extraordinary figure of a leader who not only found in the terrible events the full measure of his stature, but also bore a name which truly smacked of our land and of our ancestors. Each time I find myself in de Gaulle's presence, I feel that my mother did not deceive me and that she knew what she was talking about.

I immediately decided to follow de Gaulle to England with three of my friends, in a Den-55, an entirely new type of aircraft which none of us had ever piloted before.

The airfield at Bordeaux-Mérignac, on the 15th, 16th and 17th of June, 1940, was certainly one of the strangest places the world has ever seen. From every corner of the sky innumerable aircraft of every size and shape were coming in to land in a continual stream, piling up on the ground. Bizarre machines of which I knew neither the type nor the purpose, some of them dating from the First World War and others barely emerged from blueprint, were disgorging onto the grass passengers who were even more bizarre, many of whom seemed simply to have availed themselves of the first means of transport that had come their way.

The landing ground was thus becoming a sort of retrospective of all the prototypes which the Army of the Air had evolved in the course of the last twenty years: before dying, the French Air Force was remembering its past. The machines were less strange than their crews. I saw a young pilot of the Fleet Air Arm, with one of the most impressive displays of medals you could ever hope to see on a warrior's chest, step down from the cockpit of his fighter plane with a little girl asleep in his arms whom he must have held on his knees during the flight. I saw another pilot disembark from his Goéland plane with what could only have been a party of agreeable inmates of a third-rate provincial brothel. I saw, in a Simoun aircraft, a white-haired sergeant and a woman in slacks with two dogs, a cat, a canary, a parrot, two rolled carpets and a picture by Hubert Robert propped against the side of the cockpit. I saw a decent-looking bourgeois, his wife and two young girls, all carrying suitcases, inquiring from a pilot of a 540 Potez how much he would ask to take them to Spain, and the *paterfamilias* was wearing the ribbon of the Legion of Honor. I saw, and shall never forget, the faces of my comrades, pilots of the Dewoitines-520 and the Moranes-406 fighter planes, just back from their last combats with their wings riddled with bullets, and their young commander tearing off his Croix de Guerre and stamping it into the ground. I saw a good thirty or so generals standing around the control tower, waiting for nothing and looking like nothing. I saw inexperienced pilots, my pupils at the Air Force Academy, grabbing without orders the Bloch-151 fighter planes and taking off without ammunition, with no other hope but that of crash-diving their machines into the enemy bombers, which constant alerts led us to believe were on the way, though they never came. And always the weird, the incredible aerial fauna fleeing the shipwreck of the sky, among which the sinister shapes of the Bloch-210, the famous "flying coffins," looked like some particularly symbolic birds of ill-omen.

But I think it is our dear old Potez-25 aircraft that I shall remember best and most lovingly, together with their elderly pilots, whom we never saw without humming a popular song of the time "*Grand-père, grand-père, vous oubliez votre cheval.*" These old men of forty and fifty, some of them veterans of the First World War, had, in spite of the pilots' insignia which they so proudly sported, been employed in this other and so different war only in the lowly non-flying tasks: orderly-room clerks, scribes and the like. For months now, reassuring promises had been made to them: a little more patience and they would be trained and restored to the dignity of flying crews, for liaison duties. Those promises had never been kept; and now they were taking matters into their own hands. Grabbing such Potez-25's as were available, they were catching up, embarking on a course of self-training, and were calmly piling up flying hours, indifferent to the signs of doom all around them, calmly circling above the airfield like passengers taking swimming lessons in the midst of a shipwreck. There were a good twenty or so of these hearty men in their late forties, all convinced that they were going to be ready in time "for the first real battles," as they put it, with a magnificent show of contempt for everything that had happened or would happen before their own splendid appearance in the sky. So intent were they on their self-appointed task that, in the middle of this fantastic aerial Dunkirk, in this atmosphere of the end of the world, hovering above the heads of defeated generals, mingling with the most hybrid and grotesque fauna that had ever filled the sky, above the scheming, conspiring, desperate, treacherous heads and weak, rotten hearts, the Potez-25's of those old-timers continued with their purposeful roaring, touching down and taking off again, while, from the open cockpits, the grinning and determined faces of those ancestors, pig-headed enough to ignore despair, responded to the loving greetings which we waved to them. They were the France of good wine and sunlit anger which thrusts irresistibly upward from her deep roots, grows and blooms against all odds. They were schoolmasters, workmen, butchers, insurance clerks, grocers, bums, and there even was a priest among them. But they all had one thing in common, where it should be in a man.

On the day France fell, I was sitting with my back against the wall of a hangar, watching the warming-up of the Den-55 which was to take us to England. I was thinking of the silk pajamas I had had to leave behind in my room in Bordeaux, a terrible loss when you think that I had to add to it the loss of France and of my mother whom, in all probability, I should never see again. Three of my buddies, sergeants like myself, were with me. There was a look of cold fury in our eyes and loaded revolvers were tucked under our belts. We were a long way from the front but we were young and frustrated in our manhood, and the revolvers, naked, black and menacing, were merely symbols, a visual means of expressing our feelings. They helped us to attune ourselves to the mood of tragedy, and also served as camouflage for our sense of impotence, confusion and uselessness. None of us had done any fighting and de Gaches ironically put into words our pathetic efforts to give ourselves airs, to take refuge in an attitude and to make it plain that we would have nothing to do with defeat: "It's rather as though Corneille and Racine had been forbidden to write, in order to say later that France had no tragic poets."

In spite of my determination to think only of the loss of my silk pajamas, my mother's face kept appearing to me among all the other lights of that cloudless June. It was in vain that I then clenched my teeth, stuck out my chin, clasped my revolver; tears straightway filled my eyes and I was careful to stare hard at the sun so as to put my companions off the scent. My good friend, Belle-Gueule, who squatted next to me, also had a moral problem which he confided to us. He was a ponce in civil life and, of all his women, the one whom he preferred worked in a Bordeaux brothel. He felt, he told us, that it wasn't "regular" to clear off and leave her behind. I tried to bolster up his morale by explaining that loyalty to one's country must take precedence over every other consideration, even of the noblest nature, adding that I, too, was leaving behind me all that I most valued. I quoted the example of our third companion, Jean-Pierre, who hadn't hesitated to abandon his wife and three children in order to go to England and carry on the fight. Belle-Gueule's reply was admirable and had the effect of putting us all in our place:

"That's all very well for you," he said. "You're not in my line of business, so you just aren't bound by our moral code."

De Gaches was to pilot the plane. He had three hundred hours of flying time behind him: a fortune. With his little mustache, his uniform made for him by Lanvin and his general air of breeding, he was the very type of the young man of good family, and his presence helped us a great deal, for it seemed to give our decision to desert to England the blessing of the fine, sound French Catholic bourgeoisie.

Apart from our determination to refuse defeat, the three of us had very little in common. But we derived from everything that separated us a feeling of exaltation and an increased confidence in the single bond which united us. Had there been a murderer among us, we would have seen in his presence a further proof of the sacred, exemplary character of our mission, which made everything else futile and irrelevant, so that our differences only underlined our fundamental fraternity.

De Gaches climbed into the Den to get a few last-minute instructions from the mechanic about the handling of an aircraft none of us had ever flown before. We were to make one trial run around the airfield, then land in order to let the mechanic out, and then take to the air again, setting a course for England. De Gaches took the controls and Belle-Gueule and Jean-Pierre were the first to join him. I was having some difficulty with the belt of my parachute. I managed to fix it and already had one foot on the ladder when I saw an airman on a bicycle pedaling at full speed in my direction, waving. I waited.

"Sergeant, you're wanted at the control tower. A telephone message for you, urgent."

I was petrified. The fact that, in the middle of the shipwreck, when the roads, telegraph lines and all means of communication were in a state of complete chaos, when commanding officers had lost contact with their troops and all trace of organization had disappeared under the onslaught of German tanks and the Luftwaffe, my mother's voice had managed to reach me seemed almost supernatural.

For I had not the slightest doubt that it was my mother calling. At the time of the Sedan breakthrough, and later still, when the German motorcyclists were already touring the châteaux of the Loire, I had tried to get a reassuring message through to her, begging her to remember Joffre, Pétain, Foch and all those other consecrated names which she had so often quoted to me in times of stress, when our financial situation was filling me with anxiety, or when she was suffering an acute insulin reaction. But, at that time, there had still been some semblance of order in the tele- phone network, regulations were being strictly observed and a private conversation even of such capital importance had been out of the question.

I shouted to de Gaches to go ahead with the trial round with- out me and then to pick me up at the hangar, after which I borrowed the corporal's bicycle and pedaled off.

I was only a few yards from the control tower when the Den started off down the runway. I dismounted and, before going into the building, took a casual look at the plane. The Den was already about sixty feet from the ground. It seemed to hang motionless in the air, then it rose high on its tail, swung left on one wing, dived into the earth and exploded immediately. I stared for one brief second at the column of black smoke which I was to see so often hanging over so many fallen friends. I was experiencing the first sudden blast of that total and lightning- quick loneliness which each new loss of a comrade, more than a hundred of them, burned deep into my soul, until it left in my eyes an emptiness, and on my face an air of absence which is, or so they say, my permanent expression today. After four years of fighting with a squadron of which only five members are still alive, emptiness has become for me a densely populated place. All the new friendships I have attempted since the war have made me only more conscious of that absence which dwells beside me. I have often forgotten their names, their laughter and their voices have receded farther and farther away, but even all I have forgotten makes the emptiness at my side the most fra- ternal thing I know. The sky, the ocean, the beach at Big Sur— I always haunt those empty stretches where there is enough room for all those who are no longer there. I keep trying to fill the void with animals, with dogs, with birds, with elephants, with books, and each time a seal throws himself down from a rock and swims toward the shore, or when cormorants and sea gulls tighten their circle around me, my craving for friendship and for company takes the form of a childish and ridiculous hope and I cannot help smiling and stretching out an imploring hand.

I forced my way through the crowd of twenty or thirty generals who were going round and round in circles like a lot of herons fishing in a marsh, and headed straight for the switchboard.

Through the telephone exchanges of Mérignac and of Bordeaux, the last gasps of a country in its death throes were reaching the outside world. When Churchill hurried to France in an attempt to prevent the signing of the armistice, it was from Bordeaux that the lines carried his angry voice; it was from Mérignac that a few curious generals were still trying to discover the full extent of the disaster; it was from there that the journalists and ambassadors who had followed the Government in its retreat from Paris cabled and telephoned. Now it was all almost over, and the lines were becoming strangely silent, and over the whole country, in the dying army, the responsibility for taking decisions in the cut-off units had fallen to the company or even to the section level. There were no more orders for our generals to give and the last twists and spasms of the national agony were taking place in the tragic skirmishes of a heroic few, a matter of hours or even of minutes, just barely the time to die, short, bloody, spasmodic, silent fights which could be followed on no maps and are recorded nowhere, except in some mother's heart.

I found my friend Sergeant Dufour at the switchboard, which he had kept going for the past twenty-four hours. His face was running with the sweat of that hot June, a sweat that was coming from the very pores of France. There was a look of pigheaded obstinacy on his face and the burned-out stub of a cigarette was hanging from his lips. His cheeks were covered with a hard stubble which gave him a more than usually rough and aggressive appearance. There must have been the same angry, insolent and mocking look on his face when, three years later, he fell in the Maquis under German bullets.

Ten days earlier, when I had tried to get a message through to my mother, he had said to me with a cynical twist of the lips that "things aren't as bad as all that" and that "the situation doesn't justify so extreme a measure." But now it was he himself who had sent for me and was giving me this chance, and that fact told me more about the military situation than all the rumors flying around. He was watching me in a rage, almost with hate, all his buttons undone, and indignation, contempt and a rebellious refusal to submit and accept defeat somehow showed even in his gaping fly and in the three deep horizontal obstinate lines on his forehead—and it was his features that I borrowed some fifteen years later when, writing my *Roots of Heaven*, I was looking for a face to give my hero Morel, the man who didn't know how to despair, how to give in. He watched me, with the receiver at his ear. It was as though he were listening to music with a sort of grim delight. I waited while he stared and, under his eyelids, red and smarting from lack of sleep, there was still enough room for a spark of gaiety. I wondered what conversation he was overhearing with such *sans-gêne*. Perhaps that of the Commander in Chief with his advanced elements? My curiosity was soon satisfied.

"Brossard's off to England, to carry on under de Gaulle. I've just arranged for him to say good-by to his wife. What about you, sugar? Maybe you've changed your mind?"

I shook my head and he nodded approval. That's how I learned that Sergeant Dufour had been blocking all the lines just to give a few rebels a chance to exchange a last cry of love and faith with their families before leaving them forever. The generals, politicians and other schemers, busy with the armistice, were meeting with silence from the telephone exchange.

I harbor no resentment against the men who were responsible for the defeat and the armistice of 1940. I understand, only too well, those who refused to follow de Gaulle.

They were too snugly dug-in in their warm and nicely furnished intellectual holes, which they called "the human condition." They had learned wisdom, that poisoned draught with its sickly taste of humility, renunciation and acceptance, which the habit of living drips, drop by drop, down our throats. Well read, knowing, prudent, experienced, subtle, cultivated, skeptical, secretly aware that Man is an impossible temptation, they had sadly welcomed Hitler's victory as being in the nature of things. Conscious of our biological and metaphysical servitude, they had quite naturally agreed to give it its logical social and political conclusion. I shall even go further and say, without wishing to insult anyone, that they were right, that they had *reason* on their side—and that fact alone should have been enough to put them on their guard. They had *reason* on their side, in the sense of prudence, of refusing to plunge into adventure, in the sense of "let us keep out of this"—in the sense that would have spared Jesus from dying on the cross, would have kept Van Gogh from painting, my own Morel from defending the elephants, Frenchmen of the Resistance from being tortured and shot, and which would have united in the same nothingness, by keeping them from being born in tears, blood and sacrifice, all mankind's cathedrals and museums, all our civilizations, religions and empires.

And it goes without saying that they had not been exposed to my mother's simple-minded idea of France. They felt no obligation to risk their lives in defense of a nursery tale, of a never-never land in the heart and mind of an old woman. I cannot hold it against them that, not having been born in the wastes of the Russian steppe, of mixed Jewish, Tartar and Cossack ancestry, they should have had a more calm, realistic and level-headed view of France.

A few minutes later I was listening to my mother's voice on the telephone. I am quite unable to put down on paper what it was that we said to one another. It was a succession of cries, of words, sobs and primeval animal sounds which have nothing in common with any articulate language. I have ever since had the feeling that I can understand animals. When, in the African night, I lay in my tent listening to the voices of wild beasts, I always recognized those that were cries of pain, of terror, of utter panic. Ever since that telephone conversation, I have instantly recognized, in all the forests of the world, the cry of the female who has lost her young.

The only comprehensible words, poor, comic words borrowed from the age-old vocabulary of men at war, were the last that reached my ear. When silence had already fallen between us and it seemed as though it was all over, when there was not even a crackling on the line and the silence seemed to have swallowed up the whole country, I suddenly heard a ridiculous voice, sobbing out far, far away: "We'll get them!"

That last foolish cry of the most elementary, the most naïve form of human courage, sank deep into my heart and remains there forever. It *is* my heart. I know that it will live long after I am dead and that, someday or other, mankind will know a victory far greater than anything we can imagine.

I stayed there a moment longer in my leather jacket, with my cap pulled down over one eye, feeling as lonely as millions and millions of men have always felt when confronted by their common destiny. Sergeant Dufour looked at me over his dangling cigarette and, in his eyes, there was that sacred spark of gaiety which has always been for me, whenever I see it in human eyes, like a guarantee of survival and the only light Man has ever managed to steal from the gods.

I then set about finding another plane and another crew. I spent many hours wandering about the airfield, going from one machine to another, from one crew to another.

I had already been given a very hostile reception by several pilots whom I had tried to talk into taking me to England when I remembered a huge, four-engine Farman which had landed the previous evening. I thought it was about the right size to get me to England. It was certainly the biggest airplane I had ever seen. There appeared to be no sign of life in the monster. Prompted by nothing more than simple curiosity, I climbed the ladder and poked my head inside just to see what it was like. A two-star general was smoking his pipe and writing something at a folding table. A heavy revolver lay on a sheet of paper within reach of his hand. He had a young, nice face and gray, closely-cropped hair. As I clambered into the plane, he looked at me in an absent-minded manner, then returned to his writing. I saluted smartly, but he didn't even seem to have noticed me.

I stared with some surprise at the revolver and suddenly its meaning dawned upon me. The defeated general was writing a farewell letter before blowing his brains out. I must confess that I felt deeply moved and immensely grateful. It seemed to me that so long as there were generals capable of such a gesture all hope was not lost. What I had before my eyes was a picture of true human greatness, of tragedy, to which, at my age, I was extremely responsive.

I saluted again, discreetly withdrew and walked a few paces up and down the runway, waiting for the honor-saving shot. After a quarter of an hour or so, I began to get worried and, returning to the Farman, once more poked my nose inside. The general was still busy writing, covering the paper with his neat and elegant script. I noticed two or three envelopes already piled up under the revolver. Once more he looked at me, once more I saluted smartly and once more I respectfully withdrew. I desperately needed somebody whom I could trust and this general, with his young and noble face, inspired me with just the right confidence, and so I waited patiently for him to give a boost to my morale. However, since nothing happened, I decided to take a walk around the crew's quarters and find out what I could about the squadron's plan to seek asylum in Portugal, before going on to England.

I returned some half an hour later and climbed the ladder. The general was still writing. The sheets covered with his neat script had accumulated under the heavy revolver which lay within easy reach of his hand. Suddenly it came to me that, far from having any sublime intention worthy of a hero of Greek tragedy, the good general was quite simply dealing with his mail and using his revolver as a paperweight. Apparently we were not inhabiting the same universe, he and I. I was horribly disappointed and discouraged, and walked away from the Farman, my head low. I saw the big chief again, some time later, with the revolver back in its holster, his brief case held firmly in his hand and a look as of duty done on his calm, composed face.

A glorious sunshine lit up the bizarre aerial fauna assembled on the field. Heavily armed Senegalese troops were stationed round the machines as a protection against purely hypothetical sabotage; they were looking with an almost superstitious apprehension at the disquieting birds descending on them from the sky. I remember a pot-bellied Bréguet, the fuselage of which ended in a beam, which looked very much like a wooden leg and was as incongruous and grotesque as certain African fetishes. At the Potez section, the unconquered grandfathers of '14-'18 were still busily training for the miracle to come, and the drone of their engines was the only purposeful sound in the blue sky. When they landed, they expressed gravely their firm conviction that they would reach the front in time to take things into their experienced hands. I remember one who emerged from his Potez looking the very image of a knight of the air of the Richthofen-Guynemer period, complete with a silk stocking pulled over his head and cavalry breeches, panting a bit from the acrobatic feat involved in a man of his weight getting out of the cockpit. He gave me a slap on the shoulder and shouted: "Cheer up, old cock, we're here!"

He pushed away the two pals who had helped him to reach the ground and made a beeline for the bottles of beer waiting on the grass. The two pals, one wearing a khaki tunic with ten dangling decorations, helmeted and booted, the other crowned with a beret, his goggles pushed up on his forehead and arrayed in a Saumur cavalry tunic and puttees, gave me a meaningful wink and assured me: "We'll get them!"

They were obviously living the best moments of their lives. They were at once touching and absurd and yet, with their puttees, their silk stockings pulled over their heads, their slightly bloated but resolute faces emerging from the open cockpits, they did somehow manage to evoke the memory of more glorious days. Besides, I had never so much felt the need of a father as

I did then. This was a feeling which the whole of France shared and was the real reason why almost to a man the whole country gave itself to the old Marshal. I tried to make myself useful. I helped them into their machines, I swung the propeller, I ran to the canteen for more beer. They spoke to me of the Miracle of the Marne with knowing winks, of Guynemer and Joffre, of Foch and Verdun—in short, they spoke to me of my mother, and that was all I wanted. One of them, stiff with leather—leather leggings, leather helmet, leather jacket, leather shoulder straps and belt, leather gloves—ended up by shouting in a voice which easily dominated the roar of the engines: "F—— it all, they'll see what they'll see!," after which, pushed by me and helped by two others, he hoisted himself into the cockpit, caught his breath, lowered the goggles over his eyes, grabbed the stick and leaped into the air. Perhaps I am being a little unjust, but I can't help thinking that the dear old things were chiefly concerned with savoring revenge against the French High Command for refusing to let them fly, and that their "They'll see what they'll see" was directed against their own superiors at least as much as against the Germans.

I was making another of my fruitless journeys to squadron headquarters to see whether there was any news of the conspiracy to take off for Portugal, when one of the orderlies told me that a young woman was asking for me at the guardroom. I had a superstitious fear of going too far from the airfield lest the squadron take off for England while my back was turned. But a young woman is a young woman and off I trekked to the guardroom, where I was rather disappointed to find a childish-looking girl with narrow shoulders and waist, but wide hips and solid thighs, buttocks and calves, whose face and eyes, puffed and red with crying, gave evidence of some deep grief and also of a sort of obstinate, primitive determination which showed itself also in the unnecessary violence with which she gripped the handle of the suitcase she held. She told me that her name was Annick, and that she had been the girl friend of Sergeant Clément, known as Belle-Gueule, who had often talked to her about me as his pal, the "diplomat and writer." I was seeing her for the first time, though Belle-Gueule had often spoken of her in terms of the highest praise. He had two or three girls working for him but Annick was his favorite and he had fixed her up in a Bordeaux brothel when he was posted to Mérignac. Belle-Gueule had never made any mystery of the fact that he was a pimp in civilian life and, just about the time of the German offensive, he had been the object of a disciplinary inquiry and was expecting any day to be struck off the flying list. We were on pretty good terms, he and I, perhaps because we had nothing in common and the very extent of our difference had established, by contrast, some strange sort of bond between us. I must, however, also confess that, though I was repelled by the deplorable way in which he made his living, it had a certain fascination for me and even made me slightly envious, since it presupposed a total lack of sensitivity and of scruples, as well as a high level of indifference and callousness—indispensable qualities to anyone wanting to get along well with life, in all which I was painfully deficient. He had often boasted to me of Annick's earnestness and devotion, of her great working capacity, and I knew that he was very much taken with her. I studied her with a good deal of curiosity. She was the commonplace type of young peasant girl who was accustomed to never sparing herself, though behind the little obstinate forehead and in the clear, attentive eyes there seemed to be something more, something that went far beyond what one happened to be, what one happened to be doing, something that made the fact that she was "working" in a brothel irrelevant. I liked her at once, for no better reason than that, in my state of nervous tension, the presence of any woman could bring me comfort and peace. Yes, she said, breaking in on my description of the accident, yes, she knew that Clément had been killed. He had told her more than once that he was going to make his way to England, to carry on the struggle. She was to have joined him later by way of Spain. Clément was no more but she wanted to go to England, all the same. She wasn't going to work for the Germans. She wanted to be with those who were going to keep on fighting. She knew that she could be useful in England. At least, she would have a clear conscience and would have done her best. Could I help her? She stared at me with silent supplication, gripping her little bag in so determined a way and with that obstinate look in her eyes, so anxious to do her best, so eager to carry on as if Clément were still alive. One could not help seeing in her a basic purity and strength of character, a spark of essential beauty that no ephemeral and irrelevant soiling of the body could destroy. With her, it was less a question, I think, of being faithful to the memory of my friend than of an instinctive devotion to something that is entirely beyond the reach of any dirt, beyond what a man is or does. In the prevailing climate of abandon and discouragement, she conjured up an image of a constancy and a determination to do what was right which struck me as profoundly touching. I have never been able to accept the view that the sexual behavior of human beings is the yardstick of good and evil, and have always looked for human dignity elsewhere, at the level of the heart, the spirit and the soul, where our most infamous prostitutions are always taking place. This little Breton girl seemed to me to have a greater instinctive understanding of what is and what is not important than all the upholders of traditional morality. She must have read in my eyes some sign of sympathy because she redoubled her efforts to convince me—as though I needed convincing. The French soldiers in England were going to be very lonely: something must be done to help them and she wasn't one to be afraid of work. Perhaps Clément had told me as much. She paused a moment, anxious to know whether Belle-Gueule had, in fact, paid her that tribute or whether he had, perhaps, not thought of it. Sure, I hastened to assure her, he had told me many good things about her. She flushed with pleasure. Yes, she knew all about work, she had a strong back and could put up with almost anything. I could safely take her to England in my plane and, since I had been Clément's best friend, she would work for me—an airman always needed to feel that he had someone on the ground to care for him: everyone knew that.

I thanked her and explained that I already had someone in Nice who was doing precisely that. I also told her that it was almost impossible to find a machine bound for England, as I had recently learned to my cost, that it was quite hopeless to think of such a thing for a civilian, and a woman would not even be admitted on the airfield in the first place. But she was not a girl to be easily put off. When I tried to get out of the difficulty by telling her that she could be just as useful in France as in England, and that the French were going to need fine women like her, she gave me a sweet smile, just to make it clear that she wasn't angry with me, and then, without another word, she walked away with her suitcase in her hand. I saw her, a little later, among the crews of the Potez-63's, deep in argument, after which I lost sight of her. I have no idea what became of her. I trust that she is still alive, that she eventually got to England and did well there, that she eventually returned to France and gave us a lot of children. We could do with more women as staunch-hearted as she and I hope that her breed will multiply.

By the end of the afternoon, a rumor spread that the Mérignac air base was running short of fuel. The crews were guarding their machines in relays as there had already been several instances when pilots found their tanks emptied by fuel thieves, and there were prowlers like me looking for some means of escape and ready to grab a plane as soon as its pilot's back was turned. The air crews waited. They were waiting for orders, for instructions, for some piece of information which might clarify the situation and help them make up their minds. They were thinking matters over, hesitating, wondering what would be the best step to take, whether to go to England or to North Africa, or not thinking at all but just waiting for something to happen—they didn't know what. The majority was convinced that the war was going to be carried on from North Africa. Some were so utterly lost, so completely bewildered and out of their depth that the most harmless question about their intentions made them fly into a rage. My suggestion of going to England was always badly received. The English were unpopular. They had dragged us into the war and now they were re-embarking their troops at Dunkirk and leaving us to face the music. The noncoms of three Potez-63's crowded round me with hatred in their faces and talked about putting me under arrest for attempted desertion. Fortunately, the senior of the three, a flight sergeant, adopted a more indulgent and more human attitude. While the other two held my arms, he contented himself with punching me in the face until my nose and mouth were streaming with blood. After this, they emptied a bottle of beer over my head and let me go. I still had my revolver stuck in my belt and the temptation to use it was almost irresistible. It was, in fact, about the strongest temptation to which I have ever been exposed in the whole course of my life. But it would have been silly to start my war by killing Frenchmen, so I swallowed hard and stumbled away, wiping the beer from my face and feeling as frustrated as any man could be who had not been able to relieve himself of his most natural urges. I find it very difficult to bring myself to kill Frenchmen, and so far as I know, have never killed any. I am afraid that my country could never rely on me in a civil war and I have always refused to command a firing squad, which is probably the result of some obscure complex due to my foreign birth.

Ever since my crash, I had taken punches on the nose badly, and for several days I was in terrible pain. But I would be ungrateful indeed if I did not recognize that this purely physical suffering did a lot for me, since it helped me, to some extent at least, to feel the fall of France less acutely and to dwell less on the fact that I would probably never see my mother again. My head was bursting, I was constantly wiping blood from my nose and mouth, and I kept being seized by spasms of nausea and vomiting. In fact, I was in such a state that, as far as I was concerned, Hitler was within an inch or two of winning the war. Nevertheless, I continued to drag myself around the airfield in search of a willing crew or an unguarded plane.

One of the pilots whom I attempted to win over to my way of thinking left an indelible impression on me. He was the owner of an Ayot-372, a factory-fresh machine of the most recent type. I say "owner" because he sat on the grass beside it, looking like a suspicious peasant keeping a watchful eye on his precious cow. An impressive pile of sandwiches was set out on a piece of newspaper in front of him and he was busy devouring these one after the other. In appearance he reminded me a little of Saint-Exupéry: the same roundness of face and features, the same massive, broad-shouldered body—but there the resemblance stopped. He seemed to be suspicious and on his guard, and his revolver holster was unfastened as though he were convinced that the Mérignac airfield was crowded with cattle thieves ready to snatch his cow from under his nose—and he had a point there. I told him straight out that I was looking for a plane and a patriotic crew willing to go to England to carry on the war from there, and painted a picture of the courage and greatness of that country in my mother's best epic style.

He let me talk while he continued to absorb nourishment, at the same time examining, with some placid interest, my bruised and swollen face and the blood-stained handkerchief I kept pressing to my nose. I made a pretty good job of that speech— a patriotic, moving and inspired effort if ever there was one. Suffering though I was from violent spasms of nausea—I could scarcely stand on my feet, and my head felt as though it were filled with pieces of chipped rock—I still did my best, and, to judge from the satisfied look on the face of my one-man audience, he must have found the contrast between my sorry appearance and my enthusiastic oratory agreeably diverting. Anyway, he did nothing to interrupt me. He must have felt flattered—he was just the type to enjoy feeling important—and then, too, my high lyrical flights, with my hand on my heart, probably helped his digestion. Now and again I paused, waiting humbly for some reaction to my eloquence; since his face remained expressionless and he merely took another sandwich, I resumed my siren's song, a true call to glory and a hymn to the fatherland which Déroulède himself would not have disowned. Once, when I produced something equivalent to Hugo's *"mourir pour la patrie est le sort le plus beau, le plus digne d'envie,*" he gave a just perceptible nod of approval, then, interrupting his chewing, removed a scrap of ham from between his teeth with a dirty fingernail. When I broke off for a moment to get my breath, he looked at me with what seemed to be an air of reproach, waiting for me to continue to entertain him—he was obviously determined to make me give my best performance. At last, I finished my song—there is no other word for it—and fell silent. He saw that there was nothing more to be got out of me, took his eyes off my face, grabbed another sandwich, and looked up at the sky in search of some fresh object of interest. He had not uttered a single word, and I shall never know whether he was a traditionally prudent son of Normandy, an insensitive brute, a complete imbecile, a quietly determined man who knew exactly what he wanted but did not intend to confide his decision to anybody, a person completely bewildered by events whose nervous reaction was to stuff himself with food, or a crafty peasant with nothing in the world to care about but his cow and determined to stick by her to the end. His little eyes looked at me without the slightest trace of expression while, one foot forward, my head raised proudly, I proclaimed our unshakable decision to continue the struggle and sang a paean to honor, valor, victory and a glorious tomorrow. I must admit that there was a certain bovine grandeur about him. Whenever I read somewhere that a bullock has won first prize at an agricultural show, I always think of him.

When, at last, I gave up and turned away, he was starting on the last of his sandwiches. I, myself, had eaten nothing since the previous day. Since the German breakthrough, the menu in the sergeants' mess had been particularly tempting, French cooking at its best, worthy of our great traditions and designed, no doubt, to build up our morale and to still our doubts by reminding us of the basic and permanent values of our country. But I dared not leave the airfield for fear of missing the chance of getting away. Above all, I was thirsty, and I gratefully accepted some red wine offered me by the crew of a Potez-63 lolling on the grass in the shade of the wings. Perhaps under the influence of the strong Bordeaux on an empty stomach, I launched upon another piece of oratory; I spoke of England, the aircraft carrier of victory; I invoked the memories of Guynemer, Joan of Arc and Bayard; I gesticulated; I laid one hand upon my heart; I brandished a clenched fist; I gave myself noble and heroic airs. I truly believe that it was my mother's voice which was talking through me, because the longer I went on the more staggered was I by the astonishing number of clichés which flowed from my lips without my feeling in the least embarrassed. It was useless to feel outraged by the shamelessness of my performance: I went on and on, partly from fatigue and wine, but mostly under the influence of some strange force over which I had no control, since my mother's personality and determination had always been stronger than I. I even believe that a change came over my voice and a strong Russian accent was clearly audible when my mother conjured up a vision of our "immortal country" and spoke of our giving our lives for "this France of ours which is eternally reborn" to the interested and appreciative audience. Now and again, when I began to weaken, they pushed the bottle in my direction and off I started on a new tirade—taking advantage of the state I was in, my mother was really giving her all in particularly juicy selections from her patriotic repertory. At last the three sergeants took pity on me and made me eat some hard-boiled eggs and bread and sausage, which had the effect of sobering me up sufficiently to let me get hold of myself and put in her place the excitable Russian woman who was presuming to give us lessons in patriotism. They also gave me some dried prunes but refused to go to England since, according to them, it was from North Africa, under General Noguès, that the war would be continued. They were going to make for Morocco as soon as they could refuel their plane, which they were determined to do, even if it meant getting hold of a tanker lorry at pistol point. There had already been some fighting round it, and the tanker moved with a guard of armed Senegalese riding on top with fixed bayonets.

My nose was stuffed up with clots of blood and I had difficulty in breathing. There was only one thing I wanted and that was to lie down on the grass and stay there on my back forever. But my mother's vitality and her will power drove me forward. Indeed it was not I who was wandering thus from plane to plane but a fierce old lady dressed in gray, stick in hand, and a Gauloise between her lips, who had made up her mind that she would go to England to continue the fight and that nothing was going to stop her.

CHAPTER 32

AT 4 P.M. THE SQUADRON AT LAST RECEIVED orders to proceed to Meknès, in Morocco, which seemed to confirm the prevailing view that North Africa would remain in the war, and we left Mérignac at five in the afternoon and arrived that same evening at Salanque on the shores of the Mediterranean. We landed there just in time to learn that every plane on the airfield had been forbidden to leave the ground. Apparently, some new authority was now in control of all air movements toward Africa and all previous instructions were to be considered null and void. I knew my mother well enough to feel that she was quite capable of making me swim the Mediterranean rather than accept the surrender. Fortunately, I found a sympathetic soul in one of the squadron pilots and, without waiting for any new orders or counter-orders from our new batch of beloved leaders, we set a course for Algeria, at dawn.

Our Potez was equipped with Petrel engines, which meant that, without supplementary tanks, there was a very considerable risk that our propellers would come to a standstill some forty minutes' flying time short of the African coast, forcing us to ditch.

We took off just the same. I knew that nothing could happen to me since I was protected by a formidable power of love and also because I was still young enough to see life as a perfectly ordered work, classical and Mediterranean in its essence, as though human destiny followed a pattern of strict balance and proportion, intending a masterpiece. Such a comfortable vision of things, making justice a sort of aesthetic imperative, made me feel invulnerable as long as my mother lived: I was her victory, her happy ending. I was meant to return to her triumphant. As to Warrant Officer Delavault, though wholly unsupported by literature, he set off across the sea with a phlegmatic "Well, let's see what happens," taking with us two tires to serve as life-buoys in case of necessity.

Fortunately, the wind was in our favor, and since my mother was probably also doing some blowing in the right direction, we landed on the airfield of Maison-Blanche at Algiers with a comfortable margin of ten minutes of fuel in our tanks.

From there, we proceeded next morning to Meknès, where the flying school had taken up temporary headquarters. We arrived just in time to be told not only that the armistice had been accepted by the North African authorities as well, but also that, as a result of certain "desertions" of rebellious crews intent on reaching Gibraltar, orders had been given to ground all aircraft.

My mother was beside herself. She didn't give me a minute's peace. She was raging, storming, brandishing her cane. All my attempts to calm her were useless. She rebelled with every beat of my heart, boiled with indignation in every corpuscle of my blood and kept me awake at night, urging me to do something about it, to take things into my own hands. I kept averting my eyes sheepishly, pretending not to see her look of scandalized incomprehension when faced by a phenomenon so completely new to her: the acceptance of defeat—as though man were something that could be defeated. In vain did I beg her to control herself, to be patient, to have confidence in me. She wouldn't listen and kept on summoning all the sons of France to rally round the flag: she was profoundly shocked and hurt by the refusal of North Africa to answer her call.

The appeal broadcast by General de Gaulle, calling on all Frenchmen to continue the fight, was made from London on June 18, 1940. Without wishing to complicate the task of the historians, I think it only right to point out that my mother's rallying call was sounded on the 15th or 16th of the same month, at the Buffa Market, from Mr. Pantaleoni's vegetable stand, and numerous witnesses can bear me out on this point.

Twenty persons were later to describe to me this frightening scene, the sight of which, thank heaven, I was mercifully spared: my mother standing on a chair among carrots, beetroots and lettuces, brandishing her cane and calling on all good men to reject the shameful armistice and to continue the war from England and North Africa, shoulder to shoulder with her son, the famous writer and diplomat, who was already dealing the enemy mortal blows. Poor woman. Tears come into my eyes when I think of her winding up her tirade by opening her bag and showing around a page cut from a weekly, containing one of my short stories. Many among those present must have laughed. I don't blame them: I blame only myself for my lack of talent and stature, and for having failed to be other than I was. That was not what I wanted to give her.

Never was her presence more real to me, more physically felt than during the long hours I spent in aimless wandering around the Medina of Meknès, trying to forget, if only for a moment, in a world so completely new to me, in the exotic sea of colors, sounds and smells breaking over me, the voice that summoned me to battle with an insupportable grandiloquence swollen with all the most overworked clichés of the jingoist's repertory. My mother took advantage of my extreme nervous exhaustion to take over from me completely. My deep need for affection and care, born of too long sheltering beneath the maternal wing, had left me with a confused longing to feel some benevolent feminine power guiding my steps, so that her image never left me for a single moment. It was, I think, in those long solitary hours of wandering among the strange and colorful crowds, that all that was strongest in my mother's nature prevailed, once and for all, over what was still weak and irresolute in mine; that her breath flowed into me and replaced my own and that she became truly me, with all her violence, her lack of balance, her aggressiveness, her love of drama, all those characteristics of a nature, every feature of which was excessive and extreme and was soon to earn for me, among my comrades and with my superiors, the reputation of a hothead, to say the least.

I have to admit that I tried hard to escape from that domineering presence and did my best to escape it in the motley, swarming world of Medina. I haunted the bazaars, absorbed in contemplation of the leather and the metals worked with an art new to me; I bent over a thousand treasures under the remote and fixed gaze of merchants seated, cross-legged, on their counters, their heads and shoulders propped against the wall and the mouthpiece of a *chibouk* between their lips, in an odor of hashish, incense and mint. I visited the red-light district, where, though I did not know it then, I was soon to experience the most abject adventure of my life. I sat in Arab cafés, smoking cigars and drinking green tea, attempting—an old habit with me —to fight my distress of spirit with the sense of physical well-being. But my mother followed me wherever I went and her voice held a note of cutting irony. A little sight-seeing? While the France of my ancestors lies torn and bleeding between an implacable enemy and a gutless government? Well, we might just as well have stayed in Vilna, and spared ourselves all the trouble of coming to France—obviously I didn't have in me what it takes to make a Frenchman.

I would rise, leave the Moorish café and plunge down a side lane in a throng of veiled women, beggars, hawkers, donkeys and assorted soldiery, and in that swiftly-flowing tide of new impressions, of colors, voices, sights, on one or two occasions I did manage somehow to give her the slip.

It was then that I lived what must be one of the shortest love affairs of all time. At a bar in the European quarter where I had gone for a drink, I found myself opening my heart and confiding my most intimate thoughts to a blonde barmaid, who seemed particularly touched by my impassioned serenade. Her eyes began to wander over my face, pausing at each feature with a look of tenderness and solicitude which made me feel that

I was suddenly ceasing to be a mere rough sketch of a man and becoming the real thing at last. While her gaze shifted from my chin to my mouth and then dreamily caressed my left ear and then my right one, I felt my chest expand to twice its normal size, my heart swell with courage, my muscles acquire a strength which ten years of exercises could not have given them, and the whole of the earth became a pedestal under my feet. When I told her of my intention to desert and carry on the war from England, she took from around her neck a chain with a small gold cross and held it out to me. Suddenly and irresistibly, I was tempted there and then to ditch my mother, France, England and all the invisible but noble burdens which lay so heavy on my shoulders and settle down for good in Meknès with this unique being who understood me so well. She was a Pole who had come from Russia by way of the Pamir and Iran, and I put the chain around my neck and asked my beloved to marry me. By then we had already known each other well over ten minutes and there was no point in losing more time. She accepted my proposal. Her husband and her brother had both been killed during the Polish campaign and she told me that she had been living alone ever since, apart from the inevitable hoppings in and out of bed, a pure matter of economic survival. There was something hurt and pathetic in her expression which made me feel that I was giving her help and protection, whereas, on the contrary, it was really I who was grabbing at the first female lifebuoy floating within my reach. In order to face life I have always needed the comfort of a femininity at once vulnerable and devoted, tenderly submissive and grateful, which makes me feel that I am giving when I am taking, that I am supporting when, in fact, I am leaning. I am at a loss to say whence this strange need comes, or who is responsible for it. Armored in my leather jacket in spite of the overwhelming heat, with my cap over one eye, a real tower of strength, offering my virile protection, I clung desperately to her hand. The world was sinking rapidly around us and it drove us into one another's arms at vertiginous speed, the very speed at which it was sinking.

It was two o'clock in the afternoon, the hour of siesta, sacred throughout Africa. The bar was empty. We went up to her room and there we lay for a good thirty minutes, clinging to each other, and never have two drowning beings tried so hard to help one another. We decided to get married at once and then go to England together. I was to meet at half past three with one of my fellow pilots who had gone to see the British Consul at Casablanca in the hope of getting him to help us with our projected journey. I left the bar at three o'clock, met my friend and warned him that there would now be three of us, instead of two. When I got back at half past four, the bar was already crowded and my betrothed very busy. I had no idea what had happened in my absence—she must have met somebody—but I could see that all was over between us. No doubt she had found the separation unbearable. She was now deep in conversation with a handsome lieutenant of Spahis—I can only suppose that he had come into her life while I was away. It was all my fault: one should never leave the woman one loves, loneliness overwhelms her, doubt and discouragement set in and, in a moment, the damage is done. She must have lost confidence in me and decided to make a new life for herself. I was very unhappy but didn't feel that I could blame her. I hung about for a while with a glass of beer in front of me; I was terribly disappointed, all the same, for I had believed that all my problems were solved. She was very pretty, with something lost, beaten and defenseless about her which always inspires me and brings out the best in me, and she had a way of pushing back her fair hair from her forehead which still moves me when I think of it. I form attachments very easily. I spoke a few words in Polish to her in an attempt to arouse her patriotism but she cut me short, explaining that she was going to marry the lieutenant, who was a farmer, that she had had enough of the war and that, anyhow, the war was now over, Marshal Pétain had saved France and would put everything in order. She added that the English had betrayed us. I looked at the Spahi, who was spread all over the place, with his dashing red burnous, and I felt resigned. The

poor girl was trying to get hold of something that looked solid—
a farmer is a farmer—in the general shipwreck; I wouldn't hold
it against her. I paid for my beer and left a tip in the saucer,
together with the little chain and the gold cross. Once a gentleman, always a gentleman.

My friend's parents lived in Fez and we took the bus and went
to see them. The door was opened by his sister and I at once
saw in her a life buoy which made me forget the one I had
missed by so little at Meknès. Simone was one of those North
African Frenchwomen whose mat complexion, delicate wrists
and ankles, and languorous eyes are well known and much admired. She was gay, she was cultivated, she encouraged her
brother and me in our plan to go to England and, when she
looked at me, there was a gravity in her expression, a silent
promise of lifelong devotion which moved me immensely. Under
those eyes I felt once more whole and complete, firm on my
feet and secure in my love, and I proposed to her on the spot.
The offer was well received, we embraced under the eyes of her
tearful and delighted parents, and it was agreed that she should
join me in England at the first opportunity. Six months later,
in London, her brother gave me a letter in which Simone informed me that she had married a young architect in Casa. This
was a terrible blow, for not only had I thought that I had found
in her the woman of my life but I had already forgotten her
completely, and thus the letter came as a doubly painful revelation about myself.

Our efforts to persuade the British Consul to supply us with
false papers failed and I made up my mind to seize, by force if
necessary, one of the Moranes-315 on the airfield at Meknès and
make for Gibraltar. But first I had to find one which had not
been deliberately put out of commission on orders from our beloved leaders, or else to find a sympathetic engineer. I took to
loitering on the airfield, staring hard at every engineer I saw in
an effort to read his heart. I was about to accost one whose
pleasant face and snub nose inspired confidence in me, when I
saw a Simoun aircraft touch down on the runway and come to a

halt a few yards from where I was standing. The pilot got out and walked toward the hangar. This was surely a friendly and collusive wink from heaven, and there could be no question of letting the chance pass. A cold sweat broke out on my forehead and I felt a painful contraction in my stomach. I was very far from sure that I could get the Simoun into the air and keep it there. In my training I had never got beyond the Morane and the Potez-540. But there was no question of backing out now: the die was cast. I felt that my mother was looking at me with pride and admiration. I found myself wondering briefly whether with the defeat and the occupation there might not be a shortage of insulin in France. She could not have held out three days without her injections. Perhaps I could arrange with the Red Cross in London to send her a regular supply through Switzerland.

I walked toward the Simoun, climbed into the cockpit and sat down at the controls. So far as I knew nobody had seen me. But I was wrong. All over the field, in every hangar, gendarmes of the special air police had been stationed to prevent air-borne "desertions," several of which had taken place during the last few days: that very morning a Morane-230 and a Goéland had got away and landed safely on the Gibraltar race course. Scarcely had I taken my seat when I saw two gendarmes emerge from the hangar and run toward me. One of them was pulling his revolver from its holster. They were within thirty yards of me, and I still couldn't get the propeller to turn. After one last desperate effort, I jumped out. A dozen or so airmen had come out of the hangar and were looking at me with obvious interest. They did not make the slightest attempt to intercept me when I scampered past them like a rabbit but they had plenty of time to study my face. To cap my imbecility, still acting under the influence of the "conquer or die" atmosphere in which I had been stewing for the last few days, I drew my revolver when I jumped from the Simoun and still had it in my hand as I raced over the grass—which, needless to say, would not have helped me at all before a court-martial. But I'd made up my mind that there would be no court-martial. In my state of mind, I honestly believe that I wouldn't have let myself be taken alive; and, since I was a very good shot, I tremble to think what might have happened if I had not made good my escape. This I did, however, without much difficulty. After a while, I hid my revolver and, in spite of much blowing of whistles behind me, slowed down and calmly walked past the guard at the gate and out of the camp. I found myself on the main road and had gone no more than fifty yards when a bus drove into sight. I signaled to the driver and planted myself firmly in the middle of the road. It stopped. I got in and plumped myself down beside two veiled women and a white-robed bootblack. I heaved a sigh of relief. I had got myself into a pretty pickle but didn't feel the least bit worried. On the contrary. I had finally consummated my break with the armistice. Now, at last, I was a rebel, a desperado, dangerous, iron-willed, tough—the real thing. The war had just been declared all over again; there was no longer any question of backing out. I could feel on my face my mother's admiring gaze, and I could not keep from smiling with an air of superiority, and even from laughing aloud. I actually think, God forgive me, that I muttered something rather pretentious to her, wiping the sweat from my brow, something along the lines of "Just you wait, this is only the beginning." Sitting in that filthy bus among those veiled *moukères* and white burnouses, I crossed my arms on my chest and felt myself fully capable of doing all that she expected of me. To push my insubordination to the limit, I lit a cigar—it was forbidden to smoke in buses—and there we sat, my mother and I, for a moment or two, smoking and silently congratulating each other. I had not the least idea what I was going to do but I had assumed so threatening an air that, when I suddenly caught sight of myself in the driver's mirror, I was so frightened that the cigar fell from my lips.

I had only one regret. I had left my leather jacket in my quarters and, without it, I was feeling rather lonely. I am a poor hand at solitude. As I have said before, I form attachments very easily. That was the only shadow on the general bright scene. I clung to my cigar, but cigars have only a short life and mine seemed to be burning down more quickly than usual in the dry air of Africa and, at any moment now, would leave me entirely alone.

While I smoked, I made my plans. It was a sure thing that the military patrols would comb the town for me. At all costs I must avoid those places where my uniform would stand out against the native background. The best solution, I decided, would be to lie low for a few days, then to make for Casablanca and try to get aboard some ship about to sail. I had heard that the Polish forces were being evacuated to England and that English ships were picking them up at various ports. The first thing was to get lost, to get myself pretty well forgotten. I decided therefore to spend the first forty-eight hours in the *bousbir* —the red-light district, where, in the unceasing flood of soldiers of all armies coming for solace, I had a good chance of passing unnoticed. My mother seemed to be a little bit uneasy at my choice of a hide-out, but I at once gave her all the necessary assurances. I got out of the bus in the Medina and made my way to the red-light district.

CHAPTER *33*

THE MEKNÈS BOUSBIR, A COMPLETE TOWN IN itself surrounded by a high fortified wall, contained at that time thousands of prostitutes of all nationalities and races, living and working in several hundred "houses." Armed sentries were posted at the gates and military police patrolled the streets, but they were far too busy stopping brawls among soldiers of different armies to pay much attention to a quiet-looking fellow like myself.

The *bousbir,* on the morrow of the armistice, was seething with an activity as exuberant as it was single-minded. The physical requirements of soldiers, considerable enough in normal times, increase still more in time of war and defeat brings them to a sort of exacerbated paroxysm. The narrow lanes between the houses were crammed with troops—two days a week were reserved for the civilian population but I was lucky to have hit on a "services" day. Men of the Foreign Legion in their white *képis,* Goumiers with their khaki *tarbushes,* the Spahis in their burnouses, red pompons of the Navy, scarlet headdresses of the Senegalese, flowing white seroual trousers of the Camel Corps, eagle badges of the Air Force, coffee-colored turbans of the Annamites, faces black, yellow and white—the whole of the French Empire was there, in a deafening din of juke boxes sending cataracts of sound through the open windows—I particularly remember the voice of Rina Ketty assuring her audiences that "*J'attendrai, j'at-ten-dra-ai toujours, la nuit et le jour, mon amour,*" while the Army, cheated of its victories and its battles, got rid of its unspent virility on the bodies of a generous supply of women—Berber, Jewish, Armenian, Greek, Polish—black, white, yellow—an activity so violent and often conducted with such savagery that the provident madams had to forbid the use of beds and put mattresses on the floor in order to reduce, as far as possible, damage to their property and the cost of breakage.

From the prophylactic centers, marked with a red cross, came the smells of permanganate, black soap and a particularly sickening ointment with a basis of calomel, while Senegalese male nurses in white smocks fought with generous doses the menace of spirochetes and gonococci which, but for this sanitary Maginot Line, might well have struck another fatal blow at a thus twice-defeated army. Constant fights were breaking out among Legionnaires, Spahis and Goumiers over questions of precedence but, generally speaking, the merry-go-round turned without a stop, a girl often averaging up to a hundred men a day, in a continuous stream, each warrior following in the wake of another, for a payment varying from a hundred sous, plus ten sous for a towel, to twelve or twenty francs in the establishments *de luxe,* where the girls appeared fully dressed, instead of waiting naked on the stairs. Sometimes a girl, half-hysterical from overwork or hashish, would rush naked, screaming, into the alley, there to indulge in a display of exhibitionism which, in the interests of decency, the M.P.'s immediately interrupted. It was in this picturesque and appropriate quarter of the town that I sought refuge in the establishment run by a certain Madame Zoubida, judging, with a considerable degree of shrewdness, that I would be safer from pursuit in the midst of that apocalypse than in any other sanctuary, since the churches had lost that character which, in the old days, had been their exclusive privilege. There, for one day and two nights, I fumed and fretted under most delicate circumstances.

I found myself in a situation which could scarcely have been more painful for a man animated by the noble feelings and exalted intentions which were mine at that time and under the appalled eyes of a mother whose feelings and intentions were even more noble and heroic. The *bousbir* closed its gates at 2 A.M. At that hour, the iron grilles of the houses were padlocked and the girls sent off to bed; however, by special arrangement with the madams, and in return for certain courtesies and a fair remuneration, the police were willing to keep their eyes shut if a warrior had decided to spend a whole night with a girl. This was explained to me by Madame Zoubida a few minutes before the normal closing time of her establishment. It is not hard to imagine the nature of the dilemma by which I was faced. Until that moment, I had been scrupulously careful not to play the part of a "consumer." I attached great importance to arriving in England in good health and was not disposed to expose my blood to the contact of this sewer. It was not a matter of principle. I had been a soldier for seven years, I had seen a great deal, and done no less, and the adventurous men we were then, always in a hurry, whose lives might be cut short at any moment, and were, nine times out of ten, were not in the habit of seeking forgetfulness and release from tension only in the company of well-bred young women. It was simply that the most elementary caution warned me not to plunge into such polluted water at that particular moment. I did not wish to present myself to the leader of Free France in a physical condition which might well have made him raise his eyebrows. But the only alternative to spending the night with a girl in the establishment was to be shown the door and to fall into the hands of the military patrols on watch in the narrow streets, which at that hour were almost deserted. It would have meant arrest and court-martial. Nor was that all, since, if I wished to stay hidden in Ma Zoubida's house for any length of time without arousing her suspicion, I would have to show exemplary zeal and assiduity and justify convincingly my uninterrupted sojourn under her roof for one whole day and two more nights. It would have been difficult to feel less enthusiasm than I did in these circumstances.

My thoughts were elsewhere. Apprehension, nervous tension, exasperation and a noble-minded impatience to raise myself emotionally and spiritually to the level of the tragedy my country was living through, the thousand and one tormenting questions which I was perpetually asking myself—all this made me peculiarly ill suited to the role of a gay dog. The least I can say is that my heart wasn't in it. One can well imagine the consternation with which my mother and I looked at each other. I made a resigned gesture to express the fact that I had no choice, that once again, though in a most unexpected manner, I was determined to do my best. Then, taking my courage in two hands, I plunged head first into the raging elements. The monkey gods of my childhood must have been splitting their sides at the sight of me. I could imagine those experts in absurdity, having their fun, roaring with laughter, holding their bellies in the excess of their mirth, whip in hand, their coats of mail and their spiked helmets glittering in the shady light of their dubious heaven, now and again pointing a derisive finger at the apprentice of a lofty idealism who was now putting the final touch to his possession of the world, holding in his arms something which bore no resemblance to the noble trophies on which he had set his heart. Never had my longing for beauty and dignity received a more mocking answer than in the interminable hours I spent lying there with my face in the mud.

Twenty years have gone by and the man who has left his youth behind him can remember, with a great deal less solemnity and a little more irony, the youth he was then, with such seriousness and such fierce pride. We have told one another everything, yet we are still strangers. Was I really that quivering and idealistic dreamer, so naïvely loyal to a nursery tale and so intent on being the master of his fate? My mother had told me too many beautiful tales, and with too great a talent, in those whispering hours at the dawn of life when a child's every fiber takes an indelible imprint; we had exchanged too many promises and I felt bound by all of them. With such a longing for the heights in one's soul, every step becomes a fall. Now that the fall has truly taken place, I know that my mother's talent long compelled me to see life as the raw material for a future masterpiece and I broke my back trying to achieve it in accordance with some golden rule of beauty and happiness. My longing for perfection, my dream of dealing with life as if it were ink and paper, and with destiny as if it were literature, made me attack with impatient hands a shapeless lump of clay which no human determination can ever mold, but which has itself the frightening power insidiously to shape a human being according to its will. The harder you try to leave your mark upon it, the better it succeeds in imposing on you a form of its own, tragic, grotesque, insignificant or comic, until at last you find yourself lying on the ocean edge, in a solitude broken by the barking of a seal and the cries of gulls, surrounded by thousands of motionless sea birds reflected in the mirror of wet sand. Instead of juggling to the best of my ability with three, four or five balls, as all artists have done, I was trying to live something which can only be sung. I have wandered in pursuit of something for which art had given me a thirst but which life could not quench. I have long since ceased to be the dupe of my poetical inspiration and, if I still dream of transforming the world into a happy garden, I know now that it is not so much because I love my fellow men as because I love gardens. And I have also learned that if, for me, there is no beauty without justice, yet life cares little for logic, and can be beautiful without being just. And though the taste for perfection is still upon my lips, it is as an ironic smile —a smile that will be, no doubt, my last work of literature, if when the end comes I have any talent left.

Sometimes I would light a cigar and stare at the ceiling, asking myself how I came to be there instead of describing heroic arabesques in a sky of glory. The arabesques I was forced to describe had nothing heroic about them, and the glory I had acquired in the establishment when my marathon ended was not of the kind that leads to burial in the Panthéon. Yes, the monkey gods must have been jubilant. Their moralizing and didactic side must have made the most of the situation. One foot on my back, with how much satisfaction they must have leaned over that human hand outstretched to steal the divine fire but closing only upon the humblest clod of dirt. A vulgar laugh sometimes reached my ears and whether it was those jackals giving vent to their hilarity, or merely the laughter of the soldiers waiting their turn, I cannot say with any certainty. Not that it mattered. I wasn't yet beaten.

CHAPTER *34*

I WAS PROVIDENTIALLY RELEASED FROM MY
stretch of hard labor by a comrade who was awaiting his turn
in the infirmary attached to the establishment. He told me that
I was no longer in serious danger, that Lieutenant Colonel
Hamel, who commanded the squadron, had obstinately maintained, in the teeth of the evidence, that the attempted desertion
and theft of an airplane could not possibly be laid at my door,
for the very good reason that I had not arrived in Africa aboard
any of his aircraft. Thanks to this testimony, for which I here
wish to express my gratitude to that true Frenchman, I was not
posted as a deserter, my mother was not bothered by the Vichy
régime, and the North African police gave up looking for me.
All the same, this new situation, favorable though it was, still
condemned me to subterfuge and extreme prudence. I had left
all my money with Ma Zoubida and had to borrow from my
friend bus fare to Casablanca, where I intended to slip aboard
an outward-bound ship.

I could not resign myself to leaving Meknès without paying
one last furtive visit to the air base. It must already have been
obvious that I don't find it easy to say good-by to what is dear
to me, and the thought of leaving my beloved leather jacket behind was very painful. Never had I needed it more than now.
It was a familiar and protective carapace, which gave me a feeling of security and toughness. It helped me to hide under an
aspect slightly menacing, resolute and not a little dangerous to

those who might try to come too close or peek at me too attentively; in short, the little boy lost could feel secure and pass unnoticed. But I was never to see it again. When I reached the camp, and went into the hut I had formerly occupied, all I saw was a naked peg; the jacket had vanished.

I sat down on the bed and began to cry. How long I remained there, looking at the peg, with the tears running down my cheeks, I don't know. Now I really had lost everything.

At last I dropped off to sleep, and so extreme was my state of nervous and physical exhaustion that I slept for sixteen hours and awoke in exactly the same position in which I had fallen across the bed, my cap over my eyes. I took a cold shower and left the camp to look for a bus to take me into Casa. On my way I found a happy surprise awaiting me in the person of an itinerant vendor whose glass jars contained, among other delicacies, some dill pickles. This was proof indeed, had I needed proof, that someone who knew me well was still watching over me. I sat down on the ground and made an early breakfast off half a dozen of them. I felt better, and stayed where I was for a moment or two in the sun, torn between a longing to eat a few more and the feeling that, in the tragic circumstances in which France found herself, it behooved me to display some degree of stoicism and sobriety. I was finding some difficulty in tearing myself away from the fatherly barrow man and his glass jars. I even wondered, in a dreamy sort of way, whether, perhaps, he had a daughter whom I could marry. I saw myself very well as a dealer in dill pickles, with a loving and hard-working wife at my side and a grateful, hard-working father-in-law. I felt so irresolute and lonely that I very nearly let the Casa bus go past me. In a desperate burst of energy, I jumped to my feet, stopped the bus, and, with a good supply of pickles wrapped in a newspaper, I got in, pressing those faithful friends to my bosom. It is curious how long the child can survive in the adult.

I left the bus at the Place de France at Casablanca, where I almost immediately ran into two trainees from the flying school,

Forsans and Daligot, who like me were trying to find some way of getting to England. We decided to pool forces and spent the day wandering about the town. The gates of the harbor were guarded by gendarmes, and there was not a Polish uniform to be seen in the streets: the last British ship carrying the Poles must have left long ago. About eleven o'clock that night, we found ourselves under a gas lamp in a mood of utter dejection. My determination had begun to weaken. I told myself that I had done everything I could, that no one can be asked to do the impossible. The fatalism of the Asiatic steppe had stirred in me, and was whispering poisoned words into my ear. Either there was such a thing as destiny, in which case it had better show its hand, or there was nothing, and one might just as well curl up quietly in a corner. If some just and serene force was really watching over me, well, it was about time for it to take over. My mother had never stopped blabbering to me of my future victories and the laurels which were one day to be mine; she had made me certain promises, and it was up to her, now, to get me out of this mess.

How she managed it, I don't know. But I suddenly saw coming toward us, apparently from nowhere, a good Polish corporal. We flung ourselves on his neck: he was the first and last corporal I have ever kissed. He told us that the British cargo boat *Oakrest,* carrying a contingent of Polish troops from North Africa, was due to sail at midnight. He added that he had come ashore to buy some delicacies which would make a pleasant addition to the rations. That, anyway, was what he thought. But I knew what power had made him leave the ship and guided his footsteps to the gas lamp shining down upon our melancholy.

The heavenly corporal handed Forsan his Polish tunic, Daligot his Polish cap; as for me, I had only to bellow Polish orders to my companions to get us safely past the gendarmes guarding the harbor gate, and up the gangplank, helped, it is only fair to say, by the two Polish officers on duty, to whom I explained our situation in a dramatic whisper in the lovely tongue of Mickiewicz:

"Special liaison mission. Winston Churchill. Captain de la Maison Rouge. Intelligence Service."

We passed a quiet night at sea in a coal bunker, lulled by noble dreams of glory. Unfortunately, the Polish bugle woke me just as I was making my entry into Berlin on a white horse.

Morale was good and only too willingly assumed a declamatory form: our English allies were waiting for us with open arms; brandishing our swords and our fists against the hostile gods who thought they could reduce mankind to slavery, we would blazon upon their satrap faces the indelible scar of our dignity, in the manner of the oldest champions of our race—bad literature perhaps, but it helped.

We arrived in Gibraltar in time to witness the return of the British fleet, which had just accomplished the noble deed which will shine forever in its history, that of sinking the finest French naval units at Mers-el-Kebir. It is not difficult to imagine what effect this news had upon us. Our last hope had rewarded our confidence with a foul blow.

In that pure and sparkling light of the Mediterranean where Spain welcomes Africa, I had only to raise my eyes to see the gigantic figure of Totoche, the god of Stupidity, standing upright in the harbor, legs apart in the blue water, his head thrown back and holding his belly; his eyes closed in an apelike grimace, he filled the sky with his enormous laughter. He was wearing for the occasion the cap of an English admiral.

My first thoughts were for my mother. I could see her striding down the street, cane in hand, on her way to break the windows of the British Consulate at Nice, in the Boulevard Victor-Hugo. Her hat sat sideways on her white hair, a cigarette hung from her lips and she was summoning the passers-by to join her in an explosion of indignation.

Unable, in these circumstances, to remain a moment longer aboard an English ship, and having noticed a destroyer flying the tricolor, I tore off my clothes and plunged into the sea. My rage, horror, sorrow and confusion were absolute and, not knowing what to decide, on what saint to call, I had followed my instinct, which told me to make straight for the flag of France. While I was swimming, the idea of suicide occurred to me for the first time. But there is nothing very submissive in my nature and my left cheek is not at anyone's disposal. I therefore made up my mind to take with me into the next world the English admiral Somerville, who had so successfully carried out the butchery of Mers-el-Kebir. The simplest way would be to ask to see him and then, after saluting smartly and offering my congratulations, to empty my revolver into his hard-won medals. I would only too gladly have let myself be shot afterward, and I found the thought of a firing party far from unpleasant. It seemed to go very well with my type of beauty.

I had two kilometers to go and, the water being on the cold side, I grew calmer. After all, I wasn't going to fight for England. The foul blow which she had dealt us was inexcusable, but at least it proved her fixed determination to carry on the war. I decided that there was no reason to change my plans and that it was my duty to go to England, in spite of the English. I was, however, already within two hundred yards of the French ship and felt the need of a breather before tackling those two kilometers again. So I merely spat into the air—I always swim on my back—and having thus got rid of the English admiral, Lord of Mers-el-Kebir, I continued on my way to the destroyer. I made for the companion ladder and climbed on board. An Air Force sergeant was sitting on the deck, peeling potatoes. He saw me emerge stark naked from the sea without showing the least sign of surprise. When one had seen France accept defeat and Great Britain sink the fleet of her ally, it seemed unlikely that one would find anything surprising again.

"All right?" he asked politely. I explained my situation and learned in return that, far from returning to North Africa, the destroyer was on its way to England with twelve Air Force sergeants who were joining de Gaulle. We were in complete agreement in condemning the action of the British fleet and also in concluding from it that the English were bent on continuing the war, which was, after all, the only thing that mattered for the time being.

Sergeant Caneppa—Lieutenant-Colonel Caneppa, Companion of the Liberation, Commander of the Legion of Honor and twelve times mentioned in dispatches—was destined to fall on the field of battle in Algeria eighteen years later, having fought on all the fronts where France has given its blood—Sergeant Caneppa suggested that I should stay on board, not only to avoid having to sail under the British flag, but also to help with the potato fatigue, a most undignified job for a sergeant. I brooded over this new factor in the situation and came to the conclusion that, no matter how fierce my indignation with the English might be, I would rather take passage under their flag than give my time to household chores so much at odds with my inspired nature. With a friendly wave of the hand, I dived back into the sea.

The voyage from Gibraltar to Glasgow took seventeen days, in the course of which I discovered several other French "deserters" aboard. We made friends. There was Chatoux, later brought down over the North Sea; Gentil, who was to crash with his Hurricane fighting one against ten; Loustreau, killed in Crete; the two Langer brothers—the younger was my pilot before being killed by lightning in the sky of Africa, and the elder is still around; Mylski-Latour, who changed his name to Latour-Prendsgarde and was brought down in his Beaufighter, off the coast of Norway. There was the man from Marseilles, Rabinovitch, known as Olive, who was killed while training; Charnac, who was blown sky-high with his bombs in the Ruhr; Stone, the imperturbable, who is still flying, and others, all with more or less false names which they assumed in order to protect their families in France from reprisals, or merely in order to turn the page upon the past. But among all the "deserters" present aboard the *Oakrest*, there was one man whose name will always sound in my heart the answer to every doubt and every discouragement. His name was Bouquillard and, at thirty-five, he was far and away our senior. Rather small and slightly bent, never to be seen without his beret, with brown eyes in a long and friendly face, his apparent calmness and sweetness of temper concealed one of those flames which sometimes make France the most brightly lit place in the world.

He became the first French "ace" in the Battle of Britain before being brought down after his sixteenth victory. The roof of his cockpit jammed and he couldn't bale out, and twenty pilots standing in the operation room, their eyes riveted on the black maw of the loud-speaker, heard him sing the great battle hymn of France until his Hurricane exploded and, as I write these lines, facing the ocean whose rumble and roar have drowned so many other voices, so many other defiant cries, the song comes suddenly to my lips and I try to resurrect a past, a voice, a friend, and he rises again at my side, alive once more, and smiling, and it takes all the vastness of Big Sur to make enough room for him.

No Paris street has been christened after him, but for me all the streets of France bear his name.

CHAPTER 35

IN GLASGOW WE WERE WELCOMED BY THE pipers of a Scottish regiment who marched ahead of us in their full-dress scarlet. My mother had a great love of military marches, but the horror of Mers-el-Kebir was still upon us, and turning our backs on the pipes as they paraded up and down the park where our camp was set up, the whole French Air Force withdrew silently into our tents while those splendid Scots, touched on the raw and more scarlet than ever, continued with true British obstinacy to fill the empty glades and avenues with the sounds of their hospitable welcome. Of the fifty of us there, only three survived the war. In the hard months that followed, in the skies of England, France, Russia and Africa, they accounted among them for one hundred and fifty enemy aircraft before being felled themselves. Mouchotte, five victories; Castelain, nine; Marquis, twelve; Léon, ten; Poznanski, five; Daligot . . . But what is the point in whispering names which no longer mean anything to those who hear them? What point, since they have never really left me? All that is still alive in me belongs to them. I sometimes think that I continue to live only as a matter of courtesy and that, if I still allow my heart to go on beating, it is only because I have always loved animals.

It was shortly after I reached Glasgow that my mother stepped in and prevented me from committing an irreparable folly, the stigma of which I might well have carried for the rest of my life. I was still smarting from the injustice inflicted upon me at

Avord when I had been cheated of my officer's rank. Nothing would have been easier now than to repair that injustice myself: I had only to sew a second lieutenant's stripe on my sleeve. After all, I had a perfect right to it and had been deprived of my commission only by the treachery of a few skunks. Why should I hesitate? But it goes without saying that my mother took a hand in the matter at once. It wasn't that I asked her opinion, far from it: I did all I could to keep her in ignorance of my little project, to dismiss her from my mind. But in vain. The thought had hardly entered my head when she was there beside me, stick in hand, and the language she used was extremely wounding. That wasn't how she had brought me up, that wasn't what she expected of me. Never, never would she let me cross her threshold again if I were guilty of such an act! She would die of shame and grief. In vain did I try to run away from her in the streets of Glasgow, my tail between my legs. She followed me everywhere, brandishing her stick, and I could see her face clearly, now imploring and indignant, now with that expression of incomprehension which I knew so well. She was still wearing her gray cloak, her gray and violet hat and a string of pearls around her neck. It is the neck that ages most quickly in women.

I remained a sergeant.

At Olympia Hall, in London, where the first French volunteers were assembled, well-bred ladies from good English families came regularly to chat with us. One of them, a ravishing blonde in military uniform, played innumerable games of chess with me. She seemed determined to bolster up the morale of the poor little French airmen, and we spent many hours with a chessboard between us. She was a very good player and beat me hollow every time, and then at once suggested another game. For a French volunteer dying to do some fighting, to have to play chess with an extremely pretty girl, after seventeen days at sea, is one of the most nerve-racking experiences I know. Matters reached such a point that I found it preferable to avoid her altogether and to watch her from a distance trying *rocades* against an artillery sergeant who, after a bit, began to look as melancholy and dejected as I. There she was, blonde and desirable, pushing her chessmen over the board with a slightly sadistic gleam in her blue eyes. She was a truly vicious number, if ever there was one. Never, never have I seen a girl from a good family do more to demoralize an army.

At that time I did not speak a word of English and found it very difficult to make contact with the natives. Sometimes I was lucky enough to make myself understood by gestures. The English are sparing of gesture but I did manage somehow to make them see clearly what I wanted. Ignorance of a language can even be helpful in certain circumstances, simplifying relationships to the essentials and eliminating useless preliminaries and monkey tricks.

While at Olympia, I struck up a friendship with a young fellow whom I shall here call Lucien. After several days and nights of a more than usually turbulent good time, he suddenly decided to put a bullet through his heart. In the course of three days and four nights, he had managed to fall madly in love with one of the hostesses at the Wellington, a night club much patronized by the R.A.F., only to be deceived by her with another client and plunged, in consequence, into such gloom that death seemed to him the only solution. Actually, most of us had left France and our families in circumstances so extraordinary and tragic that the nervous reaction sometimes did not take over until some weeks later and then often in a completely unexpected manner. Some then tried to cling to the first life buoy that drifted within reach; in the case of Lucien his buoy having straightway floated off, he had sunk straight to the bottom under the weight of his accumulated despairs. I, personally, was attached, though at a distance, to a solid buoy and one which gave me a feeling of complete security, for mothers are seldom unfaithful to their sons. I did, however, get into the habit of drinking a bottle of whisky a night, in one or another of the spots where we dragged our burden of impatience and frustration—the only time in my life I had touched alcohol. We were exasperated by our sense of stagnation, longed for the controls of a bomber, longed for a skyful of juicy Germans, and night after night sought release from tension with some willing soul, or with a bottle, when the limits of human nature made themselves felt. I was most often with Lignon, de Mézilles, Béguin, Perrier, Roquère, Barberon and Melville-Lynch. Lignon lost a leg in Africa, went flying with an artificial one, and finally was shot down in his Mosquito over England. Béguin was killed dive-bombing a target in France, after eight victories on the Russian front. De Mézilles left his left forearm at Tibesti, was given an artificial one by the R.A.F., and was killed while piloting a Spitfire in England. Pigeaud was shot down, and badly burned, in Libya. He escaped from an Italian ambulance, covered fifty kilometers on foot across the desert and dropped dead as he reached our lines. Roquère was torpedoed off Freetown and devoured by sharks under the eyes of his wife. Astier de Villatte, Saint-Péreuse, Barberon, Perrier, Langer, Ezanno the magnificent and Melville-Lynch are still alive. We sometimes see one another, but not very often. All we had to say to one another has been killed.

I was lent to the R.A.F. for a few missions in Wellingtons or Blenheims so that the B.B.C. could solemnly announce that "the French Air Force bombed Germany last night, operating from its British bases." The "French Air Force" was a friend of mine called Morel and myself. The B.B.C. communiqué filled my mother with indescribable enthusiasm since, for her, "the French Air Force operating from its British bases" could mean only one thing: *me.* I found out later that, for several days, she had paraded up and down the Buffa Market, with a radiant face, spreading the good news: at last her son had taken matters into his own hands.

I was next sent to Saint-Athan and it was while I was on leave in London that Lucien, after phoning me at the hotel to say that everything was fine and morale was high, put the receiver down and killed himself. At the time, I was furious with him but my fits of anger never last long, and when I was detailed, with two corporals, to escort the casket to the little military cemetery at P—— I had quite got over my resentment.

At Reading, a bombing raid was in progress and we had to wait for several hours. I deposited the casket in the checkroom, took the receipt, and off went the three of us in search of a drink, warmth and a welcoming smile. But the atmosphere in town was scarcely what you would call gay and, in an attempt to ward off the prevailing gloom, we must have drunk more than was good for us. As a result we returned to the station in no fit state to carry the box. I got hold of two porters, handed over the receipt to them and had them put the object in the luggage van. We arrived at our destination in a complete blackout, with only three minutes in which to recover our pal, and, making a dash for the van, we had just barely grabbed the box before the train began to move off. After an hour's journey in the R.A.F. lorry awaiting us, we were at last able to dump it in the guardroom at the cemetery gate, where it was left for the night, together with the French flag to be used at the ceremony. We caught some sleep, sobered up and next morning, arriving at the guardroom, found a cowed English N.C.O., who stared at us with bulging eyes. Arranging the tricolor on the casket, he had noticed that it bore on its side, in black letters, the advertising slogan of a very well-known brand of stout: *Guinness Is Good for You.** Whether it was the porters, rattled by the bombing, who were responsible, or we, in the blackout, I shall never know, but one thing was obvious: somebody, somewhere had made a mistake. We were naturally very much upset, especially since the chaplain was already waiting, with six soldiers drawn up beside the grave to fire the funeral volley.

At last, concerned above all else to avoid exposing ourselves to the charge of irresponsibility, which our British Allies were

* The authenticity of this episode has been questioned by some, as a similar incident is said to have occurred during the First World War. Although certain details have been changed for obvious reasons, the following persons can bear witness to its veracity and to the ensuing enquiry: Capt. Gayet, Capt. Chevrier, Lt. Cdr. d'Angassac, formerly of the Free French Air Force, Sq. Leader Russel, formerly of the R.A.F.

all too ready to bring against the Free French, we decided it was too late to back out and that the prestige of the uniform was at stake. I looked the English sergeant straight in the eye; he nodded, to show that he understood, drew a deep breath and, hurriedly replacing the flag on the crate, we carried it on our shoulders to the cemetery and lowered it into the grave. The chaplain spoke a few words, we stood to attention and saluted, a volley was fired into the air and I was suddenly overcome with such a rage against the quitter who had given in to the enemy, opened a gap in our ranks, and broken the bond of our harsh companionship that I clenched my fists, words of abuse rose to my lips, tears to my eyes.

We never learned what became of the other crate, the right one. All sorts of interesting hypotheses sometimes come into my mind.

CHAPTER 36

AT LONG LAST I WAS TRANSFERRED TO ANDOVER
for training and posted to the Free French "Lorraine" Squadron
which was getting ready to leave for Africa under the command
of Astier de Villatte. Above our heads, historic battles were
being fought, and the youth of England was facing a desperate
enemy with smiling heroism, and changing the fate of the world.
They were few indeed. There were French among them: Bouquillard, Mouchotte, Blaise . . . I was not one. I wandered
about the sunny countryside with my eyes fixed on the sky.
Sometimes a young Englishman would land in his bullet-ridden
Hurricane, refill his tank, reload his guns and set off again
into the mêlée. The pilots all wore gaily colored scarves around
their necks and so did I: it was my sole contribution to the
Battle of Britain. I tried not to think of my mother and
of all I had promised her. I was overwhelmed by a feeling of
friendship and respect for Britain, a feeling shared by all free
men who had the honor to tread her soil in that July of 1940.

Our training over, we were given four days' leave in London
before sailing for Africa. It was then that an episode took place
of an idiocy unparalleled even in my career as a champion of
the world. On the second day, while a more than usually violent
raid was in progress, I found myself in the company of a young
poetess from Chelsea, at the Wellington—that great meeting
place for Allied airmen. My lady friend was a great disappointment for she never stopped talking and talking about T. S. Eliot,

and about Ezra Pound and Auden, into the bargain, gazing at
me with blue eyes literally sparkling with imbecility. I could
stand it no longer and was beginning to feel a blind hatred for
her. Now and again I kissed her tenderly on the lips in the hope
of reducing her to silence but, since my damaged nose was always blocked up, I was obliged, after a while, to abandon her
mouth in order to breathe—and off she went again about E. E.
Cummings and Walt Whitman. I was already playing with the
idea of staging an epileptic fit—it had worked before in similar
circumstances—but I was in uniform and the trick might have
been embarrassing. I confined myself to stroking her lips tenderly
with the tips of my fingers in an attempt to interrupt the flow
of words while, with an eloquent look in my eyes, I tried to
invite her to a soft and languorous silence, the only true language of the heart. But it was no good. She imprisoned my
fingers in her own and embarked upon a dissertation on the
symbolism in *Finnegans Wake*. Boredom through talkativeness
and stupidity through intellect are things I have never been
able to endure and I began to feel the sweat breaking out
on my forehead, while my fascinated gaze never left that dev-
ilish oral sphincter which kept opening and shutting, opening and shutting, until I finally flung myself upon it with
all the energy of despair, hoping, but in vain, to reduce it to
immobility by my kisses. One can imagine my feeling of relief
when I saw a handsome Polish officer approach our table and,
with a bow to my lady friend, ask her for a dance. Though the
code of the place frowned on the idea of a young woman, duly
escorted, accepting an invitation to dance with a stranger, I
smiled gratefully at the Pole and began to make desperate signs
to the waitress, determined to settle the bill and creep away into
the dark and sheltering night. I was still gesticulating wildly to
attract the waitress's attention, when my little Ezra Pound came
back to the table and at once started on E. E. Cummings, on
T. S. Eliot and on the magazine *Horizon*, for whose editor she
expressed an immense admiration. I clenched my teeth and collapsed on the table where, with my head in my hands and my

fingers in my ears, I made sure of hearing not one word that she was saying. It was then that a second Polish officer appeared. I smiled ingratiatingly. With a little luck my Ezra Pound might find other points of contact with him besides literature, and I would be rid of her. But, no—the music stopped, and she was returned to me. As I rose to my feet and bowed with true French good manners, a third Polish officer turned up. I noticed suddenly that I was becoming a center of interest, and also that the behavior of the three Polish officers was deliberately offensive. They did not even give my partner time to sit down, but whisked her away, music or no music, one after the other, at the same time pointedly looking at me with expressions of ironical contempt. As I have already mentioned, the Wellington was crammed with Allied officers, English, Canadian, Norwegian, Dutch, Czech, Polish and Australian, all of whom were now beginning to grin at my expense, since my kisses had not passed unobserved. His girl was being snatched from him and the Frenchman was making no attempt to assert his rights. The blood surged in my veins: the prestige of our uniform was at stake. I found myself in the absurd position of having to fight for the possession of a young woman of whom, for the last few hours, I had been desperately trying to rid myself. But I had no choice. Utterly ridiculous though the situation might be, duty demanded that I should not remain indifferent. I got to my feet with a pleasant smile, and, after first uttering, in a very loud voice, and in English, the few heartfelt words expected of me, flung my glass of whisky in the face of the first lieutenant, gave the second a good blow on the mug, and then, honor satisfied, resumed my seat under my mother's approving gaze. I thought that would be the end of the matter, but the hell it was. The third Pole, to whom I had done nothing, chose to consider himself insulted. While some kind Norwegians were trying to separate us, he embarked on a program of loud abuse directed at the French Air Force, and France generally, and denounced the manner in which we had treated the gallant Polish airmen. For a moment I felt a sharp uprush of sympathy. After all, I, too, was a little Polish, if not by birth at least by reason of the years which I had spent in his country—I had even had a Polish passport for a while. I very nearly shook hands with him, instead of which, my Polish sense of honor sparking within me the sacred flame of French patriotism, and my Tartar and Jewish blood blowing violently on the blaze, I rammed him full in the face with my head, since both my arms were firmly held by a friendly Australian on one side and a debonair Norwegian on the other. After all, who was I to act contrary to the Polish code of honor? He appeared satisfied and vanished somewhere under the table. Again I thought that would be the end of it, but again I was wrong. The other two Poles were now inviting me to go outside with them. I gladly acceded to their request: at last, I thought, I shall get rid of Ezra Pound, but there, again, I was out of luck. Her infallible instinct had told her that at last she was in the thick of a real "experience," and she clung to my sleeve, positively mewing with excitement. Out we went, the five of us, in the blackout. Bombs were still whining, blowing up London all around us, ambulances were dashing past, with the sweetish and nauseating sound of their muted bells.

"Well, what next?" I asked them.

"Duel!" barked one of the three lieutenants.

"Nothing doing," I told them. "No more audience, blackout everywhere, no more spectators, so no more need for heroics. Get that, you stupid asses?"

"All Frenchmen are cowards," stated the second lieutenant, with a polite Polish bow.

"All right: duel," I said.

I was about to suggest Hyde Park as a suitable place in which to settle our differences. The din of the ack-ack guns there was such that our pistol shots would pass unnoticed and we wouldn't have to worry about leaving a corpse in the dark. I was very anxious not to run the risk of disciplinary action just for the sake of a few drunken Poles. I had had enough of Poles anyway: after our bankruptcy in Vilna, they had confiscated all our possessions, and this was a God-sent opportunity to pay them back.

On the other hand, I might well miss my aim in the total obscurity. Though for the last year or two I had not been keeping up my pistol practice, I had not completely forgotten Lieutenant Sverdlovski and his lessons. Under civilized conditions, I felt reasonably sure I could make a creditable showing on the target, particularly a Polish one.

"But where?" I asked.

They argued the point among themselves for a bit.

"Regent's Park Hotel," they finally decided.

"On the roof?"

"No, in a bedroom—pistols, at five paces."

I reflected that the big London hotels do not, as a rule, let young women go upstairs to a bedroom in the company of four men and that it would be an ideal opportunity of getting rid of Ezra Pound. She was still clinging to my arm: pistols at five paces!—this was literature—there was no holding her back. We got into a taxi after a long and polite argument about who should enter first, and went to the R.A.F. club, where the Poles got out to fetch their service revolvers. I had nothing but the 6.35 which I always carried under my arm. Then we drove to the Regent's Park. Since Ezra Pound insisted on going upstairs with us, we had to pool our resources and take a suite with a sitting room. At the foot of the staircase, one of the Poles raised a finger.

"You need a second," he said.

I looked around in the hope of finding a French uniform. But there were none to be seen. The lobby was stuffed full of civilians, most of them in pajamas, who had been afraid to stay in their rooms while the air raid was on, and had come down muffled up in warm scarves and dressing gowns. The exploding bombs shook the walls. An English captain, with a monocle in one eye, was busy filling out a form at the reception desk.

I went over to him.

"I have a duel on my hands, sir," I told him, "room 520, fifth floor. I wonder whether you would be so very kind as to act as a witness?"

He smiled wearily.

"Oh, these French!" he said, shaking his head. "Thank you for the kind thought, but I'm not the Peeping Tom type."

"It's not at all what you think, sir. A real duel, pistols at five paces, with three Polish patriots. I'm a bit of a Polish patriot myself, and since the honor of France is at stake, I've got to go through with it. You understand?"

He nodded. He was of those world-weary knowing types. He told me: "Alas, the world is full of Polish patriots. Unfortunately, those Polish patriots are sometimes German, French and English—a circumstance that is apt to lead to wars. And unfortunately too, I am unable to assist you. I have a duel on my hands myself. You see that young woman over there?"

She was sitting on one of the settees against the wall, a blonde, long-legged type, in every respect an answer to the prayer of every man on leave. I suddenly realized that I was getting hungry: I had skipped dinner that night. The captain adjusted his monocle, and sighed.

"It has taken me five hours to get her to make up her mind. It took me a lot of dancing, drinking, lying, begging, imploring and whispering to get her there. Finally, she said yes. I can't very well tell her that I now have to act as a second in a duel and that she will have to wait. Besides, I'm no longer twenty, it's two o'clock in the morning and I've had it. I don't want it any longer—in fact, it's the last thing I want right now, but I, too, am something of a Polish patriot, and I can't get out of it now. I'll do what I can to defend my honor, but I tremble at the idea of what lies ahead. Why not ask the porter?"

I took another look around the lobby. Among those seated around a sickly palm in the middle was a gentleman in pajamas and overcoat, with slippers on his feet, a hat on his head, a woolen scarf around his neck, and a melancholy expression, who clasped his hands and raised his eyes each time a bomb fell somewhat too close. The Germans were treating us, that night, to a first-rate show. The walls shook, plaster fell from the ceiling, glass broke in the windows, things were falling all over the place. I studied the gentleman carefully. I can recognize instinctively the type of person in whom the sight of a uniform inspires feelings of nervousness and respect, and who can never say no to authority. I went over to him and explained that urgent reasons necessitated his presence at a duel with pistols which was about to take place on the fifth floor of the hotel. He gave me a frightened and imploring look, but, confronted by the military, he did not offer any resistance, and rose obediently to his feet with a sigh. He even found a few words admirably suited to the occasion:

"I shall," he said, "be only too happy to contribute to the Allied war effort."

Since the elevators didn't function during an alert, we walked upstairs. The anemic-looking potted plants on each landing were quivering. Ezra Pound was still hanging on my arm. She was, by now, in the throes of a particularly revolting literary seizure, and, raising her moist eyes to mine, kept murmuring, in erotic undertones:

"You are going to kill a man! I can feel it! You are going to kill a man!"

My second leaned against the wall and raised a hand to his head each time he heard the whining of a bomb. The three Poles were anti-Semites and regarded my choice of a second as an additional and deliberate insult to Polish honor. The good fellow, meanwhile, went on climbing the stairs as if he were descending into Hell, eyes shut, and muttering prayers. The upper floors were completely empty, abandoned by their inhabitants. I told the Polish patriots that the carpeted corridor seemed to me to be an ideal spot for our encounter. I also requested that the distance be increased to ten paces. They agreed and started to measure out the ground. I had no intention of suffering even the slightest scratch in this fray, and I also wanted to run no risk of killing my Pole or even wounding him too seriously, not only because Mickiewicz was a great poet but also because I did not want to get into trouble. A corpse in a hotel always gets found in the long run, and a badly wounded man cannot get downstairs under his own steam. On the other hand, knowing all about Polish honor, I asked to be given an assurance that I should not have to take on each of the other patriots in turn, should I disable the first. I must add that, throughout the whole episode, my mother did not show the slightest sign of opposition. She must have been delighted to feel that I was doing something, at last, for France. And a duel with pistols at ten paces was just up her street. She knew that both Pushkin and Lermontov had been killed in pistol duels, and it was not for nothing that she had had me trained, from the age of eight, by Lieutenant Sverdlovski. I could almost hear her sniff with satisfaction.

I got ready. I must confess that I was not my usual cool self, partly because Ezra Pound was driving me mad, partly because I was afraid that, should a bomb fall just as I was about to fire, it might make my hand tremble, cause me to miss my target or wound the damn fool too seriously.

Finally all was ready and we stood facing one another in the corridor. I aimed as best I could but conditions were far from ideal, the explosions and whining were deafening and when the referee—one of the Poles—gave the signal, I wounded my adversary more seriously than was altogether healthy for me. We carried him into our suite, where little Ezra Pound at once assumed the duties of nurse and sister while obviously having hoped for something better, as the lieutenant had, after all, been wounded only in the shoulder. It was then that I truly had my moment of triumph. I saluted my adversaries in the true Prussian, that is, Polish manner, clicking my heels and bowing to them, and then in my best Polish and purest Warsaw accent, told them loudly and clearly what I thought of them. The idiotic look which settled on their faces when the flood of insults, couched in their rich native tongue, began to pour from the lips of their French opponent was one of the most glorious moments in my career as a Polish patriot, and largely made up for the intense annoyance they had caused me. But I had not yet finished with the surprises of that evening. My second, who during the exchange of shots had vanished into one of the empty rooms, now followed me onto the stairs. His face was radiant. He seemed to have forgotten his fear and the bombs outside. With a smile which spread so widely across his face that I began to feel concerned for his ears, he took from his wallet four crisp beautiful five-pound notes which he tried to press into my hand. When I rejected this offering with dignity, he made a gesture toward the suite in which we had left the three Poles and said in bad French: "Take! Take! Thank you, thank you: they are all anti-Semites! I, too, am a Pole: I know zem!"

"Sir," I said in Polish while he was trying to slip the notes into my pocket, "*Monsieur,* my Polish honor, *moj honor polski,* forbids me to accept your money. Besides, both as a Cossack, as a Tartar, as a Jew and as a free citizen of the world, I resent your racist attitude! Furthermore, Monsieur, *Vive la Pologne,* which is an ancient ally of France, my fatherland!"

I saw his mouth gape, into his eyes came that look of monumental stupefaction which I so love seeing in human eyes, and there I left him, banknotes in hand, and ran whistling downstairs, four steps at a time, and out into the night.

Next morning, a police car came to pick me up at Odiham and, after a brief but disagreeable session at Scotland Yard, I was handed over to the French authorities at Admiral Muselier's headquarters, where I was questioned in a resigned fashion by Lieutenant Commander d'Angassac and Commander Auboyneau. It had been agreed that the Polish lieutenant should leave the hotel, supported by his two friends and acting drunk, but Ezra Pound had not been able to resist the dramatic temptation of calling an ambulance and now I was in a pretty pickle. I was helped by the fact that there was a shortage of fully-trained air crews in the meager ranks of the Free French, which made me a precious asset, and also because my squadron was about to leave for other and distant skies. But I have the feeling that my mother had been active behind the scenes, for I escaped with a reprimand—a thing that never broke anybody's leg—and embarked cheerfully a few days later for Africa.

CHAPTER 37

ON THE ARUNDEL CASTLE THERE WAS A HUN-
dred or so English girls of very good family, all of them volunteers in a woman's driver corps, and the fifteen days of our
voyage, with a strict blackout maintained on board, passed very
pleasantly indeed. I still wonder how it happened that the ship
didn't catch fire.

One night I had gone on deck and was looking at the phosphorescent wake when I heard stealthy footsteps, and suddenly
a hand seized mine. My eyes, acclimated to seeing in the dark,
had barely time to recognize the moonlit beauty of our Provost
Sergeant Major before he was raising my hand to his lips and
covering it with feverish kisses. Apparently he had arranged a
romantic tryst with one of the sweet volunteers at the very spot
where I was standing but, having come straight from the bright-
ly-lit saloon into pitch-black obscurity, he had been the victim
of a very natural mistake. I let him continue for a little while—
it was very interesting to watch a Provost Sergeant Major in
action—but, since his lips, step by step, were now reaching my
shoulder, I thought it only fair to make sure that he really
meant it, and so I said in my deepest bass:

"Darling, I'm not at all *that* sort of girl."

He bellowed like a wounded beast and began to spit, which
I thought was rather ungracious of him. For several days after
that, he blushed scarlet and spat every time we passed one another on the deck. We were young in those days and, though

most of us are now dead—Maisonneuve shot down with Roque off the coast of Egypt, Castelain killed in Russia, Crouzet in Gabon and Goumenc in Crete, Caneppa downed in Algeria, Maltcharski in Libya, Delaroche crashed at El Fasher with Flury-Herard and Coguen, Saint-Péreuse still living but minus a leg, Sandré brought down over Africa and Grasset and Perbost killed over Tobruk, Clariond vanished into the desert with Le Calvez and Davin to die of thirst, their mummified bodies found by a camel caravan nineteen years later—though most of us are now dead, our gaiety remains and I often see them, all alive and laughing, in the eyes of the young men around me. Life is young. As it grows older, it becomes merely duration. It becomes Time, it says good-by. It has taken everything from you and has nothing left to give. I often find myself in places thronged with youth, and there I try to find again what I have lost. Sometimes I recognize the face of a comrade killed at twenty. The gestures, the laughter and the eyes are all the same. Something always remains. Then I almost—almost—believe that something is still left in me of what I was at twenty, that I have not wholly disappeared. I raise my head proudly, I pull my stomach in, I take my foil, with energetic steps I go into the garden, I look up at the sky, I engage, I lunge. At other times, I climb my hill and juggle with three balls, with four, just to show them that I am still there, that I am still to be reckoned with. Them? I know that nobody is watching me, that I am surrounded by indifference, but I feel I have to prove to myself that I am still capable of that sacred naïveté. I have been defeated, but no more than that. The monkey gods did not succeed in teaching me anything, neither wisdom nor prudence, neither resignation nor indifference. The sacred naïveté of the species is still in me. I stretch myself on the sand at Big Sur and I feel all through my body the youth and the courage of those who will come after me, and I wait for them with confidence, listening to the ocean and looking at the seals and the whales who, at that season, pass by the hundreds with their minuscule spouts of white water; I shut my eyes, I smile and I know that no one has ever died, that we are all there again, ready to start once more.

My mother came almost every evening to keep me company on deck, and we leaned together on the rail, watching the white furrow astern from which the night rose with its harvest of stars. The night had a way of growing from the phosphorescent wake into the sky, where it burst suddenly into bloom, spreading its boughs heavy with golden blossoms, to keep us leaning above the waves until the first light of dawn. As we approached Africa, dawn would sweep the ocean in one triumphant leap from end to end, and there, suddenly, would be the sky in all its brightness while my heart was still beating to the slow, muted rhythms of the night, and my eyes still believed in darkness. But I am an old star eater and it is to the night that I most readily entrust myself. My mother smoked continuously and I saw her by my side with such clarity that, more than once, I was on the point of reminding her that a blackout was in force, and that it was forbidden to smoke on deck because of enemy submarines. And then I smiled faintly at my naïveté, because I should have known that, so long as she was there beside me, submarines or no submarines, nothing could happen to us.

"You haven't written anything for months," she told me reproachfully.

"There's a war on."

"That's no excuse. You *must* write." She sighed. "I have always wanted to be a great artist."

"Don't worry, Mother," I promised her. "You *shall* be an artist, a famous artist. I'll see to that."

I remained silent for a while. I could almost see her silhouette, the lighter shade in the darkness that indicated her white hair, the glowing tip of her Gauloise. I was imagining her there, at my side, with all the love, with all the talent of which I was capable.

"There is something you ought to know. I have not been altogether truthful with you."

"What is it?"

"I never really was a great actress, a great tragic actress. That is not strictly true. Certainly, I was on the stage, but I never got very far."

"I know," I said gently, "but I promise you that you'll be a great artist this time. Your works will be translated into all the languages and read all over the world."

"But you aren't writing"—there was sadness in her voice. "How do you expect that to happen if you do nothing?"

I set to work. It was difficult on a ship's deck or in a tiny cabin shared by two others, to harness myself to a full-length work; I decided to write four or five short stories, each one a hymn to the courage of men fighting against injustice and tyranny—and by injustice and tyranny I meant far more than the Germans. Once the stories had been written around the same basic theme, I would integrate them into the body of a vast narrative, a sort of fresco of our Resistance, of our refusal to accept and to submit. There would be a central character in the book, more or less patterned after myself, who would tell the stories, according to the centuries-old method of the picaresque novelists. Even if I were killed before the whole work was completed, I could thus leave behind me a few tales, a trace, at least, of my basic creed, of my hope and rebellion and faith in our victory, and my mother would see that, like her, I had never accepted defeat and had done my best. Thus the first story in my novel *A European Education* * was written on the ship which was carrying us to battle. I immediately read it to my mother, on deck, among the early whispers of dawn.

"Tolstoy!" she remarked simply. "Gorki!"

And then, as a courtesy to my country, she added: "Prosper Mérimée!"

In the course of those nights she spoke to me more freely than she had ever done before, perhaps because she imagined I was no longer a child, or because the sea and the sky were favorable to confidences, since nothing seemed to leave a trace behind it, except the white wake of the ship, itself ephemeral

* Published in the United States in 1960.

in the silence. Leaning over the waves, my eyes closed so as to see her better, I plunged myself deep into the past, into memories of words, gestures, attitudes, re-creating her in that place with all the intensity of my love, clinging to that essential faith which ran through her life and mine like a thread of light which only her heart could have woven.

"There is nothing more beautiful in all the world than France," she said, with her old childlike smile. "That is why I want you to be a free Frenchman."

"But I am now, you know."

She shook her head.

"Not yet. You will have to do a great deal of fighting."

"I have been wounded in the leg," I reminded her. "Here, you can feel the place."

I stretched out my leg with its tiny piece of lead in the thigh. I had always refused to have it removed. I was greatly attached to it.

"Be careful," she said.

"I'll be careful."

Often, during the fighting which preceded the Allied landing in Normandy, when the bursts and blasts of the shells sounded like the breakers of some savage sea against the fuselage of my aircraft, I thought of those two words, "Be careful," and could not help smiling faintly.

"What have you done with your law degree?"

"You mean my diploma?"

"Yes. You haven't lost it?"

"No. It's somewhere in my kit."

I knew perfectly well what she had in mind. The sea was fast asleep all around us, and the ship was following its gentle sighs. I frankly admit that I rather dreaded my mother's entry into the world of diplomacy, the doors of which, she maintained, that famous law degree would open to me. For ten years now she had been carefully polishing our old Imperial silver in readiness for the day when I should have to "entertain." I knew very little about ambassadors, and still less about their wives, but I thought of them then as the incarnation of tact and breeding, of discretion and good manners. In the light of fifteen years' experience I have, in that matter among others, come to see things in a more human and tolerant light. But at that time I had formed a very exalted idea of the "Career," and I was not without a certain amount of apprehension, and could not help wondering whether my mother's personality might not be a slight source of embarrassment to me in the exercising of my functions. God knows I had never voiced these doubts to her, but she had learned to read my silences.

"Don't worry," she assured me. "I'll make a perfect hostess. After all, I have been running a hotel for years."

"Listen, Mother, it's not that. . . ."

"What is it, then? If you're ashamed of your old mother, say so . . ."

"Please . . ."

"But you'll need a great deal of money. Ilona's father will have to give her a generous dowry. . . . You're not just anybody. I will go and talk things over with him. I know very well that you love Ilona, but we mustn't lose our heads. I'll say to him: 'This is what we have; this is what we are giving: a writer, a diplomat, a hero. . . . And you, what are you prepared to give?'"

I clasped my head between my hands. I was smiling, but the tears were running down my cheeks.

"Yes, Mother, yes. It will be exactly as you say. I'll do what you wish. I'll be an Ambassador. I'll be a great poet. I'll be a second Guynemer. But give me time. Look after yourself properly. See the doctor regularly."

"I'm as tough as an old warhorse. I've managed to get this far, I can go a little further."

"I have arranged for insulin to be sent to you from Switzerland: the very best insulin. A girl on the ship promised to take care of that."

It was Mary Boyd who had made that promise, and though I have never set eyes on her since, throughout several years, in fact, up till a year after the war, the insulin continued to reach the Hôtel-Pension Mermonts from Switzerland. All my life I have wanted to thank her, but I was never able to discover her whereabouts. I hope that she is well. I hope that she will read these lines.

I wiped my face and drew a deep breath. Nothing could have been emptier in the whole world than the deck of the ship beside me. Dawn was here, with its flying fish. Suddenly, with unbelievable clarity and precision I heard the silence murmur in my car:

"Hurry, Romouchka. Hurry."

I remained a moment longer on the deck, trying to quiet down, or, perhaps, trying to find the enemy. But the enemy never showed himself. There were only the Germans. I could feel the emptiness in my clenched fists, and there, above my head, all that was infinite, eternal, inaccessible ringed the arena with myriad smiles, indifferent to our ancient, to our age-long combat.

CHAPTER 38

Her first letters reached me shortly after my arrival in England. They were sent secretly to a friend in Switzerland, and then forwarded to London "Care of General de Gaulle," short notes, a few lines, usually scribbled in pencil, and none of them dated. Until my return to Nice, three years and six months later, until the very eve of victory, these letters, dateless and timeless, as though coming out of eternity, were to follow me faithfully in all my wanderings. For three and a half years her breath breathed life into me, and I was sustained by a will stronger than my own: the umbilical cord fed my blood with the fighting courage of a heart more gallant than mine. The tone of these brief commanding notes rose from week to week in a sort of lyrical crescendo; she was taking it for granted that, in my demonstration of human invincibility, I was accomplishing prodigies of skill, greater than Rastelli, the juggler, more magnificent than Tilden, the tennis player, more valiant than Guynemer, the flier. Unfortunately, my career as a champion of the world had not yet acquired either form or substance, though I was doing my best to keep myself in shape. Every morning I put in half an hour running, pushing, jumping, weight lifting, and I could still beat the hell out of my squadron buddies at ping-pong. I could still juggle with five balls and had every hope of catching the sixth. I also went on with my novel *A European Education*, and the stories, which were to run through it like a hymn to the unbreakable human spirit, were already finished. I still believed that in literature, as in life, one could bend the world to one's inspiration and restore it to what it was meant to be, that is, a masterpiece. I believed in beauty and, therefore, in justice. My mother's talent and her idealism still drove me on to achieve some miraculous perfection, both in art and in life, and her dream was still stronger than my sense of humor, than all the first insidious whispers of cynicism and maturity. I found it impossible to believe that this just fulfillment could be denied her, if only because it seemed inconceivable to me that life, that destiny, could be so lacking in art and talent. Her simple-mindedness and her imagination, that belief in the marvelous which had enabled her to see, in a mongrel child living obscurely in a remote Lithuanian province, a great French writer and an Ambassador of France continued to live on in me with all the power of beautiful stories well told. I still regarded life as an artistic medium.

I must confess that I read her descriptions of my heroic, if imaginary, deeds with no little satisfaction. "My glorious and beloved son," she wrote. "We read in the papers, with feelings of gratitude and admiration, the tales of your exploits. In the sky of Cologne, of Hamburg, of Bremen your outspread wings fill enemy hearts with terror." I found no difficulty in understanding what was going on in her mind. Whenever the R.A.F. raided a target, I was one of those engaged. In each burst of a bomb she recognized my voice. I was present on every front and made the enemy tremble, and each time a German aircraft was brought down by English fighters it was to me, quite naturally, that she credited the victory. The alleys of the Buffa Market resounded with the echo of my deeds. After all, she knew me: she knew that it was I who had won the ping-pong championship of Nice in 1932.

"My adored son, all Nice is proud of you. I have been to see your teachers at the *lycée,* just to let them know. The London radio tells us of the fire and flame you cast on Germany, but they do well not to mention your name. That might make difficulties for me here." In the mind of the old lady of the Hôtel-Pension Mermonts, my name figured in every communiqué from every battle front; it was behind each of Hitler's screams of rage. Seated in her lonely tiny bedroom she listened to the B.B.C., which spoke to her only of me, and I could almost see her smile of wonder.

The only shadow on this otherwise bright picture was that during all that time I never once managed to cross swords with the enemy. From my very first flights in Africa, it had been made clear to me that I was not to be allowed to keep my promise, and the sky around me became the tennis court of the Parc Impérial, where a young and panic-stricken clown danced a ridiculous jig in pursuit of balls he could never touch, under the eyes of a delighted audience.

At Kano, in Nigeria, our aircraft was caught in a sandstorm, touched a tree and crashed, making a hole three feet deep in the ground. We emerged from it stunned but unhurt, much to the annoyance of the R.A.F., since aircraft were hard to come by in those days and were much more valuable than the lives of those clumsy Frenchmen.

Next day, in another plane and with another pilot, I took another tumble when our Blenheim turned over on its back during take-off and burst into flame, and again we escaped with nothing worse than slightly scorched uniforms.

We had now too many crews and too few machines. Bored to distraction, trying to escape from my thoughts and frustrations in every possible way, horseback included—galloping in clouds of dust through the desert brush—I finally applied for transfer to an R.A.F. unit ferrying aircraft along the great sky highway—Gold Coast–Nigeria–Chad–Sudan–Egypt. The machines arrived in crates at Takoradi, where they were assembled and then flown across the whole continent to the Libyan battlefields.

I made only one such trip, and even so my Blenheim never reached Cairo. It crashed in the bush south of Kumasi. My New Zealand pilot and the navigator were killed. I got off without so much as a scratch, but my morale was low all the same. There is something revolting in the sight of crushed heads, in a smashed and gaping human face and in those extraordinary swarms of flies with which the jungle suddenly surrounds you. And men seem to you more than ordinarily big when you have to dig a last resting place for them with your hands. The speed with which flies congregate and glitter in the sun in all the possible combinations of blue and green with red is truly amazing. After a few hours of this buzzing intimacy, my nerves began to give way. When the rescue planes began to circle above me, I waved my arms wildly to chase them away, confusing their drone with that of the flies trying to settle on my lips and forehead.

I was seeing my mother. Her head was leaning to one side, her eyes were half closed. She had one hand pressed to her heart. I had seen her looking exactly like that, several years earlier, when she had her first attack of hypoglycemic coma. Her face was gray. She had done what she could but she had not strength enough to save all the sons in the world, only her own.

"Mother," I said, raising my eyes. "Mother."

She looked at me. "You promised to be careful," she said.

"I wasn't flying the kite."

There was some fight still left in me. There was a sack of green African oranges among our provisions on board. I can still see myself standing beside the tangled wreckage, facing the sky and juggling with five of those oranges, swallowing my tears. Each time panic caught me by the throat, I grabbed the oranges and began to juggle. It wasn't merely a matter of getting a grip on myself: it was a question of style and a gesture of defiance. It was the best I could do to proclaim my dignity, the superiority of a man over all that befalls him. I simply could not see any other way of spitting in the face of the monkey gods.

I remained there for thirty-eight hours. I was found inside the fuselage with the roof shut. The heat was infernal. I was unconscious and half parched, but without a single fly on me.

And so it went throughout my tour of duty in Africa. Each time I took off the sky flung me back to earth with a tumultuous, hollow din, in which I recognized the familiar sound of stupid, mocking laughter. I kept going down for the count with astonishing regularity. Sitting on my bottom beside my fallen mount, in my pocket my mother's last letter dwelling on my heroic deeds in a tone of absolute confidence, I stared somberly at the ground, sighed, picked myself up and once more tried to do my best.

I don't think that in five years of war spent with the Lorraine Squadron I can look back on more than four or five combat missions in which I can claim to have behaved in the least like a good son. The months passed in the tedium of routine flights. I was posted with three Blenheims to Bangui, in French Equatorial Africa, to provide air cover for a territory where mosquitoes were the only serious threat from the sky. Our exasperation and frustration rapidly reached the boiling point and, merely to express our feelings and at least do *something*, we dive-bombed the Governor's Residence with light exercise bombs, thereby discreetly indicating our mood to the authorities. We were not even punished. This sort of behavior was exactly what was expected of us. Then we tried to make ourselves as undesirable as possible and organized in the streets of the little town a procession of its illiterate and unsuspecting black citizens carrying banners inscribed: THE CIVILIANS OF BANGUI SAY SEND THE AIRMEN TO THE FRONT. Our nervous tension also tried to find release in games which, more than once, had tragic consequences. Mad acrobatics in worn-out planes and a deliberate courting of danger brought death to many a good pilot. On one such occasion, diving almost to ground level on a herd of elephants, our machine touched one of the animals and crashed, killing both elephant and pilot. Climbing out rather sheepishly, and as usual without a scratch, from the wreckage of the Luciole, I was greeted by a blow from the rifle butt of a Belgian game warden, whose indignant words "No one's got the right to treat life like that!" have long remained in my memory. I was honored with fifteen days' close arrest, during which I kept myself busy clearing the garden of my bungalow, where the grass grew each morning a good deal thicker and faster than the stubble on my cheeks. Another stretch of boredom and the friendly hand of Colonel Astier de Villatte finally extricated me from my gloomy hole, and I rejoined my squadron, which was then operating on the Abyssinian front.

I wish, here and now, to make one thing perfectly clear: I did nothing, nothing at all. When one bears in mind the hope and trust in me, not only of my mother, but of practically the whole Buffa Market, I have no excuse.

Certain incidents have completely escaped my memory. One of my friends, Perrier, whose word I would never dream of doubting, told me long after the war that once, when he returned to the bungalow we shared at Fort-Lamy, he found me under the mosquito net with a revolver pressed against my temple, and that he flung himself on me just in time to deflect the bullet. According to him, this bit of self-hatred was caused by despair and remorse and the fact that I could not reconcile myself to having abandoned in France, without resources of any kind, an aged and sick mother, only to find myself rotting, helpless and useless, far from the fighting line in some black hole under the Equator. I have no recollection of this disgraceful episode. It was not in the least like me; in my fits of despair, which are as transient as they are violent, it is against my enemies that I strike out and not against myself, and, far from cutting off my own ear like Van Gogh, it is to the ears of others that I give wistful thought. I must add, however, that the months immediately preceding September, 1941, have remained confused and vague in my memory as the result of a bad attack of typhoid in Damascus: six weeks of high fever and delirium resulted in a temporary amnesia which, even after it had gone, still left certain blank spots in my mind. So extreme had been my mental confusion under the impact of fever that the doctors expressed the view that, should I survive, my reason would be seriously impaired. I survived.

I rejoined the squadron in the Sudan but, by that time, the Ethiopian campaign was already drawing to a close. Taking off from the Gordon's Tree airfield at Khartoum, we no longer met any Italian fighters, and the few puffs of smoke from anti-aircraft guns which still greeted us resembled the last breaths of the dying. We usually returned at sunset, just in time for a visit to one or the other of the night clubs in which the English had "interned" the companies of Hungarian dancers who found themselves stranded in Egypt when their country entered the war against the Allies. After a pleasant night, we took off at dawn for another bombing of some wretched Italian garrison. It is easy to imagine with what feelings I read the letters in which my mother poured out her song of praise for my heroic deeds. Far from attaining the level of her expectations, I was reduced to seeking solace in the company of a lot of poor girls whose pretty faces grew thinner and thinner, almost while one watched, under the pitiless bite of the Sudanese sun in the month of May. We were obsessed by the feeling of manhood draining away, of stagnation and impotence while violent fighting was going on in Libya, and we did what we could do to reassure ourselves and to assert our virility.

CHAPTER *39*

MY DESPONDENCY WAS THE MORE ACUTE BE-
cause it followed in the wake of a brief moment of happiness
experienced and now gone forever, leaving only a sad and bitter
memory behind it. If I have not yet spoken of it it is from lack
of talent. Each time I lift my head and take up my notebook
again, the inadequacy of my voice and the poverty of the means
at my command seem an insult to all I am trying to say, to
everything I have loved. Someday, perhaps, a greater writer will
discover in what I lived an inspiration worthy of his talent and
then I will not have written these lines in vain.

At Bangui I dwelt alone in a small bungalow hidden in a
grove of banana trees, at the foot of a hill on which the moon
perched each night like a luminous owl. After sunset, I would
sit alone upon the terrace of the colonial club high above the
river, overlooking the black tangle of equatorial forest on the
opposite bank, where the Belgian Congo began, and listen to
the only record they had left there, "Remember Our Forgotten
Men."

One morning I saw her walking along the road by my bungalow, her breasts uncovered, on her head a basket of fruit: all
the splendor of the female body in its tender youth, all the
beauty of life, of hope, of laughter, a walk, a poise, so sovereign
in its ease that it was as if nothing had ever died. Louison was
sixteen, and when her body against mine gave me two hearts,

I knew that I had kept all my promises and accomplished everything. I went to see her parents and we celebrated our union according to the rites of her tribe. The Austrian Prince Stahremberg, whom the hazards of a chequered life had led to Equatorial Africa as a pilot in my squadron, acted as my witness. Louison came to live with me. Never in my life have I found greater joy merely in listening and watching. She did not speak a word of French, and yet talked constantly, and I understood nothing, except that life was lovely, happy and immaculate. Her voice had made me forever indifferent to any other music. My eyes never left her. The delicacy of her features, the incredible fragility of her wrists and ankles, the gaiety in her face, the softness of her hair—but what can I say here that would do justice to my memories and to the perfection I have known? And then, after a while, I began to notice that she suffered from a slight cough and, dreading tuberculosis in a body too beautiful to be safe from the enemy, I sent her to be examined by Dr. Vignes, our squadron M.O. The cough, he said, was nothing, but Louison had a curious mark on her arm which attracted his attention. He came to see me that same evening. He seemed worried. Everybody knew how happy I was—the sight of my happiness must have hurt the eyes of the monkey gods. He told me that Louison had leprosy and that we would have to part, but he said so without much conviction, guiltily lowering his eyes. I denied it. I simply denied it. I knew it was impossible: I could not believe in such a crime. I spent a terrible night with Louison, looking at her while she slept peacefully in my arms, and even in her sleep a smile of gaiety shone upon her face. Even today, I cannot say whether I loved her, or whether it was only that I could not stop looking at her. I held her in my arms as long as possible. Vignes never said a word, never insisted, never blamed me, and when I swore, blasphemed and threatened, he merely shrugged. She began treatments, but came back each night to sleep with me. Never have I clung to anything in my life with greater tenderness, with deeper pain. I refused to hear of our separating until it was explained to me, on the strength of an article in some medical publication which I did not altogether trust, that a new remedy against Hansen's bacillus had recently been tried out at Léopoldville and that the results indicated that the disease could now be stabilized and perhaps even cured. I put Louison on board the famous "flying wing" which Warrant Officer Soubabère piloted twice a month between Brazzaville and Bangui. She left me and I stood there, on the airfield, utterly lost, my fists clenched, feeling as though not France alone but the whole world had now been occupied by the enemy.

Every fortnight a Blenheim, piloted by Hirlemann, maintained military liaison with Brazza. It was arranged that I should go with him on his next trip. My whole body felt hollow. I felt the absence of Louison in every grain of my skin. My arms had become useless things.

Hirlemann's plane lost an airscrew over the Congo and crashed in the flooded forest. Hirlemann, Bequart and Crouzet were killed on the spot. Courtiaud, the mechanic, had a leg broken; for three nights and four days he fought off the red ants trying to get into the wound, and very nearly went mad. They had been my friends. Very fortunately an attack of malaria blacked me out completely for one whole week.

My trip to Brazzaville had to be postponed until the return of Soubabère the following month. But he too vanished in the forests of the Congo with that strange "flying wing" which only he and Jim Mollison knew how to handle. I was ordered to rejoin my squadron on the Abyssinian front. I obeyed the order. I never saw Louison again. Three or four times I received news of her through friends in Brazza. She was being well looked after and there were hopes of a cure. She asked when I was coming back. She was gay. Then a curtain of silence fell. I wrote letters, I made inquiries through official channels, I sent sharply worded, insolent, raging telegrams. Nothing. The military authorities were icily noncooperative. I raged and protested. The sweetest voice in all the world was calling to me from some wretched African lazaret. I was sent to Libya. I was also told to undergo an examination to determine whether I had any symptoms of leprosy. I had none, but that was poor comfort. I had never imagined that one could be so haunted by a voice, by a neck, by shoulders, by hands. What I want to say is that she had eyes in which it was so good to live that I have never since known where to go.

CHAPTER 40

MY MOTHER'S LETTERS WERE BECOMING SHORTER, mere pencil scribbles written in a hurry. They reached me four or five at a time. She was well. She was receiving the insulin regularly. "My glorious son, I am proud of you . . . *Vive la France!*" I found a table on the roof of the Royal, looking out on the steaming waters of the Nile, while mirages made the city look as though it were floating on a thousand lakes of melted lead, and I sat there, the letters in my hand, among the Hungarian dancers, and the Canadian, South African and Australian officers who crowded the dance floor and the bar, doing their best to persuade the girls to grant them their favors. They all had to pay. Only the French paid nothing, which proves that even after the defeat France had lost none of its prestige. I read and reread the loving, confident words while little Ariana, the sweetheart of one of our most popular pilot officers, came to sit with me from time to time between dances and studied me with curiosity.

"Does she really love you?"

Without the slightest hesitation or false modesty, I said that yes, she did.

"And you?"

As usual I played it tough. "Oh, women," I replied, "you know how it is. They come and they go—we say in France: one lost, a thousand found."

"Aren't you afraid she might be unfaithful to you while you're away?"

"No. Not that one. I've got a good grip on her."

"Not even if the war lasts for years and years?"

"Not even."

"But you can't really think that a normal woman can spend years alone, without a man, just for the sake of your bright blue eyes?"

"But I do," I answered. "I once knew a woman who remained without a man for years and years, just for the sake of someone's bright blue eyes."

Off we went to Libya for the second offensive against Rommel, and in the very first days six of my French comrades and nine English fliers perished in the most tragic accident we had yet had. The *kamsin* was blowing hard that morning and, just as they were taking off upwind under the command of Saint-Péreuse, the three pilots of our three Blenheims saw three English Blenheims suddenly come at them head-on out of a cloud of sand. In the *kamsin*, they had started in the wrong direction and they had the wind behind them. There were three thousand kilos of bombs on those planes and both formations had already built up to take-off speed. They were in that hundred-octane boost position—still on earth but condemned to go straight ahead —when it is impossible to maneuver. The formations crashed into one another and only Saint-Péreuse and his observer Bimont managed to avoid the collision. All the others were pulverized. For hours after, one could see dogs running about the sand with lumps of flesh in their jaws.

By good luck I wasn't flying that day. When the explosion took place I lay dying in the military hospital at Damascus. I had contracted typhoid with internal hemorrhages and the doctors who were looking after me, Captain Guyon and Major Vignes, weren't giving me more than one chance in a thousand to pull through. I had had five transfusions but the hemorrhages continued. My friends came to my bedside, one after the other, to offer me their blood. I was nursed with true Christian devotion by a young Armenian nun, Sister Félicienne of the Order of Saint Joseph of the Lesser Apparition, who now lives in her convent close to Bethlehem. My delirium lasted for a whole fortnight but it took more than six weeks for my reason to return more or less completely. For a long while after the war I kept a complaint, sent through official channels to General de Gaulle, in which I protested against the administrative error as a result of which, I said, my name had been removed from the list of the living, which meant, as I pointed out, that neither privates nor N.C.O.'s saluted me, but behaved as though I did not exist. A few weeks before I fell ill I had been promoted to second lieutenant and, after what had happened at Avord, I attached a perhaps excessive value to the insignia of my rank and the external marks of respect which were due me.

When it at last seemed obvious to the doctors that I had but a few hours to live, the Damascus air base was asked to provide the guard of honor to watch over my mortal remains in the hospital chapel. In the meantime, the Senegalese orderly had put my coffin in my room. During a momentary return to consciousness—these lucid periods usually followed a hemorrhage, which reduced my fever by draining off my blood—I caught sight of the coffin at the foot of my bed. Thinking quite rightly that it was some sort of lousy trap, I at once took flight. My legs were as thin as matchsticks, but I managed to drag myself into the garden, where a young convalescent was sunning himself. Seeing a specter tottering toward him, stark naked except for an officer's cap, the wretched man uttered a piercing shriek and rushed to the guardroom. That same evening he had a relapse. In my delirium I had put on my second lieutenant's cap with its brand-new and recently acquired golden thread of rank, and I refused to be separated from it, which seems to prove that the shock I had suffered three years before at Avord had been more severe than I knew. My death rattle was, it seems, exactly like the sound made by a soda-water syphon at its last gasp. My dear Bimont, who had made a dash from Libya in order to be present at my funeral, told me later that he had found the way I was hanging on to dear life slightly shocking and even indecent. I was insisting too much. There was a certain lack of style and elegance in my attitude toward the inevitable. It was rather disgusting, he said, almost like a miser hanging on to his pennies. And with that rather mocking smile that suited him so well—I hope he has kept it after all those years in Equatorial Africa, where he now lives—he said to me: "You really seemed to want to stay alive, old cock."

It was already a week since extreme unction had been administered to me and I realized that I ought not to be making so many difficulties. But I have always been a bad loser. I refused to acknowledge defeat. My life did not belong to me. It was but an instrument of justice. I had a promise to keep. I had to return home, my hands full of victories, write *War and Peace* and become an Ambassador of France, in short, make it possible for my mother's talent to be made manifest. I was not going to submit to formlessness. A true artist does not let his material get the better of him. He tries to impose his inspiration on the medium in which he is working, even when it is life itself, and he strives to give the magma a shape, a meaning, an expression. I refused to let my mother's life end so stupidly in the contagious ward of a Damascus hospital. All my craving for art and my love of beauty, which is to say, of justice, forbade me to abandon my lifework before it had taken shape, before I had illumined the world around me, if only for an instant, with some flash of stirring and wholly logical meaning. I was not going to sign my name to the document the monkey gods were handing me, proclaiming man's insignificance and the total absurdity of life. I could not be so utterly lacking in talent.

Yet the temptation to give in was terrible. My body was a mass of purulent sores: the needles through which the serum was administered drop by drop were planted in my veins for hours on end and made me feel as though I were wrapped in barbed wire; my tongue was rotting in my mouth; the left-hand side of my jaw, which had been cracked during that unfortunate incident at Mérignac, had become infected, and a scrap of bone had broken loose and pierced my gum, but no one dared to remove it for fear of another hemorrhage. I was still bleeding internally and my fever was so high that when I was rolled in an icy sheet it took my body exactly one minute to reach the same temperature again. To make matters still worse, the doctors discovered I had been harboring a tapeworm, which was now beginning to emerge, inch by inch, from my bloody entrails. Many years afterward, whenever I happened to run across one or another of the army doctors who had seen me through, they would look at me incredulously and say: "You'll never know where you came back from."

That may be true, but the monkey gods had forgotten to cut the umbilical cord. Jealous of any human hand that tries to give a shape and meaning to destiny, they had plunged their knives into me so deep that my whole body was hardly more than a bleeding wound. But they had forgotten to cut the umbilical cord and I survived. The will, the vitality and the courage of my mother continued to flow into me and keep me alive.

The spark of life which still glowed in me suddenly flared with all the sacred fire of anger when I saw the priest come into my room with the Sacred Elements. When I caught sight of that bearded figure dressed in white and violet advancing on me brandishing a crucifix, and realized what he was proposing to do, I thought I was seeing Satan himself. To the astonishment of the good sister who was supporting my body in her arms, I, who was no more than a death rattle, said in a loud and intelligible voice: "No dice—nothing doing."

After which I sank into unconsciousness for a few moments, and when I came to the surface again the good had already been done. But I was not convinced. I saw myself walking through the Buffa Market in my officer's uniform, my chest collapsing under the weight of my decorations and my mother on my arm. We strolled along the Promenade des Anglais, applauded by the assembled crowds: "Long live the great French lady of the Hôtel-Pension Mermonts! She has returned victorious from the wars. She has been mentioned fifteen times in dispatches; she has covered herself with glory in the Royal Air Force; her son can well be proud of her!" The old gentlemen were raising their hats; there followed a general singing of the "Marseillaise" and somebody whispered: "They are still joined by the umbilical cord"—and indeed I could see a long rubber tube issuing from my veins. I smiled triumphantly. That was art indeed, that was literature for you! I had kept my promise, I had truly achieved a masterpiece; I had defeated the monkey gods of absurdity and nothingness. And they expected me to renounce all this merely because the doctors had condemned me, extreme unction had been administered and my fellow officers in white gloves were already getting ready to mount guard in the mortuary chapel? Never! Rather than accept that—yes, I'd rather live! It must be obvious by this time that I recoil from no extremity.

I recovered. The process was slow. My fever dropped, then vanished altogether, but my mind still wandered. My fits of insanity could find expression only in a succession of lisps since my tongue was almost cut in two by an ulcer. And then, when all that was over, phlebitis set in and the doctors feared for my legs. Permanent paralysis immobilized the lower left side of my face where the infection in my jaw had cut a nerve, which is why my face today has such a lopsided appearance. My gall bladder was affected, the myocarditis persisted. I recognized no one and I couldn't speak. But the cord continued to function. And so my mind finally cleared and, as soon as I could articulate, though still with an appalling lisp, I wanted to know when we could both return to battle.

The doctors laughed. The war was over as far as I was concerned. They were not at all sure that I would be able to walk normally. The damage to my heart would probably be permanent. As to dreaming of flying an operational aircraft—they shrugged with a pitying smile.

Three months later, I was back with my Blenheim, hunting submarines above the Eastern Mediterranean with de Thuisy, who was killed some months after while flying a Mosquito, in England.

I wish to express here my gratitude to Ahmed, the obscure

Egyptian taxi driver who, for the very moderate sum of six pounds, agreed to put on my uniform and take my place before a medical board in the R.A.F. hospital in Cairo. To the English, all frogs were alike and Ahmed played the part with gusto. "He was not much to look at, he didn't smell like good hot sand," * but he passed the board with flying colors and we exchanged mutual congratulations over ice cream on Gropi's terrace.

I still had to face the medical officers at the Damascus base, Major Fitucci and Captain Bercault. There could be no question of pulling the wool over *their* eyes. They had seen me at work, so to speak, on my hospital bed. They were also aware that I was still subject to occasional blackouts and fainted at the least provocation. I was told to take a month's leave in the Valley of the Kings at Luxor before even so much as dreaming of taking my place in an air crew again. So I visited the tombs of the Pharaohs and fell deeply in love with the Nile, the whole navigable course of which I covered twice in both directions. I spent long hours on my balcony at the Winter Palace, watching the *feluccas* sailing past. I resumed work on my book. I wrote several letters to my mother to make up for my long silence. In her letters to me, there seemed to be no trace of anxiety. And yet, her latest letter must have left Nice when she had been without news of me for at least three months. But she appeared not in the least concerned. It seemed a bit odd to me. There was, however, a new note of sadness in her latest letters, something that wasn't quite said, touching and a little disturbing. "Dear Romouchka, I beg you not to think of me, not to be fearful on my account. Have courage. Remember that you no longer need me, that you are a man now, that you can stand on your own feet. Get married soon, for you will always need a woman at your side. That perhaps is the only wrong I have done you. But, above all, try to write a great book soon; then you will find it easier to be consoled. You have always been an artist. Don't think too much about me. My health is good. Old Dr. Rosanoff is very pleased

* A quotation from a Foreign Legion song.

with me. He sends you his best wishes. Be strong, I beg you; be brave. Your mother." I read and reread that letter a hundred times, there on my balcony above the slow-flowing Nile. It held an accent of sadness, a gravity and a reticence that were new to her. And for the first time my mother did not speak of France. My heart was heavy. Something was wrong, something in that letter remained unsaid. There was also that rather strange exhortation to be brave, which now recurred in her letters with greater and greater urgency. It was even slightly irritating. She ought to have known that I was never afraid of anything. But what really mattered was that she was still alive, and my hope of winning my race against time and returning home triumphant grew stronger with each day that passed.

CHAPTER *41*

I WAS POSTED BACK TO THE SQUADRON AND
spent a very peaceful time chasing Italian submarines off the
coast of Palestine. It was an uneventful occupation, and I always
took a picnic with me. Near Cyprus we attacked a submarine
on the surface. It was a sitting duck, but somehow we managed
to miss it. Our depth charge overshot by a good hundred feet.

I can say that ever since then I have known the meaning of
guilt and remorse.

A number of films and a very large number of novels have
been constructed around the theme of the warrior haunted by
the memory of acts he has committed. I am no exception. Even
today, I sometimes wake up screaming in the night and drenched
in a cold sweat: I dream that I have just missed that submarine
again. A horrible nightmare: I have failed to send a crew of
twenty men to the bottom. There is no getting away from the
simple and brutal conclusion that my feeling of guilt and my
nocturnal horrors are due to the fact that *I have not killed—*
an extremely unpleasant admission for a man who claims to
have a rather noble opinion of Man. For this, I beg forgiveness
of all. I find some slight consolation in telling myself that I am
a nasty piece of work but that there are millions, billions of
decent, sensitive human beings who are not in the least like me.
This thought does a lot to bolster my morale since what I need
more than anything else is to be able to believe in human
nature.

One half of *A European Education* was finished and I gave all my available time to writing. When my squadron was transferred to England in August, 1943, I worked even harder. I had a feeling that the Allied landing in Europe was only a matter of days and I could not go home empty-handed. I could already see the joy and pride on my mother's face at the sight of her name on the cover of a book. She would have to make do with literary fame instead of all the glories of Guynemer. Her artistic ambitions, at least, were going to be realized.

The conditions at Hartford Bridge were not ideal for literary creation. It was very cold. I wrote at night in a corrugated-iron hut which I shared with three fellow officers. Each night I would put on my flying jacket and my fur-lined boots, prop myself up in bed and write till dawn with numbed fingers, my breath rising in visible vapor in the freezing air. Under the circumstances, I had no difficulty at all in evoking the snow-covered forests of Poland in which the central action of my novel was set. About three or four in the morning, I put down my fountain pen, straddled my bicycle and went to have a cup of tea in the mess. Then I got into my Boston bomber and set off, in the gray dawn, on a mission against powerfully protected targets. When we returned to base, there was almost always somebody missing and once, on our way to Charleroi, we lost seven crews at a single blow, when we had crossed the coast at the wrong point. It was difficult in such conditions to have much heart for literature. But literature and life have always been for me intimately intermingled, and flying and writing were part of the same fight, of the same effort to discover the hidden meaning of life. I went on with my novel when my comrades were asleep. Only once did I find myself alone in the hut and that was when Petit and all his crew were shot down over France.

The sky around me was becoming very empty. Schlosing, Béguin, Mouchotte, Maridor, Gouby and Max Guedj, perhaps the most legendary hero of all Free France, fell in quick succession. Then the last of the old-timers vanished in their turn, de Thuisy, Martell, Colcanap, de Maismont, Mahé, until a day came when of all those I had known when I first arrived in England, only Barberon, the brothers Langer, Stone and Perrier were left. We often looked at one another in silence.

I finished *A European Education,* sent the manuscript to Moura Budberg, the friend of Gorki and of H. G. Wells, and heard nothing more of it. One morning, on getting back from a more than usually lively mission—the Lorraine Squadron specialized in low-level attack, often hedge-hopping for as long as two hours before reaching the target, and three of our crews had been brought down that day—I found a glowing telegram from an English publisher: he was having my book translated and hoped to bring it out within five months. I took off my flying helmet and my gloves and stood for a long time, staring at the telegram. We were born, at last.

I lost no time in sending the news to her, via Switzerland, and waited impatiently for her reaction. I could imagine her turning the pages of her first novel, sniffing with delight. Her old artistic aspirations were beginning to take shape and, with a little luck, within six months she might become famous. I could see her granting interviews, signing copies of the book, expressing her opinions on the state of contemporary fiction. She had been a late starter: she was now sixty-one. I had become neither a hero nor an Ambassador of France, not even a First Secretary, but all the same I was beginning to keep my promise and to give some meaning to her struggles and her sacrifices. Slim and slight though my little book might be, it seemed to me to weigh heavily on the scales. I waited. But in her letters there was no allusion to our first victory. She had decided to ignore it. It took very little imagination to interpret her silent reproach: what she was expecting of me, so long as France was occupied, were fighting deeds, not literature. Yet I was not to blame if my war had been lacking in brilliance. I was doing my best. Every day I was punctual at my rendezvous with the enemy in the sky and my plane often crawled back riddled with shells. I was not a fighter pilot, only a bomber, and our job was not very spectacular. We dropped our bombs on the target and then went home, or not, as chance dictated. I even caught myself wondering whether my mother had heard about the submarine I had missed off the coast of Palestine and was perhaps furious with me.

The publication of *A European Education* in England made me almost famous. Each time I returned from a mission, I found a fresh batch of press cuttings, and several news agencies sent photographers to get a picture of me heroically climbing out of my cockpit. I assumed a flattering pose, looking proudly at the sky, with my helmet under my arm, in my flying overalls. I faintly regretted that I was not wearing a Tcherkesse or Guards uniform, sitting on a white horse with a raised saber in my hand, as Mosjoukine did in *Michel Strogoff*, but I felt sure, all the same, that my mother would be delighted with these photographs and I carefully made a collection of them for her. I was asked to tea by Mrs. Anthony Eden, signed a copy of my book for her and took great pains not to stick out my little finger when I held my cup.

I spent long hours alone on the airfield, lying in the grass with my head on my parachute, fighting against the feeling of frustration in my hands, a frustration that will remain with me as long as I continue to look at life as if it were a block of marble waiting only for some Phidias to turn it into a masterpiece; against the angry turmoil of my spirit battering against its bounds.

. . . Sometimes I raise my eyes and look with sympathy at my brother the ocean: he feigns the infinite, but I know that he, too, everywhere comes up against his bounds, and hence all this fury, all this roar.

We took part in fifteen more missions, but nothing ever happened worthy of us. One day, however, we came in for a more than usually rough time. A few minutes before reaching our target, while we were dancing our crazy dance among the black puffs of exploding shells, I heard in my earphones the anguished cry of my pilot, Arnaud Langer. There was a moment's silence and then he said quietly and clearly: "I've been hit in the eyes.

I'm completely blind." In the Boston bomber, the pilot is separated from his navigator and from his machine-gunner by sheets of armor plating, so that, once in the air, neither of us could do anything for the other. And at the very moment Arnaud was telling me that he had lost his sight a violent blow struck me in the stomach. Within seconds, my hands were full of blood and I could see through my torn trousers a gaping, blood-gushing wound. I remember that my first thought was: "Business, at last." The wound didn't hurt at all and, by great good luck, we had recently been issued steel helmets to protect our skulls. The English and American crews very naturally wore the helmets on their heads but the French, without exception, used theirs to shield a part of their persons which they regarded as being infinitely more precious. I quickly lifted my steel helmet and assured myself that my essential self was safe and sound. So great was my relief that the gravity of our situation did not particularly impress me. I can say that I have always had, in my life, a sure instinct for what is important and what is not. I heaved a sigh of relief and took stock of the position. The machine-gunner, Bauden, had not been touched, but the pilot was blinded. We were still in formation and I, as navigator of the leading aircraft, was responsible for reaching the target, which was only minutes away and clearly visible already, and it seemed to me that the safest thing for us to do would be to continue straight ahead, get rid of our bombs and then concentrate on our situation, assuming that there still would be one. This was what we did, though not without sustaining two more hits. This time it was my back that was honored—and when I say "back" I am being polite. I was, however, able to release our load of bombs on the target with that pleasant feeling of relief and satisfaction which always follows with me the performance of a good deed.

For a moment or two we stayed on course, then we began directing Arnaud away from the formation and soon found ourselves alone in the sky. I had lost a good deal of blood, and the sight of my open belly and my sticky trousers made me feel sick. One of our two engines had failed. The pilot was trying to pick the splinters from his eyes with his fingers. He could still see the contour of his hand, and we cheered up considerably, as this seemed to indicate that the optic nerve was not damaged. We had decided to bale out as soon as we had crossed the English coast. But Arnaud now discovered that his sliding roof had been damaged by flak and I felt like wringing his neck for this. However, there could be no question of our leaving the blind pilot alone on board. There was nothing we could do now but stay with him and try to direct him in to a landing. Our efforts were not very effective, and we twice overshot the airfield among a confusion of Very lights. I remember at the third attempt the ground was dancing about all around us, and sitting in my plexiglas cage in the nose of the machine, I felt like the yolk just about to drop from an egg into the omelet pan. Suddenly I heard Arnaud's voice in my earphones. It was like a child's voice, and what it said was—"Jesus—Mary, save me!" I felt slightly aggrieved and annoyed that he should have put in a word for himself, and forgotten all about the rest of us and told him so in a few harsh, heartfelt and, I'm afraid, rather blasphemous words. I also wish to record, for the sake of my literary reputation, that just when the plane was going to hit the ground, I smiled, and let there be no doubt that this smile was one of my most premeditated literary efforts. In fact, I had been working for it all my life. I mention it here in the hope that it will find a place in my complete works.

I think that this was the first time in the history of the R.A.F. that a blind pilot succeeded in making a safe landing. The official R.A.F. account of the incident merely said that "during the landing the pilot managed to hold his eyes open with the fingers of one hand, in spite of the splinters of plexiglas with which the lids were riddled." This exploit was marked by the immediate award of the British Distinguished Flying Cross to Arnaud Langer. He was to recover his sight completely: the lids had been nailed against the eyeballs by the fragments of plexiglas, but the optic nerve had not been touched. After the war he became an air transport pilot. In June, 1955, he was coming in to land at Fort-Lamy a few seconds ahead of a tropical tornado; witnesses saw a bolt of lightning strike like a fist from the black clouds behind him, and hit the pilot in his cockpit. Arnaud Langer was killed instantaneously. It took this foul blow for fate to catch up with him.

I was sent to the hospital, where my injury was diagnosed as "perforation of the abdomen." But no essential organ was involved, and the wound healed very quickly. What was much more annoying was that, in the course of their investigations, the doctors discovered the generally poor state of my insides, and they declared me unfit for further flying duty. But this was only the R.A.F. speaking and we, the Free French, had a less puritanical approach to our hidden organs, and I was soon back with the Lorraine Squadron, happily bombing the Rommel line along the coast, to open the way for the Allied landing in Normandy.

It was then that the happiest moment of my life occurred, and to this day, and to my last, it will remain the happiest.

A few days earlier I had been summoned, with Arnaud Langer, to the B.B.C., where we were interviewed at length about our sortie. Knowing the requirements of propaganda and how eager the French public was for news of its airmen, I did not attach much importance to it, but I was a little surprised to see an article on the subject in the next day's *Evening Standard*.

I returned to the Hartford Bridge base, and was in the mess when an orderly handed me a telegram. I glanced at the signature: Charles de Gaulle.

I had just been awarded the Cross of the Liberation.

I don't know whether there is anybody today who realizes what that green and black ribbon meant to us. Apart from the very best of our dead comrades, only a very few among the living had received it. I am not sure whether the total of those, alive or dead, who were so honored amounts now to more than six hundred. From questions occasionally put to me by Frenchmen I realize how few of them know what the Cross of the Liberation is and what its ribbon stands for. I am glad that this should be so. Now that almost everything has been either forgotten or betrayed, it is good that ignorance should preserve and shelter our memories, our fidelity and our comradeship. We do not ask anything from the living and our pride is with the dead.

I moved in a sort of daze, shaking the friendly hands around me, and it is difficult to convey my feelings, my exaltation, my gratitude and my love. Even today I feel the need to apologize, to justify myself. When I say that I can see nothing in my poor efforts that could warrant such an honor, I know that this sounds merely like the usual display of false modesty. And yet it should be evident to anyone, if I have in the least succeeded in summoning her, in making her arise alive from these pages, that all I had been able to do was as nothing compared to what my mother expected of me, compared to all she had taught and told me about my country.

Some months later, the Cross of the Liberation was pinned to my tunic under the Arc de Triomphe by General de Gaulle and the episode of Avord thus became closed forever.

Needless to say I lost no time in sending a telegram to Switzerland so that my mother should learn the news. I also wrote to a member of the British Embassy staff in Portugal asking him to forward a cautiously worded letter to Nice at the first opportunity. I could go home at last. My book had given my mother some spark of that artistic fame she had dreamed of all her life and I was going to present to her the greatest of all French military honors, which she had so well deserved.

The Allied landings had just taken place. The war would soon be over. I could sense in the letters reaching me from Nice a feeling of joy and serenity as though my mother knew at last that the goal was in sight. There was about them an especial note of tenderness and also of apology for which I could not altogether account. "My beloved son, we have been separated now for many years and I hope that you have grown accustomed to my absence since, after all, I am not on this earth forever. Remember that I have never had a shadow of doubt about you. I do hope that when you come back and understand everything, you will forgive me. I could not have acted otherwise." What was it she had done that needed my forgiveness? The idiotic idea suddenly came to me that she had perhaps remarried. But at sixty-one it seemed highly improbable. I felt behind her words a tender irony, I could almost hear her sniff with satisfaction and catch on her face that guiltily sly look which she always assumed whenever she had behaved badly and given way to one of her eccentricities. She had already given me so much trouble! In almost all her hastily scribbled, brief notes, there was now that hint of embarrassment and apology which made me feel that, once again, she must have done something really awful. But what could it be? "All that I've done I've done only because you needed me. You must not be angry. I am very well. I am waiting for you." I racked my brains, but to no purpose.

CHAPTER 42

I AM VERY CLOSE NOW TO THE LAST WORD, AND the nearer I come to the end, the greater becomes the temptation to throw my notebook away and let my head fall upon the sand. Last words are always the same and one would like, at least, to withdraw one's voice from the chorus of the defeated. But I have only a few things to add, it is all part of the fight, and no one is going to say that I lacked courage.

Paris was on the point of being liberated and I arranged to have myself parachuted into the south of France for liaison duties with the Resistance. I was in a hurry—my blood boiled with impatience, and nothing mattered to me now except getting back to her in time. At nights I was kept awake by the apprehension that, at the last moment, something might happen to her. And a quite unexpected turn of events was now providing a truly fairy-tale ending to our strange journey from the snows of Russia to the Mediterranean shore: I received an official letter from our Foreign Office suggesting that I apply for a permanent diplomatic appointment—as a First Secretary—in the French Diplomatic Service. What made this so odd was that I knew nobody at the Foreign Office nor, for that matter, in any non-military department: I quite literally did not know a single male civilian. I had never mentioned to anyone the ambitions which my mother had entertained for me. My *European Education* had enjoyed a considerable success in England, but that was not enough to explain this sudden offer of admission into the Diplomatic Service without an examination and, as the document proclaimed, "in recognition of exceptional services rendered to the cause of the Liberation." For a long time I looked incredulously at the letter, turning it over and over in my hand. It was couched in terms which had none of that impersonal tone which is the hallmark of official correspondence; on the contrary, it breathed a sympathy, almost a personal friendliness, which deeply troubled me. This sensation of being known or, more precisely, being imagined was something quite new to me. It was one of those moments when I found it difficult not to feel that I had been brushed by a loving and smiling Providence, as if some serene and just Mediterranean, guardian of our age-old human shore, was now presiding over the scales. My mother's destiny was taking shape. But in the midst of my sunniest and most enthusiastic raptures there always remains a pinch of earthly salt, with its slightly bitter taste of experience and wariness, so that I look on miracles with a distrustful eye, and, behind the mask of Providence, I found no difficulty in detecting a somewhat guilty smile that I knew only too well. My mother had once again lent a hand, she had been up to her usual tricks. She had been busy behind the scenes, knocking at doors, singing my praises in influential quarters. I now had the explanation of that embarrassed, somewhat sly and apologetic note which had faintly sounded in her last letters and had given me the impression that she was up to no good. She had been pulling strings, knowing perfectly well that this would make me angry.

The Allied landings in the south of France cut short my parachuting plans. I arranged immediately for a "special mission order," and my friend and commanding officer, General Corniglion-Molinier, found just the right imperative and epic tone, smacking of Ulysses' return home from his travels. With the aid of the Americans—my written instructions carried the mysterious and sardonic note, so typical of the general's wit: "Nature of Mission: Urgent"—I was taken in a succession of jeeps as far as

Toulon. From there on, things became rather more complicated. The peremptory tone of the order, however, opened all roads to me, and I shall never forget the remark made to me by Corniglion-Molinier with that faintly mocking seriousness of his, when he signed the document and I expressed my thanks:

"But your mission is very important to all of us. It is very important, a victory. . . ."

And the very air around me had an intoxicating taste of triumph. The sky seemed closer and more conciliatory, each olive tree was a friendly sign, and the Mediterranean was coming toward me, above the cypresses and the pines, above the barbed wire, the silenced guns, the overturned tanks, like an old nurse opening her arms. I had sent news to my mother of my imminent arrival in ten separate messages, which must have converged upon her from all sides only a few hours after the entry of the Allied troops into Nice. A message in code had even been transmitted to the Maquis, a week earlier. Captain Vanurien, who had been parachuted into the region a fortnight before the landings, offered to get into immediate touch with her and to let her know that I was on my way. My English buddies of the Buckmaster network had promised to keep an eye on her during the fighting. I had many friends and they understood. They knew perfectly well that what mattered was not her or me, but our old human companionship, our shoulder-to-shoulder struggle and progress in pursuit of justice and reason. There was in my heart a youthfulness, a confidence, a gratitude, a singing joy, which the antique sea, the oldest and most faithful of our witnesses, must have seen so often since the days when the first of her sons returned triumphant to her shore. With the green and black ribbon of the Liberation prominently displayed upon my chest, above the Legion of Honor, the Croix de Guerre and five or six other medals of which I had forgotten none, with the captain's stripes on the shoulders of my black battle dress, my cap tilted over one eye and with a more than usually tough expression, owing to my facial paralysis, with my novel in its French and English editions in my shoulder bag, together with a bunch of press cuttings, and, in my pocket, the letter which would open the doors of the "Career," with just enough lead in my body to give it some weight, intoxicated with hope, with youth, certainty and the Mediterranean, standing, at last, standing upright in the light, upon a blessed shore where no suffering, no sacrifice, no love was ever thrown idly to the winds, where everything counted, mattered, had meaning, was thought out and accomplished according to some golden rule of art—I was coming home, after having demonstrated that the world was an honorable place, after having given form and meaning to life and thrown a triumphant light over our destiny.

Black-faced G.I.'s seated on stones, with grins so wide and glittering that they seemed to be lit from inside, as though their radiance shone from the heart, raised their automatic rifles in the air as we passed, and in their friendly laughter was all the joy and happiness of a promise kept:

"Victory, man, victory!"

We were taking possession of the world again and each smashed tank was like the carcass of a god brought low. Squatting Goumiers, with sharp-featured, yellowish faces under their turbans, were roasting an ox whole over a wood fire; among the uprooted vines, the tail of an airplane was planted like a broken sword and, between the olive trees and the cypresses, from the one-eyed blankness of cement blockhouses hung an occasional lifeless gun with its round and vacant stare of stupidity and defeat.

Standing in the jeep, in this landscape where olives and vines and orange trees seemed to come running from all sides to greet me, where the wrecked trains, the blown bridges and the twisted, tangled strands of barbed wire were, like dead hatred, swept out of sight at each turn of the road, it was only after we had crossed the pontoons over the Var that all the laughing faces and the waving hands became blurred around me, that I no longer answered their friendly signs, but stood there, clinging to the windshield, my whole being resounding with the beating of my blood and every sense, every fiber in me prepared for the familiar sight, the street, the house, the gray silhouette waiting for me with open arms under the flags of victory.

I should end my story here. I am not writing to cast a deeper shadow on the earth. It is painful for me to continue, and I will do so as rapidly as possible, quickly adding a few words, so that it may all be over and I may let my head fall back again on the sand, at the ocean's edge, in the solitude of Big Sur, where I have come to bring my story to its end.

At the Hôtel-Pension Mermonts there was no one to greet me. Those I questioned remembered vaguely having heard of a strange Russian lady who ran the place years ago but they had not met her. My friends were gone. My mother had died three years and six months earlier, a few weeks after my departure for England. But she had known that I was still a weakling then, and that I would never be able to stand on my own feet and fight as befits a Frenchman unless she were there to give me her support; and she had made her plans accordingly.

During the last few days before her death, she had written nearly two hundred and fifty letters and sent them to her friend in Switzerland. I was not to know that she was no longer there to support me—the undated letters were to be forwarded to me at regular intervals—this was, no doubt, what she was scheming with so much love when I had caught that naïve and cunning expression in her eyes, when we parted for the last time at the Saint-Antoine clinic.

And so I had gone on receiving from my mother the strength and the courage I so greatly needed to carry me through to the day of victory, when she had been dead for more than three and a half years. The umbilical cord had continued to function.

It is over. The beach at Big Sur is empty, but when I raise my head I can see the seals on one of the rocks and, on the other, thousands of sea birds—cormorants, gulls, pelicans—and, sometimes, a spouting whale passes far out at sea, and while I lie thus motionless upon the wet sand, a vulture slowly begins to circle the sky above me, coming lower and lower.

It is many years now since my fall took place, and it seems to me that it was here, among these rocks at Big Sur, that I fell, and that I have been lying here for an eternity, listening to the murmur of the ocean and striving to understand what it is trying to tell me.

I was not beaten in a fair fight.

My hair is turning gray, but that is a poor disguise and I have not really aged very much, though I must now be nearing my eighth year. I would not like anyone to think that I attach too much importance to all this. I flatly refuse to give my defeat a universal significance, and even though the torch was snatched from my hand, I still smile with hope and certitude when I think of the many hands ready to raise it once more, and to carry it further and further, until a new world will cast across the infinite its undying light. I believe in victory, and I draw no lesson from my end, no resignation; I have renounced only myself, and there is no great harm in that.

I know now that I have been badly lacking in a sense of brotherhood. It is not right to love only one human being so much, even if it is your mother. My mistake had been to believe in individual victories. Now that "I" no longer exist, all has been given back to me. Men, peoples, all our legions have become my allies, I am unable to take sides in their quarrels and I remain, with my face raised, watchful and wary, at the foot of heaven, like a forgotten sentry. I still see myself in all living and ill-treated creatures, and am wholly unsuited for fratricidal battles.

But, for the rest, take a good peek at the firmament, after I am dead: you will see, somewhere around Orion, the Pleiades or the Great Bear, another constellation, that of the human Cur, clinging with all his teeth to some celestial nose.

And I can still be happy, as I am now, this evening, stretched on the sands of Big Sur, in the gray and misty dusk, with the distant barking of the seals reaching me from the rocks, and I have only to raise my hand to see the ocean. I listen attentively, and again I feel that I am just on the point of understanding what it is trying to confide in me, that I am going to break the code, at last, that the insistent, incessant murmur of the surf is striving, almost desperately, to deliver a message, to give me the explanation, the meaning, the key.

Sometimes, too, I give up listening, and just lie there, breathing. It is a well-earned rest: I have done my best, all that I could do.

In my left hand I clasp the silver medal of the ping-pong championship which I won at Nice in 1932.

I can still be seen stripping off my coat, thrusting out my chest, lifting weights, jumping, swinging from ropes, then suddenly flinging myself down, bending, twisting, rolling—but my body keeps me well bottled and I never succeed in breaking free, in pushing back my walls. Most people think that I am merely indulging in keep-fit exercises, and a big American weekly, *Sports Illustrated,* has actually gone so far as to print a double-page photograph of me in action, as an example worth following by all middle-aged men.

I have kept my promise and I shall continue to do so as long as I live. I have served France with all my heart, since that is all that I have left of my mother, except for a small snapshot. I have also written books, made a career, and my clothes are made in London, much though I dislike the English cut. I have even rendered great services to humanity. Once, for example, in Los Angeles where, at the time, I was Consul General of France —a post which obviously imposes certain obligations—I found, one morning, a hummingbird in my living room; it had come there trustingly, knowing that it was my house, but a gust of wind had slammed the door and it had been held prisoner all night between four walls. It was perched on a cushion, minuscule and incapable of understanding, all courage gone, no longer trying to fly, weeping in one of the saddest voices I have ever heard, for one never hears one's own voice. I opened the window, it flew out and I have seldom felt happier, and I knew that I had not lived in vain.

On another occasion, in Africa, I was in time to kick in the teeth of a sportsman who was aiming at a gazelle feeding its young in the middle of the road. I could mention other similar cases, but I do not want to boast about what I have been able to accomplish for my fellow beings. I mention these matters only to show that I really have done my best, as I said I would. I have never become a cynic, nor even a pessimist: on the contrary, I have frequently had moments of great hope and anticipation. In 1951, in a desert of New Mexico, I was sitting on a block of lava, when two little lizards, entirely white, started clambering over me. They explored every nook and cranny of my person with complete assurance and not a trace of fear, and one of them, having quite calmly pressed his front feet against my face, approached his muzzle to my ear and stayed like that for several moments. One can well imagine with what fervent hope I waited, my whole body tensed by a feeling of imminence, of grace. But he said nothing or, at least, I heard nothing. It is strange, all the same, that only man is entirely visible, entirely revealed to the creatures he loves. I should not like anyone to imagine that I am still expecting a message or an explanation: far from it. Besides, I do not believe in reincarnation, nor in any such nonsense. But I must admit that I did experience then an almost violent feeling of hope. I was quite ill after the war, unable to walk the earth from fear of treading on an ant, or to bear the sight of a bug drowning in water, and then I wrote a big book, *The Roots of Heaven,* urging human beings to take the protection of nature into their own hands. What it is I see in the eyes of animals I do not quite know, but there is in their gaze a dumb look of incomprehension which reminds me of something and completely shatters me. I keep no animal with me, though, as I become attached very easily and, all things considered, I prefer to attach myself to the ocean, which does not die quickly. My friends say that I have the strange habit of stopping in the street, raising my eyes obediently to the light, and striking a pose, as if trying to please someone.

It is done, now. Very soon it will be time for me to leave the shore where I have lain so long, listening to the ocean. There will be a touch of mist tonight over Big Sur: it will be chilly and I have never learned how to light a fire and to keep myself warm. I shall try to stay here a little longer, listening, for the feeling never quite leaves me that I am just about to understand what the ocean is trying to tell me. I close my eyes, I smile, and listen. . . . I still have some curiosity left. The emptier the beach around me, the more densely peopled it appears to me. The seals on their rock are silent, and I lie here, with my eyes shut, smiling, imagining that one of them is swimming quietly toward me, and that suddenly I shall feel, against my cheek or in the hollow of my shoulder, a friendly nudge . . . I have lived.

My dear, my beloved Romouchka!
I give you my blessing, and I swear to you that your departure did not sadden me. Just as you never saddened me but gave me only joy. Be tough, be strong.

MAMA

Revived Modern Classics

Mikhail Bulgakov
The Life of Monsieur de Molière. Trans. by Mirra Ginsburg. A vivid portrait of the great French 17th-century satirist by one of the great Russian satirists of our own century. Cloth & NDPaperbook 601.

Joyce Cary
"Second Trilogy": *Prisoner of Grace. Except the Lord. Not Honour More.* "Even better than Cary's 'First Trilogy,' this is one of the great political novels of this century."—*San Francisco Examiner.* NDP606, 607, & 608. *A House of Children.* Reprint of the delightful autobiographic novel. NDP631.

Maurice Collis
The Land of the Great Image. "...a vivid and illuminating study written with the care and penetration that an artist as well as a historian must exercise to make the exotic past live and breathe for us." —Eudora Welty. NDP612

Ronald Firbank
Three More Novels. "...these novels are an inexhaustible source of pleasure."—*The Village Voice Literary Supplement.* NDP614

Romain Gary (as Émile Ajar)
The Life Before Us (Madame Rosa). Trans. by Ralph Manheim. "You won't forget Momo and Madame Rosa when you close the book. 'The Life Before Us' is a moving reading experience, if you don't mind a good cry." —*St. Louis Post-Dispatch.* NDP604.

Henry Green
Back. "...a rich, touching story, flecked all over by Mr. Green's intuition of the concealed originality of ordinary human beings." —V.S. Pritchett. NDP517

Siegfried Lenz
The German Lesson. Trans. by Ernst Kaiser and Eithne Wilkins. "A book of rare depth and brilliance…" —*The New York Times.* NDP618

Henri Michaux
A Barbarian in Asia. Trans. by Sylvia Beach. "It is superb in its swift illuminations and its wit…"—Alfred Kazin, *The New Yorker.* NDP622

Raymond Queneau
The Blue Flowers. Trans. by Barbara Wright. "…an exuberant meditation on the novel, narrative conventions, and readers."—*The Washington Post.* NDP595

Available at bookstores
Please send for our complete catalog